THE
LAST REFUGE
OF THE
KNIGHTS
TEMPLAR

"A thrilling fast-paced novel. Mann ingeniously incorporates recently rediscovered correspondence between two 19th-century Masonic luminaries, American Albert Pike and Canadian J. W. B. MacLeod Moore, in crafting this fascinating tale. He expertly weaves his intimate knowledge of Freemasonry, Templary, Rosicrucianism, alchemy, and Native American culture and beliefs into this very enjoyable and compelling adventure. Highly recommended."

JEFFREY N. NELSON, MOST EMINENT GRAND MASTER OF THE GRAND ENCAMPMENT OF KNIGHTS TEMPLAR OF THE USA

"Albert Pike is a unique figure as a Northerner who became a Confederate general, who married into the Alexander Hamilton family, who became the Grand Dragon of the Tennessee Ku Klux Klan, and an active Mason. William Mann puts life into this legendary figure as no one else can, as he was recently presented with the further honor of being appointed Grand Archivist and Grand Historian for the Knights Templar of Canada."

STEVEN SORA, AUTHOR OF *ROSICRUCIAN AMERICA*

"William Mann's charming and engrossing novel exposes fascinating facts about Albert Pike's role in Civil War history, Templar secrets, and the Mide'win Medicine Society, the keepers of Algonquin prophecy. Significant for contemporary readers is Pike's role in Civil War history that offers deep insights about the tragic fragmentation of the United States today. This book is a must-read for students of Templar lore, the marriage of Jesus and Mary Magdalene, Vatican plots for world domination, the Algonquin Seven Fires Prophecy, and for Masonic researchers. Be prepared to stay up all night!"

BARBARA HAND CLOW, AUTHOR OF *AWAKENING THE PLANETARY MIND*

"Documented history and speculative story blend into a great read that leaves one with many questions as to the actual events that make up the bonafide story of the country we call Canada or as the Cree Nation would say 'Kanata'—which is translated to mean 'Clean Place.'"

MICHAEL THRASHER, LLD(HC), INDIGENOUS STUDIES DEPARTMENT ADJUNCT PROFESSOR AT TRENT UNIVERSITY, ONTARIO, CANADA

Col. W. J. B. MacLeod Moore

THE
LAST REFUGE
OF THE
KNIGHTS
TEMPLAR

The Ultimate Secret of the Pike Letters

A NOVEL

WILLIAM F. MANN

Destiny Books
Rochester, Vermont

Destiny Books
One Park Street
Rochester, Vermont 05767
www.DestinyBooks.com

Destiny Books is a division of Inner Traditions International

Cataloging-in-Publication Data for this title is available from the Library of Congress

ISBN 978-1-62055-991-8 (print)
ISBN 978-1-62055-992-5 (ebook)

Printed and bound in the United States by Versa Press, Inc.

10 9 8 7 6 5 4 3 2 1

Text design and layout by Priscilla Baker
This book was typeset in Garamond Premier Pro with Caston, Grit, and Legacy
Sans used as display typefaces

To send correspondence to the author of this book, mail a first-class letter to the
author c/o Inner Traditions • Bear & Company, One Park Street, Rochester, VT
05767, and we will forward the communication, or contact the author directly at
www.templarsnewworld.com.

CONTENTS

Beware, thou who art tempted to evil! Beware what thou layest up for the future! Beware what thou layest up in the archives of eternity! Wrong not thy neighbor! Lest the thought of him thou injurest, and who suffers by thy act, be to thee a pang which years will not deprive of its bitterness! Break not into the house of innocence, to rifle it of its treasure; lest when many years have passed over thee, the moan of its distress may not have died away from thine ear! Build not the desolate throne of ambition in thy heart; nor be busy with devices, and circumventings, and selfish schemings; lest desolation and loneliness be on thy path, as it stretches into the long futurity!

MORALS AND DOGMA OF THE ANCIENT AND ACCEPTED SCOTTISH RITE OF FREEMASONRY,
Degree XIII, Royal Arch of Solomon
Entered according to Act of Congress,
in the year 1871, by ALBERT PIKE

ALBERT PIKE— A TRUE ENIGMA

It is easy to develop a novel around a known historical figure when the focus of your story is Albert Pike. Seen as a demigod by some and the devil incarnate by others, Pike secretly dominated several decades of U.S. history during the most turbulent time in America's past. Pike was a true enigma, a man with many secrets, many of which he took to his grave. Over a lifetime, he was seen as a thorn in the side of the collective psyche of America, reflecting a conundrum that the American people are facing today. History indeed repeats itself. Will the South rise up once more?

Above all else, over his life, Pike became a brilliant esoteric magus. Rising from New England pioneer roots, in August 1825, at the age of sixteen, Pike wrote the entrance exams to Harvard, passed, and was accepted, but he had to forgo a formal education because of the required fees and educate himself. At first he started out as a simple schoolteacher, moving from one New England town to another, then to Nashville, Tennessee, and later to St. Louis, Missouri, but his personal history following this rather innocuous beginning is the stuff of legend.

An imposing, biblical figure, Pike stood six feet, two inches tall and weighed three hundred pounds, with a flowing beard and hair that hung below his shoulders. Like most self-made men, he was a restless soul, determined to explore the West, which the United States had recently acquired through the Louisiana Purchase, so in 1831 he embarked on a hunting-and-trapping expedition to Taos, New Mexico, only to have his horse break and run. Pike was thus forced to walk the remaining thirteen hundred miles to Fort Smith, Arkansas. This foreshadowed the man's strength and determination and a spirit that would carry him through a multidimensional journey of self-examination.

It was here, in Arkansas, that Pike decided to settle and teach school and to write a series of articles for the Little Rock *Advocate.* Generating both monetary and critical success from the start, Pike was said to have made enough money to purchase the *Advocate* in 1834. However, this may be more the stuff of legend than the actual truth. In fact, just prior to his purchase of the business, he married Mary Anne Hamilton, a descendant of Alexander Hamilton, who came from a very wealthy family, suggesting that a large dowry exchanged hands. From the outset, the newspaper promoted the viewpoint of the Whig party, stoking the political volatility that existed throughout Arkansas and other Southern states during this time.

During the same period, Pike studied law and was admitted to the bar in 1837, mostly on the strength of having written a book titled *The Arkansas Form Book,* which served as a guidebook for lawyers for generations to come. At this point, Pike sold the *Advocate* and concentrated on representing the claims of many Native North American tribes against the federal government. This, of course, was extremely unusual, because most American pioneer families believed that the Native Americans had no rights to their ancestral homeland. In 1852 Pike represented the Creek nation, and in 1854 he represented both the Choctaw and Chickasaw, taking their claims to the Supreme Court. Although he was successful in defending their claims regarding their ceding of tribal lands, the American government never properly compensated the tribes in accordance with the court's rulings.

Here is the first enigma about Pike's character: although he retained his affiliation with the Whig party during the 1830s and 1840s, which adamantly opposed the rival Democrats' belief in Manifest Destiny, he remained a strong advocate of slavery. How could a man fight so hard for Native American rights and at the same time maintain such a strong belief in the right of men to enslave other men? What qualities did Pike see in Native Americans versus the African-American race, especially given his involvement in Freemasonry, which considered all men equal and free? Had he learned of something more that spoke of prior contact and strategic intermarriage between the medieval European Knights Templar and the Native North Americans?

One thing is obvious: Pike strongly believed in and fought for his convictions. Joining the Regiment of Arkansas Mounted Volunteers, he was commissioned as a troop commander with the rank of captain in June 1846. With his regiment, he fought with distinction at the Battle of Buena Vista during the Mexican War, receiving an honorable discharge in June 1847.

After his discharge, Pike became disillusioned with the Whig party, which refused to take a stand on slavery. Over the next decade, his increasing disillusionment with federalism would lead to a strong stand in support of the freedom of individual states. By 1861, he was arguing in his writings and speeches that the individual states' rights superseded national law. Thus, he strongly supported the idea of Southern secession, continuing a strong proslavery position.

It is said that Pike was one of the main Masonic entities behind the instigation of secession following Abraham Lincoln's election as president. On December 20, 1860, the state of South Carolina—headquarters of the Southern Jurisdiction of Scottish Rite Freemasonry, which by this time Pike virtually controlled—was the first state to secede, with Mississippi following the very same day. Although he had sympathy for both sides at the outset, Pike decided to take sides with the Confederates. At the same time, he continued to hold out hope for a negotiated settlement that would strengthen the states' rights of self-determination while restraining federal dominance.

But the inevitable arrived when the prospect of abolition led the nation into civil war. In 1861, at the beginning of the conflict, Pike asked to be appointed Confederate envoy to the Native Americans. The newly established Confederate States of America, under the leadership of Jefferson Davis, was more than pleased to grant his request.

Pike's first official act as envoy was to negotiate a treaty between the Confederate government and the Cherokees, led by the famous chief John Ross. The Indian-Confederate treaty led to Pike's being commissioned as a brigadier general on November 22, 1861, and given a command in the Indian Territory. Over the next six months, he was responsible for the training of three Confederate regiments of Indian cavalry.

Pike led his Native American troops into the Battle of Pea Ridge, otherwise known as Elkhorn Tavern, in March 1862. At first, they were victorious but fell into disarray during a Union counterattack. Chief Ross would forever be known for his savagery during this battle, in which his men scalped fallen Union soldiers, some still alive.

When Pike was ordered to send his troops to Arkansas in May 1862, he resigned in protest. He had given his personal assurance to Ross and the other chiefs that the natives would only fight within the Indian Territory in defense of their negotiated land claims. As a result of this protest, along with the brutal conduct of his native troops in the field, Pike was charged with insubordination and treason against the Confederacy.

In 1863, Pike, facing arrest, escaped into the hills of Arkansas and lived as a fugitive until the Confederate army accepted his resignation on November 11, 1863. Following this, he was allowed to return to his family in Little Rock, where he resumed his law practice. Between 1864 and 1866, although decommissioned, Pike continued to be heavily involved in Civil War affairs, both officially and clandestinely.

It has been purported, although never totally confirmed, that Pike was a founding member of the paramilitary espionage organization known as the Knights of the Golden Circle, which was first formed in 1854 and was intimately involved in the conspiracy to assassinate President Abraham Lincoln.

It has also been said that Pike was the only conspirator in Lincoln's assassination to escape hanging and that he was behind the founding of the Ku Klux Klan at the end of the Civil War. It is known with certainty that he was the Grand Dragon of the Tennessee chapter of the KKK, as well as its Grand Council's judiciary counsel. He also was instrumental in penning the Klan's rituals, which were based loosely on those of the Scottish Rite of Freemasonry.

With the formal end of the Civil War on May 9, 1865, Pike fled Arkansas with his wife and family and initially headed to Mexico. After a change of heart, he shifted from one state to another, narrowly avoiding arrest by Union troops. By June 1865, he had taken refuge in Canada, where he stayed for approximately two months until Lincoln's successor, Andrew Johnson, granted him a "parole" on August 30, 1865. (Pike never accepted a full pardon, which would imply that he was guilty of treason.)

Here is the second major enigma around Pike. Why was it so important to him to maintain that his commission as a brigadier general in the Confederate army and his actions in instigating the secession of eleven Southern states from the Union did not constitute treason? Earlier he had been charged with treason by the Confederate government and did not dispute that charge. Was it a matter of principle, or was there something more complex relating to his insistence that his actions were true to the Constitution of the United States?

Probably the most enduring aspect of Pike's career relates to his meteoric rise within American Freemasonry. From the early 1840s onward, Pike developed a phenomenal and distinguished Masonic career, which would lead to a remarkable series of synchronistic events in the history of North America, most of which are unknown to the general public to this day.

Pike's encounter with fraternal lodges began with membership within the Odd Fellows Lodge in the early 1840s. From there he quickly transitioned into the Masonic Lodge and rapidly rose through its state and national ranks, including receiving full Knights Templar honors in 1853 at Hugh de Payens Commandery No. 1, in Little Rock. He was elected Sovereign Grand Commander of the Scottish Rite's Southern Jurisdiction on January 3, 1859, a position that gave him absolute control over the Southern Jurisdiction for the remainder of his life.

Among many things, Pike is probably best known for having consolidated and developed the Southern Jurisdiction's thirty-two-degree rituals, which are still in use within that jurisdiction, and for having written the penultimate book on Masonry, titled *Morals and Dogma of the Ancient and Accepted Scottish Rite of Freemasonry,* which was published in 1871.

On April 2, 1891, Albert Pike died inside the Old House, which was at the time the Temple headquarters of the Southern Jurisdiction in Washington, D.C. Surprisingly, given his role in the Civil War, by a special act of Congress his remains were removed from their original burial plot and reburied in a stone crypt located within the walls of the New House, which is the current Temple Building in Washington, D.C. A larger-than-life statue of Pike dominates the Judiciary Square neighborhood of Washington, D.C. Given the current turmoil surrounding the removal of statues of Confederate generals from prominent locations across the United States, it is significant that no one has even raised the issue of removing Pike's statue.

Pike corresponded prolifically with many other high-ranking Masons around the world, including a lasting correspondence with Col. William James Bury (W. J. B.) MacLeod Moore, then Supreme Grand Master of the Knights Templar of Canada. Moore is credited with introducing Scottish Rite Masonry, Templarism, the Conclave and Rosicrucianism to Canada and North America, becoming both the first Supreme Grand Master of the Sovereign Great Priory of Canada, and Supreme Magus of the Societas Rosicruciana in Civitatibus Foederatis (SRICF). Moore provided Pike with the ancient rituals for these orders, which he had gotten during his overseas travels, allowing Pike to extend his influence over Southern Jurisdiction Scottish Rite Masonry throughout the United States.

To come full circle, approximately four years ago, in my capacity as Grand Historian/Grand Archivist for the Sovereign Great Priory–Knights Templar of Canada, I unexpectedly came into the care of a set of private letters between Pike and MacLeod Moore. The correspondence lasted Pike's lifetime, culminating in his receiving the honorary appointment of Provincial Grand Prior of the Sovereign Great Priory–Knights Templar of Canada in 1878. The contents of these remarkable letters have never been presented publicly until now.

The pages of this novel will reveal the exact content of some of those letters. As these letters are real and have been historically verified, this content is priceless in itself. When interwoven with the story that you are about to read, whispers of a secret of world proportions surpass mere speculation. I leave it to the reader to determine to what degree the following story is real and to what degree it is fictional.

MOST EMINENT KNIGHT WILLIAM F. MANN, GCT
SUPREME GRAND MASTER
SOVEREIGN GREAT PRIORY–KNIGHTS TEMPLAR OF CANADA

Orient of Washington, D∴ C∴

12ᵗʰ day of חשון, A∴ M∴ 5637.

30ᵗʰ October, 1876, V∴ E∴

Ill∴ and Very dear Brother:

Your postal card of Aug.
13ᵗʰ, and copies of your address (one corrected) and
of the proposed Statutes for Gr. Priory, came safely
and in due time to hand, but not to my
hands until a week ago, till when I was
absent, on an "Excrescence" to the Pacific Coast.

I hardly need say that I value the
address, and regret that I have it not in
pamphlet form, that I might bind and preserve
it.

I quite agree with you, that there is not
the slightest foundation for the impudent fiction that

the Knights of the Temple, after the great Order was swept out of existence, became Freemasons and under that mask continued their Templar Organization. Masonic Templarism is an absurdity. In this Country the Templar (so called) association is imposing by its numbers, but any one who is a Master Mason and can pay the fees can be a Templar; and in some places very shabby fellows, following very low modes of obtaining their living, are very good Templars. The Ritual of the Order was made here, and there is nothing of the Templar in it or in the Militia uniform they wear: and how your English Templars can recognize ours as of one and the same Order, I do not see.

I shall be glad to receive my certificate, because I set a high value upon the honour conferred on me by your Prov∴ G∴ Priory; and also because, while perfectly content with the title of Provincial Grand Prior, I really do not know, since your Sup∴ Body became a Great Priory, how I should describe myself. At all events, you can enlighten me on that point, and I beg you, by a word, to do so.

Just now I am confined to my room by an attack of rheumatic gout! Otherwise I am very well, and hope to hear in reply that you are so.

And, with many good wishes of Eminence to be

Very truly your friend and Brother

Albert Pike, 33°

Sov∴ Gr∴ Commander

Ill∴ Bro∴ W. C. B. McLeod Moore, 33°

Great Prior of Canada, Sov∴ Gr∴ Insp∴ General, and Hon∴ Member of the Sup∴ Council for the Southern Jurisd" of the U. States

THE
LAST REFUGE
OF THE
KNIGHTS
TEMPLAR

PROLOGUE
June 21, 1865
OTTAWA, UPPER CANADA

It was an exceptionally humid evening along the high southern banks of the Ottawa River, which was still swollen from the late winter runoff from the far north. Some thirty-five years earlier, the British had strategically carved their fort and settlement out of the nearby lowest valley and the highest hill, where once stood an earlier stone tower constructed by a group of medieval Knights Templar. It was said that the earliest Templar lodges, like those of the Ancient, Free & Accepted Masons before them, were located on the highest hills and in the deepest valleys. This tower had been located to take advantage of the best sight lines both up- and downriver, for the Templars protected the most valuable treasure ever—the Holy Grail—as it made its way westward.

Ottawa was located well away from easy access by American raiders across Lake Ontario for a reason. During the War of 1812, the Americans invaded Toronto, and in retaliation the British invaded Washington. Finding the American capital abandoned, the senior Masonic officers sat down to a sumptuous meal in the dining room of the house temporarily occupied by their fellow Mason, George Washington, afterward burning what would ultimately become the White House. The British were adamant that the future capital of Canada would be safe from similar attack.

The original settlement was called Bytown, named after Colonel John By, the British officer and engineer who oversaw the construction of the inland Rideau Canal system joining Lake Ontario to the Ottawa River between 1827 and 1832. An ingenious series of water locks, constructed out of huge limestone blocks carved from the local quarries by Scottish, French, Canadian, and Irish masons, compensated for the rise and fall in elevation along the 125-mile system, which joined natural inland waterways with immense, hand-dug canals.

Colonel By was a typical British army officer: the second son of an aristocratic English family; handsome and strong; educated and ambitious; and a York Rite Freemason and Knight Templar. Descended from a Norman family that had fallen on hard times, he was determined to make his own fortune in a strange new land of opportunity and fate. It didn't bother him that seventeen workers died, mainly of malaria, and twenty-two sappers or engineers died from construction accidents, during the building of the Rideau Canal. He was driven to a higher degree by other, more sublime knowledge.

John By knew that he was following in the footsteps of the Knights Templar, who had originally arrived on the East Coast of North America in the twelfth century and over the past several centuries had intermarried with the tribes who made up the larger Algonquin nation. It was their way of infusing their bloodline with new and untainted DNA while securing safe passage among the newly formed branches of their extended family trees. As they made their way westerly along ancient trade routes, they leapfrogged from one sanctuary to another, constantly looking over their shoulders for the Vatican-appointed Jesuits, whose task was to obliterate the remaining members of what was considered by the Cathars to be the Holy Grail Family—the lineal descendants of Jesus and his wife, Mary Magdalene.

On this evening in 1865, tree frogs and mosquitoes hummed in chorus from the dense underbrush below the back veranda of the elegant Victorian mansion. The mansion itself had been constructed some ten years earlier by Thomas McKay, one of the founders of Ottawa, who had emigrated from Perth, Scotland. McKay was a skilled stonemason who was instrumental in finishing the final set of locks joining the Ottawa River and the Rideau Canal. He went on to be one of the first—and richest—industrialists in Canada.

The house was built in 1855 as a gift from McKay to his new son-in-law, John McKinnon, who was to die suddenly in 1866. Afterward, the house would exchange hands several times until it was purchased in 1883 by the first prime minister of Canada, Sir John A. MacDonald, himself a Knight Templar.

As fate would have it this evening, splayed languidly on a wicker settee like an imperial rajah was the already infamous Confederate general Albert Pike. General Pike, coincidentally, was a Knight Templar under the banner of the Grand Encampment of the United States of America. Pike occasionally repositioned his excessive bulk in order to better face the northwest setting sun of the summer solstice. His face was flushed with the heat and humidity, and with an inner excitement, as he charted the sun's radiant position in his mind, rereading the letter that he had just finished penning to the president of the United States:

June 21, 1865

Dear Brother and Sir Knight Andrew Johnson, 33°, KT

First and foremost, let me officially congratulate you on your receiving the 32nd and honorary 33rd degree. If you are to allow the highest degree freely into your heart, its illumination will guide you through these very difficult times indeed.

I trust that you are most pleased with the honor bestowed upon you by my fellow officers, as deserving Freemen have received the same honor for thousands of years. Our Scottish Rite of the Southern Jurisdiction rituals link us to our ancient origins. You now follow in the footsteps of Egyptian Pharaohs, Biblical Prophets, Merovingian and Frankish Kings, and even those adepts who came before the Great Flood.

Without doubt you have heard sordid rumors of my involvement as a General of the Confederate States Army and in the assassination of your immediate predecessor, Abraham Lincoln. May God rest his soul!

I want to assure you, though, that I had no hand in such a wicked occasion. As Sovereign Grand Commander of the Supreme Council of the Scottish Rite's Southern Jurisdiction of the USA, I believe that I have been tasked by the Supreme Being to bring together the various estranged factions and to mend their differences following such a bloody and devastating civil war.

As such, my esteemed colleagues have presented to you a petition on my behalf demonstrating my civic virtue, good deeds, and positive actions. If forgiven, I offer my services in any manner deemed acceptable, no matter how small or large the task.

I eagerly await your response, as I long to return to my homeland and family.

Sincerely yours, truly,
Albert Pike, 33°, KT
Sovereign Grand Commander

Without a sound, the mansion's young owner stepped out onto the veranda and also took in the magnificent sunset. Helping himself to a glass of the cold lemonade that offered itself from an elegant side table, he found himself a wicker chair to sit in and raised the glass in acknowledgment of his guest. Pike slowly righted himself as best as he could before turning to face his host. Stroking his bedraggled white beard, Pike first sighed blissfully and then said to John McKinnon, "Blessings be, my good, younger Brother and fellow Sir Knight. On an evening such as this, it is not difficult to believe in a Supreme Being, a Great Creator, God Himself, painting such an otherworldly canvas."

McKinnon responded in kind. "Blessing and salutations be with you, my exalted Frater. I bring you sincere and fraternal greetings from my father-in-law, Brother and Sir Knight, the Honorable Thomas McKay, whom I just left. I see that you have been admiring one of our grand sunsets. The direction of the sun leading to the northwest, especially on today's solstice, reminds me that somewhere in the world, the sun is always at its meridian; and, as such, there exists a lodge in every corner of the world. Isn't that a wonderful thing?"

Pike nodded in concurrence, focusing on the key Masonic words that McKinnon had used like a code. At the same time, Pike lazily flicked away at nonexistent dust balls seemingly within his wild beard. "Yes, I agree. Freemasonry, as you know, is the central heartbeat of my very existence. Ever since I was first initiated into the fraternity back in the early 1840s, I have read everything that I could lay my hands on, trying to piece together the origins and ultimate meaning behind our many rituals and beliefs. This inner debate against my own misgivings has resulted in my realization of many spiritual matters. But this is not why I am here!"

Upon hearing these words, John McKinnon sat upright. *Here was the real reason that General Pike sought refuge in British Canada,* he thought. His father-in-law had indicated that he hoped Pike would take the young Mason into his confidence. Thomas McKay knew that Albert Pike had at times acted as a spy for Britain against the Union during the Civil War and had corresponded directly with Queen Victoria on several occasions. The British had been seeking any advantage to bring the colonies back into their empire and thought the division between the North and the South could be worked to that advantage.

Following his pronouncement, Pike cleared his throat and continued, "Now what I've been able to piece together is the result of several decades of research, along with certain secrets that have been passed down through many conduits and orders. The information that you and your father-in-law have shown me over the past few weeks confirms what's been whispered about in the dark corners of the lodges for centuries."

McKinnon drew his chair even closer to the Sovereign Grand Commander. *When my father-in-law first told me the story of how the original nine Knights of the Temple—the Knights Templar—discovered the sacred treasure under the ruins of the Temple of Solomon before the First Crusade and absconded with it to France, and then distributed it secretly to Denmark, Scotland, England, Portugal, and, of all places, pre-Columbian North America, I was skeptical. But now, here, sitting with this North American giant of Scottish Rite Freemasonry, I'm coming to realize that there truly are secrets within secrets.*

Pike pointed to the highest point above the cliffs to the west of the mansion. "It's a shame that Sir Knight MacDonald could not be available to hear what I'm about to tell you. My understanding is that he is working night and day from Kingston trying to convince various provincial bodies to join together in what he terms a confederation, which would lead the British to assent to the formation of Canada as a separate country."

Pike took a sip of his lemonade and continued, "Frankly, I'm a bit skeptical of MacDonald's potential for success. Look at what the United States of America just went through. I would hate to see Canada going the same way. There is an inherent danger of any type of nationalism being more powerful than the rights of either individual provinces or states. Most of the Founding Fathers of America, most of them Masons, of course, had slaves, and the right to own slaves was an inherent right defined in the individual state manifestos. The industry of the South depended on slavery. It will take years for the Confederate States of America to gain back a sound economic foothold; in the meantime, the North will rape and pillage the South. Southern white families will be at the mercy of those carpetbaggers. There is definitely a need to bring together those Southern survivors into a policing force of their own. Nobody else will protect them. But I digress."

Although a mist started to cloud his eyes, Pike could still see that his foray into politics was making McKinnon slightly uncomfortable. "I'm sorry, Brother John. I do get carried away at times. It's the fire in my belly, that's all! I apologize."

John looked as sympathetic as he could, while thinking: *How could a man of his stature and respect within Freemasonry actually believe in such things? Are we not taught in Masonry that all men are to be treated equal? Didn't the American Declaration of Independence speak to the freedom of all men?*

Clearing his throat, Pike changed the subject. "Ahem! I was pointing at that hilltop over there because I understand that John A. has already proposed that area for your future parliament buildings. That's a fine site. Having seen the hidden foundation remains of the earlier Templar tower that existed on the site, which you and your father-in-law showed me the other day, I can't think of a more appropriate site to continue what our medieval knights first started.

"You, of course, know the story of how the Templar Treasure, along with the surviving descendants of the Holy Grail Family, made its way to North America, and, with the help of the Native North Americans, they made their way westward, establishing several sanctuaries or refuges along the way, including right here, across the river at St. Francis du Templeton. Through my intimate dealings and sharing of rituals with the American indigenous people, I have discovered that the descendants of the Grail Family were conveyed along several different routes to the foothills of the Rockies. This was where they eventually were reunited and absorbed entirely into a few select native tribes, who became the ultimate guardians of both the Templar Treasure and the remaining Grail descendants."

Even though it had already been a long and trying day, John was quick to keep his wits about him. He knew that whatever still existed threatened the Roman Catholic Church to its very foundations. Jesuit agents for the Vatican had infiltrated the earliest French settlements from the time of Champlain's first arrival in 1604. *This certainly explains why the Jesuits moved inland quickly during the seventeenth century, establishing missionary posts across the Great Lakes, such as Ste. Marie among the Hurons in 1639. The Jesuit Nicholas Recollect even made his way as far inland as St. Anthony Falls, Minnesota, and traveled down the Mississippi River!*

Pike could see that the intelligent young man who sat across from him was quickly piecing together the puzzle. "John, I know what you want to ask and are hesitant to do so: do I know exactly where the treasure ultimately lies and how to retrieve it? Yes, I do, but for reasons that may be beyond yours or your father-in-law's comprehension, I will not reveal the final resting place of the treasure, including those holy relics and genealogical records that were recovered from the Talpiot Tomb in Jerusalem. It would surely lead to death for both you and your father-in-law, as well as for many others, I'm afraid."

General Pike had no idea that, in any case, John McKinnon would be dead within the year.

In the thick, humid air, Pike concluded his impromptu sermon: "Over the coming decades, the West will open up through the railway, and the proud, noble savage will be obliterated, not only to take their fertile land and the gold and silver that lies underneath it, but to discover the secret that they've shared with me. As for myself, I have sworn a blood oath during the native ceremonies. The secret will go with me to my grave. Of course, I'll use it as a bargaining chip as I make my way through the political labyrinth that awaits me back in the States. I'll not only survive, but thrive, and I have Freemasonry to thank for that. Secret societies must always have some secrets. That's what makes them so fascinating to the ones on the outside. Yet you and I know that is not the real worth of Freemasonry."

With that, Pike excused himself of his host's hospitality and retired for the evening. He would spend half of the evening writing and the other half reading. Sleep would not come lightly this evening to either of the two nineteenth-century Knights Templar. What had just been discussed would lie on both of their minds, and June 24, St. John the Baptist Day, was quickly approaching. St. John the Baptist Day was considered to be the holiest day of the year by the Knights Templar ever since their initial discovery under the ruins of the Temple of Solomon in 1126.

I

APPRENTICE

10:00 a.m., Thirty-three days ago

THE SCOTTISH RITE TEMPLE
1733 16TH STREET N.W., WASHINGTON, D.C.

The morning air was thick with hints of allegorical symbolism, starting with the two sphinxes guarding the Temple's main doorway. Thomas Moore could almost hear his name being called by the two outer guards and by every paper, record, and book that occupied the Temple library's stacks.

Thomas was awestruck by the size of the Temple and its library. He had recently spent many hours both in the Library of Congress and the National Archives of Canada, but there was something different about this building and its extensive collections. Both the Library of Congress and National Archives were organized and methodical, but here was a labyrinth of rooms and aisles bursting with mind-sets and philosophies—an extensive general collection covering every aspect of Freemasonry that had ever existed. There were the collections of past and present Sovereign Grand Commanders from around the world. There was the Abraham Lincoln Collection. There was the Robert

Burns Library. Other collections included the Claudy Collection, on the works of Goethe, and the L. M. Taylor Collection of esoteric literature. Finally, there was the Albert Pike Collection.

The awestruck Thomas must have appeared amusing to the scholars who had spent their lifetimes among the stacks; he also attracted the attention of the only woman present in this bastion of male fraternity. As she leaned back in her chair, she eyed Thomas with a sense of both intrigue and amusement. This freshly entered apprentice was much more interesting than the eighteenth-century text by Benjamin Franklin that she was perusing. She also noticed the leather satchel that he carried over his shoulder.

This lone female scholar, Janet Rose, was in her early thirties and was completing a PhD in Masonic philosophy and esoteric symbolism at Georgetown University. Her father, Solomon, a prominent Freemason in his own right, had thought it odd that a university established by the Jesuits would allow his daughter, an Ashkenazi Jew from New York, to study anything relating to the esoteric, especially since her bold attitudes resembled those of a modern-day witch.

It hadn't hurt Janet's chances that her grandfather, David Joshua Rose, had broken tradition and donated a very considerable sum of money to the Catholic university. He had a way of knowing how to pave the way for his grandchildren into mainstream America. His reputation as one of the foremost medieval scholars of Judaism in the United States didn't hurt Janet's chances either when she successfully applied for the prestigious George Washington Scholarship.

The relationship between ancient Masonic philosophy and esoteric symbolism wasn't Janet's only interest. Her independence and academic brilliance did not prevent her from occasionally seeking out the company of a shy and quirky academic male. She enjoyed exerting her physical and mental dominance over less assured academics, and Thomas Moore fit the bill perfectly. Tall and lanky, all arms and legs, he moved like a slightly more muscled version of Ichabod Crane. He seemed to be in a state of despair. His disheveled hair seemed too boyish for his thirty-five years, but the deep blue-rimmed glasses balanced the look and gave him the air of a millennial professor, although one with a more sinewy and athletic body than was first evident.

Something else about Thomas attracted Janet. She often made a game out of trying to guess people's professions and familial backgrounds, but for some reason she was stumped by this young man. He had a distinctly olive tint to his skin, but it was more reddish-brown than tawny. His hair was a dark, dusty brown, tending toward black. Above all else, it was his eyes that intrigued Janet—a translucent blue, speckled with green, similar to a wolf's eyes—an attractive combination when accented by the deep blue rims of his glasses.

She noticed that Thomas hadn't moved, except for his head, which appeared to be on a swivel, gazing side to side—taking everything in as if photographing the place and depositing the images in a digital file within his brain. Since no one else showed the least inclination to help this man-boy, Janet rose up from her chair and walked toward him. Her curiosity had gotten the best of her. *Ichabod Crane is searching for the Headless Horseman,* she thought.

Thomas had also noticed her. *This beautiful woman is coming toward me. Oh my God! She's extending her hand toward me! What am I supposed to do?*

Luckily, Thomas realized by her smile that she was just trying to be friendly. He instantly extended his hand and smiled back at this goddess of the Temple.

Janet grasped his hand a little too firmly and shook it enthusiastically, trying to imitate a man's grip. Keeping her voice low, she whispered, "Hi, I'm Janet Rose. I've spent most of my last two years devouring this library and its contents. It's like a candy store of esoteric signs, symbols, and tokens for someone as ravenous as myself. Can I help you find what you're looking for?"

Thomas immediately felt the uncertainty leave his body. "And, hello to you! My name is Thomas Moore . . . just like the sixteenth-century social philosopher, except with two O's instead of one. I must say that

I didn't expect any of the librarians in this place to be women. I would have thought that they had some sort of rule against that sort of thing."

Your first big mistake, Mr. Saint I-don't-care-who-you-are! thought Janet. "I'll have you know that I hold two master's degrees, one from Harvard and one from Yale, and am currently completing my PhD at Georgetown on the relationship between ancient Masonic philosophy and esoteric symbolism. I'm not a *librarian!* I was just trying to be polite because you stood there looking like a lost puppy. I must have been crazy to leave my research to offer you assistance!"

Janet's voice rose so loud that many of her fellow researchers raised their head in unison, like prairie dogs responding to a whistle. After confirming that the ruckus came from the woman who seemed to own the place, they all put their heads back down and resumed their reading.

That's when Thomas did the last thing that Janet ever expected. He chuckled. He didn't blush or stutter, but chuckled with a deep, throaty rumble. Janet at first couldn't understand if he was laughing at her or himself. *Maybe there's more depth to this man than first meets the eye,* Janet thought. *Maybe he can show me something that waits in the dark, deep waters of his eyes. Maybe he won't disappoint me the way men usually do.*

Thomas extended his left hand and placed it unexpectedly on Janet's shoulder with a rather intimate gesture. "I'm so sorry if I offended you, Ms. Rose. Please believe me when I say that it wasn't my intention to do so. It's just that I get flustered when I'm around women. My mom used to say that it's because of the many past lives that I spent as a guardian of sacred women. I always put them up on a pedestal as though they're statues that you can't touch. I know that sounds pretty lame . . ."

Janet was stunned. No man had ever talked to her like this. She was used to men fawning all over her and stuttering to find the simplest of words. She liked the power that she had over them. But here was something more. His openness and honesty disarmed her, not to mention the electricity that she felt from his strange little touch on her shoulder. And what did he mean by "guardian of sacred women"?

Thomas immediately recognized that he had made Janet uncomfortable with his comments. "I really do apologize, Janet. I do appreciate the offer of assistance, but I have no idea of even where to start. I'm surely not properly prepared. In fact, I'm not sure if I'm in the right place; I'm neither a Mason nor a scholar. I'm not even American. I'm Canadian."

"Let's start over," said Janet, recovering nicely, although the comment about Thomas being Canadian only added to the intrigue. "Thomas, if I can call you Thomas?" Thomas nodded, as Janet continued, "Thomas, how can I be of assistance?"

"I really don't know where to begin. I'm a landscape architect by profession. I live in Montreal but travel quite a bit, as my firm does a lot of international business. But that's not why I'm here. I'm actually on holiday and love the capital's architecture and planning. But that's not why I'm here either."

Janet laughed a little too loud. "Thomas, do you always ramble on like this? Maybe you should get to the point!"

"Sorry . . . did I say sorry again? It's a bad trait that we Canadians have—always apologizing. Anyway, I'm here because my grandfather passed away about a year ago. He left me a trunk full of family pictures, war memorabilia, medals, and such. My family has quite a military history. My grandfather knew that I was interested in history and our family's genealogy, so it seemed logical that he would leave these things to me. Most of my family doesn't care about our ancestry."

"Thomas, please get to the point," Janet was almost pleading with him. *This man is irritating me to no end, and I just met him five minutes ago.*

"About a month ago," Thomas continued, "I rummaged through the trunk and discovered that it had a false bottom. I removed the bottom and found three worn and stained envelopes that contained correspondence from over several decades between my great-great-grandfather, W. J. B. Macleod Moore, and an Albert Pike."

Janet involuntarily put her hand to her mouth and gave a little sigh. *The Pike Letters! They do exist, after all this time!* It was Janet's turn to lay her hand on Thomas's shoulder. "Thomas, do you have any idea who your great-great-grandfather and Albert Pike were?"

Thomas felt as though he had just been drawn into some sort of conspiracy—one that included him as the hero and the woman opposite him as the heroine. "The only thing I know is what I've read on the internet since discovering the letters. I had no idea that my great-great-grandfather was once Supreme Grand Master of the Sovereign Great Priory–Knights Templar of Canada—and that Albert Pike was once Sovereign Grand Commander of the Scottish Rite Southern Jurisdiction of the United States. Pike appears to be a real character, being a Confederate general and all. It was definitely a lot to take in, so that's why I am here. I have the letters in my satchel, but I have no idea where to begin."

Janet was flabbergasted. *How could Thomas not know about two of the most prominent North American Freemasons in the past two centuries? Within their lifetime, both men dominated Scottish Rite Freemasonry, the Conclave, Templarism, and even Rosicrucianism in North America and beyond. The esoteric philosophy and symbolism shared between these four major fraternal bodies would fill a truck. Holy crap! W. J. B. MacLeod Moore even provided rare copies of both Scottish Rite and Knights Templar rituals to Albert Pike, who further modified them for his own purposes. Pike even went so far as formulating the rituals of both the Knights of the Golden Circle and the Ku Klux Klan in part on what MacLeod Moore had conveyed to him. This will stand North American history on its head! I wonder if the signs and symbols are concealed within the letters.*

Janet was ecstatic. She had been searching for a breakthrough like this for a long time. Now standing in front of her was the prospect of original research, using original correspondence that hadn't seen the light of day for over a hundred years. She would have to tread carefully, for even though he appeared naïve on the outside, she knew that Thomas wasn't a complete fool, or a mere pawn. Her next move would be crucial to her research.

"Thomas, would you like me to introduce you to Albert Pike?"

II

FELLOW-CRAFT
10:30 a.m., Thirty-three days ago
ALBERT PIKE'S CRYPT, SCOTTISH RITE TEMPLE

W hat do you mean: Do I want to meet Albert Pike? He died over a hundred years ago. Has he risen from the dead?" Thomas stammered, obviously bewildered by both Janet's manner and apparent flippancy.

"Calm down!" Janet patted the side of Thomas's face somewhat condescendingly. "Pike's remains are entombed here in the Temple in the central crypt. When he died in 1891, his wishes were to be cremated, but instead he was buried in Oak Hill Cemetery. But then, by a very unusual act of Congress, spearheaded by a senator from Kansas—Illustrious Brother and Sir Knight Arthur Capper, Thirty-Third Degree and a Knight Templar—his remains, primarily his skull and crossbones, were removed and reinterred here inside the Temple in a stone crypt, in a sepulcher befitting his rank and talents. You must have passed it on your way in. Did you not notice the memorial bust of Pike at the central staircase?"

"To tell you the truth, I was intimidated by the grandeur of the building even before I walked up to the front door. All I've recorded in my mind since I walked in is a variety of signs and symbols, mainly Greek, Egyptian, and extremely mystical Hebrew characters, which bombarded my psyche. I can't understand anything that's around me. I've been in a trance—that is, until you walked up to me and cast your spell." Thomas blushed as he said, "By the way, how do you know so much about Albert Pike?"

Janet didn't answer the question but just stood there. *What's happening here? Did I subconsciously cast a spell over him? Oy vey! Somehow I've got to remove myself from this situation. I've got too many things to do to become involved with this man. There are my studies, and I have that paper to finish. Then I have to defend my thesis. . . . Have two years of research gone out the window now that I've learned that Thomas possesses the Pike Letters? I can't let my grandfather, David, down. He'd be so disappointed. He's been searching for the answer to Pike all of his life. Thomas must be the conduit to that-which-was-lost. I knew that Pike somehow must have rediscovered the trail of signs and symbols that lead to the crypt built by the descendants of the original Templars who came to North America. It was identical to the one they had discovered under the wall of King Solomon's Temple in Jerusalem, and it was meant to reinter what they needed to establish a New Jerusalem. Why else would Pike have been paroled by Andrew Johnson and be allowed to serve the U.S. government?*

At this point Janet experienced one of those flashback moments that she had had all of her life, going back to a time when she was the High Priestess of the Temple in an ancient time. Her grandfather had helped her control these mystical experiences to a certain degree, but she was still prone to them when she became excited. She dreamily saw herself descending a limestone staircase, wearing a white, flowing robe and glowing from her head to her leather sandals.

Her hair was a golden blonde, and she wore the colored ribbons of the High Priestess. Her vision smelled of incense and rose petals as the brilliance of the sun on the limestone acted as a backdrop to her dramatic entrance out of the cool shadows of the Temple.

During previous visions, throngs of high-ranking government officials awaited her descent from the heavens with gifts and offerings, for they hoped for a favorable prophecy. However, this time, awaiting her at the bottom of the stairs was one lone figure—the captain of the guardians of the temple.

What is his name? What was his name? I can't believe what I'm seeing. The captain looks exactly like Thomas!

The captain kneels before the priestess and bows his head in recognition of her high station. The sunlight bounces off his feathered helmet, which rests in the crook of his left arm. In his right he balances the blade of his sword, as though offering it in homage. It looks as though the captain has just completed a long journey and is reporting back to the priestess. All appears calm and tranquil, and there's an unspoken bond of admiration and respect between the two.

Janet knew in her heart that these two ancient figures loved one another deeply, but their union could never have been consummated for fear that the priestess would lose her powers of prophecy. She pressed her mind to concentrate harder. *Thomas had indicated earlier that he was a guardian of sacred women in his past life and had revered them. There would have been no temptation between these two—it was a pure love.*

Janet suddenly snapped back to the present to find Thomas studying her in the weirdest way. It was as if the gods had also given him a glimpse back into the past. "Janet, have we ever met before? I just had the strangest feeling that we knew each other, maybe in a past life?"

To dispel any notion of a past connection, Janet waved her hand and nonchalantly replied, "Oh, Thomas, I hope that you don't believe in all that hocus-pocus. Of course, the Temple was constructed to overwhelm you at first glance. It was designed deliberately to astound, confuse, and humble even the highest-ranking official. Come over here, outside of the library proper, so I won't have to whisper anymore, and I'll give you a short history lesson."

Janet wanted to make sure that she was the only one to control Thomas. He was far too valuable an asset to share with any of the other

Masonic scholars, who would have latched on to him immediately if they knew what he carried in his satchel. Janet found one of the cool stone benches that were positioned in hidden alcoves throughout the Temple and silently indicated to him to sit beside her. The architect had incorporated these resting places into the design, anticipating that visiting Masons would require secluded areas for quiet reflection after witnessing the magnificence and scale of the Temple's interior, which was designed to stimulate multidimensional experiences even in the noninitiate. This particular bench conveniently faced the plaque denoting Albert Pike's crypt.

Once they were seated comfortably, the shadows enveloping them like a morning mist, Janet continued her lesson on the Temple's architecture and history, at the same time pointing at the crypt. "The Temple was designed in 1911 by architect John Russell Pope, who modeled it after the tomb of Mausolus at Halicarnassus, one of the Seven Wonders of the Ancient World. The word *mausoleum* is derived from *Mausolus.* The original Mausoleum was a tomb built between 353 and 350 BC at Halicarnassus, which is present-day Bodrum, Turkey. It was for Mausolus, a high-ranking provincial governor in the Persian empire, and his sister-wife Artemisia II of Caria.

"Several talented architects and artists were employed to design the tomb, including Scopas, the man who had supervised the rebuilding of the Temple of Artemis at Ephesus. The tomb was actually crafted by a secret guild consisting of hundreds of other fellow craftsmen. I'm sure you'll remember that Artemisia was named after Artemis—one of the most widely venerated of the ancient Greek deities. She was the goddess of the hunt, wild animals, wilderness, childbirth, and virginity and was protector of young girls. Her Roman equivalent was, of course, Diana."

Janet waved her hand to denote a great expanse. "The tomb was erected on the highest hill overlooking Halicarnassus. The whole structure sat in an enclosed courtyard, and at the center of the courtyard was a stone platform on which the tomb sat. A stairway flanked by stone lions led to the top of the platform and at the center of the platform, the marble tomb rose as a square tapering block. This section was covered with bas-reliefs showing allegorical scenes, including the battle of the Centaurs with the Lapiths and Greeks in combat with the Amazons.

"The mathematics associated with the design of the original tomb represents knowledge directly obtained from the gods—sacred geometry, as it is known within Masonic circles. On the top of the tomb, thirty-six slim columns, ten per side, with each corner sharing one column between two sides, rose for another third of the height. Behind the columns was a perfect cube-like block that carried the weight of the tomb's massive roof. The roof, which comprised most of the final third of the height, was pyramidal. Perched on the top was a *quadriga:* four massive horses pulling a chariot in which rode images of Mausolus and Artemisia."

Janet sensed that Thomas was interested, so she continued. "In his design of the Scottish Rite Temple, Pope employed the same sacred geometry and mathematic ratios as the original but changed a few things to fit hidden Masonic symbolism. For example, there are two Egyptian sphinxes guarding the Temple's entrance instead of two golden lions. And much of the obvious reference to female goddesses and warriors has been removed. You couldn't have the prominent Scottish Rite patriarchs feeling inferior to their female counterparts, could you? The rituals of Freemasonry are based on many of the ancient cultures, so Pope did his best to mix Hellenic and Egyptian symbolism into his design, downplaying the references to the Goddess and the Amazons and to feminine symbolism. In other terms, the sacred feminine was hidden in plain sight, but it's only recognizable for those with the eyes to see. We're actually sitting within the comfort and protection of the building's womb right now.

"The thing that I find really funny is that most modern-day, high-ranking Scottish Rite Masons still do not understand that the Temple was designed and crafted not just as a tribute to a number of great Freemasons but as a *mausoleum* to a single individual; namely, Albert Pike!"

Thomas took in all of the information. It was obvious that he had an eidetic memory, yet this was far more fascinating than anything he had ever learned before. "You mean to tell me that Pike was, and still is, revered as a man-god by the Scottish Rite Masons?" Janet silently nodded. She wanted to impress upon Thomas that she was the expert, the only one who could unlock the secrets of the Pike Letters, and that she understood the craft behind Freemasonry far better than most Masons themselves.

"Yeah, it's almost as if they are waiting for the time when Albert Pike rises from the dead and assumes his rightful place within the American psyche, revered once more as the leader who will lead the people out of the wilderness—the new Messiah, if you wish. Don't get me wrong. My dad is a high-ranking Scottish Rite Freemason, a successful businessman, a philanthropist, and, more simply, a very wise and honorable man. The very fact that we're even talking about Pike and the Temple in this manner would offend his sensibilities. To most Masons around the world, Freemasonry is nothing more than a fraternal brotherhood—a self-financed, self-governing, philanthropic, and extremely charitable organization that does only good—and I would be hard-pressed to argue otherwise.

"Yet if you understand Pike's basic philosophy of life and death, as stated in his most important written work, *Morals and Dogma,* you'll realize that he believed that Freemasonry was something much more. Pike believed from the very beginning that Freemasonry was a *sovereign* state of mind. He also believed that, as Sovereign Grand Commander, all Scottish Rite Freemasons of the Southern Jurisdiction of the United States had to obey him, not the president of the United States. But he considered himself a benevolent dictator, sharing his multidimensional wisdom freely among his brothers, as long as they had taken the oath. Pike sincerely believed that he was chosen as the conduit between heaven and earth and understood God's plan for mankind's hierarchy better than anyone."

Then, as if coming to her rescue, Thomas expanded upon her

thoughts. "Perhaps they're not as much looking to resurrect Pike himself, but his philosophies, his morals, and dogma. You have to admit that the world is currently a pretty screwed-up place. Many people would love to have somebody make the tough decisions for them, like sheep looking for a shepherd."

Janet's heart skipped a beat. Again, here was a man whom she met only about half an hour ago, and he nailed the basis of her PhD thesis in one sentence. She felt at this moment as if she had known him all her life and beyond. Acting upon impulse, she quietly slipped her hand behind Thomas's neck and drew his lips to hers. *I don't care if I do lose my powers of foresight,* she mused to herself. . . .

III

MASTER MASON
11:00 a.m., Thirty-three days ago
THE ALBERT PIKE COLLECTION,
SCOTTISH RITE TEMPLE

Savoring the kiss, Thomas followed Janet hand in hand through the open door into the Albert Pike Collection room. For some reason, she appeared to have free run of the Temple. It was fairly dark, and he had to wait until his eyes adjusted to the dimness. Then a movement sensor dramatically filled the room with light. Everywhere within, the Temple dripped with symbolism—night and day, darkness and light—an analogy for rebirth. Only when exposed to the light could the grandeur of the collection and the ancient dimensions of the room be appreciated to their full effect.

Janet continued with her history lesson. "The Temple's architect certainly understood the dramatics behind the Masonic rituals and translated them perfectly into multidimensional spaces, applying both the golden mean and the perfect cube. The design also suggests that rebirth can happen through understanding, knowledge, and wisdom, gained in this case through books. Another famous Mason, Lewis

Carroll, born Charles Lutwidge Dodgson, expressed the same dramatics in *Alice's Adventures in Wonderland* and *Alice Through the Looking Glass*. The ritual of passage into another dimension through death—whether through a simple knock on the head, drowning, falling down a rabbit's hole, or even being crucified—and being reborn is the basis of most religions. Rising up once again is the essence of life itself. Native North Americans share the same passage every time they enter a sweat lodge. The darkness and warmth and sensory deprivation represents Mother Earth's womb, from which following certain ceremonies and rituals the initiate emerges into the light, reborn and renewed."

In their case, it was as though both Janet and Thomas had just emerged from their own rabbit hole. The Albert Pike Collection ceremoniously features Pike's personal library, which contains first editions and holograph copies of many of his works. The official story is that here is the Master's wisdom, in splendid arrangement, awaiting the curious fellow craftsman who has learned to follow the seven liberal arts and sciences to gain a better understanding of the sublime.

"During the years that Pike was involved in Freemasonry," Janet continued, "he wrote and compiled many books and became familiar with numerous languages, among them Latin, Greek, and Sanskrit. As such, he is regarded as one of the Masonic world's foremost scholars, philosophers, and historians. With his knowledge of languages, he conducted valuable research into ancient knowledge and practices and, of course, edited and rewrote the rituals of the Ancient and Accepted Scottish Rite for the Southern Jurisdiction. His renown as a jurist, orator, philosopher, scholar, soldier, and poet extends throughout the world, even beyond Masonry. Pike insisted that his collection could be only displayed and made available to the public if it was free. Following his instructions, all of the Temple collections are open to the public and can be viewed for free. Along with Pike's literary works sit his original desk, lamp, clock, and chair. Many of the personal items found in the Albert Pike Museum include his Masonic regalia, a representative sampling of his large collection of pipes, and a plaster-cast death mask."

Janet dropped Thomas's hand and spread her arms wide as she pirouetted in a circle. "Thomas, somewhere within this collection is a key! A key that unlocks the signs and symbols that I believe can be found in the letters that you have in your possession. When you arrange those signs and symbols in their proper order, it will reveal a secret. This will lead to a hidden crypt somewhere in North America that contains relics, ancient scrolls, and other sacred treasure that would shake the foundations of the Roman Catholic Church. Pike rediscovered the secret and took it to the grave with him, almost daring the adept to try to decipher his secret code, which leads to *that-which-was-lost*."

As he was roused from his stupor, things became very clear to Thomas. "Hold on just a second, Janet. You've been spending a little too much time reading the garbled messages that linger here and elsewhere. I recognize what you're talking about. This is the stuff that Dan Brown sensationalizes in his novels. This is the same thesis behind *The Da Vinci Code* and *The Lost Symbol*! Come on, Janet; can a scholar such as yourself actually believe that? This is *National Treasure* stuff all over again. They were all great movies, except *The Lost Symbol* was a little weak, in part, I think, because Brown himself was not a Mason. I read that somewhere. . . . Hey, I remember now. Wasn't *The Lost Symbol* even based on this very Temple?"

It was all that Janet could do to maintain her temper. *How dare you? I'm talking ancient philosophy and esoteric symbolism, and you reduce my research to the likes of Tom Hanks and Nicolas Cage. We're talking about ancient Sanskrit and the Kabbalah, alchemy, and early Christian mysteries. We're talking about the oriental mysteries. We're talking about the sacred marriage of Christian Rosenkreuz. We're talking of Sir Robert Boyle and Sir Isaac Newton, the founders of the Royal Society. We're talking about the real quest for the Holy Grail.*

But Janet maintained control of her inner demons and responded as calmly as she could. "Listen to me, Thomas, and please, listen very carefully." Subliminally, she allowed Thomas to view her third eye, which she had never before exposed to anyone on any level. "*The Da*

Vinci Code happened to hit a sublime nerve in the general population that even the author did not know existed. Ever since they first walked on this earth, humans have longed to understand their existence to a higher degree. Formal religion was invented to control the masses and to prevent them from idolizing everything from a rock to a tree to the moon and the stars. First there was the goddess; then gods aplenty, both male and female, thanks to the early civilizations; then that was reduced down to one omnipotent god; then the masses looked for a savior, and the Roman Emperor Constantine, in order to control the masses, arranged for the Council of Nicaea to develop a nice, neat package. That's when we got the Holy Trinity and the church patriarchs balked at including the Mother for fear that the Goddess would return. Instead we got the Holy Ghost.

"But it was confusing and is still confusing. The ancients understood where babies come from. They come from a union of the male and female—sperm and egg. Not by divine intervention but from love, lust, intercourse, coitus, whatever you want to call it! Of course, the idea of Jesus, the rabbi and prophet, taking a wife and having a family couldn't be suppressed forever. The church gave it a try, and it went pretty well for over two thousand years. Jesus the man became the *Christos*. Regardless, Jesus was a master magus, a supreme magus. Yes, a master magician. It was in Egypt, in the wilderness, that he apprenticed and learned to master the old Egyptian mysteries, which were passed on by the learned initiates and became the Christian mysteries. Even the Muslims revere Jesus as a great prophet. In Native North American terms, he would be a traveling shaman, a shape-shifter. In feminine form, he would be a spirit-woman.

"This, among other things, is what the Templars discovered under the Temple of Solomon a thousand years ago. They understood the power of what they possessed but also understood the absolute danger in it. The original nine knights came from rich families, most of them originating from the Jewish high priests, such as Aaron, brother of Moses. The lesser royal Frankish families, many descendants of the Merovingian dynasty, outwardly converted to Catholicism for their own protection. But they continued to pass on the secrets of the old Jewish magi. When Jerusalem was sacked by the Romans in AD 70, the Temple priests hid its most sacred treasures in the caverns, tunnels, and carved cisterns deep underground. The location of these treasures was recorded and passed down from family to family in the knowledge that one day they would be recovered.

"Once recovered, the treasures were secreted away in France. Then they were dispersed to England, Scotland, Portugal, and Denmark and also to North America, where the Templar/Grail families, direct descendants of Jesus and Mary Magdalene, strategically intermarried with the Native North Americans. The rest, as they say, is hidden history."

Janet stopped at this point, looked at her watch, and exclaimed, "God, Thomas, I can't explain what you possess any more clearly. Those letters could change the world. The question is then: are you in or out? It's that simple. Will you help me try to solve this mystery? I can't promise you anything will come of it. People have been searching for the so-called Templar Treasure for centuries. The only thing that may come of it is that you may learn on a higher level something about yourself, which otherwise you may go through life completely ignorant of. It's your choice, but make it quick. I'm famished." *For the pleasure of the sexual magic that I can teach you!*

Thomas didn't even have to think for more than a second. *She's captured my heart; that's for sure. What could be the harm in it?* "OK, you've piqued my curiosity, but where do we start? There must be thousands of pages of writings here."

Her third eye retreated back into her forehead. But before it completely disappeared, Janet caught a vision of the two of them entwined; but that would have to wait. "Thomas, we don't start here. We're going to take a shortcut. We're going to go and see my grandfather, David Joshua Rose. He's a Supreme Magus in his own right. He'll point us in the right direction, allowing us to advance to the next degree."

As they left the Temple, Thomas could have sworn that the bust of Albert Pike, which he now deliberately acknowledged, winked at him.

IV

SECRET MASTER

1:00 p.m., Thirty-three days ago

HOME OF DAVID JOSHUA ROSE, SUPREME MAGUS,
GEORGETOWN, WASHINGTON, D.C.

David Rose's house stood out from the rest of the beautiful brown-stones on the tree-lined block because of a single difference. The front door's overhead transom contained a small multicolored, stained-glass Star of David. Janet's grandfather was proud of that symbol. It meant many different things on many levels, each and every one of which was applicable to the Rose line.

Of course, the Star of David signified that Jews lived or had lived in the house, but the Rose family was equally proud to be directly descended from the House of David, the king, and through the *kohenim,* the Jewish priestly line of the tribe of Levi. It was also known as the Seal of Solomon, which spoke to the Master Builder's wisdom, which had obviously been passed down through multiple generations. The symbol also spoke to David's involvement with a historical line of Jewish mystics, starting with Mary the Jewess, who were practicing alchemists from the first century onward. The rainbow colors denoted a connection to Noah and to the knowledge (not the animals) that he preserved from before the Flood.

Although in his nineties and widowed, David Rose refused to move out of the historic neighborhood. He claimed that it kept him young at heart, with the hustle and bustle of young couples, government types, university professors and students, entertainment and eating establishments, and its real sense of American history. Being a practical man, though, he had also had the latest in high-tech security installed.

Besides, the house gave Janet an excuse to live with him, as it was close to Georgetown University. Actually it was within walking distance, even though Janet preferred to drive to school and to the Temple in her Mustang convertible.

David was especially buoyed this day, as Janet had phoned ahead to tell him that she was leaving her studies early because she had met a man, whom she was bringing home to meet him. Janet knew that this would intrigue her grandfather, since she had never before introduced even one of her many male friends to him. Besides, it was unheard of to interrupt his daily routine of prayer and study, even for his most precious grandchild.

David had volunteered to prepare a late lunch for the two, which was again rare, as he would never interrupt his day in order to eat. He believed that food during the day would cloud one's mind and require a midday nap. Buddhist monks refused to eat or drink anything that they believed would dull the senses, and David figured that if it helped the Buddhists, it would help him.

As Janet's car pulled up to the curb in front of her grandfather's house, Thomas surveyed the surroundings. *What a beautiful neighborhood and gorgeous streetscape. Judging from the quality and upkeep of the homes, I would think that Janet's family has been very successful in whatever they do.* Thomas prepared himself to meet the living patriarch of the Rose family. "Janet, your grandfather's house is tremendous. I really love the way the house fronts onto the street. I imagine that when any of the homes on this street come onto the market, they're scooped up quickly, regardless of the asking price."

Janet responded in kind. "Oh yes, you can say that. A week doesn't go by without some real-estate agent knocking on the door, trying to convince my grandfather to sell. He's so polite with them. To tell you the truth, I think he gets a kick out of the sexy real-estate agents. He's quite the rogue. If he especially likes them, he'll invite them in for tea and cookies. I expect to come home one of these days and find him in bed with one of them. To think he'll be ninety-six next August."

Responding with the same wicked chuckle, Thomas exclaimed, "Ninety-six . . . that's amazing. I wish one of my grandparents had lived to be that age. What's his secret?"

"Since you asked, my grandfather, among other things, is a practicing alchemist. Actually, among other academic accreditations, he has a master's degree in chemical engineering from MIT. In fact, he has a number of rather brilliant patents under his name, mainly dealing with metallurgy. So if you ask him his secret to a long, healthy life, he'll tell you that it's because he digests a small amount of white powdered gold every morning. He claims that it ensures that he can still get an erection."

Janet laughed out loud at the thought of her grandfather running around the house with nothing on but an erection. *Thank God that I haven't witnessed that yet.*

Ignoring the scene that Janet had just painted, Thomas continued his questioning. "Amazing . . . I can't wait to meet him." *Hopefully, he'll be fully clothed.* "Your family has obviously been very successful. What's the family business?"

Janet didn't mind Thomas's questions. *He might as well understand what he's dealing with.* "The Rose family has been involved in precious metal trading for centuries—mainly gold and silver. My father runs one of the biggest commodities-trading firms in the world. You may have seen the name before: The Rose Commodities Corporation or RCC for short? Because of that, I grew up in New York in rather elegant surroundings, and that's where my mom and dad and siblings live to this day. But my grandfather was always partial to the capital, for some reason." Janet knew the reason, but she didn't want to scare off Thomas with too much esoteric information all at once.

On the other hand, Thomas appeared to be fascinated by the information that Janet was providing. She thought for a moment. *Maybe his subconscious has been exposed to all of this before and he just doesn't realize it. I'll have to try to open up his blood memory, but now's not the time.*

As the two were exiting the car, David appeared at the front door and waved. Janet waved back. To Thomas, catching a glimpse of her broad smile as she greeted her grandfather, it was obvious that there was a deep bond between the two.

David gave his granddaughter a big hug and kissed her on both cheeks, "Janet, my precious angel, you're absolutely radiant. I can't believe what I'm seeing. Can it be that you've finally met somebody who has the mettle to challenge you? Who is this superman?"

Janet ignored her grandfather's playful jabs. "David Rose, I would like you to meet Thomas Moore." Thomas bounded up the steps and enthusiastically shook David's hand, while David eyed him up and down, all the while thinking, *Something doesn't compute here. My granddaughter has fallen for this man? He appears nice enough and all, but he certainly isn't spectacular from the outside, as I pictured that he would be. Perhaps I've misjudged my granddaughter a little. I must be missing something. It'll come to me.*

Reading her grandfather's thoughts was easy for Janet, as they were so in tune with her own. "Grandfather, I know what you're thinking. Isn't it you who always tells me not to judge the book by its cover? For your information, I just met Thomas this morning, but it seems I've known him all of my many lives. There's something else that he possesses, Grandfather—something that I know that you've been searching for most of your life. Aren't you going to invite us in?"

"Yes, yes, how boorish of me. Please come in. I apologize, Thomas, for the mess of the house. The cleaning lady comes in every other day, but as you can see, I have books lying everywhere, and she's not allowed to touch them. I can't imagine how she keeps the house as clean as she does. You can throw your satchel into that empty chair and join me in the dining room. I've already laid out your lunch."

Thomas took a look around the house as he made his way to the dining room. Beyond the books, the house's interior and contents were magnificent. Thomas recognized several Tiffany lamps and Louis XIV chairs. Portraits of family members—current and past—in gilded frames were scattered throughout, along with several jewel-encrusted Fabergé eggs in locked display cases. The living room was decorated in different shades of royal blue. *The New York auction houses would be beating down the doors if they knew what existed here. Maybe they do. What've I gotten myself into? I'm certainly not in Janet's league, not by a mile!*

David could sense Thomas's unease. "Thomas, please ignore the trappings of an old man. I collect things, not for their monetary value, but because of the history that they carry. If you concentrate enough, they will speak to you."

Janet declared, "Yes, Thomas, I confess: my grandfather talks to the furniture." Then she spied the lunch offering in the dining room. "What a magnificent setting, Grandfather! I see that you had your favorite kosher deli deliver; please serve up our lunch. But there are only two settings. Aren't you going to have anything?"

"My dear granddaughter, you very well know that I don't eat lunch. I will have some Earl Grey and green-tea mixture with you, though. I did make that!" Janet and Thomas took their seats and settled into the lunch, which allowed David to continue leading the conversation: "Thomas, please excuse my forwardness. Believe me when I say that I'm most interested in you and your family's background and all that, but above all else, my granddaughter has piqued my curiosity. What is it that you possess that has captivated my granddaughter so much?"

Thomas looked toward Janet, who sheepishly nodded in concurrence. *Go ahead, Thomas, reveal your secret to the Secret Master.*

Putting down his fork, Thomas looked hesitantly into the eyes of David Rose and admitted, "Mr. Rose, according to your granddaughter, what I possess will apparently astound you. In my satchel out in the hallway I have three envelopes that contain what your granddaughter refers to as the Pike Letters."

Janet watched her grandfather, trying to judge his reaction, but the old fox was too clever to give anything away. But deep inside, David Rose's heart was racing. *The Pike Letters . . . I had given up all hope of ever seeing them in this lifetime. Now, to my absolute delight, my granddaughter has delivered them to me, along with this somewhat befuddled young man. His knowledge of the secrets must be quite limited. No mind, there will be time to teach him. I can see that he has the capability already, to some degree, as long as he realizes his inner confidence. If I'm reading my granddaughter correctly, she will give him the confidence. She's definitely taken with him. Perhaps he will take the white powder freely.*

David reached out with both hands and put one on each of Thomas's and Janet's, as if giving his blessing to a future union. Clearing his throat, he asked as humbly as possible, "Thomas, would you mind if I studied those letters for a while? I'm sure that my granddaughter has given you some indication of what they purportedly contain. Albert Pike was a Supreme Magus, like me. For all of his faults and misguided ways, he must also be revered and admired, not only in Masonic circles but in all mystical circles. He was mostly self-taught, unlike me, who had a great mentor—my own father—God rest his soul. However, I believe that it was the Canadian MacLeod Moore and Pike's other friend, Albert Mackey, who guided Pike in his quest."

That's when Janet dropped her bombshell. "Grandfather, MacLeod Moore was Thomas's great-great-grandfather."

"Yes, Janet," David's eyes didn't leave Thomas's; "I figured as much. Your grandfather still holds a few secret ways of knowing things before they're revealed, ways that you're not even aware of." He could feel his granddaughter's eyes boring down on him, but he ignored them. Instead he repeated his request to Thomas, "So, Thomas, will you grant this old man his wish?"

Thomas didn't really know how to respond, so he followed his heart. "Sir, it would be my honor and pleasure to have such a learned and honorable man study those letters for as long as you desire. I have to fly back to Montreal early tomorrow morning for several business commitments, but I could be back here in about a week. I'll leave the letters with you while I'm gone, if that's OK. My office will be surprised when they learn that I intend to take a month off, but it's time that my colleagues learn to make decisions on their own. Besides, with your approval, I would like to spend some more time with your granddaughter. I know this sounds irrational, but I think I'm falling in love with her."

Janet couldn't help smiling at Thomas's honesty, but she was raised to respect her elders' wishes. She had always acknowledged that she still required her grandfather's and parents' blessing, but she was sure that they would all say yes, even though Thomas wasn't Jewish. She too knew that she was falling for this man, although they had just met.

"Thomas, nothing in the world could make me happier," David smiled.

V

PERFECT MASTER

6:00 p.m., Thirty-three days ago

THE GEORGETOWN INN, WASHINGTON, D.C.

David, Janet, and Thomas spent the next few hours talking about nothing really important in light of what was in Thomas's satchel. David Rose didn't want to alarm Thomas by rushing off with the Pike Letters while Janet and Thomas remained in the house. He had waited his entire life to examine the letters, so another two or three hours didn't matter.

On the other hand, Janet had volunteered to drive Thomas back to his hotel—the Georgetown Inn—which was fairly close to her grandfather's house. After a cordial farewell to David, Thomas found himself in the passenger's seat of Janet's convertible, which was pulling up too soon to the front door of his hotel. Although it had been only eight hours since he first met her, he was emotionally exhausted with so many things, on so many levels, that were swirling around in his brain and his heart.

Janet was the first to break the silence. "Nice pick of a hotel," she offered. "There must be a little synchronicity involved here, what with you choosing the Georgetown Inn to stay in while you're here in Washington, being so close to my grandfather's house. I've always loved this hotel. Many people think it's historic, although it only opened in 1962. But that's what I love about it. It was designed to fit into the historic architecture, but it has all of the modern amenities. There is even a butler assigned to each floor. They really did a lovely job on the exterior and the interior. Its tasteful, edgy design and great service have attracted a lot of actors and actresses over the years. Although I understand that the most notable guests of the Georgetown Inn have been the rather 'horsey' Duke and Duchess of Windsor. Oh, sorry, with you being Canadian and all . . ."

Thomas let out his low chuckle once again, ignoring Janet's comments about the royals. "Yes, I love this hotel too. That's why I chose it. Many of my colleagues stay here while on business. I have to say that, Janet, you seem to be rambling a bit, which I've not seen before, although I have known you for less than a day. If I didn't know better, I would take you to be nervous. Here, let me get right to the point: would you like to spend the night with me?"

Janet let out a big sigh as she placed her hand on Thomas's shoulder. 'Thomas, nothing in the world would make me happier. I would love to. But I have to confess, I'm more of a proper old-fashioned Jewish girl than I appear. Normally I would have no qualms about falling into the sack on the first night, but our relationship is different. I want it to be different. You need to go back to Montreal without visions of me in your bed tugging at your heart, among other things."

Thomas held up his hand to stop her right there. He wanted to assert his manhood at least a little in the conversation. "And what makes you think that I haven't entertained those lustful visions already?"

It was Janet's turn to chuckle. "Yes, I imagine that you have, especially after all the signals that I've been sending you. Do you know that you have amazing eyes? A girl could get lost in those . . . oh, what am I doing? Listen, I promise you that when you get back from Montreal, I'll make you so content that you'll be begging me to leave you alone.

There will be plenty of time for me to teach you about all the magic and delights of a Jewish princess. I'm a master of them all! I'm my grandfather's esoteric prodigy in more ways than one. I guarantee that our lovemaking will be perfect. I want it to be perfect. Now please, get out of this car before I change my mind."

With that, Janet teasingly reached across Thomas's lap and flipped the door handle to the passenger door. Simultaneously, she gave Thomas a sensuous yet fleeting kiss and then gave him a gentle push.

Without looking back, Thomas mockingly obeyed Janet's command, bounded out of the car, and vanished through the front doors of the Georgetown Inn. Janet pulled the passenger door shut rather sullenly, threw the stick shift into first, and gunned the car away from the hotel entrance, doing her best to concentrate on her driving and leave her thoughts of Thomas back at the hotel. She kept on telling herself that a week wasn't that long, and besides, she needed to help her grandfather. She knew all too well that once he started to concentrate on something this important, he would totally forget to eat, sleep, or even brush his teeth. Time and space stood still for him at times like this. It would be like the seventeenth-century alchemist retreating to his laboratory for days on end, trying to execute the perfect transmutation.

Back at the hotel, Thomas wasn't faring any better. If he had had his wits about him, he would have noticed the handsome, sharply dressed man sitting in the corner of the foyer, nonchalantly scrolling through his cell-phone messages. As Thomas made his way to the front desk, he might even have noticed that every few seconds the cell phone would be righted to enable its owner to take a photo of Thomas. Love has a way of turning the fool into mush, and at this point, Thomas was the archetypal fool, but he didn't care one iota. He had just found his Tarot princess.

As Thomas approached the desk, the pretty concierge recognized him as the one who had asked for directions to the Temple earlier that morning. She came around from her desk and initiated the conversation once again. "Ah, Mr. Moore, I see that you're back. Did you find the

Temple Library, and were you able to complete your necessary research?"

The man in the corner was eagerly awaiting a reply, as he had arranged the conversation in the first place. The concierge was more than pleased to assist in the ruse, especially after he had handed over a $100 bill as a tip. As far as she knew, the handsome man hiding in the corner was playing a trick on his good friend, Thomas, looking to surprise him in person later that evening.

Thomas pulled himself away from his dreams and answered, "Yes, thank you very much for all of your help. The day was certainly a busy one. The Scottish Rite Temple definitely lives up to its billing. What a magnificent building! I understand now why it was voted one of the top five architectural gems in all of the United States. And the library certainly met all of my expectations. Truly unbelievable!"

The concierge tried to speak a little louder than normal without giving anything away, "That's terrific, Mr. Moore. Were you able to find the information that you were looking for?"

Thomas, still dreamily thinking about Janet, only half-listened to the question. "What? Ah, sorry." But he recovered nicely, finally noticing that the young woman bore a striking resemblance to the Canadian actress Rachel McAdams. "Unfortunately, I really wasn't able to delve into my research in any great detail. I found the material overwhelming. Regardless, I have to fly back to Montreal early tomorrow morning because of business. But I'll be back in about a week to dive into my research. I'm exhausted. I need a good shower and to go to sleep early. I had a late lunch, so I won't be having dinner, but I do need an early-morning wake-up call for three o'clock, if that's possible? I'll take Uber to the airport."

The concierge thought her acting coach would have been impressed with her performance. "Yes, of course, Mr. Moore. Three o'clock a.m. it is! Have a good evening."

Thomas made his way to the elevators and was sound asleep within ten minutes of entering his room. He slept deeply for most of the evening, only once dreaming of Janet lying naked beside him, peering lovingly into his eyes and stroking his chest. He subconsciously focused on that image, trying to ignore the figure of Albert Pike sitting in the corner of the bedroom watching the two of them. Before he sank back into a deep sleep, Thomas made a subconscious note to read Pike's *Morals and Dogma* before he returned to Washington.

As soon as Thomas disappeared into the elevator, the ordained Jesuit, Philippe De Smet, rose from his chair and walked silently across the foyer toward the concierge. Smiling widely, he slid his well-manicured hand into his pant pocket and produced a business card of sorts, which he handed to the young woman. "I couldn't help overhearing that Thomas was exhausted and was taking an early flight back to Montreal. No matter: I won't surprise him tonight. I haven't seen him for five years, so another week won't matter. I really want it to be a surprise." *He'll definitely be surprised when I judge the perfect time to expose myself.* "If I could ask you to do me one more favor, I would be eternally grateful. As soon as Mr. Moore arrives back in Washington next week, could you phone me and let me know?"

The concierge was smitten with De Smet's good looks and well-schooled manners. As a student of theater, she prided herself on her ability to identify different dialects and determined that he had a touch of the Boston accent, which made him all the sexier. "Yes, of course, Mr. De Smet, it would be my pleasure." She looked down at his business card and saw that it identified him as Dr. Philippe De Smet, "I'm sorry, I mean Dr. De Smet. Very interesting, are you a GP or specialist?"

Philippe found the young woman shallow and almost repugnant in her assumption that he was a medical doctor. In reality, he had a doctorate in divinity and ancient philosophy. But he knew that he needed to court her some more, as she was a valuable little snitch. As Philippe turned to leave, to feed the charade a little more he said, "I'm very much a specialist. Now remember, it's our secret. By the way, you could be an actress, you know?"

The concierge glowed as Philippe breezed through the front door and was gone.

The young woman wouldn't be the first female to fall under Philippe De Smet's spell. From the time that he turned thirteen and started to grow and fill out faster than most of the other boys from his Boston neighborhood, Philippe found that he possessed a power of sorts over most women, young and old. The fact that his father was French and his mother Irish, producing rich, dark hair and smoldering dark eyes, didn't hurt. By the time that he had graduated from high school and entered Boston College, he had a number of conquests already under his belt. And by the time he completed his undergraduate degree in ancient philosophy, he had made a name for himself as the all-time bedding champion on campus. But the rumors of sexual kinkiness and sadistic abuse were starting to catch up with him. One girl even pressed a rape charge against him, but those were quickly swept under the carpet. Conveniently or otherwise, Philippe entered divinity school around that time, and the rumors faded away.

Unfortunately, Philippe had witnessed his fair share of domestic violence from an early age, thanks to his rough and abusive father. The first time that he actually saw his father punch his mother, he felt sickened and wanted to run to her side and defend her, but he was too afraid. Instead, he confided in his teacher, an old Jesuit priest named LaFortune. Many would have thought that this was the right thing to do, but what LaFortune told him would everlastingly warp Philippe's perspective on the world. His teacher explained that woman has sinned from even before the time of the prostitute Mary Magdalene, and if Philippe's father had hit his mother, then she must have deserved it.

Being only eight at the time, Philippe eagerly discovered a refuge in the church and a substitute father in LaFortune. From then on he savored every word that the old Jesuit spit out, starting with the concept of the devil inhabiting a female form that forever tempted men. Of course, it was only natural that men would fall for the devil's female guiles, but all men should turn the tables on the devil. Men needed to satisfy their primary lust but also needed to punish the temptress during and after her seduction.

For his part, LaFortune recognized Philippe as a future Jesuit, a true Black Robe, who would protect the church against those who claimed that Jesus had married Mary Magdalene and produced a Holy Family. Philippe did not recognize it at the time, but his fate had been sealed from the very moment that he first approached Father LaFortune, innocent and scared.

None of this bothered Philippe as he strode down the street, making sure that nobody from the Georgetown Inn was following him. He even smiled at the thought of what he would do to the young concierge once he no longer had any use for her.

He allowed himself to drift back to his secret ordination by Pope Benedict XVI—Joseph Ratzinger—some twelve years before. He relished the coldness of the limestone tile as he was splayed like Christ on the cross and fought back tears as the pope knelt on one knee to assist him in rising as a newly ordained soldier of Christ, a Jesuit. He also knew that his was a special, secret ordination, arranged by the most powerful Jesuits, who had high hopes for Philippe. The pope asked him if he was prepared to go forward, not as an ordinary parish priest, but as a special envoy of the Vatican—an envoy who would work in the shadows, rooting out all enemies of the true faithful.

Again, Philippe found himself fighting back the tears as he returned to the present. As if to distract himself from the past, he reached into his jacket pocket and retrieved his phone. Without breaking stride, he hit #9 on his speed dial and waited for it to be answered. The voice on the other end came on with the greeting, "Jesus suffered and died on the cross." Philippe took a deep breath and replied, "In order for mankind not to suffer." Always conscious of his surroundings, Philippe took a quick look around before continuing, "This is Philippe De Smet. I will be sending you a number of digital photos. Several are of our main subject, Thomas Moore. He definitely was at the Temple, and it appears that he possesses the letters. I need all of the information that you have on him. The other photos are of what appears to be a seductive Jewish princess. I'm sure that we have information on her also. There is a close-up of her car's license plate. Start with that. I need to understand the relationship between these two."

Philippe listened for the confirmation code; then he disconnected the call and returned his cell phone to his inner pocket. His razor-sharp mind was his greatest weapon, even though he made sure that the molded-plastic Glock was always neatly positioned under his left armpit for easy access. *It's funny,* he thought. *My background instructions were to follow this Thomas Moore and to discover if he indeed possessed the Pike Letters. Then once I've determined if it's true, to retrieve the letters and dispose of Mr. Moore. Though nothing was mentioned of a woman being involved? Oh well, all the better. Those evil Jewish bitches are all the same. This one certainly had the look of a temptress, perhaps even a high priestess. By my holy oath, sealed in my own blood, I'll make sure that she eventually disappears, just as Mary Magdalene did over two thousand years ago!*

VI

INTIMATE
SECRETARY

June 24, 1868

WASHINGTON, D.C.

By the combined light of a small oil lamp and side candle, Albert
Pike had just finished one of his many letters to his lifelong friend
and fellow Mason and Templar, William James Bury MacLeod Moore.
Correspondence between the two would continue until MacLeod
Moore's death in the spring of 1890. It was as if their two Masonic
souls were intertwined, although the two couldn't have been more different in appearance and familial background. For over thirty years, the
two Masonic brothers exchanged their innermost intimacies and con-
fidences on a number of topics, which ranged from the mundane and
secretarial to the esoteric and arcane.

In fact, it was MacLeod Moore who would provide Pike with copies of degree rituals relating to Ancient Scottish Rite Freemasonry,
which he had gathered in his travels back to his homeland of Ireland
and Scotland. Pike had earlier entered the Scottish Rite at Charleston,

March 20, 1853, receiving its degrees from the fourth to the thirty-second. He received the thirty-third degree in New Orleans in 1857.

Conversely, while on a visit to the United States in 1863, MacLeod Moore visited New York and there received the thirty-three degrees of the Northern Jurisdiction Scottish Rite and immediately afterward received honorable membership in their Supreme Council. Following his appointment, Macleod Moore set about to establish the Ancient and Accepted Scottish Rite in Canada. On May 6, 1868, the Supreme Grand Conclave of England and Wales granted a patent authorizing him to establish chapters and consistories in the Ontario cities of London, Hamilton, and Toronto.

The Colonel, or W. J. B., as he was commonly known, was also instrumental in formally introducing Templarism to Canada. Templarism there first dates from 1764, when a British field encampment is known to have existed in Halifax, Nova Scotia. In 1800, a second Templar warrant was issued under the authority of Craft Lodge No. 6 at Kingston, Upper Canada. But neither of these lodges flourished, so the continuous history of the Canadian Knights Templar actually dates from October 7, 1855, when MacLeod Moore exchanged the dormant Craft Lodge warrant for a new one issued by the Supreme Grand Conclave of England and Wales to establish the Provincial Grand Conclave at Kingston, Canada West, named after the original Grand Master of the medieval Knights Templar, Hugh de Payens. On May 11, 1868, following the confederation of Canada, the Provincial Grand Conclave's name was formally changed to the Grand Priory of Canada. Subsequently, at the first annual meeting of the Grand Priory on July 7, 1884, the organization became a "Supreme and Independent" body under the title of the Sovereign Great Priory of Canada, Knights Templar, with MacLeod Moore as its first Supreme Grand Master.

In the United States, it is said that Templarism was first established through St. Andrew's Royal Arch Chapter of Boston. Records show that on August 28, 1769, a William Davis was initiated as a Knight Templar. However, it is believed that as far back as 1762, the British

Army Field Lodges, either organized under the Grand Lodge of Ireland or through the Grand Lodge of England, which were located in and around Boston, brought Royal Arch Masonry with them. Royal Arch Masonry is the first component or series of rituals included within York Rite Masonry, which was formally established by English Masons in 1717. In order to become a higher order Knight Templar within York Rite Masonry, the candidate must first move through the Royal Arch degrees and prove himself worthy.

Unlike the well-established orders of Templarism that were carried to North America by British army officers, the Scottish Rite degrees became jumbled across various jurisdictions, mainly because of the sentiments leading up to the American Civil War. Consequently, Pike saw it as his duty to correct the many versions of degree rituals relating to Scottish Rite Freemasonry that were practiced throughout the Southern states, concentrating them into one jurisdiction.

Pike was made Sovereign Grand Commander of the Scottish Rite, Southern Jurisdiction, in 1859, and immediately took it upon himself to begin to rewrite its rituals and reshape its degrees, some of which existed only in rough outline. Unfortunately, the Civil War started soon thereafter, and his endeavors would have to cease for five years. During this dark period, he looked north of the American border for continuing support from his longtime friend.

June 24, 1868

Most Illustrious Brother and Fellow Sir Knight W. J. B. Macleod Moore, 33°, KT

On this most illustrious day of St. John the Baptist, June 24th, 1868, may I be the first to formally congratulate you on your fraternal efforts to re-establish your Provincial Grand Conclave under the Grand Priory of Canada. Our friendship and solidarity has thus been strengthened even more, as I am eternally grateful for the illumination and greater understanding that our friendship has provided me. Your sending of the collection of Ancient Scottish Rite degrees that

you amassed while overseas have helped me immensely and provided
the basis for my editing and expansion of the 33 degrees, which is a
significant number indeed. The secrets that you have conveyed have
caused me to think a great deal inward. I wish that I possessed the
Wisdom of Solomon and was able to readily decipher the many layers of
symbolism that the three sojourners discovered in the original crypt.

I long to travel to the ancient lands but I am afraid that the current
federal government is still suspicious of my past activities; and, as such,
constantly monitors my daily activities. I am most grateful for the
respites from the tedious that yours and other exalted Brothers provide
me in my darkest hours. The many native delegations who constantly
arrive in Washington for high-level discussions with the federal
government also offer me some light, as they invariably ask for me to
provide them with counsel. As you may imagine, theirs is a far stranger
and more ancient Brotherhood than you and I share, yet their secrets
are much the same.

Your eternal Intimate Secretary and Brother,
Albert Pike, 33°, KT,
Sovereign Grand Commander

As was his custom with any correspondence, Pike read and reread
what he had written, all the while blessing the fraternal bond between
his friend and himself. He was certain that the Colonel would recognize the signs, seals, and symbols that he had carefully concealed within
his writings. The code that the two had developed earlier was unbreak-
able, for the only two who understood it had veiled its secrecy in an
oath sworn on the blood and body of St. John the Baptist.

Smiling ever so slightly, just before sealing the letter in an envelope with the seal of the Sovereign Grand Commander of the Southern
Jurisdiction Scottish Rite of the United States of America, Pike silently
acknowledged the current circumstances in the reference to the United
States of America. *United States of America, indeed! The South will rise*
up once more, but until then I will have to kowtow to my new masters. No

bother, I will do their bidding in the humblest manner. I have survived this far and will continue to survive and ultimately serve a far greater Master. All the time, our great Masonic legacy will grow! The Blackfoot, Blood, and Piegan delegation will be here tomorrow. They are rightly upset that the white men are invading the foothills looking for gold and silver. The fools in Washington, of course, will try to bargain with the noble chiefs as though they are children. Do they not understand that the noble savage possesses the key to unraveling the final piece of the puzzle to the Ancient Mysteries? Instead, I'm positive that they will see the light when I expose certain things to them.

The Sovereign Grand Commander stood up and stretched his weary bones. It was time to sleep, but it never came easy to him, as his mind raced constantly. Some suggested certain medicines, but he needed to keep his mind clear. He was happy that his family was provided for through his law practice, but he was becoming restless. The secrets that he possessed were calling out to him, urging him to constantly seek *that-which-was-lost.*

He decided to dim the lights and try to sleep while sitting upright in his favorite chair, which reminded him of the Master's chair in the Lodge. As he dozed, his thoughts raced across the northern landscape, envying the newly formed country of Canada and the solidarity among its provinces, which had agreed to a confederation under the British North America Act of 1867.

Pike also knew that this agreement required the building of a transcontinental railway from the eastern end of the country to the western end. This troubled him, because he realized that the railway would lead to the genocide of the North American Indian. *The West will be overrun by the whites, and the indigenous people will be forced either to fight or die.* Pike slept badly that evening.

Upon receiving Pike's letter, MacLeod Moore immediately withdrew to his study and slowly examined the red wax seal that was affixed to the envelope. As Pike had done earlier, Macleod Moore smiled ever so slightly, as the unspoken bond between the two constantly grew stronger, both physically and spiritually.

The red seal on the white envelope denoted a portion of that bond, for here were the colors of the Knights Templar. The red represented the blood shed by the medieval crusaders, who had taken Jerusalem and the Holy Land from the infidels on several occasions, only to eventually lose it once and for all. The white represented the purity of the mind and body of the knights, denoted by the white tunic and lambskin apron that they wore during their sacred rituals.

MacLeod Moore allowed his mind to wander. *But all had not been lost! The original nine knights had discovered a treasure trove of secrets under the Temple wall—secrets that would threaten the Roman Catholic Church to its very core. The immediate result was that the Vatican and pope, in 1129, formally acknowledged the formation of the order of the Poor Fellow Soldiers of Christ and of the Temple of Solomon and granted it absolute sovereignty, solely answerable to the pope himself. Over the next two hundred years, the order grew in wealth and power throughout Europe, only to be double-crossed by Philippe le Bel, king of France, and Pope Clement V on the fateful night of Friday, October 13, 1307.*

As was his practice, after allowing his mind and body to totally relax, MacLeod Moore continued his thoughts once again. *But again, all was not lost. The Templars possessed the finest spy network in all of Europe, as well as the finest fleet in the world. They had been informed of the plot against them beforehand and had arranged for what remained of the treasure to be secreted away from the Paris Temple to the maritime port of La Rochelle. It had even been agreed upon by the Supreme Grand Council beforehand that the Grand Master, Jacques de Molay, would sacrifice himself and remain behind, knowing that he would be captured and tortured.*

MacLeod Moore involuntarily shuttered at the thought. *The poor bastard; he was tortured by the inquisitors for seven years and then burned at the stake. But he never gave up the true secrets. Instead he confessed to a number of outrageous blasphemies, only to recant his confession while being burned alive. Little did his enemies realize that the inner circle of Templar families had foreseen their fate shortly after the treasure reached their homes in France in the early twelfth century. It took a lot of spiritual insight to systematically distribute the treasure to the far ends of the Earth some two hundred years before their absolute betrayal. And to think that over the centuries the treasure was first divided and dispersed, only to be consolidated here in North America, where it remains to this day, protected by the silent guardians. Now let's see what my friend Albert has to tell me.*

The engraved silver letter opener silently lifted the wax seal, which was deposited upside down on a piece of paper that MacLeod Moore had laid out on the desk in front of him. Then he inserted the letter opener's tip into the upper right-hand corner of the envelope and carefully slid it across the top of the envelope. The opener sliced through the expensive linen paper effortlessly. In his mind MacLeod Moore was envisioning the slicing of the Grand Master's skin by his torturers. *The poor man must have suffered much like Christ on the cross. How could someone withstand being tortured for seven years, and then burned at the stake? The story is that de Molay's feet were roasted over the hot coals until the flesh had melted and his bones had dropped away. Then he was forced to hobble to the fire pit while holding the bones in his hands. Unbelievable! I hope that his sacrifice did not go for naught.*

MacLeod Moore sighed and then gently unfolded the one-page letter. *Let's see what my good friend and Brother has to say on the higher level.*

VII

PROVOST
AND JUDGE

10:00 a.m., Twenty-seven days ago

WASHINGTON DULLES INTERNATIONAL
AIRPORT, WASHINGTON, D.C.

Janet watched intently through the window of the arrivals' lounge in the shadow of the morning sun as it playfully moved from east to west along the runway concrete. Thomas's plane had just landed from Montreal and was taxiing up to the gate almost too slowly for her patience to bear. Janet and Thomas had spoken at length on the phone every day since he left six days ago, but her anxiety was at an all-time high. *How could I have fallen in love with this man over an eight-hour period from the time that I first met him?* she pondered. *If it's not some kind of predetermined destiny between the two of us, then what is it?*

But before she could receive the answer from the celestial world, the inner door was opened by the attendant, and there he was, beaming with schoolboy anticipation. Without hesitation, Janet rushed into Thomas's arms and gave him the most sensuous kiss that he had ever experienced. Then she began to gently shudder and cry, pressing her face into his chest.

Taken aback, Thomas held her tight and stroked her hair. "Hey, come on now. What happened to the tough, dominant woman that I left less than a week ago? You couldn't have missed me that much!"

With that, Janet pulled herself away from Thomas and tried to control the tears. "Oh, Thomas, I'm so glad that you're here. I didn't want you to see me like this, but last night was terrible. My grandfather locked himself in his basement laboratory with the Pike Letters ever since you left. The place is built solid and is secured better than a Templar castle. Every so often I would tempt him to come out of his lab for some food, but he only picked at it. He was completely preoccupied. I even went to his favorite kosher deli and bought him the cheese blintzes he loves so much. You could see his mind racing all of the time. He's done something similar to this before when working on an alchemical experiment, but I've never seen him so obsessed."

Thomas felt he should break the tension. "Here, take my handkerchief. There now, it'll be OK. Don't worry about the people around us staring. Actually, I find it kind of flattering. I've never had a gorgeous woman hold me tight like this before."

Janet pulled herself together, enough to give an unladylike snort, which caused the people around her to jump a little, and then continued, "Thomas, just stop it!" She good-naturedly pounded his chest with her fist to give the arriving passengers another little something to think about. She continued, "Then last night Grandfather came up from the basement around ten o'clock almost in tears. He looked so downcast and defeated. He's such a gentle and honorable man. It's unjust for such a caring soul to carry such a burden. Anyway, he confessed to me that he was stumped. He had pored over the letters for days on end. He searched for invisible watermarks and ink, identifiable signs, symbols, and tokens, but he simply couldn't find anything resembling Masonic, Kabbalistic, ancient Egyptian, Zoroastrian, Druidic, or alchemical coding. You should have seen the state he was in! It's as though he had been unjustly accused of murder. He was a broken man."

Thomas was shocked after all that had gone through his mind over the past week. He had stayed up late every evening and read Pike's magnum opus—*Morals and Dogma of the Ancient and Accepted Scottish Rite of Freemasonry*—from cover to cover. The more he pored over Pike's writings, the more he was fascinated by the man. *My God! The man was a voracious reader, a brilliant poet, a journalist, a philosopher, a lawyer, a soldier, a provost, a judge, a true survivor, a magician of sorts, and a defender of the Native North Americans. Pike even taught himself to read and speak fifteen different languages, many of which were extinct, including one that I had never even heard of—Avestan! Pike was a true enigma!*

At that very moment, Thomas felt a little cheated because he had expected Pike's secrets to have revealed themselves to Janet's grandfather already. But it was here that he had also met this beautiful, brilliant woman, who appeared destined to be his partner for life. As if this wasn't enough, there was the promise of mystery and intrigue in the letters. In his wildest dreams, he never would have thought that he could have even one such adventure, let alone both. The women who worked at his business couldn't get over the fact that the boss was, for the first time ever, taking a holiday longer than seven days and that it involved a woman whom he had met at a library, of all places.

But before Thomas could feel the least bit sorry for himself, Janet blurted out the rest of her story. "Then, just as suddenly, Grandfather clutched his chest and started to breathe heavily. I could see his heart pounding in his chest. He collapsed in a chair, while I ran and got him aspirin tablets and some water. Then I called 911. Thank God that the ambulance came in less than three minutes. They got him stabilized and took him to MedStar Georgetown University Hospital. They have the most magnificent doctors there. They told me to go home, as he was out of danger, but I was so scared, I couldn't sleep at all last night. I'm so sorry; I must look a terrible sight." Janet tried to dry her eyes, trying to catch her breath. "I phoned this morning, and they indicated that they're still running tests and won't tell me anything over the phone."

Thomas was fascinated by how Janet had transformed into a little girl right before his eyes. He knew then and there that she was going to be with him for the rest of their lives. He felt a great need to protect her, but at the moment he also found her physically irresistible. Her vulnerability and openness almost broke his heart for the second time in less than a week. Chuckling ever so slightly, he wiped away the last tear beneath Janet's eyes with his thumbs, "Well, that's it then. Let's go see how David is faring. The silly old bugger . . . he should have known better."

"Oh, Thomas," Janet's face broke into a big grin, as his simple comment took all of the strain out of her body, "I do love you. Thank you for caring. Yes, let's go see my grandfather!"

Meanwhile, standing off to the right in the morning shadows was Philippe De Smet. He was looking out the window as though he was waiting for the arrival of another plane. Looking like any other innocent bystander, he prided himself on being able to make himself almost invisible. The technique of watching a developing scene unfold through the reflection in the window was brilliantly simple. To be able to focus his hearing back over his right shoulder was a little bit more complicated, but he had heard enough. He would use the time that Janet and Thomas would take visiting the grandfather to search the Georgetown home for the letters.

As previously arranged, Philippe had been tipped off to Thomas's arrival by the concierge, who had carefully scanned the hotel reservation list every day since Thomas had left to go back to Montreal. On the fifth day, she phoned Philippe with the news that his friend was returning to the capital the following morning. She appeared surprised that the reservation was for a month, even though many out-of-town businessmen used the inn as their base while in Washington.

The Jesuit assured her that it was typical of Thomas, in that once he had discovered a place such as the Temple library, he would take as much time as required in order to satisfy his fascination. In turn,

Philippe assured himself of her ongoing part in the conspiracy by suggesting that the two could have dinner sometime. She had giggled at the thought of a romantic rendezvous with the handsome man. She knew that her friends wouldn't believe her when she told them, but that didn't matter. She would make sure that she captured the moment on her cell phone.

Philippe had spent the previous five days learning everything that he could about both Janet and Thomas. The Jesuit research group had been placed at his disposal, and he had demanded the impossible from the team. He was always amazed at the amount of information that they could produce on any given subject or person. In this case, once Philippe had the opportunity to sift through the stacks of information that had been collected, he developed a very accurate profile of both subjects. What amazed him was the physical and spiritual attraction between the two, as evidenced by the scene that had just unfolded.

If Philippe had been a betting man, he would never have put the two of them together. In his mind, they were a complete contradiction. He grudgingly had to admire Janet's mental capacity and physical beauty. It was obvious that she was well bred and came from an ancient family, but with Thomas, it was the exact opposite. Despite his connection with MacLeod Moore, Thomas was tentative, almost too shy, and not very worldly at all, considering that he did business around the world. His recorded conquest of women appeared haphazard and awkward at best.

Philippe was a Jesuit, though, and knew that the human heart had no bounds. He chalked the union of Janet and Thomas up to a trick played by fate on the two of them. He had concluded earlier that the attraction between them was more on a spiritual plane than a physical one. He wasn't superstitious, but he believed in the Almighty and His omnipotent power. To him, anything was possible if God allowed it. And he felt that God was delivering these two to him because of their sins.

What had also been confirmed was the fact that Thomas was in possession of the Pike Letters. Their existence was part of Masonic lore and the subject of great conjecture among the Masonic scholars. It had been whispered for over a hundred years in certain circles that Pike must have had a secret source of information about the ancient Scottish Rite rituals that provided the basis for his development and expansion of the thirty-three degrees. Several researchers had revealed a definite connection between ancient French esoteric ritual and that of the Scottish Rite. The connection had even contributed to the employment of the original Scots Guard by the French monarchy, starting in the 1600s.

As Philippe drove the short distance to David Rose's Georgetown home, he pieced together the seemingly unconnected information that was in the back of his brain. His brilliance lay in his ability to file vast amounts of information and then to formulate a properly layered, composite formula explaining it, which inevitably turned out to be correct. In this case, he reasoned that the ancient material concerning the Scottish Rite rituals had been collected by MacLeod Moore through his military and overseas connections and then provided to his Masonic brother Albert Pike.

Perhaps Macleod Moore realized that Pike was the only one who had the mental and spiritual capacity to make sense out of the mishmash of esoteric ritual that existed in Ireland and Scotland at the time. After all, Pike was a brilliant self-taught scholar, having been accepted into Harvard at the age of sixteen, whereas MacLeod Moore was first and foremost a soldier. Yes, that must be the connection, the explanation for their lifelong friendship.

Philippe was proud of himself for his reasoning and his surefire conclusion. He allowed himself to hum a little missive hymn to himself that he first learned as a child. It reminded him of his mother, of all things. He rarely thought of her anymore in such a loving way. No matter: the sun was shining and his prey was in sight as he drove slowly past the Georgetown brownstone and parked around the corner, two blocks away.

Given the time of the morning, Philippe was surprised that more people weren't walking the streets, but this didn't raise any alarms. He considered himself invisible. It was as though he was on a mission from God Himself as he bounded up David Rose's stairs. The Seal of Solomon above the door was a sign that he had the right house. He was certain that in a short time he would have the Pike Letters in his hands.

Reaching into his pocket, he extracted a small black box with a switch on its side. He immediately flipped the switch, and a small red light positioned in the upper right-hand corner of the box started to flash. This indicated the presence of high-frequency sensors, which in turn indicated the existence of an elaborate alarm system. This was no problem for Philippe, as he had been trained in a variety of dubious skills. He started to count backward from thirty as he inserted the pick locks into the key tumbler. There was a second button on the black box, and his index finger gently slid into position, ready to render the house's entire security system inert as soon as he opened the door.

VIII

INTENDANT OF THE BUILDING

MEDSTAR GEORGETOWN UNIVERSITY HOSPITAL, WASHINGTON, D.C.

The trip to the hospital had taken no time at all, since Janet used the fresh morning air and speed of her Mustang to unloosen and relax a little bit more. In the relatively short time that it took to reach her grandfather's room, she was once again smiling and back in control of her body and emotions. But as they walked down the hallway, hand in hand, neither Janet nor Thomas really knew what to expect. They both were walking blindly into a situation that neither of them had ever experienced before, at least in this life.

No one could have expected what awaited them around the corner. As Thomas opened the glass door to David Rose's private room and slid back the gray curtain, he was greeted with a booming, "Hello, Thomas, my dear boy. Come in, come in. I must say that you're a better sight looking this morning than my granddaughter, who looks as though she's seen a ghost."

Astonishing as it was, propped up by several pillows, David Rose sat, looking as cheery and fit as the last time Thomas had seen him. To top it off, he was having a lunch of scrambled eggs mixed with lox and onions, stewed tomatoes, and bacon. Sitting in the corner watching over the scene was an attractive, fifty-something doctor, whose name tag announced her as Dr. Sarah Cohen, chief cardiologist.

Janet just stood there, but Thomas quickly smiled and then pronounced, "For someone who is supposed to be dying, you look pretty fit to me! I was told that you were moving toward the Light and Truth, but from where I stand you look as though you're enjoying life too much here on Earth." Thomas walked around the bed and shook David's hand, while nodding and winking to Sarah, who instinctively returned the wink. "Your granddaughter certainly had me expecting a more gruesome scene. Here you are, eating like a pig, and to top it off, eating bacon, no less. What would the local rabbi say? Is this a hotel or hospital?"

"Ah, Thomas, he probably would say, 'Good for you, and let me have a slice.' I never knew that food could taste so delicious. I'm sure that God will allow me this one indulgence in life. To be fair to Janet, I must admit that even I scared myself. I should have listened to my granddaughter and tempered my activities. May I introduce, by the way, my guardian angel: Dr. Sarah Cohen, chief cardiologist here at the hospital. She was just telling me that, unfortunately, her husband passed away prematurely about five years ago of a massive heart attack." David gave a conspiratorial wink back to Thomas.

Sarah shook her head at the innuendo, rose from her chair, and shook both Thomas's and Janet's hands. "So very nice to meet the two of you. Janet, you certainly have your hands full. Don't let him fool you. He was in terrible shape when he came in last night. Just to calm your mind, though, there was no heart attack or stroke. The old fool was suffering from extreme dehydration and angina, that's all. I must say that I've never met anyone in their nineties fitter and sharper of mind. The plate of food was a bribe, actually. He threatened to check himself out if we didn't order him something from that favorite deli of his. We had it Ubered over to the hospital. Funny, I've never heard of kosher bacon before. Is it true what he claims: that he takes a small amount of white powdered gold every morning?"

Janet had finally regained her senses enough to respond. "Oh yes, Dr. Cohen. My grandfather is a practicing alchemist, among many other things. Did he also tell you that he eats small children every full moon?"

Dr. Cohen laughed. "Oh yes, and he's already propositioned me three times. He even asked me if I wanted to see his morning erection, by the way. No shame whatsoever. Putting that aside for the moment, I would like to keep him in the hospital for another day or two, in order to run a few more tests. Would that be all right with you? We did a full CT scan on him this morning, and the technician claimed that he saw your grandfather levitating while in the cylinder. If he does have a certain level of precious metal coursing through his body, I guess that could explain it. I'll save a few children from being eaten while I'm at it."

Sarah concluded her impromptu stand-up routine: "In all seriousness, David is one remarkable man. He reminds me so much of my late husband, although he was forty years younger than your grandfather, of course. I'll leave the three of you alone. I've spent too much time with the old fool as it is! David told me that the two of you met only a week or so ago. You do make a smart-looking couple. May the birth of your first child be a festival of joy!" With that she vanished beyond the curtain.

"Oh, Grandfather," Janet leaned over and hugged David, minding the intravenous tubing that extended from his left arm. "You had me so worried. I didn't sleep at all last night, thinking about how I would live without you. By the way, Dr. Cohen seems quite taken with you, even though there might be a forty-year age difference."

David was glowing. "Stop it, Janet. Your grandmother, bless her soul, still wouldn't allow me to even consider it. I must tell you, though: I found her mind quite stimulating. Her qualifications and experience are really quite impressive. She has world-class medical credentials, and she obviously has a deep sense of appreciation for life. Maybe I'll have to make a sizable donation to the research center that they have here. Or maybe she has a favorite charity. Anyway, I think that I'll stay that day or two and allow her to conduct a few experiments on me. It should be interesting. Come to think of it, she really is quite attractive. And to think, she's Jewish to boot!"

Thomas chuckled to himself. *Is this family crazy? Or are they just so brilliant that they find humor in everything that surrounds them? They certainly have a love for life. I want so much to be part of what they possess.*

It was David who brought everybody back to earth. "Thomas, I'm so sorry that I've failed you. Honestly, I searched the inner reaches of my brain and used all of my magic tricks to discover something hidden within the Pike Letters, but I'm stumped. I called upon every deity that I knew, including Lucifer and Asmodeus, but achieved nothing. I was so eager to have the Pike Letters reveal their secrets to me that I even forgot to drink the purified water that I have in my lab."

Listening with a newfound intensity, Thomas said, "Forget it for now. Your health comes first. I'm here for at least twenty-seven days and will attend to everything that you need, so there's no cause for you to rush. You can spend as much time with Dr. Cohen as you like. Janet and I will try to put our minds together and figure this thing out. She has the feminine right side of the brain—analytical, logical, and reasoning— and I'll bring the male left side of the brain: creative, emotional, instinctive. Or is it the other way around? No matter: if there's something to find, we'll discover it together. By the way, where are the letters now?"

David thought for a moment before he answered. "Now that's a very good question. To tell you the truth, I'm not entirely positive, as I was in an altered state of mind. Come to think of it, I think the letters are spread about on the central table in my lab. God, I hope that I closed the door behind me."

Janet stopped to think for a moment herself. *I hope that I turned the alarm system on back at the house before I left this morning. . . . Yes, I'm certain that I did.* "Thomas, we should get back to the house as soon as possible, just to make sure the letters are safe." Thomas nodded in agreement. "Grandfather, are you certain that it's OK for us to leave you? Is there anything that you need before we go?" Janet asked.

David's response was somewhat surprising. "Yes, Janet, there is something that you can do for me. I've been too self-indulgent lately and immersed in my alchemical experiments and, as such, have forgotten the bond between father and son. Could you phone your father for me and explain the situation to him? Now don't alarm him. You know how he gets. He'll want to take charge of all of us."

Janet was pleased with what she was hearing. The recent distance between David and Solomon Rose had begun to alarm her. "Yes, of course, Grandfather. There's nothing in the world that would make me happier. I think that it's time that Father got to meet Thomas also, don't you?"

"Yes, of course, my darling granddaughter. There is one other thing that you could do for me. Stop being so prudish and make love to Thomas. I can feel the sexual tension between the two of you. It's not good to build up so much negative energy. You have to let it be released."

After that comment, both Janet and Thomas were blushing as they left the hospital room. As they rounded the hallway corner, they could still hear the faint laughter of Janet's grandfather.

Settling back against the pillows with a contented sigh, David Rose pushed the button for the attendant. He needed the empty plate to be taken away so that he could think. He was missing something with the letters. He was sure of it. *Or maybe I need a one-time key, which had been developed between Pike and MacLeod Moore?*

Even though Janet was in a hurry to get back to the house, Thomas insisted that they needed sustenance of their own, so they stopped at the same deli where David had ordered his lunch. Although it was primarily a take-out place, there were several booths along the front windows where one could sit down and order off a menu.

Janet was astonished when Thomas ordered cheese blintzes with a double helping of sour cream; a giant dill pickle for two; a large beef knish with gravy; and a tray of lox, cucumber, and tomato, along with two plates and two large cherry Cokes.

David laughed at Janet's amazement. "What, you don't think that we have any deli in Montreal? We're famous around the world for our deli."

"Thomas, you keep pulling those little rabbits out of your hat. You really have amazed me today, and we're not even home. I do want to thank you for being so kind to my grandfather. He's really taken a shine to you. You have an ancient soul, I can tell. Maybe I'm not deserving of you."

The food arrived just in time. But before the two dived in, Thomas made sure that their union was sealed. He leaned over and kissed Janet, who savored the kiss as much as she savored the food that they started to devour.

Having satisfied their cravings for the moment, the two left a generous tip and departed from the deli hand in hand, oblivious to Philippe's black Audi idling across the street. Thanks to the tinted windows, Philippe felt that it was safe enough to be so close to his prey. Normally, like a big-game hunter, he would have allowed them to come to him, but this situation was different. Philippe realized that the fate of his own soul depended on the success of this mission. A spiritual triangle had been formed between the three.

Philippe's thought was broken by the growl of Janet's Mustang as it roared past his car. *They're definitely heading back to the house, that's for sure*, he thought. *There's nothing that I can do but listen to their conversations from this point on. The letters must be in the old man's lab. Who would have thought that he would have such a sophisticated security system installed in that house of his?*

As Philippe pulled his car away from the curb, Janet and Thomas arrived at her grandfather's house. Making sure that the Mustang was locked behind them, Janet slowly walked up the steps with Thomas. It was her habit to knock on the door before opening it, but this time she didn't, thinking it would look silly. Gently gliding her key into the front-door lock, she felt relieved to hear the click of the tumbler as she turned the key to the right. *Thank God, I did lock the door when I left this morning,* she mused.

She stopped in her tracks. Something definitely wasn't right. Normally she should hear the quiet ping and see the faint flashing light of the central alarm box. This indicated that they had thirty seconds to allow the retina scanner above the key pad to verify the caller's optical signature. Only then could the system be deactivated through an eight-digit pin code. Janet's father had had the most sophisticated high-tech security system installed throughout the house. Both Janet and her grandfather had their retinal and digital signatures programmed into the system. Her father insisted that she be able to access the system in case of an emergency. Her father turned out to be a prophet, but Janet had never experienced a situation where the system appeared to be dead, paralyzed, or suspended in animation.

IX

ELU OF THE NINE

HOUSE OF DAVID, GEORGETOWN,
WASHINGTON, D.C.

Janet had just gotten off the phone with her father and was returning to the kitchen, where Thomas was finishing off the blintzes he had discovered in the fridge. Outwardly, everything around the house seemed to be in place, but Janet had the odd feeling that an intruder had been present. Her inner High Priestess was speaking to her.

Laying down her cell phone on the island countertop, Janet reported to Thomas what was happening. "I finally got hold of my father and explained the situation. He's at the Ritz in Paris at the moment, attending some important EU monetary conference. I first explained the situation with David and then told him about the disruption of the security system here at the house. Because of the terrorism level in France nowadays, the head of the company's security division, Danny Sullivan, is with him, along with a full security detail. My father can't get away just now, but he's sending Danny over, along with his second-in-command, Jimmy O'Reilly, who's a high-tech wizard, on the RCC company jet.

"The trouble is that they have to land in New York tomorrow morning and then drive down because they want to bring some gear to check out the house top to bottom. So considering the time change, they may not be here until the morning after tomorrow. In the meantime, just to be on the safe side, Father has arranged to have some plainclothes detectives watch the house and the hospital until the cavalry arrives. Thank goodness Grandfather has chosen to remain in the hospital for a few days. This would just add to his anxiety and stress."

Thomas, finishing his last piece of blintz, put down his fork and asked, "Janet, isn't that a little excessive? We don't even know if someone has been here. I don't know much about alarm systems, but can't they just malfunction at some point, maybe because of a power surge or something similar?"

"That's exactly the point, Thomas. The security system that Jimmy installed a couple of years ago has its own power source that's completely inaccessible. Even if the whole Eastern Seaboard was blacked out, the security system would still be functioning. And the only person who can access the main programming for the system is my father, with the assistance of Danny and Jimmy. They may sound like the leprechaun twins, but those two are ex-Navy SEALs and CIA operatives. They're the best at what they do. Jimmy is already running a remote diagnostic check on the system from his control pad in Paris. Father says that the system should be back up and functioning within the next half hour. Meanwhile we're to hang tight and disturb as little as we can. I see that you found the blintzes."

At that moment, as if by magic, all nine security units in the house pinged simultaneously, indicating that the system was back up and functioning properly. The house was locked down tight once more.

Janet laughed as Thomas jumped off his stool. "See, as if by magic. It's amazing what they can do nowadays from anywhere around the world, from the Himalayas to Etruria. By the way, the security system installed in this house is exclusive, military-grade top secret and not yet available on the open market, so I wouldn't go telling your friends about it."

Grabbing Janet around the waist and drawing her close, Thomas whispered in her ear, "Right now you're the only friend that I care about. Do you mean to tell me that we need to find something to do for the next two days? If that's the case, then I'll need to test both your virtue and your fortitude."

"Down, tiger!" Janet said, as she patted the side of Thomas's face. "There will be plenty of time for that. I remember what my grandfather said. He likes to pretend that he's a randy old goat, but deep down inside he's still devoted to my grandmother. I wish she were still alive. She had a very mystical way about her. I think she would have liked you very much. Meanwhile, you're forgetting something. Let's check out David's lab and see if the letters are where he said they were."

Taking Thomas by the hand, she led him to a staircase, where they descended into what first appeared to be a labyrinth of sorts. Surprisingly, the hallway had nine arches positioned overhead with four doors on either side. At the end of the corridor, a shiny steel door stood ominously, reflecting the hallway lights. Thomas noticed immediately that a second retina scan panel was positioned next to the door, blinking red to denote that it was functioning and ready for use. Thomas also noticed that there was no handle on the door.

Positioning herself in front of the security system, Janet stared straight into the viewing pane and pressed the *ENTER* button. Following the retina scan, the blinking red light turned yellow, upon which Janet keyed in the eight-digit code and then the *ENTER* button again. This caused the light to go green, but nothing happened. Janet then applied her right thumb to the retina panel, and finally, following a proper reading of her thumbprint, the solid-steel door withdrew into the wall, exposing what amazingly appeared to be an early seventeenth-century alchemist's laboratory—David Rose's inner sanctuary—the sanctum sanctorum.

Thomas stood there with his mouth open.

Janet smiled slyly and then asked, "Pretty amazing, isn't it? I don't know if you'll believe me, but after he discovered this lab in Istanbul, Grandfather had the whole thing carefully dismantled, packed, shipped, and meticulously reassembled here in his basement. The only difference is that he's added a few modern-day pieces of equipment. The centrifuge, spectrometer, and metal-analysis computer are prototypes of the models that are being installed at MIT as we speak."

"This is unbelievable. I would have no idea that something like this ever existed. It's like an ancient crypt. That whole thing that you did with the security system to get in here was pretty slick also. It was like something out of *Star Wars*."

"Yes, it is pretty amazing, when you think about it. The whole system is programmed to allow access only to Grandfather or me. There's a three-step process to the unit upstairs at the front door, but a four-step process with this unit downstairs. If there was someone in the house, he or she may have been able to disable the front-door unit, but the additional degree was designed to stymie the intruder when he came to this unit. The fourth step, the thumbprint, was an added feature that Jimmy came up with. Wait until you meet Danny and Jimmy. They're both wizards with this type of stuff. They're also deadly, come to think of it. You'll get a kick out of them."

"I'm sure I will." Thomas retorted a little too sharply. *Janet isn't helping my confidence here, going about talking about these two ex–Navy SEALs that way. Maybe she has a thing for one or both of them.*

"Thomas, stop being jealous right now. It shows weakness on your part, and I was just beginning to like your newfound assuredness. It's you I've fallen in love with, in part because of your vulnerable side, but a little too much vulnerability just makes you appear to be a wimp, which is totally unappealing. Besides, both Danny and Jimmy are close to sixty, you knucklehead. They're the same age as my father, for God's sake!"

Thomas tried to quickly change the subject. He had spied the letters on the central table. "There they are. They're safe and sound, from the looks of them. Let's leave them arranged as they are. David may have done that on purpose, trying to fit them together like pieces of a puzzle. Can we go to bed now? I'm exhausted. It's been a long day."

Leaving the letters exactly as they had been found, Janet readily agreed. She too was exhausted, as she had been awake for more than twenty-four hours. So again with Thomas in tow, she hit the *CLOSE* button on the inside pad, which allowed the door to shut tight and reset its lock after they exited the lab. The two of them, feeling safe and secure, slowly made their way to the upstairs bedrooms.

Once on the second floor, Janet pointed to the spare bedroom. "Thomas, you're in there. There's an adjacent washroom with all of the masculine necessities. My older brother and his wife use this spare bedroom when they come to visit. There's even a few sets of pajamas in the wardrobe if you so desire. I'm sorry, but I'm exhausted. Good night!" Janet didn't appreciate his pouting and decided to teach him a quick lesson.

The problem was that Thomas, being emotionally drained from the day's activities, accepted the rejection without reservation. After saying good night, he meekly proceeded to his bedroom. Janet shrugged and stomped off to her room.

Thomas took a quick shower and was lying naked on the bed in the dark, dreamily thinking about Janet. There was a faint glow to the room from the moonlight, which seeped through the front window. Even though he was especially tired, he couldn't sleep. *God, she can be exasperating at times. At any moment she's dominant, and the next moment she's this little girl looking for comfort and shelter. At one moment it's as though she's been transmuted into an enlightened High Priestess and the next moment, she's cold and calculating. Just when I think that I have her figured out, she switches up on me. Could it be that she's scared? She's been pretty independent most of her life, and now I'm asking her to share the rest of her life with me. She's also been her grandfather's protector for so long, and now she must feel helpless, what with him in the hospital.*

As if to provide an answer to his thoughts, the door to the hallway opened slowly, exposing the sensuous, sleek outline of a naked Janet. She whispered, "Thomas, don't say a word, or I swear that I'll turn around and leave you forever. Please just do what I ask."

Thomas let Janet slide in beside him. The moonlight appeared to focus its soft light on the two of them. As he turned to face her and put his arm around her, he could feel an unusual energy surging from her body. He was immediately absorbed by the moment and let all doubts slip from his mind.

As he melted into Janet, he didn't notice that she had set down a small-caliber gun on the side table, cleverly disguising that movement by letting out a little sigh.

She then brought up her right hand and gently caressed Thomas's mouth, running her forefinger around his moistening lips. Not surprisingly, Thomas was too absorbed with the sensuousness of the movement to taste the small amount of white powdered gold that she was spreading across his lips. As the powder was quickly absorbed into Thomas's bloodstream, he sensed a sudden surge of energy course through his veins.

The next two days were a blur of ecstasy. It was as if time stood still. They made love many times between small fits of sleep, caressing each other. Every time they climaxed together, it was as if they had ascended to a higher level of out-of-body consciousness. Thomas had never experienced anything like this.

At one point, Thomas silently acknowledged that Janet's grandfather had been right. All of the negative tension had disappeared, only to be replaced by a total acceptance of love and commitment to each other.

Over the two days, Thomas had one dream, over and over. It was of himself dressed as an ancient soldier, a captain of an elite guard that had just landed by ship on a sacred island.

His servant had readied a majestic white horse and helped him mount. As he spurred the horse into action, wings grew out of the animal's sides, and he found himself flying over the landscape. Then he could see where they were headed. Atop the highest mountain, which lay just ahead of them, was a small temple.

But before he could reach his destination, he always awoke to Janet's murmurs or caresses. It was as though she could read his dream and wanted to prevent him from seeing who awaited him.

X

ELU OF THE FIFTEEN

Twenty-five days ago

HOUSE OF DAVID

Around six o'clock on the second morning, Thomas woke to the sound of a running shower. The bedroom looked like a war zone. The sheets were on the floor, pillows strewn everywhere. Even one of the lamps was lying on its side on the floor. Janet had made sure that the gun had mysteriously disappeared so as not to alarm Thomas. He lay there innocently and smiled, faintly piecing together the events of the last two days.

As if that wasn't enough to jog his memory, Janet emerged from the bathroom wearing nothing more than a towel. Leaning down on one knee across the bed, she kissed him gently. "Good morning; I must say that you didn't disappoint me."

Thomas drew her closer and kissed her more intensely. "I had a good teacher. Promise me that we'll never share a bad word between the two of us ever again."

Janet appeared to be all business this morning. "Yes, of course, I promise. Now hurry up and get showered and dressed. Danny and Jimmy may appear any minute. I've put coffee on and prepared a few things, but I need to dress, so I'll see you down in the kitchen."

Thomas happily did what he was told and soon found himself sitting at the kitchen counter. He was drinking coffee and half-watching the early news on CNN from the small flat screen on the wall when the doorbell rang.

As he got up to answer the door, Janet bounded down the stairs looking radiant. She was wearing, of all things, a navy-blue Chanel pantsuit with a frilly white blouse and had her hair pulled back and tied with a powder-blue ribbon. *My God,* thought Thomas, *this woman is a chameleon.*

Smiling wickedly as she quickly moved past Thomas, she opened the door to two of the largest men Thomas had ever seen, dressed immaculately in the latest made-to-measure, European-style suits. The only thing that said *military* was their rather short haircuts and the fact that the lead man sported a three-inch scar from his right ear to his neck.

Janet allowed both men to enter and then threw her arms around the first one, squealing with delight. "Oh, Danny, I'm so glad to see you two again. It's been too long." Then she released herself and silently hugged the second man, who was carrying what appeared to be two black cases. At the same time, she addressed Thomas over her right shoulder, "Thomas, I would like you to meet two of my family's closest and dearest friends: Danny Sullivan and Jimmy O'Reilly. These two men have been my personal keepers since I was a teenager. Danny, Jimmy, please say hello to Thomas. I'm sure that my father has mentioned him," she said, rolling her eyes.

If Janet was looking for any sign of overreaction, she wouldn't be getting it from these two. They had seen and heard it all before. Instead, Danny effortlessly extended his huge right hand to Thomas. "It certainly is a pleasure to meet you. It's good to see that Ms. Rose has finally settled down with just one man. Why, just the other day, Jimmy and I were sharing a laugh over the time we caught Ms. Rose with those fifteen bikers under the Brooklyn Bridge."

Janet good-naturedly punched Danny in the shoulder before he could utter another word. "OK, stop that, you two. Thomas, don't pay any attention to these Irish lunatics. They still think that the United States is a collection of thirteen colonies and we're fighting for independence. Now come to the kitchen, all of you. There's fresh coffee, croissants, toast, and jam. And just for you, Jimmy, I forced myself to make a pot of that stupid oat porridge you always rave about. We'll tell you the full story while you eat."

In unison, Danny and Jimmy muttered, "Yes, ma'am," which produced a loud guffaw from Thomas and a resulting stern look from Janet.

The two men had enormous appetites. Thomas sat across from them and stared in amazement as the food and coffee disappeared in no time. All the while, Janet was filling them in on the entire story, starting with Janet's and Thomas's initial encounter in the Temple Library.

Finally Danny wiped his mouth with a napkin and addressed Thomas directly. "Well, Thomas, first of all, I must congratulate you. I never thought that I would see the day that Ms. Rose would find somebody who could challenge her grandfather or father for her affection. I have no idea what you did, but keep it up."

With that comment, Jimmy almost choked on his last spoonful of porridge.

"OK, enough of the wisecracks from you two." Janet obviously adored the two men. "Danny, let's you and I and Thomas go down and check out Grandfather's lab, and we'll show you the letters. Meanwhile, Jimmy can do whatever he does with those black boxes and determine if there was an intruder. We'll meet back here in the kitchen."

This time all three men chimed in unison, "Yes, ma'am." The laughter rang throughout the house.

Half an hour later, Danny, Janet, and Thomas were back sitting around the kitchen island, enjoying a fresh pot of coffee, when Jimmy popped in holding what looked like Harry Potter's magic wand. But it was the items in his other hand that fascinated the trio when he deposited them on the countertop. They were no bigger than a nickel but were made of a sleek black plastic.

Danny spoke first. "Are these little buggers what I think they are?"

Jimmy responded immediately, displaying a slight Boston lilt in his voice, "Yup, the latest in military-grade listening devices. Fascinating little things, aren't they? I think they're made in Israel. Anyway, I found them in every room of the house, hidden in places you wouldn't even think of looking unless you had my magic wand. There are fifteen of them in all!"

Danny picked up one of the chips and flipped it around in his fingers like a poker chip. "I'm going to assume that you rendered these useless?" Jimmy nodded. He really wasn't much for words, so Danny continued without missing a beat. "That settles it, then. We definitely had an intruder, an intruder who's been listening to everything that you've said, even the slightest noises that you've made, ever since you arrived back at the house." Janet and Thomas cast a quick look at each other as their eyes glowed with shock.

Danny caught but tried to ignore the expressions on their faces. "What can you tell us, Jimmy, from your audit of the security-system programming?"

By this time, everybody had picked up a black chip and was playing with it. Jimmy put his down to make sure that he concentrated fully. "Well, for the life of me, I can't figure out how the intruder rendered the main floor unit useless. He used something that I'm not even aware of, and trust me, I'm aware of every little black gadget around, even the stuff that the North Koreans are producing nowadays. Luckily I had the forethought to add that additional step to the scan downstairs. I got the idea from the fact that the original basic Irish Craft Lodge degrees numbered four instead of three, including a fourth, Knight Templar degree. The Scottish Blue Lodge went down to three in 1818 with the formation of the United Grand Lodge, thanks to those English bastards." Jimmy easily gave away his Irish Boston roots.

Thomas perked up when he heard the reference to Freemasonry. "Hold on a minute. Do you mean that the two of you are Scottish Rite Masons?"

Even Janet cast a grin when Danny chuckled before responding, "Yes, Thomas, both Jimmy and I, even though we're church-going Boston Catholics, are 33° Scottish Rite Freemasons. So is Janet's father, Solomon, and her grandfather, by the way, and they're Jewish, of course. It's a common myth, even still, that you have to be Protestant to be a Freemason. That's silly. You only have to believe in a Supreme Being. Some of the other higher orders, especially related to York Rite Masonry, the English version, such as Knights Templar and the Red Cross of Constantine, are referred to as 'Christian Masonry.' You may find it interesting that we received our three initial Masonic degrees at an army field camp in a Middle Eastern desert, much as some of the British army officers did throughout the eighteenth century. What's fascinating here is the mystery surrounding the Pike Letters and their association with Scottish Rite Masonry and the Knights Templar."

Janet jumped in. "Thomas, you have to understand that my family has no secrets when it comes to these two gentlemen. The Masonic Brotherhood between them, my grandfather, and my father, means everything: absolute trust and tolerance, especially when dealing with these two's shenanigans. Seriously, I consider Danny and Jimmy to be extensions of my father. In fact, I would trust them with my life—with your life, for that matter. These two men, along with my father, are three of the finest gentlemen I have ever known, and I attribute that, in part, to Freemasonry. The only thing that annoys me about their fraternity is that they only allow men to join, which is pretty chauvinistic and sexist."

"Now, Ms. Rose, we won't get into that. You know that Freemasonry has its roots embedded within the ancient Egyptian mysteries, among other ancient rites. The High Priestesses, the goddesses, of that era had their own secret societies, if I'm not mistaken?"

Just as Janet was about to start to debate the issue—it was a sore point with her—Danny went on, "Sorry to cut you off, Ms. Rose, but we need to sort out the current situation. From what you've told me and from what I know, Thomas hasn't told anyone other than you and your grandfather that he discovered the Pike Letters, and that he still possesses them? Outwardly, the letters do have a certain historical value, but as for their purported esoteric value, even your grandfather couldn't discover anything."

It was Thomas who interjected, "Right on both counts!"

"Then we need to think. Who or what organization has the knowledge, means, and capability of, first, clandestinely discovering what you know? Who or what organization has the technology and skill to invisibly penetrate what for all intents and purposes is a miniature fortress? Who or what organization has the means not only to penetrate this fortress but to leave behind some black-ops listening devices? Remember, the questions relate to the still unknown secret that lies within the Pike Letters."

All four of them sat there pondering the questions that Danny had presented.

Thomas was the first to pipe up, "Could it be the CIA?"

Danny and Jimmy glanced at each other. Danny just shook his head. "No, Thomas. I can assure you that it's not the CIA, NSA, FBI, Interpol, or any other intelligence group within the Free World; and it's not the GRU, the new KGB. However, there is one other organization that it may surprise you to learn has all of the capabilities that I've described."

"What organization is left, apart from those that you described? Wait a minute, it's not the Mafia?" Thomas was wide-eyed by this time.

The other three just laughed. Janet reached over and patted Thomas on the cheek. He was beginning to hate it when she did that. Jimmy had the answer: "Thomas, I think you've been watching too many late-night movies. The answer may shock you. It's the Vatican. More precisely, we're talking about the secret police of the Vatican—the Jesuits."

"The Jesuits . . . the Vatican? You mean to tell me that the pope and the Vatican have their very own secret police? Come on, guys: I realize that you're far more worldly than I am, but I find this hard to believe. Even if it were true, what would be their interest in a set of letters between two old friends and Brothers?" Thomas looked appealingly at Janet. "Janet, you told me that Freemasonry was nothing more than a fraternity. Will someone please tell me what's going on here?"

Janet nodded her consent for Danny to educate Thomas. He said, "Thomas, I think you'd better sit down for this. I'm going to give you a lesson in global politics of which I guarantee 99 percent of the world's population is totally unaware. I'm going to explain why certain seemingly unconnected current events around the world appear to be converging into a nuclear holocaust. Many of the evangelicals attribute it to the apocalypse foretold in the Bible, but that 1 percent of us look at it in a more human way. There is a struggle going on between the world's three great religions for total world domination, along with a fourth wild card, namely atheistic communism. This struggle has been going on for over a thousand years. Now let's take our coffee into the living room. We might as well get comfortable, because this story may take a while."

XI

PRINCE AMETH
(ELU OF THE TWELVE)

FROM WASHINGTON TO PARIS

Everyone took their respective seats in the living room and prepared themselves to receive Danny's summation. Danny rubbed the scar on the side of his face, as though it would stir his memory. Then he started. "I want to provide a context to what I'm about to tell you so you can understand what we're dealing with. Since time began, it's been basic human nature to try to survive and preserve life, first and foremost your own. Unfortunately, over centuries, man has forsaken that basic human instinct for survival and has learned to justify his killing of others or himself, based on certain beliefs, usually in the name of God. Now I want to tell you the story of how I got this scar, and that will set the context for everything else that I'm about to tell you."

Janet was amazed by Danny's proposed revelation. Even though she had asked at least twelve times over the years, he had always been reluctant to even broach the subject of his scar with her. She leaned forward to hear every last bit of the story as he continued. "It was about thirty years ago, shortly after Jimmy and I had become Navy SEALs, that we were sent to a hellhole of a place in the Middle East to kidnap a territorial Muslim warlord. This fellow was a nasty piece of work. Under the guise of Islam, he had been running amok among his own people, terrorizing and killing people who did not belong to his own familial tribe or sect.

"Our mission was to drop in by sea at night, hump about five miles inland to his village compound, neutralize all of those guarding him, infiltrate his lair, sequester his rather large family, and extract him by helicopter before dawn.

"Everything went smoother than we expected. We were a little suspicious of the information that had been provided, but it was bang on. Of course, the warlord had to be somewhat persuaded to come along quietly. I remember him spitting in my face. For that I gave him a real shot with my fist and flattened his nose.

"Anyway, we had to move him through his own inner compound to reach the other side of the village, where there was a landing zone big enough for the helicopters that had been called in. As we moved this fellow through the room where two other SEALs were guarding his family, they all start to wail and cry for this guy, even though Intel had told us that he viciously abused his own family.

"Just as we thought that everything was calmed down and we were in the clear, one of his wives leaped onto my back with the speed of a mountain lion. Now I'm a strong guy, but for the life of me, I couldn't shake her off. She then drew out a curved ceremonial dagger and drove it into the side of my face, just below my right ear, and started to drag the blade toward my jugular. I'm sure someone had trained her to do that. Luckily, Jimmy blew her off my back with his ball-bearing shotgun, which he favors over the M16. He still claims that he can open steel doors with it."

To which Jimmy replied, "Saved your fat ass, didn't it?"

Danny nodded. "Yes, you did just that. So there we were, loading this guy into the lead helicopter, with me bleeding like a stuck pig, when the whole house disintegrates in smoke. It turns out that this guy's favorite son, who was only about eight, was wearing an explosive vest. His father had instructed him to destroy his own family if the patriarch was ever killed or kidnapped."

Janet and Thomas sat there aghast. There was nothing that anyone could say.

The silence allowed Danny to continue. "Can you imagine? The idiot would rather have his whole family obliterated than exist without him, all in the name of Allah. He believed that they would all be joined together in heaven. How can you defend against that?

"So as I lay in the army hospital back in the States, recovering from my near-death experience, I explored the deep recesses of my mind. I just couldn't fathom the actions of the father, mother, and son. What saved me was simply the bond that Jimmy, Janet's father, and I had developed through Masonry. It was my saving grace. This grinning goofball over there came every day to let me know the results of the interrogation of our prisoner. It turned out that the guy had personally been responsible for the death of hundreds of his own countrymen, twelve U.S. Special Forces personnel, and one prince of the Saudi royal family. He was also planning a strike on U.S. soil twenty years before Osama bin Laden. After hearing that, I had no qualms about what had happened back there."

"I also took every chance that I could to remind him that I saved his ass!" Jimmy chimed in gleefully.

"Pay no heed to him. I returned the favor on a number of occasions. But that's what I was trying to demonstrate with that little fairy tale. In the end, it's all about the brotherly bond that we have with one another here on Earth.

"Now I'm not advocating that Masons honor their bond before their love of their family. Not at all! But when it comes to surviving and protecting your family, it's almost impossible to go it alone. That's when it comes down to faith, family, fidelity, fellowship, and fraternity.

"These were the five points of the star, the five pillars that the original Knights Templar swore to uphold a thousand years ago. They became the guardians of the light in this world. And this is where we get into current world politics. Tell me, Thomas, how much do you know about the medieval Knights Templar? Janet told her father over the phone that you didn't appear to know much about their history other than what you've learned through summer blockbusters like *National Treasure*." Danny leaned closer to Thomas and gave him a stern look, as if he would be judging Thomas's response on a higher level.

Clearing his throat, Thomas felt as though he was back responding to his elementary-school teacher. "Not really much at all. As I told Janet when we first met, I wasn't even aware that my great-great-grandfather was a Templar, let alone the first Supreme Grand Master of the Knights Templar of Canada, until I did some digging on the internet."

From the look in Danny Sullivan's eyes, Thomas appeared to have passed some kind of test. Danny clearly had the ability to judge when people were not telling the absolute truth. "That's good, Thomas. Your honesty will serve you well. And don't worry about not knowing anything about the Knights Templar or your great-great-grandfather's involvement in the Order. There are only a very few who truly understand the significance of the Templars' involvement in world affairs over the past thousand years. What you get through movies such as *The Da Vinci Code* and *National Treasure* is the watered-down, grade-five version: *Templar Light,* just like *Knightfall*!"

Danny took a sip of coffee before continuing. "Now let me tell you the real story. The original nine knights, who traveled to Jerusalem before the First Crusade, were on a secret mission. Outwardly, the story was that they were there to protect the early Christian pilgrims. One thing that you should know is that the knights were all members of aristocratic families who could trace their ancestry back to the high priests of the Temple such as Aaron, brother of Moses. Although all of them were outwardly Roman Catholic, they continued to practice and maintain the secrets of the old Jewish magi, including the location of certain treasures that had been hidden under the Temple when Jerusalem was sacked by the Romans in AD 70. Thanks to *The Da Vinci Code,* many think the treasure consists of relics and other priceless things, including proof that Jesus married Mary Magdalene and that union produced a Holy Grail–type family, which lives on to this day.

"That may be the case, but here is where it gets really interesting. The moral to the story is always to look beyond. The purported secret relating to Jesus and Mary is not the ultimate Templar Treasure, if that's what you want to call it. Within Masonic tradition there is a deep belief that speaks to sacred knowledge that's been preserved from before the Great Flood.

"Many people assume that the population that existed before the Flood was almost animalistic. That wasn't the case at all. The ancient human race was far more technologically advanced in many ways than we are now. For thousands of years, certain inner circles have believed that this knowledge would enable its possessor to destroy the entire world. What we're talking about is death star from within type of stuff, to put it in layman's terms.

"Now we do know that once they were recovered, portions of the Templar Treasure were secreted away, first to France. Then they were systematically dispersed to England, Scotland, Portugal, and Denmark, and also directly to North America, where the Templar/Grail families, direct descendants of Jesus and Mary Magdalene, strategically intermarried with the Native North Americans. Secret information has it that all remaining portions of the treasure were brought back together and ultimately hidden in a crypt somewhere in the American West. The direct descendants, or guardians, of the original nine knights built a crypt identical to the one that was discovered under the wall of King Solomon's Temple in Jerusalem in order to reinter what they needed to establish a New Jerusalem.

"Albert Pike somehow must have rediscovered the trail of signs, symbols, and tokens developed by the descendants of the Templars who came to North America, which still lead to the crypt. Or maybe he had access to the purported journals of one Prince Henry Sinclair. Why else would Pike be paroled by Andrew Johnson and then allowed to serve the U.S. government? Why else was he appointed the government's top Indian agent after the Civil War? Some say that even the president of the United States deferred to Pike. Regardless, the inner circle of the Scottish Rite of the Southern Jurisdiction supported the Supreme Grand Commander even after he died. Why? Because it was believed that Pike knew where the final resting place of the crypt lay and, quite ingeniously, hid the coordinates for that final temple of sacred knowledge in letters that he wrote to his lifelong Masonic Brother, Colonel W. J. B. Macleod Moore. He trusted MacLeod Moore with the ultimate secret because of the original key that MacLeod Moore shared with him.

"Can you imagine the power that would be gained by the organization that recovered that knowledge? They could threaten to blow up the Earth itself unless the entire world paid homage to them. The Vatican and the pope would finally be able to regain control and impose their form of Christianity upon the world. Thomas, this is why we are certain that your intruder, your stalker, is a Jesuit! The Jesuits are fanatics. They're the pope's personal storm troopers, who will stop at nothing to regain world dominance."

Everyone sat in silence, contemplating what Danny had just outlined. It was as if a miniature bomb had exploded within the living room.

Thomas was the first to speak up. "OK, now I get it. So tell me: how do we first eliminate this stalker and then go about finding this sacred knowledge before someone else does?"

"Thomas, I'm so glad you understand," said Janet. "Danny, Jimmy, and I have already agreed on what we have to do. My father agrees too. I'm sorry for not involving you sooner, but you needed the background to this whole thing. Anyway, you and I are flying to Paris this evening and will pretend for several days to be enjoying ourselves. Maybe we'll even take a riverboat cruise, sort of like a mini pre-honeymoon." Thomas smiled at the thought while Janet continued, "We're sure that our intruder will think that we have taken the letters with us to get some second opinions on their hidden content or to explore some clue mentioned in the letters. All the while, Danny and Jimmy and some other select men will shadow us constantly, hoping that our stalker slips up and shows his hand. Don't worry: we'll be entirely safe every step of the way."

Thomas wasn't naive enough to believe that they would be totally out of danger. But if Janet noticed the concern on Thomas's face, she didn't give it away. "After we leave, it's been arranged that Grandfather will move back into this house, with rings of invisible security, of course. Danny and Jimmy have also arranged for the finest cryptographers from CIA headquarters at Langley to join Grandfather tomorrow, and hopefully, with the latest in modern equipment, he can direct their efforts in cracking the letters. Once that's done and our adversary or adversaries are eliminated, then we can get on with rediscovering *that-which-was-lost*."

Regardless of the plans, if any of the four had bothered to look out the front door that morning, they could have easily caught a glimpse of the mysterious stalker. Down the street from David Rose's house was a Catholic private school, which had a fenced-in playground. On most days it wasn't unusual to see a pickup basketball game being played on the court closest to the street. What was unusual this day was that the game consisted of a number of older students playing a group of thirty-something males, some of whom weren't that bad as basketball players. In fact, the most talented and most competitive individual was Philippe De Smet.

For Philippe, an incentive was added to this morning's game by the realization that his listening devices had suddenly gone dead, which meant that the two older gentlemen, who had arrived at the house in the early morning, were something more than they first appeared.

Philippe called for a break, outwardly to check his cell phone, but he needed time to think. He walked over to the quiet corner of the court facing the house. As he pretended to check for phone messages, he tried to sort out his next move. He didn't need to think hard. He suddenly received a text message from the ever-obliging concierge at the Georgetown Inn.

Apparently, Thomas Moore had just phoned the inn, canceling his month-long reservation, indicating that he unexpectedly had to fly to Paris that evening. *Very well, Mr. Moore, Paris it is! I presume that your Jewish wench is going with you. The Paris Temple was the headquarters of the Crusaders in the fourteenth century, when the king of France and Pope Clement V crushed them. But they were unsuccessful in obliterating the order, which appears to have risen from the dead. It's never been proven that the Masonic Knights Templar, who showed themselves in North America in the mid-1700s, were directly connected to the medieval Knights Templar, but they've carried on with portions of the earlier secrets. Albert Pike and MacLeod Moore had seen to that through the expansion of Scottish Rite Masonry. The pieces to the puzzle are beginning to come together. Very interesting indeed!*

XII

MASTER ARCHITECT
Twenty-four days ago

THE RITZ PARIS HOTEL

The overnight flight was made much easier by the Rose Commodities Corporation, which had arranged to fly the brand-new Boeing 777 Daydreamer from Washington to Paris. Janet and Thomas slept for most of the flight, thanks in part to the small bottle of pills that Janet had the forethought to tuck away in her purse before they left for the airport.

Of course, they weren't ordinary pills. They were David Rose's special mixture containing just enough white powdered gold to keep Thomas's confidence level at an all-time high. Janet needed to be sure that if there was trouble, Thomas would rise to the occasion. One benefit of the powder is that it enabled one to focus and to block out all negativity.

Meanwhile, Danny and Jimmy had driven back to RCC headquarters in downtown Manhattan. Both men had a lot to do before they boarded the corporate jet at 2 a.m. They didn't need that much sleep, as thirty years flying around the world on a moment's notice as SEALs and CIA operatives had trained their bodies to exceed their natural limits. They also enjoyed the benefits of the white powder.

Amazingly, the speed of the Learjet ensured that Danny and Jimmy arrived at the Ritz in Paris the next morning before Janet and Thomas. The two were there, flanking Janet's father, Solomon, when Janet and Thomas entered their lavish suite.

Even before Thomas could drop his carry-on bag onto the suite's living-room floor, Solomon had risen from his chair and approached him with his hand extended in greeting. The broad smile on his face soothed Solomon's otherwise stern composure. It was good for business and also reflected his reaction to the briefing that he had just been given by his two security experts. Thomas never wondered how the three had gotten into the luxurious suite, but he did take in the father's rugged good looks and toned physique. Solomon's hair was jet black, and his blue eyes sparkled with wisdom. *Wow, is the entire family descended from the Egyptian gods or from the ancient Hebrew kings? I guess those are really the same.*

"Thomas, it is indeed a pleasure," said Solomon. "My daughter is certainly taken with you, and Danny and Jimmy tell me that you're catching on to all of this sorry state of affairs rather quickly." Thomas shook Solomon's hand enthusiastically as the latter continued, "Unfortunately, we've found ourselves in a world of upheaval. There is a constant battle between good and evil being fought for world supremacy. Most of the world's population can't comprehend it, but the combination of the Brexit vote, terrorism throughout Europe and the world, the yellow vests, the Israel-Palestinian question, the rise of the alternative right, the United States versus Russia, the refugee question, climate change—you name the rest—has put the world in turmoil.

"My immediate job right now is to try to prop up the EU economy until it can get back on its feet, so you can see that I'm a little preoccupied. I apologize in advance if I don't have much time to spend with you and Janet. But I want you to know that my daughter's happiness and safety, along with the health of my father, take precedence in my heart over everything else. That's why I've personally assigned Danny and Jimmy to this situation. They are two of the finest men and soldiers whom I've ever had the pleasure of being able to call friends and Masonic Brothers. Did Janet happen to mention that my two guardians are also modern-day Templars?"

Thomas stood there, looking first to Janet and then to Danny and Jimmy. All three appeared to have sprouted the goofiest grins. Janet just shrugged her shoulders in a moment of attempted ignorance. Thomas was both impressed and not impressed. "No, I'm afraid that none of the three happened to mention that piece of information. I take it, Mr. Rose, that the only reason you're not one yourself is because of your Jewish background?"

"Yes, Thomas, that's exactly right. I truly admire the qualities and foundation of the Poor Knights of the Temple of Solomon. You probably aren't aware that the original Knights Templar had made a pact with influential Jewish sects throughout Europe and the Middle East right from the start, for Jesus is still seen as a powerful rabbi and prophet in Jewish eyes.

"The Jews also financed the original endeavors of the knights until they secured their own monetary supply, which they turned into the first real banking system in the world. Once the Crusades had taken hold, it was the Knights Templar who reciprocated by safeguarding the rights and property of the Jews. But the Templars had also very early on realized that they ultimately could not defeat the Muslims. Once they developed a stranglehold on the papacy as a result of what they had discovered beneath the Temple, they entered into secret pacts with the Muslims.

"The Knights Templar believed that the holiest of holy cities—Jerusalem—and the place of the Temple ruins could be shared by Christians, Muslims, and Jews. Unfortunately, the Vatican had other ideas. If you didn't believe in Jesus Christ as the Son of God, your head was chopped off and put on a spike as a deterrent to others. Of course, the smarter ones quickly converted to Roman Catholicism.

"Thomas, are you aware that the tenets of Christianity were decided upon during the First Council of Nicaea in AD 325? The Roman emperor, Constantine, a pagan until just before his death, decided that he needed to control the outbreak of Christianity among the slaves who formed the bureaucratic ranks of the Roman Empire. Constantine indeed had the final say on what formal concepts, such as the Holy Trinity, Gospels, rituals, holidays even, would remain to form the basis of the Holy Catholic Church. Unfortunately, that ended the true understanding of Christianity as practiced by the earliest Christians for about three centuries. The church became patriarchal, centered on Peter, burying the earlier goddess concept, and ever since has ruled with an iron fist. Need I mention the Spanish Inquisition?"

Jimmy had to chime in, quoting Monty Python, "Nobody expects the Spanish Inquisition!" To which Danny answered, "Be quiet, you Irish mug!"

Thomas thought Janet's father would be angry at the interruption, but he just laughed. "Sometimes, Thomas, I even admire the Irish. Unbeknownst to many, the Irish secretly maintained the tenets of true Christianity and even provided some of the earliest routes to the New World. Imagine Brendan riding the backs of right whales across the Atlantic. And although the church has done its best to suppress the Irish people, there are still a few enlightened Irishmen who share our desire to disarm the Vatican and its inner circle, which is tightly guarded by their keepers, the Jesuits. I shudder to think what could happen if those fanatics, or anyone else, got their hands on the ancient technology. Can you imagine a lunatic taking us to the brink of extinction, all in the name of God?"

Solomon started to slowly make his way to the door. "Before I must go, Thomas, there is one more thing that I should tell you." Thomas reacted in his usual self-deprecating manner, thinking, *Oh, here we go; here's the punch line to all of this. I'm sure that we're all going to die.*

Solomon reached for his daughter's hand. "Janet has always been the smart one in the family. In fact, I think that she may rival her grandfather on the levels of both esotericism and pure brilliance. In her younger days, her mother and I tolerated her wild ways because we believed that it was best to allow her to get it out of her system. Without Danny and Jimmy there, I shudder to think what would have happened to my precious princess. She has certainly been blessed in the eyes of Adonai. In any event, I know that she still believes that she needs our blessing before she gets married. If that is the case, then I've already made my judgment: the two of you have mine and Janet's mother's blessing. *Shalom!*"

Janet threw her arms around her father and kissed him on the cheek. "Oh, Father, thank you, thank you so much. You've made me so happy. I promise you a wonderful grandson and granddaughter of your own. We'll name them Solomon and Eliza, in honor of you and Mommy." Without further fanfare, Solomon exited the suite to be greeted and escorted back to the closed-door conference by two elite members of RCC's security team.

Danny and Jimmy stood there with their jaws open. Danny was the first to bring everyone back to reality. "OK, you two, enough of the sentimental whatever-that-was. I never thought that in all eternity I would live to see the great and wise Solomon Rose turn into mush. I suggest that we get back to the present situation."

Janet walked over to Thomas and kissed him silently on the cheek. Then she reached for his hand and led them over to the table, where Danny and Jimmy, still grinning ear to ear, had taken a seat. Thomas realized that he had just witnessed the special bond between a great man and his equally great daughter. He felt privileged to be in that room when the stars and the heaven opened up for the faint moment when God's presence made itself known.

Spread out on the table before them was a large tourist map of Paris, along with an itinerary for both Janet and Thomas for the next three days. Thomas had been to Paris on business several times, but he had not played tourist since his university days.

"I have a real surprise for you two. Courtesy of the Rose Commodities Corporation, you have won an all-expense-paid, five-star vacation for two, including four days in Paris and a magnificent eight-day, seven-night riverboat cruise up the Seine to Normandy and back. Now doesn't that sound lovely, especially after receiving the formal blessing to fornicate anywhere and anytime that you desire?"

Jimmy almost hit the floor laughing. Danny, in the driest of moods, just looked at Thomas and said, "And I won't even tell you the time that Jimmy picked up this young lady in Morocco only to find out in the morning that she had stolen his passport, his wallet, and his gun. Boy, did he get taken that day."

The only response that Danny got from Jimmy was, "But man, she was worth it. I'll never forget what's-her-name." After that, time was called, as general laughter broke out around the table. But Danny and Jimmy knew what they were doing. It was common for the warrior-monks to kid around before they went into battle. It didn't hurt for Janet and Thomas to join in on the fun.

As the laughter subsided, Danny pushed over the itinerary for both Janet and Thomas to review. "Here's the scoop: we'll leave you two love-birds alone today. Since you're jet-lagged, you'll probably want to sleep until eight o'clock this evening, Paris time. Then I suggest that you stroll down to the main dining room at nine o'clock for a late, candle-light dinner. Your reservation is already booked. Ms. Rose, I took the liberty of getting you one of those next-to-be-famous-designer cocktail dresses that you favor so much. It's hanging in the closet. There's also quite a nice French silk suit for Thomas.

"As it's your first night in Paris, you'll be expected to go for a stroll along the Seine. I suggest that you don't make it a long one and take an umbrella. It always rains in Paris this time of year. Actually, I'm told that it's quite romantic. Then off to bed, because tomorrow you have a full itinerary. You have a car and a driver, already booked. You'll visit the Louvre before the tourists really start to come out and then have lunch and walk along the Champs-Élysées for an afternoon of shopping. Then it's back to the hotel for a quick change and then off to the Eiffel Tower restaurant for a long and romantic dinner in a stunning setting.

The light show on the tower begins at dusk. It's a must-see, for sure."

Janet had already realized that Danny and Jimmy wanted to make this a special treat for Thomas and her, even though a deadly game of chess was on the board. She leaned over and kissed Danny on the cheek. For the shortest of moments, she could have sworn that she saw his eyes welling up with tears. Danny and Jimmy had always thought of Janet as the daughter that neither had ever had.

Trying to move on, Thomas perked up and questioned the two men. "I see from our itinerary that you have us going from one public place to another, pretty much out in the open. I suspect that this is your intention in order to draw out our stalker. What if he isn't here in Paris?"

Unexpectedly, it was Janet who answered, "He's here, Thomas. I can feel him."

Thomas wasn't about to question Janet's source of intuition at that moment. Instead he continued with his own line of reasoning. "Then I see that we take a somewhat more sequestered riverboat cruise, where we'll more likely be able to get separated or even worse." Nobody said a word. "I presume that Jimmy here will be fitting us up with the latest GPS tracking and listening devices?"

Taking his cue, it was Jimmy's turn to deadpan, "Thomas, you have once again been watching too many late-night movies. That's old hat. Don't worry, you won't see us, but we'll be with you every second. Anyway, your stalker won't make a move until he's certain that you have the letters with you. Even then, he'll probably follow you in order to see what you're searching for here in France. Now I suggest that the two of you have a nice afternoon nap. You'll need it."

"Come on, Danny, you can buy me an expensive Scotch down in the bar. Maybe we can sit on the same stool that Dodi Fayed and Princess Diana sat on the night that they were killed. I know that sounds morbid but when in Paris . . ." And with those words they were gone.

Janet and Thomas looked at each other. The next ten days were going to be like a honeymoon, even though somewhere out in the shadows lurked a madman, a knight of a different color. Thomas was thinking,

Are we just two pawns in a global game of chess? The morbid joke about Princess Diana didn't sit well with either of them. On their way from De Gaulle airport their driver had made a special point of showing them the memorial to Diana at the entrance to the Pont de l'Alma road tunnel. The driver had surprised even Janet when he pointed out that the site of the accident is an ancient, sacred site, dating back to before the time of the Merovingian kings. In pre-Christian times, the Pont de l'Alma was a pagan sacrificial site. She was impressed, thinking that the Paris tourist board had certainly done its homework with the limo drivers, trying anything to draw back the tourists after several terrorist incidents.

As Janet closed the drapes to the many windows around the suite, she convinced Thomas to forget about the two wisecracking Irishmen. At this point they really were too jet-lagged to care. Yet Thomas had all of his clothes stripped off and was under the covers before Janet even had her blouse off. As she slipped in beside Thomas, she reminded herself to tell her grandfather when she next saw him that this batch of white powdered gold certainly did the trick.

For the faintest moment, the two were content enough just to wrap their arms around one another. It was a moment of pure bliss that they would cherish for a long time in the City of Lights. "Thomas, there's an interesting story about Albert Pike that you may not know. There is a commonly believed hoax perpetrated by the church. It says that Albert Pike received a vision, which he described in a letter to Giuseppe Mazzini in 1871. Mazzini was an Italian revolutionary leader as well as the purported director of the Illuminati in Europe. Ostensibly this letter graphically outlined plans for three world wars that were seen as necessary to bring about a New World Order. The contents of the supposed letter rather too accurately predict the advent of the first two world wars, even identifying the Nazis by name, along with speaking of a third world war of epic, biblical proportions."

Thomas thought about Janet's comments for a second, then, pulling her even closer, he whispered in her ear, "If it's my last day on earth, then I can't think of a better place to be than in your arms."

XIII

ROYAL ARCH OF SOLOMON

August 21, 1871

WASHINGTON, D.C.

Albert Pike had become increasingly restless and finally decided to abandon any attempt to go back to sleep. Instead, he lit the oil lamp, sat at his writing table, and allowed his sleepy eyes to adjust to the faint glow. Finding his favorite pen and ever-present writing paper, he wrote another letter to his friend and Brother, W. J. B. MacLeod Moore. Most of the time, the contents of his letters were rather philosophical or secretarial in nature, but this letter carried with it an invisible black stain of self-doubt and foreboding.

August 21, 1871

Most Illustrious Brother and Fellow Sir Knight W. J. B. MacLeod Moore, 33°, KT

    My Most Illustrious Brother, I must confess that I have been having such fitful sleep. I am working almost too hard on my Morals and Dogma of the Ancient and Accepted Scottish Rite of Freemasonry. *Unfortunately, my demons of old seem to be haunting me again. Like the earliest Christian monks, St. Peter and St. Anthony, I sense that I must take to the wilderness to be rid of them. Only then will I be able to truly escape my horrible dreams, such as the one that I experienced in early August of this very year. For the first time in my life I was truly afraid, as the hand of the Supreme Being eluded me.*

It was so vivid and real that I felt compelled to convey my visions this past August 15th to Director Giuseppe Mazzini. I believe that he is in Paris at this moment. During our last meeting here, he indicated that he had also met you on occasion and was most impressed by your ancient knowledge.

As you are aware, I have come to believe that among all the ancient nations there was one faith and one idea of Deity for the enlightened, intelligent, and educated, and another for the common people. Wherefore nothing forbids us to consider the whole legend of the Royal Arch of Solomon as but an allegory, representing the perpetuation of the knowledge of the True God in the sanctuaries of initiation. By the subterranean vaults we may therefore understand the places of initiation, which in the ancient ceremonies were generally underground.

The luminous pedestal, lighted by the perpetual flame within, is a symbol of that light of Reason, given by God to man, by which he is enabled to read in the Book of Nature the record of the thought, the revelation of the attributes of the Deity.

The lion, the altar, still holds in his mouth the key of the enigma of the sphynx.

The time is early morning and I have been rambling of late. I long for the sun to be at its meridian.

Albert Pike, 33°, KT,
Sovereign Grand Commander

Pike almost cried after completing the letter to his friend. In the faint darkness of his room, the demons were closing in, tempting him with visions of the flesh—evil temptations. He had found Justice. Now he was searching for Fortitude and Temperance. He had earlier broken out in a cold sweat and believed that by conveying his thoughts to MacLeod Moore, he could control the visions. The sunrise saved him. Its warmth and assurance allowed him to wrestle the demons back into the inner reaches of his soul.

The rising of the sun always brought reason and logic back to Pike. As he basked in its warmth, he concluded that he was on the right path. Reason told him that he was just physically exhausted. That was all. For years he had worked at a breakneck speed, absorbing as much sacred knowledge and learning as many ancient languages as he could before he felt comfortable enough to write his magnum opus.

He certainly believed that his was the penultimate work on Scottish Rite Freemasonry and that it would become the basis for all Masonic research far into the future. He wasn't a man for personal accolades, but given his dark periods of late, he allowed himself a fleeting sense of self-satisfaction this morning.

Little would he realize the enormity of his life's work. *Morals and Dogma,* an immense collection of thirty-two essays, would provide a philosophical description and rationale for the degrees of the Ancient and Accepted Scottish Rite, but it would be written so as to not reveal the Masonic secrets and to provide a background to the Southern Jurisdiction's thirty-two degrees of ritual through comparative ancient and esoteric religion, history, philosophy, and symbolism.

Philippe De Smet had flown out of Boston in order to avoid a potential and unnecessary confrontation with his two subjects. Having access to unlimited funds and resources, he flew first class. The Society of Jesus was depending on their rising star and therefore didn't mind Philippe's occasional self-indulgences, monetary or otherwise. As long as he completed his mission, he was the golden child as far as the Inner Circle was concerned.

The Society of Jesus was first formed in Spain in 1534 by Ignatius of Loyola, a Basque nobleman from the Pyrenees region. At that time, Ignatius and six other young men, including Francis Xavier and Peter Faber, gathered and professed vows of poverty, chastity, and later obedience, including a special vow of obedience to the pope in matters of mission, direction, and assignment.

Ignatius came from a noble and military family, and accordingly, the order's members were instructed to consider themselves soldiers of Christ. Ignatius's plan for the order's organization was approved by Pope Paul III in 1540 in a bull containing the Formula of the Institute. From that time forward, the Jesuits had rooted out and systematically obliterated any adversary of the pope or the Catholic religion.

Although it was actually the Dominicans who created the organization, the Jesuits were a fundamental element of the Spanish Inquisition. Simply stated, the Inquisition was a religious tribunal or court established in Spain from 1480 to 1820, but most active from 1492 onward, following Columbus's supposed discovery of America. It was responsible for the jailing, trial, torture, and execution of thousands of heretics, mostly Spanish Jews or Muslims, who were accused of not completely converting to Catholicism.

Philippe always smiled when he recounted the history of the Society of Jesus. Ostensibly the Society paid homage to the pope himself, but for the past four hundred years it had become an entity unto itself. His current masters believed as he did: Pope Francis, although a Jesuit himself, was weak and ineffective. It all started out well when he chose Francis as his papal name in honor of St. Francis of Assisi. At the time it was hoped that this pope from Argentina would take a strong stand against the weekend Catholics of North America and Europe and demand that they return to the rigors of the church.

The last thought that Philippe had before he slept aboard the plane that evening was concerning the future of his beloved church. *When I personally return the lost ancient knowledge to its rightful place, the rock upon which the church was built, Peter will rise up and smite those who do not bow before his tomb. Only then will I be able to ascend to heaven.*

Arriving in Paris just ahead of the Washington flight, Philippe took a taxi to a small boutique hotel that he had chosen on the internet. He noted from the reviews that it was centrally located, clean, and quiet and above all else offered central heating and air-conditioning. Philippe considered this a must, given that Paris was built on a swamp. The weather conditions at any time of year were extreme at best.

Having quietly checked in under a completely profiled alias provided by the Society and confirming that the room was satisfactory, the first thing Philippe did was retrieve his gun from the hidden compartment in his suitcase. Although he knew that all suitcases were routinely X-rayed, he had been confident that the molded-plastic components would not set off any alarm. He patted the gun as if to reassure an old friend and then hit #9 on a disposable cell phone previously provided to him.

A different voice, this one with a slight French accent, came on the other end but with the same familiar greeting, "Jesus suffered and died on the cross." Philippe replied without hesitation, "In order for mankind not to suffer." Then waiting for a few seconds, he continued, "This is Philippe De Smet. Have you determined where the two subjects are staying?"

The voice replied, "Oui, they are at Le Ritz. At this moment, they are having a nap, but they have a dinner reservation for nine o'clock in the main dining room."

Philippe was grateful for the Society's efficiency. "Do you have any other information?"

Again, the voice replied, "Oui, you should be aware that there are at least three eight-man security details from the Rose Commodities Corporation working inside the hotel around the clock. The hotel is locked down for the EU monetary conference. Representatives from all over Europe are attending the conference hastily called by the head of the IMF. There are three external perimeters manned by the local Paris police, regional police, and the republican military respectively."

Philippe had expected as much. *No matter,* he thought, *it's better to allow the two to provide him with the information that is required to activate the ancient knowledge when it was retrieved.* He was certain that this was the main purpose behind the couple's visit to Paris. He had reasoned that they were in pursuit of clues left by the Knights Templar before that evening of Friday, October 13, 1307. Philippe focused back on the voice. "Do you know their future itinerary?"

For once, the voice showed a slight bit of emotion, indicating that here was the prized information. "Oui, starting tomorrow, they are essentially sightseeing around the city for three days before they board one of the riverboats for a seven-day cruise on the Seine, traveling north to Normandy and back. I will text you their entire ten-day itinerary." The cruise along the Seine intrigued Philippe. *Perhaps there are locations outside of Paris proper that possess the necessary signs, symbols, or tokens. It's along the same route that the Vikings took when they first attacked and sacked Paris over a thousand years ago.*

Philippe was more than pleased. "Merci. Your group has done well. If I require anything else, I will call. Meanwhile, if any further information comes that you feel is relevant, just text me with the number 9. I will get back to you as soon as possible."

The voice became slightly more human but was disciplined enough to follow established protocol. "We are all God's soldiers." With confirmation that his instructions would be followed completely, Philippe disconnected the call. Having immediately assessed the situation, he decided that he also needed a nap. He would need his wits about him if he was to follow his two subjects without being spotted himself. Flipping off his fine Italian loafers and shoving his now-loaded Glock under his pillow, he lay back on the bed and closed his eyes. He was immediately asleep.

Awaking at exactly seven o'clock in the evening, Philippe felt he could indulge himself a little, so he took a long hot shower, followed by a blast of freezing cold water to shake the cobwebs from his brain. Then he changed into his trusty old runners and gym clothes. The transformation was immediate. No one would really take notice of a middle-aged, athletic jock out for a jog in the cool evening air, especially since he hid his eyes behind his sunglasses. As far as he was concerned, he was invisible once more.

Exiting past the front desk, since he knew that the owner would be having supper at that time, Philippe stood just outside the hotel entrance and smelled the early night air. He had been in Paris on a number of prior assignments and often marveled at how the air, despite its faint, humid odor of garbage mixed with sewage and stagnant water, was oddly appealing.

No matter: he had chosen his route carefully, making his way toward the river and then across the Pont des Arts to the Left Bank. From there he would make his way past the Louvre and up Rue Saint-Honoré to the Place Vendôme, where the Ritz was located. Then he would circle back across Pont Alexandre III, down the Rue Marechal Gallieni, and make his way back to the hotel. If he was feeling hungry, he decided that he might try one of the street-side cafés located along Rue Saint Dominique. He loved the fact that the French offered so many amazing food choices, whether at a small café or a five-star hotel such as the Ritz.

He would make sure that he passed the Pont d'Alma and the eternal flame to Diana, almost where the crypt of past Merovingian kings lies under the Seine. He wouldn't be paying homage at any time to Princess Diana, or any past moon goddesses, who are said to visit the kings every twenty-eight days during the rising of the full moon. He much preferred the story of how two proud kings met on the bridge and fought to the death for the honor of being crowned the ultimate king of the Merovingian kingdom, which preceded the kingdom of Francia. As he ran past the throngs who continued to commemorate the twenty-year mark since the death of Diana, he thought, *Stupid people. Don't you realize that Diana was just a pawn in a larger game?*

Philippe had no qualms about being stopped by the police. In his small running pack strapped around his waist he had his false credentials, which identified him as a high school art teacher from Boston, just in case some sharp-eared policeman noticed the slight lilt. (Although he had taken some speech lessons to rid himself of a strong Boston accent, like all Bostonians, he was proud of his heritage.) He wouldn't be taking his gun. There was no need.

In fact, he silently hoped that he would be stopped.

XIV

PERFECT ELU

Twenty-one days ago

THE DOCKS OF THE SEINE, PARIS

The two lovers spent three days of romantic perfection, touring the best of what Paris could offer before they made their way in the late afternoon sun to the docks where they would embark on the riverboat. Over the past three days, their lodging had been exquisite in every detail. Their lovemaking had risen to a higher degree, and the French food was almost as sensuous. Janet and Thomas felt as though they had died and gone to heaven.

During their seemingly endless touring of Paris, Janet was impressed with Thomas's love for the landscape and his knowledge of the evolution of the city's design. From Le Notre to Le Vau to Pierre Charles L'Enfant to Haussmann to Le Corbusier, he rambled on about vistas and allées, distant focal points and trompe l'oeil. He even regaled Janet with an impromptu lecture comparing the design of Paris to that of Washington.

In turn, Janet exposed Thomas to the ancient esoteric philosophy that lay beneath Paris and its many layers of deity dedication and symbolism. Thomas couldn't believe that he hadn't noticed the many references to the goddesses Columbia, Artemis, and Venus; to the gods Mithras and Apollo; to the Egyptian mysteries; and beyond. Nor could he believe it when Janet trumped his lecture and compared the esoteric design of Paris to that of Washington. Of course L'Enfant had been primarily responsible for the final design of both republican capitals.

The Masonic symbolism first applied by men such as L'Enfant, Eiffel, and Verne was carried on through modern designers, landscape architects, architects, and planners on both sides of the Atlantic. In Paris especially, Masonic symbolism oozed through the goddess's pores, much like the ancient odor of sewage that whiffed gently from the underground catacombs up through the street grates.

Thomas couldn't get over the fact that five-pointed star patterns had been woven into the two designs. *How did I not know this?* He asked himself. *Janet has taught me so much—how to look beyond the obvious. It's through her that I've become so enlightened in such a short time. She has opened my soul to the divine nature of everything that surrounds us, the many levels of subconscious understanding that awaits enlightenment. God, these past three days have been so perfect, almost sublime in intensity, as if driven by a divine spirit.*

Nudging Thomas out of his dream, the hotel's limo pulled up to the dock's VIP entrance to reveal something that looked as if it had been taken out of Jules Verne's *Twenty Thousand Leagues under the Sea*. Waiting for them at the end of the gangway was a newly designed riverboat that resembled Captain Nemo's *Nautilus*.

They looked at each other and laughed in unison at their common thought. From its shiny, silver exterior to the central, circular design of the main foyer, the riverboat resembled a sleek dragon boat, preparing to rise up and cut through the river water like a knife. Thomas paused for a moment and thought, *Surely, I must be living a dream. I've died, only to be reborn into a parallel dimension.*

Janet slipped her hand into Thomas's and whispered into his ear, "Come on, our water chariot awaits us."

The two of them quietly exited the limo, as though they were afraid to wake the sleeping dragon, and strode hand in hand down the gangway to where they were greeted by the boat's captain. *"Ah, oui,"* he exclaimed, "Mademoiselle Rose and Monsieur Moore, I presume. My name is Captain St. Clair, Jean St. Clair. Welcome to your home away from home for the next seven nights. Never have I seen a couple more in love. *Très bien.* It will be our pleasure to serve you. Please, follow our head purser to your suite. Your luggage has already arrived and been sorted for your pleasure. And please do not hesitate to request as much privacy as you desire. Although I hope that you will join us for at least some of our scheduled tours and events, *mais oui?*"

Janet giggled at the captain's not-too-subtle innuendo. She loved the French way of assuming that the two of them would be spending most of their time in their suite. Without thinking, she reached out and embraced the captain and kissed him on both cheeks before declaring, "Captain St. Clair, it is indeed an honor and privilege to meet such a wise and distinguished gentleman such as yourself. Of course we would love to join you as often as we can. May I introduce Thomas Moore?"

Thomas extended his hand and clasped the captain's. To judge by the look on his face, Janet's charm had worked its magic once again. Thomas thought that if Janet had asked the captain to sail across the Atlantic to the United States he would have done so gladly.

After the introductions, the head purser, a lovely young woman from Bulgaria, showed the two to their suite, which was positioned amidships, on the upper deck. Everything in the room looked magnificent, and the sliding balcony door was opened to allow a gentle breeze through the linen drapes. Janet recognized her father's hand in the way that they had been received. There was even a large basket of fresh fruit, champagne, and chocolates awaiting them on the side table. Glancing at the card, she smiled inwardly, as the card simply said, "Congratulations! With all of our love, Mom and Dad."

The moment was interrupted by the head purser. "Ahem, excuse me, Mademoiselle. But first I must tell you that we depart at eighteen hundred hours with the tide, and there will be a cocktail reception on the upper deck. Dinner will be at twenty hundred hours, and I am also to tell you that the captain has requested your presence at his table, if you would be so kind?" Janet nodded her consent as the purser continued, "Your full itinerary is outlined in the blue folder on the side table. As all tours are included, we just ask that you give us twelve-hour notice if you plan to skip any." The purser gave a conspiratorial wink but recovered nicely. "It's so that we know how many buses we need. If there are no questions then, I will go? Oh, one more thing: if you require any other services day or night, just pick up the phone and press digit number 7."

Thomas stood by the door politely holding it open, thumbing a large American bill as a tip. The purser saw the money but didn't take it. Instead she commented, "No, no, Mr. Moore. I cannot take your money. A very gracious tip for all of the crew has already been provided through the Ritz. I guarantee you that every crew member will gladly see to your every wish." Then she was gone.

Looking at Janet, Thomas inquired, "Your father?" To which Janet sheepishly replied, "Yes, my father. What can I say? I'm his princess."

Thomas came across the room and picked Janet up and twirled her around. Planting her back on solid ground, he kissed her neck and started to make his way to her lips.

Surprisingly, Janet held up her hand between them. Thomas quickly stopped and looked curiously into Janet's eyes. "What's wrong? Am I smothering you too much?"

Janet put the fingers of her right hand to Thomas's lips, as if to signal him to be quiet and to listen. "Thomas, I have a confession to make. Ever since we left the United States, I've been clandestinely feeding you small amounts of my grandfather's white powdered gold. Not as much as I've been taking, but enough to quell self-doubt in you. I'm afraid that the powder is doing the talking and not you. It was just that we were thrown into this situation so fast. I was afraid that it would be too much for you to comprehend without the white powder."

Thomas took her fingers lovingly and kissed them and then confessed himself. "Janet, I've known all along that you've been feeding me that powder. Do you think that I don't know my own body? The first surge of energy was remarkable. I want to thank you for the clarity and confidence that you've brought me. It's as though a door opened up to a whole new world, one that I can taste, feel, see, hear, and touch. My senses are alive, thanks to you. Besides, your grandfather's mystery powder doesn't affect the heart, the soul. That's where I know that I love you—with my heart and soul."

Janet's eyes filled with tears. She didn't know what to say, so she just allowed Thomas to finish: "Hey, now, why the tears? I really hope that those are tears of joy. . . . Oh well, I was going to wait for the right moment, but now seems better than most." With that, Thomas walked over to his carry-on and fished around the bottom of it.

Having found what he was looking for, he held out a blue and gold Tiffany box. "Those two big lugs, Danny and Jimmy, are full of surprises. When you were having your massage yesterday, they personally escorted me to the jewelry store and actually haggled the price after I had selected the ring that I thought was perfect for you. I think that the jeweler was intimidated by the size of those two lions. I know that it's not the biggest or the most expensive ring, but I believe that it perfectly suits you." Thomas popped open the lid to expose something quite unique. The engagement ring had a small band of intertwined gold and silver, almost Celtic in nature, and sported a three-quarter-carat white diamond surrounded by a smaller blue sapphire, ruby, emerald, topaz, and jet-black onyx.

Thomas dropped to one knee and stammered a proposal. "Janet Rose, I have known you for only two weeks, but will you marry me?"

Janet dove forward toward Thomas with so much force that he fell over backward, as the ring went sideways under the desk. Janet landed squarely on top of Thomas, but he appeared not to mind being smothered with kisses. Every so often, Janet would come up for air, repeating one word over and over again: "Yes, yes, yes!"

After the one-sided wrestling match appeared to have subsided a little, Thomas caught his breath and asked, "Janet, there is one thing that I need to ask you."

By this time, Janet had retrieved the ring and was sizing it up on her finger. "Oh, Thomas, it's so beautiful, almost Druid in style! I love the way the various jewels dance around the sun diamond. It's as though I have my own little universe. Yes, what is it, Thomas? Ask me anything."

Thomas hesitated for a moment. "Could you up my dosage of powder to be comparable to yours? I want to be on the same spiritual level as you."

Janet sat upright and indeed pondered the request before replying, "I don't imagine that it could do any harm. If you promise to let me get some sleep. I wonder what dosage Grandfather takes. We'll need to phone him and let him in on our news; we'll ask him then. Oh, Thomas, I never in my wildest dreams would imagine that being married to someone would mean so much to me. I don't know where all this emotion is coming from."

After extricating himself from Janet's leg lock, Thomas stood before responding, "Look, both of us have been on edge ever since your grandfather was taken to the hospital. Now there's this game of cat and mouse being played, with us as bait. That's got to take a toll on our nerves. We'll be fine after we have a cocktail and eat something. I wonder if they have dancing onboard. I love to dance."

Here was another thing that Janet didn't know about her new fiancé.

"That sounds wonderful, Thomas. Here, let me freshen up and put on something special. I think we should hold off on upping your dosage until I can talk to Grandfather. I don't want to be a widow before I'm married."

Thomas lay back on the bed with his hands clasped behind his head, admiring Janet in the large mirror that was positioned above the writing table, thinking how lucky he was.

At exactly eighteen hundred hours the riverboat lurched forward, as if the dragon had been awakened. Thomas, who was half-dreaming, heard a small cheer rise from the top deck. *People must already be cel-ebrating our departure. Janet's in the shower, so I'm going to grab a few winks of sleep.*

But before he could drop off, Janet popped out of the washroom wearing the now-familiar too-short towel, along with a towel wrapped around her hair. "Hey, sleepy bones, you can't doze off now. You need to get spruced up. I would hate to disappoint Captain St. Clair and the crew and not show off my new engagement ring. I love it that much, Thomas."

Thomas rolled onto his side. He suddenly became serious once again. Propping himself up on a pillow, he started to quietly proph-esize. "Janet, I've been thinking about Albert Pike. He seems to have gotten into my brain, and I can't get him out. Assume for a minute that Pike had truly discovered the whereabouts of the lost crypt and knew how to access it successfully and safely. He was a Confederate general and Sovereign Grand Commander of the Scottish Rite of the *Southern Jurisdiction* of the United States. Why didn't Pike take advantage of the ancient sacred knowledge to bring the North to its knees?"

Realizing that Thomas had just proposed a very perplexing ques-tion, she replied, reflecting his mood. "I think that I know the answer to your question. Albert Pike was an intellectual, a genius. He believed in a God different from the one worshipped by the masses. He lived by a collection of his own morals and dogma and must have felt privileged to belong to a Sovereign Brotherhood that knew no bounds.

"I actually feel sorry for him because of the moral dilemma he must have faced every day. What a burden to shoulder! He certainly must have been haunted by the fact that he possessed a secret that could have changed the very nature and makeup of the United States, and prob-ably the entire world. No, I believe that with the guidance and support of men such as your great-great-grandfather, Albert Pike made the right decision. I believe that he finally came to the conclusion that he would leave well enough alone and take the secret to his grave. Perhaps he didn't think he was worthy enough in the eyes of his God, because of some of his darkest deeds. Perhaps he believed that human nature was ultimately more good than evil. I somehow doubt that he was really involved in the assassination of Abraham Lincoln, but we'll never know."

"But, Janet, we may someday be faced with the same dilemma. If we can get rid of the Jesuit question, and your grandfather, along with the CIA, can crack the letters, then there's nothing to stop us from retrieving that knowledge for ourselves. The point is: I'm not sure that I'm worthy either."

Leaning across the bed, she gently kissed him on the lips. "Thomas, there's a depth to you that is subtle yet extremely powerful. Now go get ready for cocktails."

While Janet sat at the mirror brushing her hair, Thomas jumped into the shower. The Jesuit in question was directly across the river from them. He had joined a number of tourists and locals who come out to see the riverboats arrive or leave. Many had expensive cameras and were trying to capture the perfect moment of the sun reflecting off the shiny boats. They liked to fantasize that they too were on the cruises, for the rivers were the original highways throughout Europe and beyond. Statues of Poseidon and Lady Liberty waited to greet them a little way upriver.

Philippe leaned back against the sporty Peugeot that he had rented in order to follow the boat on land and lifted the high-powered binoculars, training them innocently on the boat. He knew that his two subjects had embarked but didn't really believe they would be on the upper deck to celebrate the boat's departure. It appeared, to him anyway, that the two were spending an inordinate amount of time wrapped up together in bed.

Janet froze mid-brush, as a shiver went down her spine. She knew instinctively then and there that their stalker was somewhere nearby.

XV

KNIGHT OF THE EAST OR OF THE SWORD

6:00 p.m., Twenty-one days ago

ABOARD A FIVE-STAR RIVERBOAT CRUISE, SEINE RIVER, NORTH OF PARIS

Janet decided that she wasn't going to tell Thomas about her intuition. It was too dark and frightening. Besides, she sensed that the stalker was on land and not on the boat. As a High Priestess, she knew that the surrounding water and the shiny dragon that she rode would protect her. She also knew in her heart that her modern-day guardians, Danny and Jimmy, were nearby. For years, she had been comforted by the thought that she was protected. She had no idea how they managed to constantly go undetected, but they were always there.

The Jesuit's brooding presence still bothered her, though, as she dried her hair. The simple act of Thomas walking out of the bathroom with a towel wrapped around his waist broke the darkness. He too was drying his hair, roughly toweling his head. "Hey," he declared, "come on, get a move on! We're going to be late. What have you been doing?"

Janet forced a smile, "Oh, I was just doing some additional thinking. Maybe we are rushing into all of this a little too fast. I mean, we've only really known each other for two weeks. I read somewhere that couples are really in love for only the first three months of their meeting, and then they have to learn to live with one another for the rest of their lives. Have you given any thought to where we would live? Of course I need to finish my doctorate, and then you have your business back in Montreal. How is that going to work?"

Thomas laughed. *Is that all she's worried about? I thought that she had one of her premonitions again.* "As a matter of fact, I was just thinking about all of that while I was taking my shower. Once this ordeal is over, you definitely need to complete your doctorate. On the other hand, I'm fascinated with your grandfather's alchemical experiments and teachings, so I was wondering if he would like to take me on as an apprentice. In that way, once I've mastered the basics, at least, you and I could pass on our combined esoteric knowledge to our children. Imagine having a couple of little wizards running around the house. That would be really cool. We could travel the world seeking lost secrets. Who knows? We might even improve the world a little if we could expose some of those secrets."

Once again, Janet was taken back by Thomas's developing wisdom. "Thomas, I would really love that. I'm sure that Grandfather and Father would also love that. And I'm sure that Grandfather would love to have us stay with him and share the house. I warn you, though: he may outlive both of us. And what about your business and your family?"

Thomas turned serious. "As you already know, my parents' health is failing, and they are in a very nice retirement home. Mom's got premature dementia, and Dad is slowly dying with her. It's pretty sad, given that they're only in their early sixties. Besides me, there's only my sister, who is a high school teacher. She lives just outside of Toronto. Her husband is pretty successful, but they are a standard Canadian family: two boys, both into hockey, and a golden retriever who thinks he runs the joint. I imagine that she would love to be able to come and visit us in Washington.

"As for my business, I have four senior associates who would love to buy the company from me. They're a lot better at the business end than I've ever been, and they deserve to own it. They'll love it when I tell them that I'm going to get married to an American and become an alchemist's apprentice. So you can stop worrying about our future. It's all mapped out."

Janet got up to walk back into the bathroom. Time was moving on, and they needed to get ready for the cocktail reception, but as she passed Thomas, he gently grabbed her wrists. As he pushed her lovingly back on the bed, both towels fell to the ground. Before she could protest, he whispered in her ear, "We can be a few minutes late. From what I can tell, the captain and the crew are counting on it. So we really can't disappoint them, can we?"

It was just past 6:30 as they walked hand in hand down the short corridor into the lounge. They descended a small glass staircase, feeling like a prince and princess making a grand entrance. Many of the guests who had gathered for the cocktail reception, along with the captain and the crew, smiled at the happy couple.

Not to be rude, after surveying the two, the crowd resumed its conversation, but it was obvious that the couple was indeed in love. The glow of their faces confirmed the fact. As if to calm the two, out of the crowd walked the captain, beaming as if he had a royal couple on board, "Mademoiselle Rose and Monsieur Moore, it is so nice to have you attend our welcoming reception. Ms. Rose, may I say that you look radiant tonight, and it is indeed an honor and pleasure to have the daughter of such a great man, Solomon Rose, grace us with her presence."

"You know my father?" Janet's eyebrows slightly lifted as she held out her hand to the captain.

"*Mais oui.* Yes, of course, I thought you already knew. We are both members of the Grand Orient de France Lodge of Paris, among other things. My family is one of the oldest Norman families in all of France to have belonged to the Lodge. It is something that we take very seriously. I always kid my guests by saying that you have taken the other

Grand Orient Express. Of course, we make our way upriver a little bit more leisurely." The captain shrugged, replicating one of the oldest of French gestures.

Janet laughed again at the captain's love of life. She thought just for a moment, *Well, this is going to be one of the most interesting trips that I've ever taken. I wonder if the captain has been tasked with keeping an eye on us. Did he just assume that it was Thomas or me coming down the gangway, or was he made aware of our presence even before we appeared? It certainly looks as though he could handle anything that comes his way.*

Captain St. Clair broke Janet's train of thought. "Our cruise director, Giselle, is just about to do a presentation on the highlights of the cruise. Please, you and Mr. Moore should find a seat, and I will have the waiter bring you two of our special chocolate martinis. They are very delicious."

Thomas nodded his thanks and immediately found two adjacent lounge chairs that faced the front of the boat, where an attractive young lady in a navy-blue pinnacle suit was sorting her notes for the last time. Thomas remarked to himself, *I think that the hiring requirements on the boat are all the same: Eastern European, long-legged, multilingual blondes. It must keep the older male passengers entertained. An effective yet simple marketing plan indeed!*

Everyone else also appeared to be finding seats and settling in for the presentation. Thomas was next surveying the variety of passengers and commented to himself that this cruise was just like Noah's Ark. *There are two of every kind of passenger one could imagine.*

Thomas eyed an older couple who appeared as though they had just come from the English countryside, large bonnet and airy scarf and sandals. Another couple looked as though they were straight out of Wisconsin, sporting matching Green Bay Packers jerseys. Scattered about were also a number of twenty- and thirty-something men and women who were already sizing each other up. *I wonder if they all came for the art history lesson.*

Thomas was feeling a little superior and perhaps even a little vain, knowing that more than one set of eyes was checking out his fiancée. Feeling Thomas's vibes, Janet leaned over and gently chastised him. "I know what you're thinking. You should be ashamed of yourself, judging other people like that. Now accept your drink that the waiter is about to deliver with dignity and appreciation. Many of the Eastern Europeans who work these cruises are actually better educated than you or me. It's all about situational luck as to where and to whom you were born. Remember that kindness to others is the greatest virtue. I will forgive you this time, because you are feeling cocky after our little interlude. I may have to think twice about upping your dosage after all!"

Janet was right. Thomas had, at least mentally, stepped out of the bounds of appreciation and acceptance. He sheepishly accepted his drink, with mumbled thanks to the waiter, and was thankful when the lounge lights were dimmed for the presentation.

The enthusiastic tour director stepped forward with microphone in hand. "*Mesdames et messieurs,* ladies and gentlemen, lovers and lovers of history, welcome to your floating castle on the Seine for the next eight days and seven evenings. My name is Giselle, and I am from Budapest. We have crew members from over eighteen countries on board, who speak a total of fifteen different languages. I apologize to any Cajuns who are on board, because we do not have anybody from Louisiana on our crew this time around." Everybody around the lounge laughed in unison.

After giving a slight bow in acknowledgment of the laughter, she continued, "I am sure that most of you have met Captain St. Clair. The captain has over fifty years on the Seine, as he grew up on this very river. Yes, his parents owned a riverboat. I am told that his ancient family has been living on and traveling these waterways ever since the Vikings first came and occupied the countryside under Rollo, the first duke of Normandy. This means that the captain is also a Viking. So rest assured: we are prepared to repel any intruders who may try to overtake the boat!"

Again the crowd broke into laughter, throwing in a smattering of applause, but this remark caused Janet and Thomas to glance at one another with a slight frown. The cruise director's joke had hit a little too close to home.

Janet sensed Thomas's unease, especially after her scolding, so she patted his wrist as if to provide assurance. She leaned over and whispered in his ear, "Don't worry. I see you looking around. The Jesuit is not on board. I sensed him earlier. He's following us along the riverbank by car." Immediately she remembered that earlier she had sworn not to alarm Thomas. *What am I doing? I shouldn't have mentioned anything to him. How stupid of me!*

Thomas almost jumped out of his chair. He was about to question Janet about how she knew these things and what power she actually possessed, but the older lady from England, who was sitting directly next to him, shushed him.

Although the cruise director sensed a little unrest in the area by Janet and Thomas, she ignored the slight commotion and continued with her presentation. She had given the same presentation over a hundred times, but she had a knack of personalizing it each time for the passengers. She was on a roll and prided herself in her ability to get everybody excited about something on the cruise.

"Now please turn your attention to the screen. What you will see before you is a map of our planned itinerary. I will break down our trip on a daily basis, highlighting our planned excursions, which have all been included in the price of your trip. I am sure that many of you have booked this cruise specifically because of your interest in art, ancient history, or the history surrounding World War II, and I am sure that none of you will be disappointed.

"I hope that everyone enjoyed their time in Paris beforehand. As you can see by the map, we are currently sailing upriver to Vernon, for a choice of guided visits tomorrow morning to either Claude Monet's stunning gardens at Giverny or the magnificent Bizy Castle. For those art lovers, Monet painted his famous Water Lilies series while at Giverny." As the cruise director talked, the slides on the screen magically changed to pictures correlating to her main points of attraction. The assembled crowd gasped with delight when several slides of Monet's most famous series of paintings flashed on the screen.

"From here, we will continue to Les Andelys with its Château Gaillard, built by England's King Richard the Lionheart, a Knight Templar, in 1196. Richard led the Third Crusade, along with the French king Philippe II. The captain will schedule his arrival so that you will be able to view the castle on the hilltop in the early-morning sun. Art lovers, again, may recognize Les Andelys as the childhood home of the most famous Renaissance painter, Nicolas Poussin. It is said that Poussin depicted the French countryside around his childhood home in his most famous painting, *The Shepherds of Arcadia.*

"Then we sail on to Caudebec, where you have an excursion to the Normandy landing beaches. You have a choice of venues: Omaha for the Americans or Juno for the British and Canadians. We ask that you indicate by the sign-in sheet at the front desk what beach you will be going to for bus purposes. Unfortunately, the drive is about two hours either way, so we can't take you to both beaches.

"On your return, we overnight again at Caudebec, where the next morning you can take a tour to the medieval town of Honfleur, where Samuel de Champlain set sail for the New World. This is one of the only Norman towns along the northern coast that was left intact from bombing during the war: the Germans never really occupied the town, as it had no potential landing beach. There is a lovely inner harbor that was painted by many of the Impressionist artists. Or you may be interested in the timber-structured church built by the pagan Vikings who embraced Christianity.

"The next day, after arriving in Rouen, you will have a chance to visit Joan of Arc's historic birthplace, including Rouen Cathedral, which Monet painted, not once but nineteen times. There will be a walking tour of the Old Town, including the spot on which Joan of Arc was burned as a heretic. There is also the oldest medieval tavern still in existence, for those passengers who would like a glass of wine or beer.

"The next morning we find ourselves in Conflans, where you will be able to choose between a visit to Vincent van Gogh's Auvers-sur-Oise or Napoleon and Josephine's elegant Château de Malmaison before heading back along the Seine to Paris in the late afternoon.

"During your last day on the Seine, a local expert will come on board and show you some of the famous sights after we dock, such as the Arc de Triomphe, Eiffel Tower, and more! This is actually my favorite part of the tour. The captain times our arrival to coincide with dusk, when the city starts to light up for the evening. Once your City of Lights tour is completed, it's back to the boat, where you will sleep one more time and depart the next morning."

After such a dramatic presentation, the rest of the evening was a blur. The evening meal was exquisite, and the crew made sure that the wine was flowing, so that the dance floor was packed way beyond midnight. Janet and Thomas discovered that they enjoyed dancing with each other, so they made a night of it and happily collapsed into each other's arms, exhausted, around two o'clock in the morning. Sleeping soundly, they both forgot about the evil that lurked along the shoreline, somewhere in the dark.

Philippe De Smet was also enjoying himself, having found a little bed-and-breakfast just on the edge of Vernon. As his father's family came from the northern border of France, the drive alongside the Seine allowed his mind to wander and to remember his father's insistence that he understand his French heritage. When he wasn't drunk, his father would regale him with stories of Vikings, chivalrous knights, French kings and queens, the First and Second World Wars, the French Resistance, and, of course, Charles de Gaulle.

Philippe's favorite story was about a collateral ancestor of his, although he was considered to be Belgian, not French. His name was Pierre-Jean De Smet, a Jesuit priest who was active among the Native American peoples in the midwestern and northwestern United States and western Canada in the mid-nineteenth century. Philippe loved the story about how Father De Smet had convinced the Sioux war chief,

Sitting Bull, to participate in negotiations with the United States government for the 1868 Treaty of Fort Laramie. Philippe was also familiar with the assertion that Father De Smet had mentored Albert Pike, both in his early years and during Pike's early time as the U.S. government's official head Indian agent.

XVI

PRINCE OF JERUSALEM
Thirteen days ago
THE LOWER SEINE DOCKS, PARIS

Surprisingly, the riverboat docked at a different area of Paris from where it had departed. The passengers suspected that it was a maneuver to thwart any terrorist attempt to hijack the boat and its many foreign passengers. The crew knew differently. Other riverboats were embarking at the other dock, and this location was more accessible to the airport during the morning rush hour, from which many of the passengers, including Janet and Thomas, would be catching flights home.

The two lovers were among the last passengers to disembark, as they had a midmorning flight scheduled back to Washington, D.C. Both Janet and Thomas were grateful for the small respite; they had made the most of their last evening on the boat, savoring the flavors and smells of Paris itself. Besides, it gave them a chance to partake one last time of the crew's hospitality and the chef's amazing fare.

As they sat at their usual table overlooking the river, enjoying a breakfast of steaming hot coffee, chocolate croissants, toast, French marmalade, and various cheeses, the captain came and briefly joined them, "*Ah, très bien.* I see that the two of you cannot live on love alone. That is good." The two smiled and thanked him for his gracious hospitality.

The captain nodded and continued, "You're very welcome. Of course, it is my job, but it brings great pleasure as a Frenchman when I can share my country and some of its treasures with foreigners. Unfortunately, world events are changing that. As such, would you mind visiting my office before you disembark?" Janet and Thomas displayed alarm, but the captain was charming. "Please, there is nothing to be concerned about. Now I must go and bid *adieu* to our remaining guests. *Bon voyage!*"

The brevity of the captain's visit and the request to visit his office shattered the euphoria that Janet and Thomas were feeling. They had all but forgotten their stalker, and only once more had Janet felt his presence, while they were walking around Honfleur. The two had even forgotten to question whether Janet's father had any purpose in arranging this particular cruise.

Quickly finishing their breakfast, they collected their carry-on luggage and made their way back along the corridor to the front of the ship, where the captain's office was located. Knocking on the door, they found that it was opened by Jimmy, who sported a wide grin and a chocolate croissant in his hand. "Well, well, Danny, look who we have here: the two randy lovebirds."

Sitting behind the captain's desk, enjoying a croissant of his own, along with a steaming cup of coffee, was Danny Sullivan. He didn't spare a moment to join in on the surprise. "Yes, it's certainly the same two lovebirds who left their suite at the Ritz in such a shambles. Jimmy, from the look of the bags under their eyes, I would say that they continued their wicked ways for the last eight days also. Wouldn't you?"

"Yes, Danny, for a while there I thought that the boat was going to flip right over in the water, what with all of the rocking."

With that, they took another bite of their croissants. Thomas stood there dumbfounded at how calm the two could be, and at how much they could eat.

Janet, thinking a little differently, exclaimed, "OK, you two knuckle-heads, act your age, and tell us what you've been up to. I hope that some-how the two of you don't have pictures of us over the last ten days."

Danny assumed his normal deadpan, but there was something in his eyes that told Janet that something wasn't normal. Danny knew that Janet could read his thoughts, so he decided to come clean. "No pictures, just lots of film! But what we really needed was the time to get ahead of the game. Sending you upriver was all that we could think of on such short notice. But it did the trick. It was Jimmy who first identified him, your stalker. Man, the guy is good, but don't worry, we're better. It was first in Honfleur, actually, which is quite interesting considering that's where Champlain set sail for Montreal. Thomas, are you aware that the Jesuits who followed after the founding of Montreal in 1632 didn't even stop there for a breather? They immediately made their way inland, ostensibly to establish a mission, still known as Sainte Marie among the Hurons. I believe it's located near a place called Midland, Ontario. This means that the Jesuits had inside information that the secret treasure had moved inland past Montreal some three to four hun-dred years before.

"But that story can wait. Here's your man. We took pictures of him in the airport, waiting to fly back to the States a day ago, which means that you two have nothing to worry about on your own trip back to Washington." Danny slid over a folder of large photos. Some were not that good, but a couple definitely caught the brooding features of Philippe De Smet.

While Thomas and Janet leaned over the captain's desk to stare at the face of their stalker, Jimmy continued the narrative. "As I was say-ing, this guy is good. We had three teams following you all the way, and they couldn't pick him out once. Now that we know who we were look-ing for, we tried to trace his steps backward for the past ten days and came up with nothing the first time around. Anyway, using you as bait was the key. The two of you walking around so in love, hand in hand, must have driven the guy nuts!"

At this point Janet was extremely confused. "Jimmy, what in the name of the goddess Columbia are you talking about?"

Danny held up his hand to quell Janet's irritation and continued, "Once we have a face and know who we're dealing with, then it's easy. You wouldn't believe how much profile there is available on just about anybody in the world. That's if you know where to look. Anyway, De Smet is an ordained Jesuit priest, of all things. But he's also a pretty nasty fellow, from all reports. He started out as an ordinary kid from a working-class family in a tough Boston neighborhood. His father was of French Catholic origin, and his mother was Irish Catholic. He had a rough childhood, as his father was more often drunk than sober. At around eight years of age, a prominent Jesuit priest by the name of LaFortune took him under his wing, identifying him as gifted, and manipulated and molded him into what he is today."

"And what exactly is he?" Thomas blurted out.

Danny finished what was left of his coffee and croissant and then focused on the pictures. "Well, what he isn't is just an ordinary ordained priest. The Society of Jesus molded him into their ultimate trouble-shooter. It turns out that he's been implicated in about twenty murders, but nothing's stuck. As soon as things get a little hot, the Society closes ranks, and he disappears into their colleges for a while, teaching ancient philosophy, of all things. We couldn't access his divinity-school records, but rumor has it that he has a doctorate in human behavioral psychology, as well as his divinity doctorate.

"Apparently, he's a pretty good athlete and could have been a pro basketball player if he'd stuck with it. The Celtics would have loved him. He's even run the Boston Marathon a few times. He also speaks five languages and, they say, is quite an actor."

Janet was getting frustrated, "Good for him; so he's a Jesuit rock star. There's something else that you're not telling us, Danny. Tell us everything."

Danny looked to Jimmy, who nodded back to him. "OK, here's the real nasty part. This guy is a complete psychopath. To boot, he's a sadistic son-of-a-bitch. During his undergraduate years at Boston College, a shrink had him under observation for a semester. Sadly, it turns out that De Smet was so depraved—something to do with a love-hate relationship with his mother—that the shrink had to seek his own counseling. De Smet graduated that year and disappeared into the ranks of the Jesuits. Here, Jimmy, you explain how we pegged the guy."

Jimmy was caught midbite with a piece of evil-smelling cheese, which he quickly put down on his plate. "Janet, do you remember being slightly jostled while you and Thomas were touring the Viking church in Honfleur?"

As she concentrated, it quickly came back to her. "Yes, yes, I do. I sensed his presence, but it turned out that the person who bumped into me was the older English lady who was on the ship with us. She just politely cautioned me to carry my purse in front of me, as she suspected that there were pickpockets around. I remember the church being quite full of tourists. I'm confused."

"Don't be!" Jimmy tried to calm Janet. "The English lady was one of our agents."

"You mean to tell me that the older woman on the boat was actually reporting our activities to you?" Thomas almost fell on the floor.

"That older woman is a top professional, Thomas. That's the beauty of it. She carries with her a lot of intuition, and in this situation, it was what was needed. She felt that something just wasn't right with the good-looking thirty-something male who first appeared to be a pickpocket. That's not unusual. Pickpockets invariably try to dress the part depending on what group they're trying to infiltrate. But the older English lady felt that our pickpocket was spending just a little too much time focused on Janet. So she quietly caught a profile of him in a photo that she took of the timberwork inside the church. It wasn't much to start with, but here's the photo."

Jimmy sorted through the pile of photos and slid a smaller picture across to Janet and Thomas for their consideration. The profile of De Smet wasn't the greatest, but it was at least a start. "Then the big break came. Given his psychological profile, the sight of the two of you constantly being lovey-dovey really must have been extremely frustrating to him. Here he was, thinking that you carried with you the Pike Letters, and somewhere on your travels there was the big key that would unlock the letters' code. We think he became extremely frustrated and finally threw in the towel. He probably figured he would have better luck back on U.S. soil. He drove back to Paris two evenings ago and booked a flight back to Boston for yesterday."

Waiting for Jimmy to tell a story was almost as bad as waiting for him to finish a meal. It just kept going on, and Janet and Thomas's limo would be arriving in ten minutes to take them to the airport. Danny jumped back in. "Anyway, De Smet checked back into a small boutique hotel not far from the river and the Eiffel Tower, where the prostitutes come out at night. This guy must have been ready to blow with frustration."

Danny paused for effect. "So off he goes in his guise as a jogger and starts to proposition this prostitute under one of the bridges. Apparently, the guy was bargaining for some real kinky stuff, speaking perfect French, but the prostitute indicated later that he had a slightly funny accent. That's when one of the roaming French military twosomes started to walk toward them. It really spooked him when the military got close. Normally something of this nature doesn't alarm them. They treat the business under the bridges as a way of life, but with the terrorism level being so high, they were required to question the prostitute and to send in a report. I think that it was the graphic nature of the report that caught Jimmy's eye early yesterday morning, as he has pored through thousands of reports just like this every morning for the past ten days. He's developed a program, which amazingly correlates thousands of seemingly unconnected facts in seconds."

That was a cue for Jimmy to pick up the story again. "I tell you; I've met a lot of sick puppies in my day, but this one takes the cake.

What struck me was the prostitute's description of her conversation with her potential client. He wanted some sick stuff but also asked her if she was a Catholic and if she went to church regularly. She must have been a bright girl, because she noted to the military that it was almost as though he wanted her to confess her sins before they executed the transaction."

Jimmy was on a roll now. "Putting two and two together, we quickly located the two military personnel back at their barracks. Luckily, one of the guys knew the young lady under the bridge quite well and knew where she lived. You wouldn't believe this, but she has a fairly nice apartment overlooking Les Invalides and is studying art at the University of Paris. Long story short, we woke her up around seven o'clock and showed her the picture of De Smet from Honfleur. She was convinced that it was the same guy. She indicated that even though he kept to the shadows, he was quite tall, dark, and handsome, well mannered.

"I then went to work, using Interpol's facial recognition and profiling digital library, crossed it with all of the security cameras positioned throughout France, and came up with our man. I knew for sure that it was him, because his travel schedule coincided with yours. But the bugger used three separate aliases, switched cars four times, never with the same rental company. He never stayed in the same place twice, except here in Paris. He's a bloody ghost! But the Interpol facial recognition program caught him on camera for good when he was checking in at the airport."

Stammering, Thomas blurted out the question, "And you arrested him, right?"

Janet laid her hand on Thomas's arm. "Thomas, calm down. Danny and Jimmy already indicated that he flew back to Boston yesterday. Besides, what were they going to arrest him for—being horny? Remember that these two are not military or CIA anymore. They head up Rose Commodities Corporation's private security division. We'll get through this, but right now I need you to focus." She thought, *Did I give Thomas his powder this morning?*

Just then there was a knock on the door. When it opened it was Giselle, the cruise director. "I beg your pardon, but your limo has just arrived. Your luggage has already been transferred to the car, and the driver says that you must hurry, as the traffic has been heavy all morning."

Danny and Jimmy stood up. Danny came around from the desk and wrapped his arms around Janet, quietly speaking, almost whispering, into her ear. "Don't worry, everything will be fine. We'll get through this, you'll see. Good always triumphs over evil. The limo driver on this end is one of our European team, and the driver at the other end is another one of the team. The monster has gone back into his lair to lick his wounds. Go home to your grandfather, the old goat, and celebrate your engagement. He'll be thrilled. And don't worry about the Georgetown house. We have it locked down." Danny kissed Janet on both cheeks.

There was nothing more to be said. The trip home could be described as efficient and mostly uneventful. Janet and Thomas were exhausted, so both easily slipped into nap mode in the first-class pods once the plane was in the air.

While Thomas slept, Janet fell once again into a trancelike dream sequence and found herself back in time, back to the Temple on the sun-drenched Mediterranean hilltop. As High Priestess, it was her assigned responsibility once a day, when the sun reached its meridian, to enter the inner sanctum and read the reflecting bowl for prophetic visions. Today she had a foreboding of a terrible event. Peering into the sheer black surface of water within the bowl, she foresaw a series of events that left her speechless.

The holy city of Jerusalem was being sacked by the Babylonian king Nebuchadnezzar. The violent destruction and persecution of the Jewish population caused pain in the priestess, almost causing her to collapse. Twice she gasped as Zedekiah, king of Judah, was brought forward before the king in chains and beaten until he knelt in subservience. Zedekiah had just been forced to watch his entire family being slaughtered, as he was of the Davidic line, but that wasn't the worst of it. The

High Priestess forced herself to focus on the king's face. What she saw made her skin crawl. Where Zedekiah's eyes should have been, there remained two bloodied caverns of empty despair. The king's eyes had forcibly been ripped from their sockets. The last thing that he would ever witness was the slaughter of his royal line. Having seen enough, the priestess fell to the ground exhausted, with her attendants running to her aid. Just before she blacked out, she wondered where on earth was the captain of the temple's elite guards.

When the plane was over Nova Scotia, Janet broke out of her trance, covered in sweat. She realized then and there that the deadly game that she and Thomas were involved in was not over, not by a long shot.

XVII

KNIGHT OF THE EAST
AND WEST

7:00 p.m., Thirteen days ago

HOUSE OF DAVID, GEORGETOWN

David Rose was there to open the front door to his Georgetown home even before Janet and Thomas were able to exit the limo. Although extremely tired, Janet managed to wave enthusiastically to her grandfather, silently indicating that it was good to be home. She had forgotten about how much pride and comfort she took out of living in such a magnificent house.

Thomas was more apprehensive, knowing that the Jesuit could be watching them at that moment. It had unnerved him to learn that the stalker had gotten so close to them on their cruise. Thomas stood and looked around, up and down the street, but he couldn't see anything out of the ordinary. *Maybe I'm just imagining things. Why aren't there marked police cars sitting at both ends of the street?* He was tired, and his imagination was starting to get the best of him.

Luckily, he was broken out of his paranoia by David Rose's loud appeal for him to come inside. Looking up, he noted that Janet had already wrapped herself in her grandfather's arms. Thomas took strength from the fact that he appeared to be his old self again. Then came a surprise. Standing just past the shoulder of David Rose and Janet was a smiling Dr. Sarah Cohen. *Well, well, well,* Thomas thought, *now that's an interesting development.*

Thomas couldn't wait to hear the story behind that situation and suddenly found the energy to run up the steps. David greeted him emotionally. "Thomas, my son, *shalom!* Congratulations! The two of you have made this old man quite happy. I must say, though, that I didn't expect a formal engagement so soon, but as soon as I heard about it from Solomon, I lit a candle in your honor. Well done, well done!

"Come in, come in; your luggage will be seen to by the driver." David was almost thrusting Thomas through the door into the living room. "I see you eyeing Dr. Cohen." Sarah sheepishly acknowledged Thomas's nod. David was beaming with pride. "Before you ask, Dr. Cohen is here strictly on a medical basis," David laughed. "It turns out that she is fascinated with my level of good health and well-being, given my age. And then there's my intellectual capacity!" He let out a wicked chuckle.

Janet looked to Dr. Cohen to fill in the details. She didn't disappoint them. "Don't look so surprised, you two. I really am here out of medical curiously. The old goat is in perfect health. We've done every test that we could think of, and he's passed them with flying colors. Of course, it's gone to his head. The one on his shoulders, I mean. I just can't believe that he has a seventeenth-century alchemist's lab in his basement, from which he produces monoatomic gold, among many other things. Either he's brilliant or all the rest of us are idiots!"

Grabbing her grandfather's upper arm, Janet responded in a lighthearted tone, "Oh, he's brilliant all right. Come on into the kitchen, everybody; I don't know about Thomas, but I'm famished. We ate and drank our way across half of France but never appeared to be full. I believe it's dinnertime here in Washington."

Janet's grandfather could not have been happier. "Oh, Granddaughter! Do you really think that your grandfather would not plan a small celebration for your return? We are going to celebrate life: my life, your life, all of our lives, and future life. I see by Thomas's glow that you have been giving him my powder. That's good. The babies will soon be coming. Now come into the dining room."

It was Sarah's turn to jump back in, as the group rounded the corner and took stock of what only could be described as a temple feast: "I told David that he ordered too much food, but he wouldn't listen. He must have stock in that favorite deli of his because they went all out. I've never seen such a variety of kosher food for four people. And he had them run across town to get a case of his favorite Israeli wine."

As everyone took their seats, Sarah started dishing up the plates, heaping pile after pile of hot food on top of cold food on top of hot food. Both Thomas and Janet looked at each other and laughed. It certainly appeared that Dr. Cohen had made herself right at home.

David sensed the acknowledgment and decided to pay some acknowledgment himself. "May we thank God that the two of you have arrived home safely. Yes, Janet, I have been talking regularly with your father, along with his two warrior-monks, and know about everything that has happened, including the news concerning this mysterious Jesuit priest. Now let's eat; I'm starving."

The two looked at one another in slight alarm and then looked at Dr. Cohen, who didn't give anything away.

David continued, "Will you two please stop being conspiratorial? I've let Dr. Cohen in on every little secret that the family has. She needs the information for her research anyway."

Nodding in agreement, Sarah dove right back in between heaping forks of thin, tender beef strips and pickled beets. "David's not kidding. What he has been producing through his alchemical experiments has tremendous promise for cancer and geriatric medical research. Is either of you aware of the theory that the pharaohs digested a substance similar to your grandfather's white powdered gold? Could this have been the key to the elixir of life, the Holy Grail itself? The Comte de St. Germain was seen by three generations of eyewitnesses. Did he have the secret to that gold of your grandfather's? They say that his sexual prowess was legendary.

"I've been doing some reading in your grandfather's ancient texts. I needed his help to translate, of course. It amazes me that there are some scientific tenets in the mysticism that he has been exposing me to over the last ten days."

Janet couldn't help thinking that something was happening between the two of them. She looked at Dr. Cohen and then at her grandfather. *I hope that's the only thing that he's exposing. Although Dr. Cohen doesn't appear the least bit put off by Grandfather's age.*

Sarah was definitely enjoying herself. "It appears to me that the earliest concept of God as Light possibly derives from the clarity of mind and higher level of understanding brought upon those who took a form of the powder on a regular basis. That's not to imply that there are no other ways of accomplishing the same thing. For example, the medicine men of the indigenous people of North America attain the same state of enlightenment through their ceremonies and ingestion of stimulants like peyote. But I'm interested in the alchemist's ability to achieve that state through elemental chemistry."

David chimed in at this point. "Janet, I want you to know that Dr. Cohen and I have come to an agreement—a professional agreement. Anything that is developed between us in terms of medicinal pharmaceuticals or other lifesaving proprietary information is going to a not-for-profit charitable foundation that the two of us are establishing in the name of your grandmother and Sarah's deceased husband. Any monies generated through patents and other means—and I have a feeling that the sums will be considerable—will go toward furthering cancer, geriatric, and cardiac research. It'll be our gift to the world. I wanted to tell you in case you were worried in any way about your inheritance. Of course this house and all of its contents will go to you. You and your siblings will surely be more than well-off with your controlling shares of Rose Commodities Corporation."

Janet threw her arms around her grandfather and kissed him on both cheeks. "Grandfather, I think what you and Dr. Cohen are proposing is wonderful. Your experiments are based on ancient mysteries that most of us don't understand. I think it's the perfect collaboration. And you know that I like to live comfortably, but the amount of money that this family generates is almost obscene. I've already been given the greatest gift that one could ask for: a loving partner and the opportunity for a family. I was beginning to give up on both, you know."

At this juncture, David Rose was feeling a little philosophical. "Did you know that the Gnostics derived their leading doctrines and ideas from Plato and Philo, the Zend-Avesta and the Kabbalah, the sacred books of India and Egypt, where East meets West?"

Janet and Thomas didn't know where this was going but nodded to try to show their enthusiasm. David went on: "The same dogma was then introduced into Christianity. Thus the cosmological and theosophical speculations, which had formed the larger portion of the ancient religions of the Orient, joined the Egyptian, Greek, and Jewish doctrines, which the Neoplatonists had adopted in the Occident."

Sarah said, "OK, David, you have us stumped. What exactly is the point that you're trying to make?"

David paused for effect before continuing. "I want everybody here to be the first to know that, thanks to the brilliant personnel from Langley who have been working with me over the past week, I have made significant progress with the Pike Letters, and I believe that I have figured out how to break their code."

The remaining three almost jumped out of their shoes. Janet squealed with delight, "Grandfather, this is terrific! I was so afraid that the Pike Letters would be the death of you. . . . But hold on: you indicated that you figured out how to break the code. Are you telling us that you haven't deciphered the secret yet?"

"That's exactly what I said, but I know that you two are very tired from your flight. What with the time change, you'll soon be deflating and won't be able to comprehend what I need to explain in detail. Sarah and I also want to hear about your holiday. I want to hear about your impressions of the art, architecture, symbolism, and atmosphere of everywhere that you visited. I also want you to tell me about what your father is up to, and I want to hear about those two Irish mugs. So I have to ask you to be patient. We'll certainly have enough time to explore everything relating to the letters. Are we all in agreement?"

Everyone chimed in, "Yes, of course!"

Sarah watched the two as their eyes began to droop. "David, we definitely must leave it for this evening. I sense that both Janet and Thomas are exhausted. Let's allow the young ones to go to bed."

Agreeing, David made sure that Janet and Thomas were helped up the stairs and comfortably settled in the spare bedroom. He watched as only a grandfather could while the two dreamily drifted off, unable to fully comprehend what they had heard this evening. As he closed the bedroom door, David whispered to them, "Sweet dreams, my two love-birds. May your hearts soar above the clouds."

Janet and Thomas fell into a deep alchemical sleep; David had seen to this by adding a pinch of tincture to their tea. He knew that they would sleep long and hard and wake up refreshed and full of energy. He needed the two to be fully capacitated, for he too was a little worried about the Jesuit. He thought back to his wilder, younger years. *Evil has a way of seeping into your pores, no matter how hard one tries to be pure. Temptation is all around us, forever tempting us. God, please protect these two.*

The captain of the elite guards had received word from the attendants that the High Priestess was gravely ill. Riding his trusty winged steed, the captain flew all night over prairies and forest and water to be by her side. He felt guilty for being away so long, traveling far away across the vast expanse of ocean to the new and exciting holy land. He had hoped that one day he would be able to take her with him to the ancient New World temple, to a place where she would be safe and comforted forever by the natives. For far too long now, the temptations were growing between them, but the priestess needed to remain pure. His task, assigned by the gods, was to forever be her guardian, and her task was to forever safeguard the sacred treasure from the usurpers, using her gift of vision. He was confident that no one would find the key needed to unlock the numerological sequence of degrees.

XVIII

KNIGHT ROSE CROIX
Twelve days ago
HOUSE OF DAVID, GEORGETOWN

The two lovers woke from their slumber somewhere close to noon. The sun's rays shone brightly through the front bedroom window, casting light on everything they touched. It was as though Janet and Thomas were reborn. Refreshed and content, she was the first to wake up, and she had lain next to Thomas for the longest time, absorbed in his shallow breathing. The combined anxiety and excitement that they had shared over the past ten days had been replaced by warmth and peaceful contentment.

The only disturbance of the morning was a faint knock on the door, followed by her grandfather's voice, gently declaring that lunch was being served downstairs in half an hour.

Although she was wearing the upper half of Thomas's pajamas, Janet rather modestly scurried from under the covers into the bathroom. She barely escaped just as Thomas rolled over to draw her body back into his. Groggily accepting that the warmth was gone from the bed, he slowly stood up. Roughly half an hour later, the two were sitting at the kitchen island enjoying dark-roasted coffee and a heap of scrambled eggs, toast, and thickly sliced tomatoes.

The noon-hour news was on quietly in the background when suddenly a missing person's bulletin, with picture, flashed across the screen. Although he instantly recognized the person in the picture, Thomas didn't react completely until a picture of her place of employment also flashed up on the screen. "Hey, I know her. She's the concierge from the Georgetown Inn. She's been missing for more than forty-eight hours, and her parents and friends say that it's out of the usual . . . Hang on! They've just updated the bulletin to say that her body has been located in a dumpster somewhere across the Potomac. What a shame! She was such a pretty and outgoing young lady. She was always so helpful."

Janet's grandfather was quietly reading the *Washington Post* at the other end of the island, but put the paper down when he heard Thomas's exclamation. Suddenly he had a premonition of things to come. The white powder was working its magic. Then he looked to Thomas and said, "Thomas, think back. Could this Jesuit priest, Philippe De Smet, have been aware of your staying at the inn and had some interaction with the concierge? Weren't you staying at the inn when you and Janet first met? And didn't you have a reservation to stay there after you came back to Washington, but got sidetracked by my going to the hospital?"

Immediately grasping the web of suspicion that her grandfather was weaving, Janet brought her hand up to her mouth and exclaimed, "Oh my God! Grandfather, you're absolutely right. He must have been following both Thomas and me all this time. I'm willing to bet that it was De Smet who broke into your house and hid the listening devices. Danny and Jimmy even indicated that he flew to Boston two days ahead of us because he was, apparently, sexually frustrated. Oh, the poor girl. What did she do to deserve this? Are we the cause of her death?"

Thomas wrapped his arms around Janet to provide what comfort he could. "Hey now, we don't know for sure if De Smet was involved. It could be just a horrible coincidence." But everyone sitting around the kitchen island knew better. David was right: evil had a way of entering a room no matter what precautions had been established.

After thinking for a moment, Janet appeared to have drawn strength from a special inner sanctum. "I'm going to phone Danny and Jimmy right now. I don't know where they are, but they'll know what to do. They have contacts throughout the investigative world. I'm sure they would want to follow up on the possibility. It's the least that we can do for the poor girl."

Thomas started to say something as Janet turned to go out of the kitchen in search of her phone, but David caught his eye, indicating that he should let her go. He laid his hand on Thomas's forearm and said softly, "Thomas, please listen to me carefully. I think that my intuition will prove right. There's some sort of powerful synchronicity happening here. There's almost a global game of good and evil being played out before our very eyes—a game that's been waged for centuries. The original nine Knights Templar realized this when they set in motion a series of events a thousand years ago. Here—while Janet is busy on the phone, there's something that I want to show you."

David Rose went over to the small writing desk to the side of the dishwasher, opened its drawer, and produced a plastic folder. He slid it across the granite countertop to Thomas. "Here's letter number 18 of the Pike Letters. The numbering corresponds to the date it was written. That's what I wanted to show you last night, but you and Janet were so tired, you wouldn't have been able to comprehend what I needed to explain."

Thomas was about to examine the letter, but Janet returned to the kitchen sooner than expected. She was almost out of breath. "I got right through to Danny and Jimmy. Believe it or not, they're here in the capital. They'd caught the news earlier and already made the connection. They've been in contact with the police and FBI, who are following up on their lead. They'll be here in about an hour. They said we should just stay put until they arrive."

Janet eyed the plastic folder and asked, "Hey, were the two of you going to discuss something without involving me?"

"No, of course not," replied David. "I was just trying to take Thomas's mind off this awful situation until you were finished with Danny and Jimmy. I must say, they do work fast, those two. Now come and sit and have the rest of your coffee while I explain what I've discovered."

Janet did as she was told, and then David began, "The problem that I had, which ultimately put me in the hospital, was that I was making everything too complicated. I was looking for hidden signs, symbols, and tokens within the letters. I figured that Pike and MacLeod Moore had developed or used a code based on their understanding of the Kabbalah, the Egyptian mysteries, alchemy, Zoroaster, Sanskrit, ancient Masonry, the Zend-Avesta, the Jewish codes, the Gnostics—either separately or a combination thereof. I had myself convinced that once I unveiled their coded messages all I would need was the key to unlock the code. The trouble was that I wasn't thinking about the foundations of a Scottish Rite Mason or a Knights Templar. Instead of complicating things, I should have simplified things. In other words, I should have worked backward to their origin—their original purpose and tenets. I must confess that it was a young cryptologist from Langley who helped me unlock the riddle."

Thomas shook his head. *For the love of God, I have no idea what David is talking about. Maybe the powder has taken over his mind. Maybe Sarah was right. Nobody has studied the long-term effects of ingesting the white powder over a lifetime.*

Janet intercepted those thoughts before they could reach her grandfather and said, "Grandfather, that's so brilliant in its simplicity. Albert Pike and MacLeod Moore must have been geniuses in their own right. That's one reason they became lifelong friends. They obviously related on the highest level to one another. Why didn't we see it all along? Thomas, are you aware of the basis of all civilizations, all cultures, all languages?"

Thomas shook his head again. He couldn't figure out what was going on between grandfather and granddaughter. Here was a level of synchronicity that he had never been exposed to before.

Answering her own question, Janet exclaimed in delight, "Numerology! Since the start of mankind, humans have watched the sky and identified patterns, sequences, anything that would help them reason out their existence. The moon was full every twenty-eight notches on a stick. A trek to a water hole was three suns and two moons away. Two seemingly unrelated tribes could communicate in the simplest manner: sunup and sundown, a moon's rising and setting, and that developed into an ordered pattern of numbers. Commerce developed in the same way. I'll trade you two goats for three pigs." To emphasize her point, Janet held up two fingers and replaced them with three.

Janet continued, splaying her hand in front of Thomas. "Humans had five digits on each hand. One of the earliest symbols painted on cave walls by Cro-Magnon man was his hand. The Knights Templar and Native Americans both believed in the divine nature of all things. They believed that there was order in all of nature and therefore they could be one with nature. It's how we classify everything from plants to animals. DNA has a structure, a numbered sequence. A hand is made up of one thumb and four fingers; again, a numbered sequence, which can be repeated infinitely."

David had never been prouder of his granddaughter. Codes started out as nothing more than patterned numbers. Signs, symbols, and tokens were just more complicated reflections of numbers. Computer coding was nothing more than a patterned set of numbers. David wanted Thomas to understand this. "The Pike Letters were contained within three envelopes for a purpose. The first envelope contained fourteen letters. The second contained four, and the third contained fourteen. See, there's a number sequence that I should have twigged into right from the start. How stupid of me not to have recognized it at the beginning!" David grabbed Janet's hand and held it up higher in order to emphasize his point. "It was right there, like a slap in the face!"

"Grandfather, sometimes you're too hard on yourself." Although Janet was trying to console her grandfather, she realized that he should easily have recognized the letter patterns as a clue.

David dismissed Janet's attempt at consolation with a wave of his hand. "Thomas, understand this: Scottish Rite Masonry is made up of three levels of degrees. In order to move from one degree to the next, the initiate had to demonstrate a fundamental understanding of the speculative, or philosophical, nature of the previous degree. So in Scottish Rite Masonry, you can only move on to the higher degrees once you've completed the first three degrees of a Blue Lodge Master Mason. That's standard for everyone. Degrees 4 to 14 are contained within the Lodge of Perfection. Then degrees 14 to 18 are known as the Rose Croix, while degrees 19 to 32 are known as the Consistory. Degree number 33 is actually an honorary degree, bestowed on those who have demonstrated extreme dedication to and understanding of the Scottish Rite, either in word or in deed. So the numerical pattern of degrees is 14–4–14, mirrored images of the number 14, much like the two-headed phoenix that graces the Scottish Rite motif."

David then grabbed onto the plastic folder and passed it to Thomas. "Now take a look at letter number 18. It coincides with the 18th degree of Scottish Rite Masonry, which Pike identified as the *Knight Rose Croix*—the Knight of the Red Cross. Look at the date, and let's see what you can make of it."

June 22, 1880

Most Illustrious Brother and Fellow Sir Knight W. J. B. Macleod Moore, 33°, KT

My Most Illustrious Brother, Thrice-Greatest, once again I am forever in your debt. Without your prior introduction to Prince Rhodocanakis of Greece and your providing to me the Ancient Rosicrucian degree work, my appointment as Supreme Grand Magus SRICF would not have been possible.

As you are aware, within the Scottish Rite, the Knight Rose Croix teaches three things, which symbolize the three pillars of the old Temple, with three that have already been explained to you. If any see within this degree also a type of the sorrow of the Craft for the death of Hiram, the grief of the Jews at the fall of Jerusalem, the misery of the Templars at the ruin of their Order, and the death of Grand Master De Molay, or the world's agony and pangs of woe at the death of the Redeemer, it is the right of each to do so.

The obligations of our Ancient Brethren of the Rose Croix were to fulfill all duties of good and scrupulously to avoid evil and every other kind of vice. They took their philosophy from the old Mysteries of the Egyptians, as Moses and Solomon had done, and borrowed its hieroglyphics and the ciphers of the Egyptians, the Hebrews, of the Sanskrit and the Kabalah.

The key to their true meaning is not undiscoverable.

Albert Pike, 33°, KT,

Sovereign Grand Commander

The letter was obviously written with an underlying message for the intended reader, but to Thomas these were just the philosophical ramblings of a man who lived much of his life on a totally different plane.

Janet knew otherwise. She reached across the kitchen island and snatched the plastic folder containing the letter so that she could examine it more fully. She pondered just for a second before proclaiming, "Grandfather, you'll be pleased to know that the money that you donated to Georgetown University didn't go to waste. Here's your numerological key right here. First, look at the date: June 22, 1880. It's the day after the summer solstice, but when the date is reduced to its numerological value, you get 6 + 2 + 2 + 1 + 8 + 8, which equals 27. Now the number 27 can be broken down to its cube roots: 3 x 3 x 3. The number 3 is prominent throughout Pike's letter. What you're looking for is the symbol that relates to the perfect numerological sequence: the tau cross, T, which has three points. The earliest Christians, those before the Council of Nicaea, believed that the tau cross represented the very essence, the spirit, the word of God. The later Christians, following the Vatican's tenets, developed the triple tau, which is said to represent the points of the crucifixion cross."

"Yes, yes, you're absolutely right, Janet," David agreed, but there was obviously something else. "Janet, Thomas, I don't know if either of you are aware of another hidden association that Pike alludes to in this letter. No? Pike was made Supreme Magus of the Rosicrucian Society in the United States on May 17, 1880.

"I believe that here we're witnessing an extension of Pike's enlightenment and spiritual advancement. Throughout his letters to MacLeod Moore, he is not only referring to the advancement of knowledge through the various degrees of Scottish Rite Masonry and Templarism, but he is instilling his knowledge of Rosicrucianism on top of that. Those three elements make a powerful formula! You might say that he combined three very fundamental elements of Christian Masonry into one. He was indicating that, through his own advancement, he had reasoned out the true meaning of God, the Supreme Deity, who evolved from a combination of earlier deities."

David gained a reprieve from further questioning by the ringing of the doorbell. Danny and Jimmy were as prompt as ever.

XIX

GRAND PONTIFF

1:30 p.m., Twelve days ago

FROM BOSTON TO WASHINGTON
AND BACK TO BOSTON

After checking the remote split-screen video recently set up in the kitchen, David Rose went to the front door to allow Danny Sullivan and Jimmy O'Reilly to enter. Both men were carrying brown paper bags containing a variety of steaming hot bagels. They always appeared to be hungry and made sure there was enough food not only for themselves but for David, Janet, Thomas, and anyone else who happened to stop by. This was their way of deflecting any sense of danger, but it was evident from the bulges on their left hips under their suit jackets that they had come armed and ready for anything. Both David and Janet realized this even before the two men took their jackets off but said nothing in order to keep Thomas calm. Janet had spent too much time with her guardian knights not to recognize the signs. Janet did meet her grandfather's eyes, however, acknowledging that their visit wasn't entirely a social call.

The two guardians tried to keep it light. Jimmy was the first to drop his bag on the countertop and dove right into the fridge, looking for something to complement the bagels. "See, I told you, Danny—they wouldn't let us down. I spy cream cheese, onion, lox, capers, and lemon. Hey, is that a strawberry torte? Man, I am going to have myself a piece of that after a couple of bagels."

Everyone laughed as they settled back to watch Jimmy retrieve a couple of plates from the cupboard and start to create a feast for himself and his partner. Meanwhile Danny had deposited his bag on the countertop and was proceeding to pour himself a cup of coffee. "*Shalom!*" Danny exclaimed. "Me and the human garbage disposal over there have some news for you to catch up on, but I'm just not sure how to deliver it."

"Since when have the two of you ever worried about delivering bad news in any way other than your normal damn-the-torpedoes style? Come on, out with it," Janet countered.

Danny shrugged and pulled a stool up to the kitchen island while Jimmy thrust a plate full of bagels in front of him. The rather short preliminaries had been completed. Now came the punch line.

"Well, if that's the way that you feel, don't tell me that I didn't warn you." The following moments of silence were filled with foreboding. "Jimmy and I twigged early this morning to the possibility that the young lady's disappearance and murder were tied to our Jesuit priest. The timelines were just too much of a coincidence. Anyway, the FBI has taken over the investigation, since the body was found in another state, even though it's a short drive from where she was last seen to where her body was found.

"With our assistance, along with the initial forensics, the FBI psychologist has already developed a profile of the murderer's psyche, and it isn't for the fainthearted." Danny paused and looked around the kitchen to make sure that everyone was prepared for the gory details. "Whoever committed the murder is definitely one sick puppy. The poor girl was tied up and raped, brutally sodomized, then strangled with a bungee cord. Her body was also mutilated with a small, serrated army knife; some of this was inflicted on her before she died. I'm guessing that this guy gets a higher thrill inflicting pain while he goes at it. The strangest thing is that the head wasn't touched at all—no bruising, no nothing—and she was laid out in that dumpster as neatly as she would have been at a funeral home. Her hands were folded, and a small gold chain and crucifix that her parents had given her for her first communion, which she wore around her neck, were found cupped in her hands, as if in prayer."

Danny could tell by the expressions on everyone's faces that the complete gravity of the news hadn't sunk in, but he continued anyway. "The FBI profiler indicates that we're definitely dealing with a multiple-personality, sadomasochistic psychopath, with a whole lot of other sicknesses and depravities thrown in. This guy's handler must be just as sick. After all my years, I still can't believe that an organization like the Catholic Church allows someone like this to run around doing these things."

Thomas sat quietly, unable to believe how everyone around him was accepting the news so calmly. "Hey, you guys, it really doesn't matter who is involved or who's controlling whom, all in the name of God. I really feel sickened about what happened to the concierge, but the question that remains is: how does this affect what we're trying to accomplish, and are we in danger? And why can't the authorities just arrest this guy? There must be enough evidence to implicate him in the murder."

Now that he had devoured both of his loaded bagels, it was Jimmy's turn to add to the conversation. "The problem, Thomas, is that everything we've talked about so far is just speculative. All of the evidence is circumstantial at best. As we said, this guy is an unholy ghost—a real spook. There's nothing yet that can tie him to the crime in any way. You can't just snatch people off the street, even if you know what they've done." Thomas was stunned by Jimmy's opening remarks but let him continue. "More to the point, the question is how do we use the three of you to lure this freak out of hiding and get him to commit himself?"

Jimmy let what he said sink in for a while and took a sip of coffee before continuing. "The young lady's phone is missing, and we can't get its signal. If they did communicate, it probably was by text. Nothing in her past phone records indicates anything out of the ordinary. The local police have interviewed her colleagues at work, but the problem is that she interacted with so many people at the hotel—fellow workers and guests. It also appears that she had a pretty active social life. Anyway, this guy would have kept his personal contact with her to a minimum. So far, the coroner says that the body had no obvious external excretions on or in her. I'm willing to bet that they won't be able to come up with a DNA sample at all. There are also no eyewitnesses or closed-circuit cameras around the area where she was dumped. I tell you, this guy is a specialist. He's very good at what he does, so we should all remember that. Now I'm going to have a piece of that strawberry torte."

Things were becoming far too complicated. Both David and Janet realized that at some point, once they had cracked the code, they would be led to the sacred crypt. They couldn't be doing this while constantly in danger from Philippe De Smet. Janet decided that the best tactic was to meet the question head-on. "OK, you two, out with it. Don't tell me that you haven't come up with a plan. How do we lure the Jesuit out of the dark and into the light?"

Janet's grandfather instinctively moved closer to her, intuiting that Janet was the best bait in this situation, although he didn't like it one bit.

After finishing off the last piece of his second bagel and wiping his mouth with a napkin, Danny responded, "Like in any unorthodox game of chess, we're going to expose our queen."

Aside from feeling the effects of driving from Boston to Washington and then back to Boston in a span of twenty-four hours, Philippe De Smet was buoyant this morning as he made his way to his holy appointment. The adrenalin from murdering the young concierge, as well as from the images of her pleading for her life, was still coursing through his body. What made Philippe De Smet feel this way would have kept a dozen psychiatrists busy for the remainder of their natural lives.

But this would never come about. Philippe had realized very early in his ordained life that he was either destined to be killed or to spend the remainder of his life enjoying the spoils of his triumph in monklike isolation and prayer. He thought to himself. *Whatever I do over the next week or so will ensure either my legacy or my martyrdom. Either way, I will receive my reward in heaven.*

Accepting what he considered to be his preordained destiny, Philippe made his way across the Boston Common to a little-used chapel that had seen better times. Walking around the side to the priest's entrance, he inserted an old skeleton key into the outer door's lock and turned the key. Rather surprisingly, the lock accepted the key silently and smoothly. Someone was regularly maintaining the chapel. Philippe pushed the door open effortlessly to expose a well-traveled nave. Shutting the door behind him and locking it, he made his way by speckled sunlight to the side confessional, where he entered and shut the lattice door behind him.

As soon as he knelt before the confessional window, the sliding door separating the two sides slid open, faintly exposing the shriveled and decaying profile of Father LaFortune. Although the adrenalin rush was wearing off, De Smet felt an odd glow fill his body as the old priest recited the Jesuit acknowledgment, "Jesus suffered and died on the cross." To which Philippe responded, "In order for mankind not to suffer."

LaFortune sighed, as he too felt the glow rise in his body. He was extremely proud of his protégé, regarding him as the son that he never had. The old priest was also very perceptive and felt a deep unease in Philippe. "Tell me, Philippe, what is troubling your heart? I thought that by giving you permission to commit that small indiscretion last night it would help alleviate your anxiety. Remember that all of us are sinners. That is why Christ sacrificed himself for us. You do God's work as His soldier. He will forgive you."

Philippe shifted slightly on his knees. The old basketball injury to his right knee was acting up lately, but he put it out of his mind and answered his mentor. "I'm sorry, Father. I didn't think that my anxiety would be that visible. I should have known, though. Ever since I first came to you as a child, you've been the only one to truly understand me. I feel that I'm letting down the Inner Circle, as well as you. I have been unable to get close enough to the letters to possess them and to rid the world of Thomas Moore. He, that woman, and her grandfather now have the help of two highly trained professionals. What can I do? I'm just one soldier against many."

This last comment alarmed Father LaFortune. He had never seen this level of self-doubt in Philippe before, especially less than a day after a bloodletting. The older priest realized that he had to give some additional incentive. "My son, do not despair. You must be patient and wait for the opportunity that will surely come your way. You must remember the pain and suffering that the High Priestess has caused mankind throughout her past lives. She foresaw the future and didn't do anything to alter it. Mary Magdalene was the same. She foresaw Christ's suffering but didn't warn him, didn't seek to help him when the Jewish priests denounced him to Pontius Pilate, and didn't do anything to alleviate his suffering on the cross."

This caused the adrenalin to rise once again throughout Philippe's body. He almost shouted but caught himself before his answer could reverberate within the confined space. "Yes, Father LaFortune, you are absolutely right, as you always are. How could I have not seen it before? The Jewish woman is feeding falsehoods to my prey, making him think that he is stronger than he really is. I see it now. His lust for her will be his downfall. He will soon wander aimlessly, and I will be there, waiting to pounce. Killing both will cleanse my soul once and for all. I'm sure of it!"

Father LaFortune was pleased with himself. He was now certain that Philippe would complete his task. He needed to add one more incentive. "Philippe, listen to me. I have spoken to the Inner Circle. We are all too aware that Pope Francis is weak. He has forgotten the promises that he made to us, his fellow Jesuits. Soon he will be abandoned to the wolves, like Ratzinger before him. The Inner Circle has authorized me to tell you that if you're successful in your mission, your name will be put forward for pontiff. With the ancient technology that you will possess, the world will kneel at your feet. God, in a breath, through you will rock the Earth."

Philippe let out an involuntary cry of joy and started to weep. This potential honor was beyond his wildest dreams.

The older Jesuit, tiring, spoke for the last time. "Philippe, do you remember the allegory of St. John, the favorite apostle and the depositary of the secrets of our Savior? Do you remember that he wrote in numbers so that he wouldn't be understood by the multitudes? Do you remember what he said?"

The younger Jesuit drew a breath and replied, "Let him who hath knowledge, understand! Let him who understands, calculate!" To which the older Jesuit instructed, "Then calculate your next move carefully. Now go and perform your duty as God's soldier."

With that, the sliding window closed. Philippe understood what was expected of him. As he rose to go, he uttered a small prayer: "St. Anthony, help me find *that-which-was-lost*."

XX

GRAND MASTER OF ALL SYMBOLIC LODGES

Eleven days ago

BACK TO THE CAPITAL

As Philippe De Smet drove from Boston back to Washington, reflecting on the conversation with his mentor, he allowed his mind to wander. He was euphoric at the possibility of being crowned as pontiff and thus afforded himself a little self-indulgence.

To think, in an odd sort of way, I have Masonry to thank for this potential supreme honor. For centuries, Masons have been at odds with the Jesuits. America's Founding Fathers were mostly Masons, and the Jacobite Masons were responsible for the French Revolution. All the while the Jesuits fought to maintain the aristocracy. Masons are taught to be freethinkers, to reason like the ancient philosophers, while the Jesuits followed their rule to the letter, neither questioning nor deviating from their instructions.

But somewhere in the shadows of mankind, they must have shared a common origin, a common understanding of a Supreme Being, of the essence of God. Even Albert Pike wrote within his Morals and Dogma *that Jesuitry was first taught under the mask of Freemasonry. No matter: when I sit upon the throne of Peter, all religions will return to one belief— a belief in our Savior, Jesus Christ. If they do not buckle under, then they do not deserve to exist in God's eye. Earth will be destroyed once and for all. It was Simon de Montfort, during the French crusade against the Cathars, who declared, "Kill them all. God will know His own!"*

Putting aside his thoughts, he fiddled with the car radio, seeing if he could catch the news about the murder of the concierge. Although he was confident that he had erased all signs of his involvement, including retrieving his business card, just hearing about the unsolved mystery stirred his loins. He knew that when he became part of the Inner Circle, he could exercise any depravity that his heart desired. He would resurrect the Spanish Inquisition. Only then would his appetites be truly satisfied.

De Smet then heard the announcement that an amazing find had just been made by a doctoral candidate at the Scottish Rite Temple Library. Apparently the student had just found a previously unknown letter from Albert Pike.

The newscaster went on to say that the discovery had Masonic historians clamoring to examine the letter, as it purportedly was the last to be written by Pike to his longtime Masonic Brother, Colonel William James Bury MacLeod Moore. The newscaster went on to describe the doctorate student as Ms. Janet Rose, of the renowned Rose family, owners of the biggest private commodities firm in the world.

The newscaster then finished with a quip. He reckoned that the letter could lead to another Templar Treasure, like the one discovered in *National Treasure,* except for real this time. Philippe smiled and thought, *Fool! You might be closer to the truth than you imagined! So, the High Priestess has served her purpose. Father LaFortune was right. Be patient and God will deliver!*

Philippe sped up, winding between cars, some of them blowing their horns at the seemingly reckless fool. A wicked smile came across his face as he formulated a brilliant scheme not only to secure all of the

Pike Letters but to disgrace the Rose family while eliminating those who were involved with the letters.

Meanwhile Janet Rose had spent the entire morning and most of the afternoon fielding calls from around the world. Most of them were from major news outlets and conglomerates, which surprisingly had some historical or contextual association with Masonry. She was even scheduled to appear live on several prominent newscasts around the dinner hour. The problem at this point was being able to schedule all of the requests.

Research departments at the news corporations had been hard at work since the first announcement. They zeroed in on the fact that Pike had been a Confederate general and that a statue of him still stood unmolested in the heart of Washington while other Confederate statues had become focal points for racial tension throughout the United States.

Janet tried her best to keep an academic spin on things, citing her and others' research into the relationship between ancient philosophy and esoteric symbolism, but it was the negative aspects of Pike's life, including his involvement in the Knights of the Golden Circle and the Ku Klux Klan, that went viral.

Technically, the letter belonged to the Scottish Rite Temple, but a secret arrangement had already been made between the current Sovereign Grand Commander and David Rose. Janet would be given credit for the discovery of the letter and exclusive rights to its use in her doctoral thesis, as long as the original remained the property of the Temple. If truth be known, the letter's existence had already been proven for over a year, since its original discovery by Janet. But without the other thirty-two letters, the thirty-third letter was just a curiosity at best and had remained in the bottom drawer of the Grand Historian and Archivist's desk in his Temple office since Janet first revealed it to him. Neither the Grand Historian nor Janet had a clue about what to do with the letter before this set of events. Every so often, however, Janet had reached out secretly to examine the letter, but every time it appeared to be nothing more than a tantalizing hint of things to come.

The plan was for Janet to announce on the six o'clock news that in seven days a new exhibit would open up at the Scottish Rite Temple's Albert Pike Library. Its centerpiece would be the newly found letter, and Janet would be the author of a new catalogue issued in honor of the find. After the ceremony, the exhibit would be free and open to the public, just as Pike had decreed.

Hastily written invitations had been already sent to Masonic leaders around the world, and at least a hundred Masonic dignitaries were expected to attend, dressed in their ceremonial regalia. This was going to be an immense celebration of the worldwide Masonic fraternity, and even the president of the United States would be present. It was destined to be a time of celebration; the world was going to once again turn its eye on those noble gentlemen.

The trap was set.

Of course, Philippe De Smet recognized it for what it was, but he vowed to change the game to his advantage. His appointment in the capital wasn't until six o'clock, so he slowed down and decided to blend in once again with the seemingly endless line of cars going, from his point of view, nowhere.

At the same time, Danny Sullivan and Jimmy O'Reilly were arranging a meeting with a select group of ex-SEAL buddies who had all gone on to high-level positions in the FBI, CIA, Secret Service, and Homeland Security. The meeting was scheduled at one of the better Washington steak houses, where everyone could enjoy good food and drink. A private dining room had been secured, and Jimmy swept the room for listening devices. An electronics scrambler was set up in the corner, preventing any of the attendees from using their cell phones during the meeting, even for emergencies.

As the impeccably dressed middle-aged gentlemen filed in and greeted each other, the usual quips, on topics such as getting fat and soft, losing what was left of their hair, or being unable to sit down on their bulging wallets, zinged through the air. Old warriors have forever been the same the world around. In this case, though, they were still fighting the enemy, one that was more sophisticated and technologically advanced than those thirty years before.

Following the usual fraternal greetings and salutations, Danny took control of the meeting, "Greetings, Brothers! We've asked you here because once again the devil is at our door. Unfortunately, in this case the threat has become extremely personal, because they're targeting a family that is very dear to both Jimmy's and my heart—the Rose family." Nobody made a comment or showed any emotion.

Danny continued uninterrupted. "Jimmy is going to pass around to each of you a portfolio of the information we have to date." Manila folders made their way around the table. "The picture of the suspect was recently taken in Paris. His name is Philippe De Smet, and he's an ordained Jesuit priest. Yes, you heard right. Sadly, he is one of God's soldiers, and unfortunately he's very good at what he does."

The assistant director of the FBI, who was sitting at the other end of the table, quietly whistled and then spoke up with a question: "And what exactly is it that he does?"

"Let's just say that he eliminates any problems that the Vatican may have, especially if they directly relate to the pope. He has been tied to twenty unsolved murders or disappearances over the ten years since he was ordained, and there are another dozen or so unproven rapes or murders of seemingly unrelated women. It appears that the bastard needs a little bloodletting just to calm his nerves before or after he does a job."

The tall, lanky gentleman from the Secret Service quipped, "Hell, I just have a few shots of bourbon when I need a release!" This comment caused a few guffaws around the table.

"Yeah, right," Danny replied, "just a few shots. I happen to remember that time in Angola when you drank four bottles of rotgut over three days after you whacked that Amazon general. I knew that you had a thing for her. Now let's get serious, guys. This priest is deadly, and what he's after could destroy the world."

It was the CIA man who spoke up next. "What are we talking

about, Danny? Is it nuclear, or a hydrogen bomb of some kind?"

Jimmy felt that it was his turn to join in. "Nothing of the sort. What we're talking about here is apocalyptical in scale. Something straight out of the Bible—the end of time, hell and brimstone, Ark of the Covenant stuff, the wrath of God—*Indiana Jones* meets *The Exorcist*!"

Everyone knew Danny and Jimmy long enough to take the threat seriously. Since 9/11, everyone was prepared to take any threat seriously.

The CIA man asked the obvious question. "If you say it could be catastrophic, then I for one believe you. Besides, I never did like the Jesuits and their damn secret police. What is it that you want us to do?"

"Two things," Danny held up two fingers as he spoke. "One, he can't be working alone. We need to know where he's getting his intelligence from. He's like a virtual spook. I don't want to believe that he's tied into one of our organizations, but he always appears to be a step ahead of us. Two, we need to locate him, to get a read on him. Between all of you and your facial-recognition profiling and ability to access all of the CCTV here in the capital, we figure that someone should be able to locate him."

There really was no need for any sign of acceptance from anyone around the table. Everyone knew that if any one of them had a problem where the others could help, it was an unsaid rule. The motto of the SEALs said it all: *The only easy day was yesterday.*

Noting everyone's quiet acceptance of the assignment, Jimmy stood and walked over and opened the double doors. It was time for the waiters to bring in the main course. As they entered with several sizzling-hot trays of filet mignon, porterhouse steaks, lobster, and crab, Jimmy spread his arms wide and declared, "Beats powdered eggs and canned beef anytime!"

Prior to his own meeting, Philippe De Smet stopped at a McDonald's to get a drive-through meal. The smell of the cardboard and paper always reminded him of his student years, when he tried but failed to fit into his fellow students' eating and social habits.

Thinking back one last time, he shrugged before gently knocking on the senator's office door. The staff had been let go early and were probably gathered at one of the trendy bars that had sprung up all over the capital in recent years. The greeting of "Y'all come on in!" that sounded from the other side of the door seemed friendly enough, but Philippe knew that this senator was an extremely ruthless man, having also been raised and schooled by Jesuits.

Philippe entered and closed the door behind him. The white collar of a priest suddenly stared across the room at the senator: Philippe had thought that his priestly collar would have an authoritative effect on the overbearing man. To judge by the surprised look on the senator's face, the collar had worked its magic. "Ah, *Father* De Smet, I presume! When my old Jesuit mentor called me and asked me to embrace a Philippe De Smet and do whatever he asks of me, I assumed that you were a Jesuit scholar, as I once had been. I mean, I didn't actually think that you were a priest."

Another pompous and presumptuous idiot, thought Philippe. "No problem, Senator. As God's soldiers, we come in many forms. Anyway, thank you so much for seeing me on such short notice. I won't take up much of your time. I have a rather odd request of a man like you, in such a high position within the government."

"Yes, of course, Father, anything for the church. But I haven't been asked for anything for forty years. Why now?" The senator had been taken aback by Philippe's entrance. The priest was young, yet possessed a raw and confident energy. He had never met such a man before.

"Our duty is never to question the Inner Circle!" Philippe realized that this was going to be easier than he had thought. Clearing his throat, he pointed at the senator in an accusatory manner. "Senator, the Inner Circle put you here, and they can remove you just as easily. Remember that! They allowed you to join the enemy, the Freemasons, because it suited their purpose. Now you have risen to become one of the thirty-three members of the Supreme Council of the Scottish Rite of the Southern Jurisdiction of the United States. That's quite impressive indeed! Now here's what I request of you."

Upon hearing the request, the senator turned white with fear.

XXI

NOACHITE OR PRUSSIAN KNIGHT

May 21, 1881

OKLAHOMA TERRITORY

As the train rolled along the tracks, making its way westerly through the Indian Territory, the conductor made his own way up the aisle of the first-class coach. Counting as he went, every six rows of seats he announced that they would be arriving in Oklahoma City in less than one hour. Upon hearing his pronouncement, many of the passengers, who had slept or read over the past three days from the capital, started to stir and prepare for arrival.

One such passenger was Albert Pike. But as he didn't require a lot of sleep, over the last three days he had mostly allowed his mind to wander through the window and across the open territory. Having deeply reflected on his prior life history during that time, he silently gave thanks to the Supreme Deity for allowing him a second life, a chance to be reborn.

Albert Pike was indeed a true survivor, having come through both the Mexican War and the Civil War without a scratch. Freemasonry saved him beyond that, affording him the time and space to present his reason and logic—his *Morals and Dogma*—to the world through the thirty-three degrees of Scottish Rite Masonry. Now, as the lifetime-appointed Sovereign Grand Commander, he was afforded the opportunity to search for *that-which-was-lost* from the time before the Flood.

This time Pike wasn't traveling in his capacity as Sovereign Grand Commander. Instead he was fulfilling his duty as the head Indian agent for the United States. Trouble was brewing among the remaining Choctaw, Cheyenne, and Cherokee, who had been driven west out of the Alleghenies and Ohio Valley in the years prior to the Civil War. Pike had at one time represented their interests, and now he had been asked by the federal government to do the same.

Sighing at the inevitable, as it related to the collective destiny of the Native North Americans, Pike took out the letter that he had recently penned to his friend and Brother, and, as was his custom, read and reread it:

May 21, 1881

Most Illustrious Brother and Fellow Sir Knight W. J. B. Macleod Moore, 33°, KT

My Most Illustrious Brother, oddly enough, I find myself traveling to the west into the wilderness in search of that which I have shared with you. It is the evening of the 21st, and I find the sun still high in the sky, suggesting that somewhere an ancient lodge is conducting its ritual upon the square, 3 times 7.

Tomorrow I will be meeting with the remaining chiefs of the western First Nations. They remind me a great deal of the lost tribes of Israel seeking a New Jerusalem—so noble yet so desperate, wandering aimlessly across the desert. Or were they? Brigham Young understood this and ventured forth to the Prime Meridian, seeking the same as you and I. For all of our virtues, it is most fortunate that he did not fully

*understand the signs, symbols, and tokens left behind by our fellow
Knights Templar who covenanted the Goddess.*

*I find that I must remind myself constantly of our temperate ways,
as we are constantly surrounded by temptation. It will help my pain to
share the ceremonies and degrees of our Mide'win Brothers, who share
the blood of our ancestors. It is in their lodges that I find myself most
humbled and modest toward the Great Architect of the Universe.*

*I want to assure you that it has never been my intention to impugn
His Wisdom, nor set up my own imperfect sense of Right against His
Providence and dispensations; nor attempt too rashly to explore the
Mysteries of God's Infinite Essence and inscrutable plans and of that
Great Nature which we are not made capable to understand.*

Forever will I steer far away from all those vain philosophies.

Albert Pike, 33°, KT,
Sovereign Grand Commander

Pike was pleased with the letter, the twenty-first to be sent to
MacLeod Moore. As the train whistle blew to signal ahead that it was
arriving, Pike assessed the situation in his mind. *God has given me the
strength to endure and to triumph over the evil that resides in all men.
For this, I will be eternally grateful. He, in his Infinity, has wisely allowed
me, over my lifetime, to receive his voice of reason, to comprehend his very
existence. Therefore, I now realize that I am, as he was and is and ever
will be! I truly hope that my eternal Fellow and Brother has grown as I
have grown, for it is only through our duality that the secret can be safe.*

People were stirring and starting to lift their luggage and belong-
ings down from the overhead racks. The vainer passengers would wait
for the half-breed porters to come on board once the train had stopped.
Pike watched carefully as they chose of their own free will which virtues that they would live by.

He wouldn't have much time to complete his self-assessment, as the
squealing brakes sounded throughout the coach. The train was lurching
to a stop. *I pray that I am granted enough time to complete all thirty-*

*two letters—my half of the chess board. How ironic that a Scottish Rite
Mason must complete all thirty-two degrees of ritual in order to truly see
the light, in order to gain their honorary thirty-third. I chose to be the
black squares, while William agreed to be the white. 32 x 2, 64 squares
in all, 8 x 8. I am glad that it was William who freely agreed to accept
the burden that I carry in my heart, the location of the crypt. I belong to
the south and William is of the north. Black and white—the colors of the
Beauséant—the Templars' banner, which had flown at the front of the
warrior-monks' column as they rode into battle. I am proud to say that
the medieval knights had been spiritually enlightened through the same
ancient rituals to a level where they had no fear. They understood that
they served God for the betterment of mankind.*

As Pike stood to exit the coach, his one last thought confirmed his
ultimate decision. *There, I've decided once and for all! It's better for the
secrets of the crypt to remain where they lie, to never be disturbed, for only
death and destruction would come of their discovery and use. I have laid
down the foundations for Masons to continue to possess the capacity for free
will. Let a better man than I somewhere in the future decide what to do
with the ultimate secret.*

As Pike exited the train, the small entourage of Oklahoma City
Masons, who had gathered to greet him, broke into spontaneous
applause. Here were the fruits of his labors, which he brought about by
his long and arduous studies. Pike had come to understand the ancient
philosophies, which had been consolidated into the thirty-two degrees
of Scottish Rite Masonry, which he had subsequently labored for a lifetime to return to their rich and dark meaning.

The Freemen who stood before him understood this. They would
be eternally grateful for his labor, after completing the thirty-two
degrees themselves. Freemasonry is said to take good men and make
them better. Here was evidence of that result. Here was the nucleus
of the upper middle class—the merchants and the bureaucrats—from
which Oklahoma would ultimately become a state.

But off in the western distance, sitting atop their horses, were the other pieces to the puzzle. The great chiefs of the Western Plains' First Nations silently awaited the man, whom they also considered to be their Brother. Pike sensed their presence and turned toward them to acknowledge them. As he shielded his eyes against the setting sun with his left hand, he hailed the chiefs in the usual Masonic manner with the right.

Having received his acknowledgment, the chiefs spun their horses around and rode back to their camp, which had been established beyond the railyards and outside of the city proper. The homesteaders of Oklahoma City could never understand why the natives established their camp where they did, but the natives knew better. For centuries, long before any foreigner had invaded their land, this was a traditional spring meeting place, where the Plains tribes would meet their blood brothers from the north, south, east, and west. It was where the traveling shamans would come to share their traditional secrets relating to astrology, healing, and the spirit world. Here was a sacred gathering place where the Mide'win would gather and practice their ancient rituals, seeking the truth concerning their very existence.

Here also was a place where the medieval Knights Templar who had escaped the wrath of King Philippe le Bel and Pope Clement V had traveled on their journey to a New Jerusalem. Over several generations waves of Templars and their descendants had been passed from one Algonquin nation to another, all the while intermarrying among the various tribes. Not only did this strengthen the warrior bloodline, but allowed the DNA memory bank of the eastern monks and western medicine men, the holy princesses of the east and the west, to come together. The ancient spiritual bond between the red and white man, the colors of the Templars, became eternally connected.

The Sovereign Grand Commander was heralded through the streets by coach to his hotel. Given the young age of Oklahoma City, which had evolved from a stagecoach stop fifty years earlier, the hotel could be considered opulent. But Pike was too tired to appreciate the richness of the proffered comfort. He thanked his fellow Masons for fraternally greeting him with enthusiasm and asked their forgiveness. He assured them that he would indeed attend their lodge during his brief stay and promised to provide an appropriate lecture on the merits of the Brotherhood. This appeared to appease them, so they bid farewell and made their way to the hotel's bar for refreshment and socializing.

Pike opened his hotel room door and entered, immediately sensing an evil presence in the room. *Of course he couldn't wait until I got settled. Such an impatient and shallow man,* Pike thought. He then closed the door behind him to prevent the evil spirit from escaping.

As the looming figure in full priest's cassock standing near the window turned to greet the Sovereign Grand Commander, Pike threw the key to the room onto the side table and bent over the lamp to raise the wick higher, in order to fully illuminate the intruder. Slowly, out of the dark of the coming night, the full bulk of Father William Hoffman came into focus. W. J. Hoffman was the secret protégé of Father Pierre-Jean De Smet. Prior to his death, De Smet had also been an early mentor for Pike and would go on to explore and Christianize much of the Western Plains, including the traditional territory of the Cree, Chippewa, Nez Perce, Blood, and the Blackfoot.

It was Father Hoffman's appointed task to convince Albert Pike to reaffirm his childhood devotion to the Jesuit cause, denounce Freemasonry, and reveal the location of the crypt to the Jesuits and the pope.

Pike did not hold back his ever-growing contempt for the organization represented by the man who stood before him. "Father Hoffman, I thought that we came to an understanding the last time we met. Do I truly have to spell it out to you? Your mentor, Pierre-Jean De Smet, pestered me constantly, and my answer was always the same. I will never give up the secret that your Inner Circle covets more than anything else in the world. I have come to realize that you do not wish to help the indigenous peoples but to annihilate them if they don't bend to your tenets."

Father Hoffman appeared not to be put out the least bit, but inside a hellfire was raging. Using every skill that he had been taught by De Smet, he decided to use guilt as his weapon of choice. "Albert, how can you think such a thing? We are talking about saving millions of wretched souls here, including yours. I know the burden that you carry. Father De Smet was most specific in the information that he provided me prior to his passing. God rest his soul."

Father Hoffman crossed himself before continuing. "Albert, do you truly believe that your soul can make peace with the Lord after what you have done, after what you have set in motion? Not only have you killed personally, but your so-called Knights of the Golden Circle and the odious Ku Klux Klan have killed hundreds, maybe thousands, in the name of what—self-determination, states' rights, free will? What about your purported involvement in the assassination of President Lincoln? Your Masonic teachings are misguided. The ancient philosophers such as Plato, Socrates, and Pythagoras tried to reason faith, refusing to accept something which is unexplainable. Come, I am prepared to accept the burden of your confession. I will show you the pathway to heaven, to the Light."

Pike was incensed. *How dare they send this Jesuit priest to persuade me? How dare he accuse me of past regressions? Will these Black Robes stop at nothing to attain what they desire? Does the Inner Circle really consider itself the most powerful force on earth?* Controlling his rage, the Sovereign Grand Commander stuck out his immense chest and straightened to his maximum height as he made his way to the door. Without looking around, he opened the door to the hallway once again and silently waited for Father Hoffman to fully comprehend the implications of his actions and depart.

As Father Hoffman shrugged and moved toward the door, Pike quietly whispered to him, "I know that you have been trying to infiltrate the Mide'win and their rituals for years and will continue to do so. You will not succeed in learning their secrets, but I will provide a warning to you. If you do not stop, you will ultimately be inexplicably drawn to their teachings and start to question your own faith. Self-doubt comes in many different ways, and yours will send you straight to hell."

Father Hoffman moved past Pike and continued out into the hallway, as though paying no heed to Pike's warning. But the Sovereign Grand Commander was astute enough to know better. From the slight twinge in Father Hoffman's shoulders, Pike knew that the Jesuit's faith had started to crack. He slowly shut the door and locked it. The Jesuits would never again attempt to enter Pike's inner sanctum.

Pike moved on and started to unpack his suitcases. He had a change of rough wilderness clothing for visiting the Indian encampment, as well as formal attire for his visit to the Masonic lodge. The valise that contained his Masonic regalia was tucked under the bed with the knowledge that a six-shooter lay underneath in a false bottom.

Pike laid the letter to MacLeod Moore on the side table to remind himself that it had to be mailed first thing in the morning. He undressed and prepared to get some sleep. The next three days were going to be busy, and Pike would need a fresh mind and spirit. Turning the wick down on the oil lamp, he had just turned the blankets down on the bed when a faint rap occurred at the balcony door. There were three quick knocks, followed by a pause, and then seven longer knocks.

Following an instant recognition of the only person whom it could be, Pike quickly moved to the balcony door and unlocked it, allowing his visitor entrance.

Not the least bit surprised, Pike stepped back and allowed Peter Pitchlynn Jr., hereditary chief of the Choctaw, to enter, encased by the moonlight. The chief greeted Pike in the usual Masonic fashion and then commented, "It is good to see the Sovereign Grand Commander once again."

To which Pike replied, "And it's good to see you, Peter. I'm sorry that the last time we saw one another was at your father's funeral in Washington, back in January. Your father was a great man and fought hard for the Choctaws' rights. He was also a great warrior, riding alongside me during the Civil War. I will miss him forever. Now tell me, what is happening in the West?"

Chief Pitchlynn looked around and into the darkness to make sure that the two were alone. "As you can see, the whites are moving into the territories in droves. They press our people and do whatever they can to drive us forever farther into the foothills. The buffalo have all but disappeared, and the traders fill the young warriors with bad spirits. The Choctaw are suffering from famine and disease, and our women are being enticed by trinkets. I've taken up my father's cause to no avail, and the federal agents and soldiers all but laugh at us."

Pike laid his massive hands on the shoulders of this proud warrior. In spite of the darkness, he could see the sorrow in the depths of his eyes. "Peter, my fellow Brother, you have my word as a Mason and a longtime blood brother of your father that I will do whatever I can to intervene on behalf of the Choctaw with the federal agents. The president himself has asked me to speak on your and the Cheyenne's and the Cherokee's behalf."

"Thank you, Brother. You will come and sit among the Mide'win tomorrow and share the stories of our despair. We will tell you the truth that lies within our hearts. But I see from the shadows that I was not your only visitor tonight. The Black Robes carry nothing but disease and poverty in their pockets and in their hearts."

Pike knew that most people considered the Indians to be nothing more than savages, but here he was, standing before a wise, well-educated hereditary chief of one of the noblest nations in the world. At this point, even Pike felt inferior to this noble being in wisdom and spirituality. *He surely must be of the Grail bloodline himself,* thought Pike.

Then came the ever-present question, "Brother Peter, is there any news of the crypt?"

Peter was about to disappear the way he came but stopped and turned toward Pike. "The Blackfoot elders have arrived. You can ask them yourself, tomorrow, during our ceremonies."

XXII

KNIGHT OF THE ROYAL AXE, OR PRINCE OF LIBANUS

Ten days ago

GEORGETOWN

Preparations for the Pike exhibit were in full swing, as was the constant spinning of the spider's web. Danny was determined to catch his prey before any more harm could be done. He had called in every favor ever owed to him through a lifetime of playing in the covert shadows, but he was no further ahead. His adversary was his match—and the Society of Jesus was just as powerful as the CIA.

Danny Sullivan wouldn't give up. Sitting at his desk in a borrowed corner office at one of Rose's subsidiary business units in Washington, he scrolled down his daily influx of emails, all the while thinking about Janet and her stalker. *Jesus, I must be missing something. Either that or De Smet must really be a ghost. After college, it's like he stepped off the edge of the Earth. He pops up every so often to do a job and then vanishes down the rabbit hole again. What am I missing?*

163

As quickly as Danny could search the far recesses of his mind, his laptop quietly pinged, indicating that he had just received another email. As he scrolled to the top of his inbox, his eyes lit up when he saw the sender of the email, followed by the subject line: *Society of Jesus, Re: One of God's Soldiers.* Danny thought for a moment. *What the hell is going on? What's this all about?* However, being a professional, before opening the email he clicked on the little icon in the bottom right-hand corner of his laptop. This ensured that his location couldn't be traced or that the email didn't contain any Trojan horses or malware.

When the icon went from red to green, indicating no other sinister programming had piggybacked on the email, he clicked on the subject line, opening it to find just a few lines of text. *Mr. Sullivan, you and I share the same objective. We are the same dutiful servant but to a different Master. We are like the two-headed phoenix, rising from the ashes, black and white. Or are you St. Anthony and I, St. Paul, two hermits forever battling our temptations? No matter, I think that we should meet. Would you not agree?*

Danny reached for his cell phone and hit speed-dial #1. Jimmy O'Reilly, who was sitting in his own borrowed office down the hall at the time, answered immediately. Even before Danny could say something, Jimmy answered, "You have to admit that he's got balls. We're tracing the IP source right now, but I doubt if we'll be able to follow it to its origin. He's too clever for that. He also knows that we have him in our sights. I wonder what he's up to now."

Danny couldn't help responding to Jimmy's comments with a laugh. Was he supposed to be angry or thankful that Jimmy was screening his emails remotely? *No matter, as long as we catch this bastard.* Danny thought a little longer and then decided. He reached out to the keyboard to respond but hesitated for a moment. *I hope that Jimmy is making sure that the bastard can't track this email's location. Oh well, here goes nothing.* The email that he crafted was simple and to the point: *OK, where and when?*

Danny almost jumped when a response to his email arrived almost simultaneously with his own. Watching the icon go green, he opened up the email to find a riddle of sorts: *In a day's time when the sun is at the Prime Meridian and no shadows are cast on the water. Please come alone. I would hate to have to kill someone for no reason.*

Following the reading of De Smet's latest email, Danny produced a note pad and pencil from the top drawer. *Well, you've got to give him full marks for cleverness. Let's see now: In a day's time, that's twenty-four hours. The Prime Meridian established by L'Enfant runs north-south through the capital at 77 degrees, 32 minutes and 6 seconds west. The capitalization of the two words, PM, means at noon, when the sun is at its meridian, but it also suggests that the sun will then move to the west. No shadow in the third degree? No reason to kill—certainly not in the vicinity of a philosopher, a Mason?*

While sorting out the email, Danny pulled up Google Maps and zeroed in on Washington. He ran his finger across the screen as he pieced together the clues. *A lot of people get confused when they talk about the Prime Meridian, because four meridians have actually been established for the capital. The Prime Meridian is actually the first longitudinal line set by L'Enfant in 1791. It's known as the Capitol Meridian and passes through the Capitol, not the White House, as many believe.*

Before Danny could decipher the entire message, Jimmy came hurriedly into the corner office and exclaimed, "Bloody cheeky of him, making reference to the three basic Masonic degrees like that: 1, 2, 3— the three squares of a knight's move in chess. As we're aware, in the old Irish lodge the fourth degree was a Knight Templar. He's completing the square. You don't suppose that this Jesuit priest is also a Mason and a Templar? His mother was Irish and his father was French, I believe? Do you know the location he's referring to?"

Danny smiled, "Yes, of course. He's referring to the Ulysses S. Grant Memorial, which is located just west of the Capitol. Fronting the memorial, to the west, is the Capitol Reflecting Pool. Were you aware that Grant's first name was Hiram? It's evocative of Hiram Abiff, the Master Mason who's killed in the third degree, only to rise out of the shadows

once again through the lion's grip. Ulysses S. Grant was no philosopher, that's for sure. He was a soldier's soldier, plain and simple. It is said
that he believed that the easiest way to defeat the South was just to kill
more Southern soldiers than the South killed Northerners. By the way, I
checked: Grant was never a Mason, but his father and all brothers were.
He definitely didn't believe in reason and logic, just good old practical
blood-and-guts warfare. March forward, and the last man standing wins."

"You've got to admit," said Jimmy, "that's an odd way of conveying
a message. So, noon tomorrow. We should start to prepare our surveillance. We should be able to nab the bastard this time." Jimmy was itch-
ing for a fight.

Holding up his hand to quell Jimmy's enthusiasm, Danny shook his
head. "No, we're going to do it his way. He's too smart not to realize if
it's a trap. Besides, I want to see what he has to say."

Jimmy wanted to stay with the General Grant issue for a moment.
"OK, you got it. Were you aware that Grant was elected president after
Andrew Johnson was impeached for his sympathies with the South?"

Danny looked up intently, as if to indicate for Jimmy to continue.
"Once Grant secured the presidency, one of the first two things that
he did was urge the ratification of the Fifteenth Amendment and said
he would approach Reconstruction calmly, without prejudice, hate, or
sectional pride, as well as recommending that the proper treatment of
Native Americans be studied, advocating their civilization and eventual
citizenship. Given Grant's rather abrupt style, these sentiments sound
more like Pike's words."

"You're right, Jimmy. Things aren't really as they appear. Listen, I
need you to dig into everything that you can get your hands on concerning our Jesuit priest. There's something more to his story that I just
can't pin down. I need an advantage when I meet this bastard tomorrow, and I need it fast. He claims that we're the same *dutiful* servant but
we just serve two Masters. Now what the hell does that mean?"

Jimmy nodded and spun around to make his way back to his office
and his sophisticated technical equipment. He knew from the tone of

Danny's voice that he was desperate to get a leg up on De Smet. One could feel the tension rising throughout the building.

The same thing could be said across town at the Georgetown brownstone. Janet was feeling overwhelmed by the media requests and desperately needed some time to work on the exhibit's catalogue. At the same time, Thomas was feeling helpless and forgotten. It was as though he was the odd man out. Even David Rose had been assigned a task in the great conspiracy and was down in his lab examining the Pike Letters in a new light.

Janet was working at the side table in the kitchen, trying to catch up on her influx of emails when Thomas snuck up behind her and wrapped his arms around her. But instead of accepting the gesture as a sign of affection and support, she snapped and jumped up so quickly that her head glanced off Thomas's chin. It was like a jolt of reality. Thomas quickly backed away and excitedly exclaimed, "Hey, what's going on? I was just trying to show some affection."

Janet turned on him like a cornered lioness. "Thomas, grow up, will you? Can't you see that I have a lot of work to complete? This is so important to my studies, and besides, we're trying to lay a trap here for a known killer. God, we're not teenagers anymore." Then she said it. "Sometimes I wish that you never had walked into my life that day in the Temple."

As soon as she said it, she totally regretted it. The look on Thomas's face was one of shock and despair. His shoulders sagged, and tears welled up in his eyes.

Janet moved forward instantly, reaching out in an attempt to reconcile the situation, but the damage was done. Confused and deflated, Thomas recoiled. He quickly turned and headed down the hallway toward the front door. Before she could utter any protest, Thomas grabbed his satchel, which contained his phone, wallet, and passport, and bounded out of the house, slamming the door behind him.

Stunned, Janet staggered back down the hallway to her desk and collapsed in the chair, sobbing. *Oh my God, what have I done? I've*

driven away the only man I've ever let into my heart. Fate's told me that
this was the right man, the only man, my soul mate, and now he's gone!

Having heard the door slam, even from his lab in the basement,
David Rose ascended the stairs to investigate. Then he heard Janet's
sobs and went into the kitchen to see what the problem was. Upon sensing her grandfather's presence, Janet jumped up and buried her head
into his chest. Through great sobs she exclaimed, "Oh, Grandfather, I've
done the most terrible thing. I've let my own duties get in the way of
my relationship with Thomas. I said the most terrible thing to him; he
was smothering me, and I lashed out. He's gone, just left. I have no idea
where he's going and if he'll ever come back."

"There, there, my child, these things happen. He'll come back;
wait and see. You've both been through a lot the past couple of weeks."
David was trying his best to comfort Janet, but he had a nagging feeling
that this wasn't just a lover's spat.

"Don't you see, Grandfather? I think I purposely turned on him to
drive him away. I'm afraid, regardless of what Jimmy and Danny say. I'm
afraid of the Jesuit priest. I'm afraid of losing you. I'm afraid of leaving
Thomas alone, especially after how deeply he's fallen in love with me.
Oh my God, I'm so confused." Janet's body was racked with guilt, and
her sobs started to blend into a crescendo.

David knew that he needed help with this situation. First, though,
he had to calm Janet down. "Janet, listen to me. You are the strongest
woman that I've ever known, even stronger than your grandmother.
Right now I need you to stop this self-doubt and to go lie down. I'm
going to give you a small sedative, which lasts about two hours. You'll
awake refreshed and renewed. While you're resting, I'll be on the phone
with Danny and Jimmy and your father. This is getting out of hand."
I'll also phone Sarah. She'll know what to do about Janet's anxiety.

The sobbing started to cease immediately. Janet's grandfather continued with his reassurance. "Now there, that's better. Think now!
Where would Thomas go?"

With one last sniffle Janet responded, "I really don't know. The only two places that he's really familiar with are the Temple and the Georgetown Inn."

"Then we'll start with that." David was formulating a notion in his head. "Come now, let's get you settled."

With that accomplished, David saw to his granddaughter's immediate needs. The small packet of powder that he retrieved from the kitchen drawer was mixed into a glass of water and given to her. The effects were surprisingly quick. Janet fell into an exhausted sleep, only to find the inner recesses of her mind searching for answers to why she treated Thomas so badly. Her mind had no idea where it was heading.

Thomas had no idea where he was heading either. As he stumbled down the street, seemingly in a trance, he once again saw himself and Janet in the ancient land where the Oracle's Temple stood on top of the sun-drenched hill.

The captain of the elite guards had just returned the High Priestess to the Temple on his winged horse, but something was different. There were no attendants to greet her, and the wind even appeared to be angered by the thought that the Oracle had given in to temptation. The loss of her virginity also meant the loss of her ancient powers. She no longer had the ability to foresee events in the future. The only sound emanating from the Temple's inner sanctum was a faint whimpering. Immediately realizing the gravity of what they had done, the High Priestess and the captain ran up the steps of the Temple and into its dark shadows, cast by the thirteen pillars of the Temple. Upon reaching the heart of the Temple, they spied the overturned bowl, from which a mixture of water and blood flowed. The priestess realized what this meant and ran around to the other side of the limestone pedestal to find what she feared most. Lying on her back, with her eyes looking skyward, was her young apprentice. The priestess bent over her but knew that the end was near, as her white gown had turned crimson red. The priestess knew that in order to appease the gods, the other attendants believed that they needed to offer a blood sacrifice. Who better than her virgin apprentice? Downcast, all the priestess could do was stare into those empty, lifeless eyes. At this point, the captain believed that he was the cause of all of the turmoil and quietly faded into the background.

If Thomas had his wits about him, he would have noticed the tall, handsome priest who was fast approaching from the other direction. Only when they were side by side did Thomas look up, but it was too late. Thomas was jolted out of his trance when the priest's gun suddenly appeared from nowhere, only to be rammed into his side.

"What the heck? Oh my God, it's you! What do you want?" Thomas was instantly terrified.

Philippe just smiled and then whispered, "Now then, Mr. Moore. If you don't want any harm to come to you or your fiancée, I suggest that you do exactly as I say." Thomas nodded in compliance.

"That's good. Now you and I are going to go for a little ride. My car is just up the street from where I came. Please, do not shout out or I will be forced to kill you. I think that you know by now that I will do so without hesitation." Thomas nodded again.

Philippe returned the gun to his holster in one swift move and moved down the street, with Thomas in tow. "Nice and normal now," Philippe whispered to Thomas. "We wouldn't want to disturb such an idyllic street, would we?"

The car wasn't very far at all. Philippe assisted Thomas into the passenger's side and then slipped behind the wheel of the Audi. All the while Thomas was motionless, very much aware what the priest was capable of.

Driving through the streets of Washington, Philippe pulled up in front of a mansion, which had seen better days. He commented, "She's beautiful, isn't she? The house was built as the manse to an adjacent church over one hundred years ago, but unfortunately the church burnt down ten years ago. The house is now used as a retreat of sorts. Of course, it was vacated and put to my disposal by the Inner Circle. My understanding is that once I'm finished here, the house will be torn down and the property will be redeveloped for assisted and subsidized housing. It will be made available primarily to Catholics, of course. It's one way to assure that the flock is forever in gratitude to the church."

Thomas didn't know what to say, so he kept quiet.

Philippe continued to ramble on about the history of the house as he pushed a small button on the car's console. The big, old iron gates parted, and the priest slowly drove up the long, tree-lined driveway, which split off and curved to the back of the mansion. Philippe hit the button again, and the door of the attached garage opened, allowing Philippe to drive right in without any prying eyes on them. With a definitive thump, the garage door slammed back down, giving Thomas a feeling of being sealed inside a coffin.

As Philippe was about to exit the car, he hesitated for a moment, as though deep in thought, before speaking to Thomas. "Mr. Moore, please understand this. You can be my guest or my prisoner. In some ways, I wish you would resist, but I don't think that you will. I can see that David Rose's white powder is already wearing off. Unfortunately, that's the problem with alchemy. Unlike an everlasting faith, chemical effects never last. They strive to achieve the Philosopher's Stone and then what? The funniest thing is that no alchemist has gotten that far."

With that summation, Philippe exited the car, walked around to the passenger's side, and opened the door for Thomas to exit. Philippe couldn't help but get in one last jab before they entered the manse: "Thomas, I forgot to mention that it was here that I had the pleasure of spending her last evening with the young concierge from the inn." Thomas stood up, stunned.

A wicked grin appeared across Philippe's lips. "I told her that the house had belonged to a dear old aunt, who had just passed away and left it to me. The first half of the evening we made wild love. She was a hungry one, that's for sure. But the second half of the evening was even better. At first, she thought that I was just upping the kinkiness a little. After that, I tortured her to the point that she would have committed any depravity that I demanded, if I would let her go. She begged me to stop, the whore. I absolved her of all of her sins before I strangled her."

XXIII

CHIEF OF THE TABERNACLE
Nine days ago
THE CAPITAL

The tension at the Georgetown home was unbearable. After seeing to Janet, her grandfather had phoned Danny Sullivan and reported Thomas's abrupt departure and disappearance the previous day. Fearing the worst, the full power of the Rose family went into hyper speed. Danny immediately arranged an all-points bulletin through the police and the FBI. Meanwhile, Jimmy urged their entire list of covert contacts to monitor the capital's closed-circuit cameras and cellular airwaves for any facial or voice patterns resembling those of Philippe De Smet.

The biggest problem was that when Janet woke from her induced sleep and learned that Thomas had disappeared, she became unhinged. David had never seen his granddaughter act like this. She was normally a rational, mature, and controlled person. He was so alarmed with her emotional state that he asked Dr. Sarah Cohen to come as soon as she could. Luckily, Sarah was due for a forty-eight-hour break in her schedule and arrived at the house almost immediately, only to spend the evening in one of the spare bedrooms after giving Janet another sedative. Janet's visions still continued after that well into the night before she calmed down and fell into a heavy sleep.

To top it off, the two guardians hadn't turned up a single piece of information concerning the Jesuit priest outside of the general profiling listed on several Vatican and church websites. As far as the internet was concerned, Philippe De Smet was an ordained Catholic priest and a brilliant scholar who had obtained doctorates in divinity and behavioral psychology and was a guest professor at Boston College and other Catholic universities. It struck Jimmy as ironic that Dr. De Smet was identified as the Vatican's expert on the Spanish Inquisition.

Janet's cell phone had also been incessantly ringing, with further inquiries from the news outlets and even a few preliminary approaches from publishers and movie executives. It seemed that the public had embraced the story surrounding Albert Pike. There was even social media chatter that the alternative right and left were going to stage rallies in front of the Temple on the day the exhibit opened.

Meanwhile, Jimmy had called in several senior teams from the Rose CC security company in New York. As a result, the entire floor of the RCC Washington office had been commandeered. Now there was a flurry of battle-hardened veterans going about their work, with many of them trying to electronically infiltrate the meeting site.

Finally, the time was quickly approaching noon, with Danny preparing to meet De Smet in front of the Grant Memorial. Although he didn't want to leave the command center that had been set up in the office between his and Jimmy's, he had an inkling that Philippe De Smet was involved in Thomas's disappearance. Still, it wasn't a meeting that he was looking forward to, since he would be going in blind—no backup, communications, or gun. He couldn't have felt more vulnerable.

Just then, Jimmy popped his head into his office. "Danny, your car is all set. Are you ready to go?"

Danny had been staring out the window at the Washington

monument but turned to acknowledge Jimmy. "Yes, I'll be there in a moment. I was just thinking."

Knowing that Danny always got a little melancholy before going into battle, Jimmy knew that talking was the best thing for him. "Listen, Danny, Thomas may have gone to a friend's house or an all-night diner for all we know."

Danny appreciated what Jimmy was attempting to do. "Jimmy, do you remember when Janet took off one night because her father refused to let her go to that New York nightclub? Her parents were frantic, and so were we. Finally we get a call the next morning from that Catholic priest down at St. Patrick's saying that he found her curled up on one of the pews, sound asleep. I don't know what freaked Solomon more: her disappearing all night or the fact that she sought refuge in a Catholic church."

They both laughed. It was exactly what Danny needed. "OK, let's get this over with. You're sure that the guys will have the site under remote surveillance by the time I arrive?"

"If there's an installed camera or microphone nearby, whether it's public or private, we'll have tapped into it before you even get there. That's a promise. Leave your cell phone on silent just so we can track you and, hopefully, pick up the conversation between the two of you. We can't use a drone because of the restricted airspace, but don't worry. I'll be there if your ass needs saving."

The quip was wasted, as Danny was already going down in the elevator before Jimmy could finish the last sentence.

Danny arrived at the parking area ten minutes early. The sun was almost directly above him. He got out of the car, took off his raincoat, and threw it back into the car before locking it. He proceeded toward the memorial. Once there, he stood around, admiring the statue of Grant sitting atop his horse and the scene that unfolded before him. Grant appeared to be pointing stoically to the west.

Danny took in the entire scene. The air was still, so there was barely a ripple on the reflecting pool; the water appeared almost black. Here and there, tourists had stopped to take pictures, and one or two joggers were kicking up their heels along the pathway. The setting was perfect for surveillance, out in the open and very public.

Just as Danny was feeling a little bit more at ease about the situation, a young boy, no more than twelve, rode his bike up to him and stopped. The boy asked, "Are you Mr. Sullivan?" Danny responded, "Yes, I am." The boy seemed pleased that he had picked the right man. "Your friend told me to tell you that he's sitting under those trees over there waiting for you. He said that it was much cooler than standing in the sun." The boy pointed to just north of the memorial, where a small grove of leafy trees afforded a considerable amount of shade. Danny nodded to the boy and groped in his pocket for a $20 bill. Handing it to the boy, he commented, "That's great. He's an old friend whom I'm looking forward to meeting. Here's a tip for your trouble."

The boy went to halfheartedly protest, as the other man had also given him $20, but Danny was already on the move. The boy just shrugged and rode away, quite happy with the $40 that he had earned for five minutes of work.

Making his way into the shadows under the tree canopies, Danny immediately spotted his prey. Philippe was sitting on a wooden bench, acting as though he was on his lunch break. Rather odd, given the circumstances; Philippe waved to Danny to come on over, as though they were old friends. Danny warily approached Philippe, only to be greeted as though they certainly knew each other: "Ah, Danny, come and sit down."

As Danny went to sit down, he spied the leather satchel lying flat on the bench between them. He immediately recognized it as belonging to Thomas. The stakes of the game had been raised once again.

Danny wanted to try to get the upper hand in this rather bizarre game within a game. "Philippe De Smet, I presume?" Philippe nodded in reply before Danny continued, "I see that you have Mr. Moore's satchel. I therefore presume that you know his whereabouts."

Philippe smiled with the wickedest of smiles before replying, "Yes, of course. To answer your silent question: he is safe, for the moment.

May I also commend you on the fact that you came alone? I can see that you are an intelligent man." It was Danny's turn to nod.

Continuing, Philippe reached into the satchel and produced another one of his little black boxes, which he then switched on and placed on top of the satchel. In this case, Danny discerned a very minor hum emanating from the box. Even though he immediately knew the purpose of the box, he allowed Philippe this little victory. "Ah, Mr. Sullivan, I can see by your eyes that you know what this little box can do. Fortunately for me, your Mr. O'Reilly is not the only one well versed in cybersecurity and countermeasures. This little black box is preventing your cell phone from transmitting our GPS location or our conversation and is jamming any directional listening devices within one thousand meters. Don't you just love modern technology? The Vatican is equipped with several larger versions of this device. They're great when the pope wants to pray without cell phones going off all around him." Philippe chuckled at his own joke.

Danny had heard enough. "Cut the crap. What is it that you want?"

"Fine, if that's the way you want to play it." Philippe adjusted his position to face the reflecting pool. "I desire a simple exchange: Mr. Moore's life for all thirty-three of the Pike Letters. There's one other thing: Ms. Rose and Mr. Moore must then hold a press conference at which time they confess to forging the letters and making the whole thing up. This will take place on the same evening that the Pike exhibit is supposed to open, with all of the Masonic dignitaries present. Now that's not too much to ask, is it? I think it's an extremely fair exchange."

Thinking fast, Danny countered, trying to drag any bit of information out of Philippe that he could use to his advantage. "That's it? What's to prevent us from copying the letters and presenting them to the world as the originals?"

"You could try, but as you very well know, the Vatican is very good at producing a bevy of experts whose singular purpose is to dispute the authenticity of anything that threatens the church. Look at Dr. Karen King and her Gnostic fragment, which said that Mary Magdalene was the wife of Jesus. Ms. King's academic reputation was ruined, and she was forced by her university to recant her words. Even when we were dealing with fiction such as *The Da Vinci Code,* the Vatican rolled out a number of renowned theologians who dispelled the myth with a single stroke of the pen or a single interview."

Philippe then got serious. "But you won't break our deal, because you realize that I'm your match and regardless of how long it would take, I would hunt down your precious High Priestess, Ms. Rose, and her captain, Mr. Moore, and kill them both. No, Mr. Sullivan, you're much smarter than that. You have my word as the next pope that if I receive the original letters and the Rose family accepts the embarrassment and shame of confessing to forging the letters, it all will be over. With any luck, the question of Albert Pike's so-called genius will also come to light, to the point that Freemasonry will be exposed once and for all for what it is—a devious cult aimed at undermining the Vatican."

"Ah, I see it more clearly now. You want to restore the Catholic Church's dominance over the world, and to do that you need to eliminate the freethinkers and philosophers. To you, *free will* must be an evil attribute."

Philippe waved his hand as though he was already addressing the multitudes. "I must say, you're very astute. You know, the Vatican could use a few good men like yourself and Mr. O'Reilly. After all, you were raised as Irish Catholics."

Danny almost spat out his next comment. "Yes, we were raised Catholic but as Irish-Americans, we were allowed to make our own choice. It was the Irish monks who took to the windswept outer isles and beyond in order to preserve the true Christian tenets before the church fully developed. Through their shedding of all earthly goods, they came to be closer to God than any other so-called men of God. They were the ones who reconciled the ancient mysteries with the Christian mysteries. These ultimately became the basic beliefs of Christian Freemasonry. Through a lifetime of studies, Pike was able to follow this thread all the way back to its origin in order to *reason* the very essence of God. This is what you fear the most, isn't it, Philippe?"

The reason and logic presented by Danny Sullivan bit Philippe De Smet right in his soul. However, the Jesuit priest showed no emotion. Instead he pocketed the black box and stood up to leave. But as was his practice, he left something for Danny to ponder. "There are four days to go before the exhibit. I will send you an email tomorrow with instructions as to how and when the exchange will occur. Just to prove to you that I am not bluffing, you may keep Thomas's satchel as a gift. Within it, you will find his wallet, phone, and passport. If you access his phone, there is a short video showing that he is still alive. You will also get a glimpse of his fate if you deviate from my instructions in any way whatsoever. I hope that I've made myself clear, Mr. Sullivan?"

The Jesuit priest then turned and triumphantly walked away, not waiting for Danny to respond.

Danny sat on the bench and recounted the surreal meeting. Perplexed and frustrated, he reached into Thomas's satchel and extracted his phone. He turned it on and saw that it had been fully charged. Danny couldn't help but smile. *Typical Thomas: no password or PIN number in use.*

Scrolling through the various apps, Danny thumbed the video icon and waited as an image appeared on the screen. It was of Thomas, who was securely strapped to a heavy wooden chair. As the video ran on, he watched Thomas's head loll to one side and then the other. It was obvious that he had been drugged. Sitting in his lap was this day's *Washington Post,* clearly illustrating that he was still alive.

Then the video faded and another one appeared. This one was even more disturbing. It showed the young concierge, stripped naked and bound to a heavy iron-railed bed by leather straps at her wrists and ankles. She had a wild stare in her eyes. *Total fear!* The video only went on for less than thirty seconds, but he would remember her pleas for the rest of his life. Between sobs and screams, she was offering to do anything for her freedom, even willing to confess to her sins. *The bastard was smart enough not to put himself into any frame of either of the two videos.*

Danny shut off the phone. Tears were welling up in his eyes. *To think: all in the name of God.*

XXIV

PRINCE OF THE TABERNACLE

Eight days ago

THE CAPITAL

Although Danny had briefed his entire security team the moment he returned to RCC headquarters from his meeting with De Smet, he deliberately kept the occupants of the Georgetown home in the dark. He knew that the contents of the two videos would devastate not only Janet but all those around her. The brutality and sickness reflected in the two thirty-second clips were beyond anything he had encountered in more than thirty-five years on the job. Besides, he needed time to think about how he was going to cut the heads off this three-headed snake once and for all.

It was midmorning at the office, and Jimmy had close to twenty-four hours to analyze the two videos. What he was shown also deeply disturbed him, especially because the perpetrator was an ordained priest who suggested that he could become the new pope. As Jimmy walked down the hallway toward Danny's office, all he could imagine was

De Smet walking out onto the Vatican's papal balcony to the cheers of a million followers.

Reaching Danny's door, he gently knocked on the glass partition and then entered. Danny was sitting at his desk and looked up from behind his upright laptop screen. "Come on in. I was just about to call you. Do you have anything?"

Jimmy gently laid Thomas's phone down on the edge of Danny's desk and took the seat directly opposite Danny. "Unfortunately, no. I can't believe that this guy hasn't made one mistake by now. He disabled the GPS tracking somehow, so that Thomas's movements for the last three weeks have been wiped clean. I can't even get a ghost mapping from his main server or from any Wi-Fi that he's accessed. I scanned the videos frame by frame, dot by dot. There's nothing there that can provide a clue to the whereabouts of his hideout. The only thing that we can assume is that it's probably within the District somewhere, but I can't even say that for certain. Thomas uses for the most part one of the three major service providers out of Canada and has a roaming package that allows him to tie into all major servers here in the United States. It's like his social footprint has been obliterated."

Danny sat quietly, pondering a Google image of the capital that he had pulled up before him. He leaned back before expressing his frustration. "Jimmy, this guy has us over a barrel. He practices plausible denial as though it was a religion. To tell you the truth, I'm stumped. I just don't know what to do next."

Never had Jimmy seen his best friend so desperate. Although they never really spoke about it, the two had a close bond between them that was intense. Nonetheless, Jimmy knew what they had to do next, no matter how painful. "Danny, we have to tell them sometime. We're working to that bastard's timetable, and we really have no clue what is next, other than we're now only four days away from the grand opening."

"Yes, I'm quite aware of that. OK, let's take a run over to Georgetown and break the news to Janet and the others. Even if we don't show her the contents of Thomas's phone, the news is going to break her heart, although I know what she's going to do. She's going to agree to the bastard's terms. She'll do anything to keep Thomas safe. It could mean the downfall of RCC and the Rose family itself, Freemasonry as we know it, and possibly the beginning of the end of free will around the world. I really couldn't blame her, though. The guilt that she must be feeling is probably eating away at her." Jimmy nodded in agreement.

Having decided to relay what they now knew, Danny stood up from his desk. He was just about to push his laptop screen down when his email pinged, signaling a new message. Sitting back down, he scrolled to the top of his inbox. Danny sighed as his eyes fixed on the heading: *Society of Jesus, Re: One of God's Soldiers II.*

Danny once again waited for the bottom-right icon to turn green, and then he opened the email. It read: *Mr. Sullivan. I believe by now that you have decided that the exchange is the only alternative. With this in mind, I will expect Ms. Rose to present to me personally the thirty-three Pike Letters tonight at ten o'clock sharp, right in front of the Grant Memorial. No attempts at any tricks, please. If I am satisfied, I will then indicate to you via email where Mr. Moore can be found, safe and sound. Otherwise I will indicate where his parts are scattered.*

Jimmy had shifted to allow himself to look over Danny's shoulder and read the email simultaneously. He whistled out loud after he finished the last sentence and then remarked, "What a bastard! He knows that Thomas is his ace in the hole. We can't even set a trap for him, or Thomas is dead. I'm sure of that. No riddles anymore. He spits just plain venom this time."

"Yes, it appears so. Well, we have our instructions. Let's go and tell them the bad news."

The two warrior-monks drove silently from their temporary headquarters to David Rose's house. Although it was quickly approaching noon, neither of them appeared to be hungry. Both men feared breaking the terrible news to everyone, especially to the woman they considered their surrogate daughter.

Since they phoned ahead only to say that they were coming over, as the car pulled up to the curb Janet was at the front door, anxiously awaiting their arrival. She instinctively knew that Danny and Jimmy had news concerning Thomas. Peering over her shoulder were both her grandfather and Sarah Cohen. Janet wasn't the only one who was concerned beyond the breaking point.

As Danny walked up to the front door, it was as though he was carrying the fate of the world on his shoulders. Sensing this, Janet instinctively drew her hand to her mouth and exclaimed, "Oh my God, Danny, it's about Thomas. I know that it is. I can sense it. Is he dead?"

Danny held up his hand as though to signal that any news of this nature should be discussed in private, so Janet, her grandfather, and Sarah all backed away and allowed Danny and Jimmy to enter the hallway. Jimmy quietly closed the door behind him.

"No, he's not dead. For now, he's very much alive, but I need all of you to listen to me very carefully. We don't have much time, and fateful decisions have to be made—decisions that will determine if Thomas dies or lives. So I need everybody to focus." Danny grabbed Janet by the arms and gazed into her eyes. "Janet, look at me. Do you understand me?"

It was as though a switch had been thrown on. Janet stood upright and stared back into Danny's eyes, almost boring a hole into his skull. She knew then and there what she had to do. She could always read Danny's mind. "Danny, you don't have to ask the question. You already know my answer. We'll somehow figure this out and prevent that monster from fulfilling what he believes now to be his eternal destiny. But for now we have to follow his instructions."

Jimmy shook his head in amazement. He had stopped trying to figure out how Janet could read his and Danny's thoughts, even though they had tried on numerous occasions to develop the skill to block her out. Janet's intuitive powers were too strong for the both of them combined.

"Let's go into the living room, and we'll brief all of you." Danny looked toward David, who shook his head just enough for Danny to understand that they had no alternative but to give in to De Smet's demands.

They all made themselves as comfortable as possible before Danny outlined the dire scenario. "De Smet has provided us with an ultimatum. Janet is to bring the thirty-three original Pike Letters to the Grant Memorial tonight at ten o'clock sharp. That's where the exchange will happen."

Sarah Cohen, who had remained quiet all of this time, felt the urge to present a positive viewpoint. "That doesn't sound so bad. We can make copies of the originals and authenticate them using other historical references. From the small bit that I understand, if David and Janet can't solve the puzzle, then neither can De Smet."

"If it were only that simple," Jimmy jumped in. "There's a lot more at stake here. De Smet is nobody's fool. So far he's avoided implicating himself in any of this. Even his email threatening Thomas can be dismissed as nothing more than a zealous outrage." Jimmy looked to Danny for guidance in terms of telling them about the two videos, but from their eye contact, Jimmy understood that he shouldn't mention either Thomas's current state or the filmed murder of the concierge.

Danny picked up where Jimmy left off. "There's one other thing. Janet and Thomas are to hold a press conference before the exhibit, at which time they are to confess to forging the letters and making the whole thing up. This would most probably be the beginning of the end of the Rose family's reputation, and we all know that the commodities business is based on trust and integrity. De Smet is also demanding that all of the invited Masonic dignitaries from around the world attend the same press conference. By association, he wants to embarrass Freemasonry beyond repair."

Being the first to realize what this meant, David Rose exclaimed, "Not only that but, by extension, both the Jewish and Muslim faiths would be implicated, because those religions are also associated with the ancient mysteries. What a simple but devious plot! The only religion to benefit would be Catholicism. As for decoding the letters, the

Jesuits have resources and information that is beyond our knowledge. They'll eventually unlock Pike's secret and use the ancient technology to threaten the world into submission."

"Exactly!" shouted Jimmy, more animated than anybody had ever seen him before. "And if we don't go through with the deal, then we know that Thomas is dead, and Janet and probably the rest of us will be hunted animals for the rest of our lives." Jimmy was on a morbid roll. "And given how good the bastard is, I don't give any of us more than a year."

Danny glared at Jimmy for the brutal comment, but Jimmy just shrugged.

"Oh my God," Janet almost blurted out the words. "OK, I'll do it. Saving Thomas is our first concern. That will buy us some time. If Thomas and I have to confess to forging the letters, then I'm prepared to do that also."

"We both figured that would be the case," Jimmy sighed. "We're going to follow the priest's instructions to the letter. Heaven help us."

Enveloped by the nighttime shadows cast by the memorial's lighting, Janet stood and stared upward at General Ulysses S. Grant silently resting atop his horse. As she waited for Philippe De Smet to show himself, she thought it odd that Grant was staring due west into the darkness. *I wonder what he's searching for. Could he be thinking of the thousands of young soldiers who died on both sides of the Civil War? For what?* Janet pondered. *Come on, come on, you snake; let's get this over with.*

Suddenly he was there. Janet had sensed his presence and turned around just in time to confront her own personal demon. Except, in this case, the demon was a startlingly handsome man with eyes like two hot coals. Janet shuddered as he drew himself closer before saying, "Good evening, Ms. Rose. It's a lovely evening, isn't it?"

Janet, taken aback by Philippe's casual demeanor, froze and said nothing in reply.

"Ah, I see, the cat's got your tongue. No matter; I also see that you've brought what I desire above all else." Philippe pointed to the large manila envelope in Janet's right hand.

Janet couldn't take her eyes off this man; his power was that great. She stood there and raised the envelope in complete and utter defeat.

Reaching out, Philippe gently eased the envelope out of Janet's hand, politely saying, "Thank you!" He opened the envelope's flap and pulled out one of the letters. *Ah, letter number 18: Prince Rhodocanakis of Greece and the Rosicrucians. He must have provided one of the last pieces of the puzzle for Pike and MacLeod Moore.*

Satisfied, Philippe looked back at Janet and said, "Very good, Ms. Rose. You've shown that you are not a stupid person. I admire that. It really is quite unfortunate that we will not be able to get to know each other in a more physical way. I could easily show you that fine degree between pain and pleasure."

A cold chill overcame Janet. De Smet's words made her skin crawl.

"Now remember the second part of our bargain," he continued. "You and your beloved Thomas will act as though everything is normal, but when it comes time to open the exhibit with a press conference, with all of your Masonic guests surrounding you, you will confess to forging the Pike Letters for your family's personal gain. Do I have your binding word on that?"

Janet managed to nod her head and to whisper, "Yes, I agree."

De Smet gave her a cruel sneer. "Fine. If you do that, you have my word that you can live out your life in peace and solitude. You and your beloved captain, though, will have to find a quiet, secluded place to live out your lives together. No matter: I imagine that the Rose family fortune will see to that! What's left of it, that is, after I finish destroying your entire family's legacy."

Managing to gather her goddess courage, Janet lifted her head and once again became the High Priestess of the Temple. Startled by the sudden transformation, Philippe took an involuntary step backward. Janet's skin started to take on the glow of countless centuries of enlightenment and feminine wisdom.

"You will not triumph. Evil never triumphs over goodness. I want you to understand that."

De Smet regained his composure. "Really? It appears to me that I've already won the game. Just to show you that I am a man of honor and not entirely evil, your precious Thomas can be found just over in that grove of trees passed out on a bench. Don't worry; he's just sleeping . . . a mild sedative. I've made it look as though he's a street person, liquor bottle in a paper bag and all. I want him to be bright-eyed for your press conference in three days. Now please remember: no tricks, or I will come back and haunt you and your entire family. By the Holy Trinity, I pledge that I will hunt you down one by one."

With that unholy proclamation, he spun on his heels and was gone, confident that he wouldn't be followed. The little black box humming in his jacket pocket assured him that all electronic devices had been disabled and would continue to be so.

Just to be on the safe side, he would continue to assure himself that Mr. Sullivan and Mr. O'Reilly and company would not be following him back to the manse. Knowing that the drugs he had given Thomas would cause some short-term memory loss, he was confident that Thomas couldn't lead them there either. Of course, he wanted to examine the letters himself, one by one, but as he had waited a lifetime, a few hours more wouldn't hurt. He knew that the Inner Circle would also be delighted. He could almost feel the papal dress weighing gently on his shoulders, along with the pope's miter on his head.

As fast as Philippe was, Janet was faster. She sprinted to the adjacent grove and located Thomas curled up on one of the benches within the dark shadows, just as Philippe had indicated. She glided next to Thomas and checked to see if he was breathing. Relieved, his breathing was steady. Amazingly, Thomas was sleeping as though he hadn't a care in the world.

Janet reached into her jacket pocket and retrieved her phone. The signal was once again at full strength and she hit her speed dial. Danny immediately came on the line: "Thank God, it's you. Are you OK?"

Almost breathless, Janet responded, "Yes, I'm fine. I'm just a little startled, that's all. De Smet took the letters and left. As some sort of warped peace offering, he also left me with Thomas. He's been given a sedative and is sleeping."

Danny almost yelled into the phone. "Janet, don't touch him. I don't trust De Smet one bit. We've finally picked up the GPS signal on your phone. Jimmy will be there with a team in less than five minutes. They'll do a full electronic and medical scan on Thomas. We can't be too careful. Do you understand me?"

"Yes, of course." With that, Janet sat cross-legged on the ground next to Thomas. It was only then that, overcome with emotion, she quietly wept.

XXV

KNIGHT OF THE BRAZEN SERPENT

Seven days ago

GEORGETOWN

Following the recovery of Thomas and the RCC medical team's assurance that nothing had been done to him other than being sedated, everybody returned to the Georgetown brownstone. Here Dr. Cohen determined that all Thomas needed was to sleep off the effects of the sedation. But just to make sure that he was fully hydrated, she hooked him up to an intravenous bag full of electrolytes.

Janet, on the other hand, needed another of her grandfather's mild sedatives in order to be able to sleep. The ordeal of coming face-to-face with such a brazen serpent had really shaken her. It was around midnight that Janet made her way up to the spare bedroom, where Thomas was laid out comfortably.

With a sigh of relief that could be heard throughout the house, she gently slid beside Thomas and protectively wrapped her left arm over his chest. Even though he could not hear her, she whispered, "Thomas,

I'm so sorry—so sorry for driving you away to fall into the clutches of that snake. Don't worry my love, we'll think of something—we have to think of something." Then she was asleep, continuing the same dream that haunted her.

As the evening mist started to roll in from the sea, the High Priestess found her captain of the guards lying peacefully in what appeared to be the fields of Elysium. She knew all too well the temptation to which they had succumbed. She also knew that their actions had angered the forces of Nature—Mother Earth—so she thought it strange that such an idyllic place would remain surrounding the Temple. As she approached, she could see that her lover's eyes were wide open but blank—staring at the twinkling stars and moon above in the blackened sky. It was then that she noticed the bloody sword resting in his hand and the spreading scarlet stain across his tunic and armor. It was evident that the captain had sacrificed himself in order to try to save her.

Every bit of the priestess's soul went dark as she knelt beside her lover. Tears streamed down her face. As she fell beside the captain, her aura was fading. The flow of cosmic energy ebbed out of her body. Her last desperate motion was to lay her arm across her lover and to draw herself into him. As the darkness enveloped both of them, she spoke to the Goddess—to Venus—asking forgiveness for all her sins. It was as though Isis and Osiris had melted into an androgynous form—neither male nor female—one inert element.

Satisfied that both Thomas and Janet were safe and fast asleep, Danny, Jimmy, David, and Sarah, all sitting in the living room, turned their attention to the problem at hand. Before summarizing the situation, though, Danny had helped himself to a cold plate of blintzes and sour cream. Sarah had also distributed four large mugs of strong hot coffee, along with a plate of cheeses and meats, from which everyone helped themselves. It was a mildly good sign that everyone appeared to be getting their appetites back.

Wiping his mouth with a napkin, Danny started, "Once again, De Smet outfoxed us. I thought for sure that he would dump Thomas somewhere after he had taken the letters from Janet and authenticated them. He knew that he could make good on his escape if we were pre-occupied with Thomas. The arrogance and vanity of the man know no bounds."

It was late at night, and all of them were exhausted, but it was Janet's grandfather who had the revelation. "Danny, that's it! That's the key to defeating this black knight at his own game. You've got to play on his vanity. It's apparently his only weakness. I bet that right now he's sitting back at his lair perusing the Pike Letters and gloating like he's already won the game."

Jimmy had found his own plate of blintzes while everybody else was talking, but he put his plate down when David started to talk. "As far as it appears, yes, he's won. Now all that is left to do is to see that Janet and Thomas confess to forging the letters. May I remind you it's a death sentence for all of us if they don't go through with the press conference as agreed?"

"But don't you see?" David Rose was quite animated at this point. "Philippe De Smet believes that he is all powerful. This guy truly believes that his divine destiny is to become the next pope. Given as much, I can't believe that he will not want to witness the downfall of the Rose family and Freemasonry in person. I'll bet my life on it!"

Danny sat quiet for a moment. "Mr. Rose, I believe that you've hit on something. Why didn't I think of this before? Of course he'll want to be there to witness the climax of his grand scheme—his ultimate triumph."

"But how do you draw him out at the right moment?" Sarah Cohen didn't want to be an outsider in contributing to the possibility of turning the odds in their favor.

"I can think of only one way of making sure that Mr. De Smet attends the press conference in person. For the remaining two days, we go on an all-out media offensive. We'll have to use Thomas and Janet once again, but I think that they'll buy into the plan. We need to double down on the publicity and social media surrounding the grand opening of the Pike Letters exhibit. We won't say anything about the originals not being available."

Danny thought for a second and then continued, "Part of that increased effort should focus on drawing the church into the fray. Let's have Janet claim that the Pike Letters speak of Pike's discovery of a definitive link between Scottish Rite Masonry and an advanced technological civilization that existed before the Flood. That will drive the creationists crazy."

David chimed in again, "Which will play against De Smet's self-assuredness and vanity. He may actually start to doubt whether Janet and Thomas are going through with their end of the bargain. As a result, he will want to be there in person to make sure the agreement is met. I would think that he may even make himself be known, trying to throw the fear of God into Janet and Thomas once more. Since the press conference is going to be held within the foyer of the Temple, it shouldn't be too hard to spot him, no matter how he's disguised."

"With that, then," David paused in order for everyone to absorb the faint ray of hope that presented itself, "I suggest that everyone finish their food and get some sleep. I've learned from experience that sleep is crucial to being able not only to function but to thrive. And we will need our wits about us for the next few days if we are to defeat the rule of evil and darkness."

Both Jimmy and Danny looked at David in absolute bewilderment. Sometimes the words of wisdom offered by Janet's grandfather were incomprehensible to even those who possessed the thirty-third degree of the Scottish Rite.

One person who would have understood what the aging Supreme Magus was saying was sitting at the head of a massive dining-room table, the centerpiece of the furniture left in the old manse. Here, over two hundred years ago, members of the Inner Circle had gathered regularly in order to absorb the power generated by the underlying patterns of Washington.

Here too, over a hundred years ago, both of the earlier Jesuit priests,

Father De Smet and Father Hoffman, would have sat—a fact that would not have been lost on Philippe, for he believed he was following in their sacred footsteps. The two priests had been seeking the same thing that he now had access to, if only he could decipher the secret.

Poring over the Pike Letters, Philippe was vainly trying to decipher the hidden message, the coded secret that they contained—a secret that led to a hidden crypt containing an ancient knowledge that could be used to control the world.

Indeed, for centuries, learned adepts such as the Founding Fathers of the United States understood the dual powers that balanced America and the world itself. For centuries before the American Revolution, the inner circles of the Spanish Jesuits and the French Sulpicians also understood this need for balance and battled for its control. The inner circles of the Knights Templar and the European royal families also understood that the continent that the natives called Turtle Island balanced all of the Earth's inner powers. Here was the real reason the battle for the control of North America had been waged for four hundred years. Knowing how to unsettle that balance would ultimately lead to the control of the world.

Seeking the same enlightenment, Philippe was presently absorbed in this other world—a world he understood all too well—where the active and passive powers of Nature taught the initiates in the ancient mysteries that the rule of evil and darkness is but temporary, and that the rule of Light and good is eternal.

Unfortunately, many modern initiates, including Philippe, believed that Albert Pike had discovered a way to harness Nature's power. In one sense, Pike did discover the higher power of the divine essence, but Philippe was unable to understand this, because his ego and his vanity prevented him from opening his heart to the truth.

The truth was that the location of the crypt had been revealed to Pike by the guardians—the Mide'win—the secret elders of the Grand Medicine Society as a reward for defending their rights against a hostile federal government. Pike had realized early on in his legal career that the indigenous peoples of North America maintained a far higher level of ancient enlightenment than Freemasonry.

The Mide'win believe that the truth can be found in the mind—in the soul—not outside of the body. In other words, the initiate must look inward, to his very self. Through a succession of seven degrees performed within the lodge, the initiate comes to understand how one truly relates to the universe. Having successfully moved through the seven degrees, one comprehends the eighth degree of infiniteness, which is forever perpetuated by the delicate balance between the human and spirit worlds. The adept is thus able to ascend to a higher level, enabled by the conductor—*Migiis.*

It is Migiis who possesses the ancients' knowledge and understanding of Mother Earth, the Creator, and the forces of Nature. His symbol is the Migiis seashell, whose interior spiral reflects the golden mean of sacred geometry. He is the teacher of astronomy and mathematics, of medicine and the arts, of agriculture and animal husbandry.

The practitioners of Mide'win taught the prophecy of the Seven Fires. Each fire represents a prophetical age, marking phases, or epochs, in the life of the people on Turtle Island. The Seven Fires prophecy, which represents key traditional teachings for North America, suggests that the different colors and traditions of all human beings can come together on a basis of respect.

The Algonquin are the keepers of the Seven Fires prophecy wampum. What many people do not realize is that what is known as the Larger Algonquin Nation covers an area that stretches from the East Coast all the way west to the foothills of the Rocky Mountains. Included within this larger nation are fifty-six independent nations, including the Algonquin, Ojibwa, Chippewa, Odawa, Potawatomi, Choctaw, Cherokee, and Blackfoot.

Albert Pike was granted the opportunity, rare for a nonnative, to glimpse the powerful spirit world, which affected him beyond comprehension.

XXVI

PRINCE OF MERCY

May 22, 1881

OUTSKIRTS OF OKLAHOMA CITY,
INDIAN TERRITORY

If any of the good citizens of Oklahoma City had encountered Albert Pike as he strode through the early-morning darkness toward the Indian encampment at the edge of town, they would have gotten the scare of their lifetime. Pike presented an imposing figure, all three-hundred-plus pounds and six feet, two inches of him, with flowing white beard and hair and piercing eyes. He wore a rare, much-prized, white buckskin body mantle over his woodsman's clothes—an outer tunic that bore a red Templar cross made of intricate native beadwork centered on his chest. After he had been initiated into the Grand Medicine Society, the natives had given him the name Great White Bear.

Dangling from Pike's left hip was an ornate Templar sword, sheathed in a richly engraved gold and silver scabbard. This was the sword he had carried throughout the Civil War during his command as a Confederate general. He also wore the purple-and-white and gold-braided apron and ornate purple-and-gold cuffs of the Sovereign Grand

Commander of the Scottish Rite of the Southern Jurisdiction of the United States of America.

As he hurried along, Pike's breath turned to mist as it met the cold, damp air. He knew he had to make the entrance of the Mide'win wigwam prior to the rising of the sun in the east. To be late would have been unacceptable to his Mide'win brothers, for part of their initial ceremonies was to give thanks to the Creator for once again sending the sun and its light and warmth.

Moving through the scattering of prairie teepees, which surrounded a central cooking fire and ceremonial circle, Pike was aware of many suspicious eyes that surveyed him from the shadows. Of course, they were looking more out of curiosity than malice, as word of the Great White Bear had spread throughout the Larger Algonquin Nation. The effect of seeing this legend up close was more than the children could comprehend, and they squealed in amazement. In an odd way, it was as though Santa Claus had been caught sneaking through the living room on Christmas Eve.

As he approached the long wigwam situated along the riverbank, Pike was confronted by two young braves who had been tasked with guarding the eastern doorway to the Otherworld. Both of them carried modern Remington rifles, suggesting that at one time or another they had either fought for or against the U.S. Army. Although they were several inches shorter than the hulking mass that approached, the larger of the two braves forcefully held up his hand, silently commanding Pike to stop.

Doing as he was told, Pike stopped in his tracks and proceeded to undo his oversized belt buckle. As his sword fell away, he effortlessly swung it up in his hand and offered it to the sentry, who grabbed it and then stepped aside. At the same time, the other sentry came far enough forward to run his hand over the beaded Templar cross, saying something in a language that Pike didn't recognize, except for a smattering of Welsh in the mix. The sentry appeared to stand at attention and salute before he bent down and pulled back the doorway's leather curtain, revealing the warm glow of the nearest fire.

It took considerable effort for the big bear of a man to bend down and crawl into the wigwam, but once he was through, he was able to stand back up without having to stoop. Looking toward the west end of the lodge, he recognized a number of old, familiar faces seated cross-legged on the ground. Here were some of the natives he had commanded during the Civil War. Yet he knew that he had to first pass scrutiny by the inner guard before he could relax and be officially received.

Greeting him was no other than Peter Pitchlynn Jr. himself, who came forward and exclaimed loud enough for all to hear, "Great White Bear, greetings! Do you come in peace?" To which Pike responded, "I come in peace." To which Peter exclaimed, "Then come in peace!" The outer guard moved in close and gave Pike as much as a bear hug as he could manage, given the size of the man who stood opposite him.

Peter stepped to Pike's right, grabbed him by the forearm, and conducted him to the west. They walked past the first three fires and stopped at the fourth. Peter bent down and reached inside a wooden bowl that lay just off to the side. Finding a handful of a mixture of tobacco, cedar, sage, and sweetgrass, he touched the earth and then lifted the mixture to the sky while giving thanks to the Creator. Next he threw the mixture into the fire, where it crackled and sparked, sending exploding embers in all directions.

Taking his cue from his conductor, Pike did the same, grunting slightly with satisfaction as the fire once again sparked and flamed after his mixture was offered up through the smoke. The two resumed their walk past the fifth fire, the sixth, and the seventh, finally arriving in the far west, before the elders.

The head shaman sitting before Pike stood to greet him. Although they were great friends and brothers, neither of the two showed any sign of recognition. Maintaining his silence, the shaman formed a square with his hands and then held up his right hand with his elbow bent to form a ninety-degree angle. In the background, a silent attendant constantly moved from fire to fire, ensuring that the coals were stirred and the fires glowed brightly. The smoke, taking the form of a serpent, wistfully made its way up and out of the wigwam through eight squares neatly cut and spaced along the top ridge line. There was no need for a smudge, as the swirling smoke had cleansed the entire assembly.

The remaining group of shamans also remained quiet, but they were obviously tense, as though waiting for something to happen. Then it came, gradually at first, and then in a staccato fashion. Starting with the first square in the east, the sun's first rays of the morning penetrated the wigwam with a shaft of light angling toward the ground. As it hit the second shaft, then the third, then the fourth, and so on, the wigwam was lit with a spectrum of light, like a quartz prism. The little spirit people danced around the firepits and center poles as the eighth shaft of light appeared to pierce Pike from the back.

Although he had sensed it before, he was still amazed at the energy that he felt. His skin tingled and glowed, as if the spark of life had entered Mother Earth's womb. Albert Pike was symbolically reborn that day. He had come a long way in his journey, having offered the repentance necessary to purify his soul. He managed to hold back his tears.

Witnessing the cleansing of his fellow Brother, the great shaman, known as Raven Who Sees All, threw his thin arms around Pike as best he could. Instinctively, Pike bent his head down and whispered just one word in the shaman's ear, "Golgotha." To which, the shaman replied, in broken English, "Place of the skull."

Satisfied with the proper greeting, the head shaman let out a whoop. Raven Who Sees All then pronounced, "Great White Bear, it is my honor to receive you in the lodge of the Mide'win—the Grand Medicine Society. We have gathered here to discuss the white man's encroachment into the last of our sacred native lands. You must help us argue our case before the Union's president. Come and sit in our place of honor." Raven Who Sees All pointed to a spot on the ground to the right of him.

Pike grunted in acknowledgment and deposited his massive bulk on the hard ground, which luckily had been covered with several layers of buffalo hide. The sun's warm glow, along with the many fires, was causing him to sweat, but the warmth was welcomed. Pike's body began to relax to the point where he allowed himself to easily enter the netherworld. Here he was safe and protected, buffered from the outer world by an invisible barrier. Some would call it a parallel dimension. Others saw it as ascending to another plane—a plane where the animal spirit world meets the physical, human world.

Seamlessly, without any signal that Pike detected, the eastern doorway was opened once again to a long line of women carrying wooden and clay vessels of food. There was bison, moose, deer, elk, rabbit, duck, and goose cooked in clay; dried strawberries and blueberries; bannock and other grain breads; and gourds with strange liquid concoctions, both hot and cold. The combined aromas overwhelmed the senses.

Following a small prayer of thanks to Mother Earth and the Creator, Raven Who Sees All indicated to the others that the feast was ready to be consumed. Albert Pike was amazed to see that Mide'win and Horn Society shamans were present from tribes extending to all boundaries of the Larger Algonquin Nation: Mi'kmaq from the eastern coast; Algonquin and Nipissing from northeast of the Great Lakes, Blackfoot, Nez Perce, and Blood Piegan from the west, and Cherokee and Choctaw from the south. There were even Ojibwa, Odawa, and Potawatomi of the Three Fires Confederacy. As each shaman shuffled past Pike, they all nodded in deep respect, as tribute to the honesty and integrity that he had brought to his position as intermediary.

Each medicine man ate in silence, with only a contented sigh or grunt being heard, for each man realized that others in the village were going without in order for this feast to be offered in honor of the Great White Bear. It was customary for the more able-bodied warriors and shamans to ensure that the women, children, and elderly were fed first, but this was a special occasion.

Everyone there knew that the Native North Americans were quickly losing their traditional hunting and fishing territories to the constant onslaught of white explorers, miners, and settlers. They were also aware that the federal government was systematically attempting to either assimilate or eliminate the indigenous peoples.

Raven Who Sees All did not eat much at all, as his heart was heavy with sorrow. As a result, he was the first to finish and stood to address the assembly of still-proud warrior-shamans. Holding up his arms to the sky, he pronounced, *"Bashoo, kwey, kwey, mino gigizheb! Ginoondezgade na? Ningashkendam!"* Then he exclaimed, "In honor of Great White Bear, I will attempt to speak in his native tongue." Shamans were quietly interpreting for those who didn't speak English as Raven Who Sees All continued to speak: "Since the beginning of time, our people have roamed this earth, through the mountains, over the water, across the windswept grass; following the fish, the buffalo, the elk, the deer; always recording our way by the sun, the moon, and the stars. We have moved our camps to follow the four seasons. We have done so because the ancients made a sacred oath with the Goddess—Mother Earth—to be her guardian. Everyone here knows that the Mide'win have always respected and followed the ways of the ancients, keeping the truth in our hearts. We have practiced our traditional ways and ceremonies in our sacred locations, giving thanks to Mother Earth, the forces of Nature, and to the Creator. We have been the stewards and guardians of the land and water for seven generations and will continue to do so, even as the white man presses farther westward. Even as our people die as fast as the buffalo dies, we have maintained the old ways. Remember, it is foretold in our prophecies that we will still be here when the white men are all gone."

Some of the younger medicine men within the group started to show their restlessness and unease at the mention of the white man's intrusion, but Raven Who Sees All fixed his eyes on them to be quiet. His black glare was enough to silence even the most outspoken of the group.

The head shaman appeared to be weighed down by the souls of all of those who came before him as he continued, "Many moons ago, the keeper of the Seven Fire prophecies, our Algonquin brothers, told us to leave our many great villages and to disperse into the wilderness, as white men from the east would be coming to tear us apart and destroy us. But they also told us that before that, a great warrior would be arriving. How would we know him and his signs? We would know him from the eight-pointed red cross that stands on his white chest. We would know him from the secret signs of the red people that he already possesses, including his love and respect for all that we know. We would know him from his great wisdom about the Earth and the sky, how to heal our people, and how to travel under the ground that we stand on."

Albert Pike knew that the head shaman was talking about Prince Henry Sinclair and the group of Knights Templar, who acted as guardians to the Holy Grail descendants at the end of the fourteenth century. Pike gently nodded his head in recognition as the head shaman continued, "We would also see that they knew how to make weapons from the rocks, using fire, and how to catch fish using nets. It was all of this that they gladly shared with us, and in return, we shared everything with them. But they too warned us of others who would be coming to search for and destroy them as well as us.

"That is when we agreed to keep their sacred secret, and they agreed to keep secret our sacred ways. The bond between us was sealed when those knights married into the various nations. Indeed many of you are direct descendants of those unions. The mixing of sacred and noble blood has kept us strong, and the combined magic has allowed us to survive among the chaos."

As Pike listened, he was reminded of stories that his Jesuit teachers told him of the original Knights Templar and how they found the Temple Treasure under the Temple of Solomon and spirited it away under the noses of the Muslims. He knew too that many of the ancient rituals of Freemasonry, especially the Scottish Rite, perpetuate some of the story. He often wondered how the Jesuits knew the stories to be true and, if everything was a secret, why they would have confided in him.

Finally, Raven Who Sees All said, "All my Brothers, the sun will always rise but will always set. Our power is waning like the sun at dusk. But do not shed a tear. We will once again rise up from the ashes. The raven will become the crow, feed on the carcass of the white man, and one day will change back to the trickster. On this day our people will once again dance and rejoice in the abundance of Mother Earth. On this day Nature will provide us with more food than we can eat and more water than we can drink. The prophecies tell us that we must remain strong and on guard until this day comes."

As if on cue, one of the fire keepers moved quickly down the line of fires and threw a small handful of gunpowder into each one. The resulting flash and smoke produced the desired dramatic effect.

Raven Who Sees All continued, "As warriors and guardians, we have protected the crypt of those who came before us, which contains the ancient knowledge and understanding. We have kept our promise to the red crosses and will continue to do so. Let Great White Bear, who is of the red crosses, witness this continuing oath. In return, he has promised to speak on our behalf when he returns to the white man's main village. He will convey to the white man's great chief that the red man has kept its promise and expects the white man to keep his. Our people are dying, slaughtered by the white soldiers. This is not our agreement. Why are we being punished? Did we not receive the original red crosses as our friends and Brothers?"

In the following silence, Pike could do nothing but sit with his eyes closed, contemplating the fate of these proud natives. *The federal government in Washington has betrayed these people. I will do my best to argue on their behalf, but I doubt it will make any difference. Christianity has taken root too deep. The wave of Manifest Destiny is too strong. The prairies and mountains offer too much good earth and lumber and gold and silver. It's obvious that the younger natives will fight until they can't fight any more. I just hope that the crypt remains hidden and intact until the world is ready to accept its contents.*

With the end of the head shaman's proclamation, all that was left was to initiate two young braves into the Grand Medicine Society's first three degrees. Pike knew that he could leave anytime, but out of respect he remained for the next three days and nights. He felt that it was the least that he could do, as he had been welcomed into the natives' secret society with open arms. His heart felt heavy, given the immense responsibility and trust that had been put on his shoulders.

Pike wished he could spend his remaining days with his honorable Mide'win Brothers. The otherworldly comfort and security of the wigwam was the most powerful mystical world he had ever experienced, far away from the distrust and evil that Pike felt in Washington.

XXVII

KNIGHT COMMANDER OF THE TEMPLE

7:00 a.m., Four days ago

HOUSE OF DAVID

The past twenty-four hours had been a flurry of activity. Both Thomas and Janet had awakened early the day before and spent the first hour in bed alone, holding each other and giving thanks that they were still alive. Neither appeared to have suffered any real physical effects from their shared ordeal, but they were still very upset about what was required of them.

The evil taste that Philippe De Smet had left in their mouths was almost too much to bear. Although they felt a little stronger by the time they came down to breakfast, after Danny briefed them on the plan to go forward, their trepidation once again set in.

The previous day had been filled with rushing around, preparing for the press conference, scheduled for five o'clock today, and the official opening of the exhibit immediately following. Janet and Thomas were purposely scheduled to spend the day concentrating on social media concerning the events. In this manner, the deadlier issue surrounding the Jesuit priest's threats would be pushed to the back of their minds. That plan had worked the previous day, but this morning it would be different.

As if on cue, Jimmy came rushing into the kitchen with the news. "Hey, guys, I hate to tell you this, but Danny and I were just informed that some influential senator who sits on the Scottish Rite's Supreme Council has convinced the council that moving the press conference outdoors to the steps of the Temple would be a major public-relations coup for Freemasonry!"

Janet was dismayed. "They can't be serious. What benefit does the Supreme Council see in exposing us even more to this madman?"

Danny had quietly taken his seat at the kitchen island and put down his coffee cup, which had seemed to be an extension of his very being for the past forty-eight hours, and said, "Janet, you have to appreciate that the Supreme Council is unaware of anything that is occurring outside the norm. As far as the Masonic world is concerned, what's been discovered should be shared with as many people as possible. They see this as a major triumph of scholarly endeavor by the one person—Albert Pike—who made the definitive connection between the ancient mysteries and modern Scottish Rite Masonry, proving the connection between heaven and earth, between God and man. For far too long, Freemasons have been seen by some as a covert, evil cult, bent on destroying civilization, normalcy, and formal religion, with Pike leading the battle. The Anti-Masonic movement of the 1800s never really died out. The Supreme Council has made the decision to finally come out of the shadows and into the light."

Sarah Cohen seemed almost besides herself with this new revelation. "But won't that expose Janet and Thomas to the point where you can't protect them? They won't have any chance of surviving if Philippe De Smet is in the crowd."

Danny Sullivan put his hand on Sarah's shoulder. The two had quickly become close. Even though he had spent a lifetime on the front lines, Danny had a keen spiritual awareness. "Hey now, what's going on? Remember that Jimmy and I are true present-day knights. We've devoted our lives to protecting you against evil and treachery. You've got to have faith in our abilities. But we can't execute our plan if all of you don't concentrate on our objective!"

"Danny's right," Thomas interjected. "If we're going to catch De Smet at his own game, we need to be at the top of our game. Now let's go over the plan once again."

Thomas was obviously feeling much calmer, partly because he was back on David's white powdered gold. Both Sarah and Janet raised their eyebrows at Thomas's positivity. It appeared to have an effect on everybody in the room.

Then Jimmy came back into the kitchen, killing the mood. "Hey, you all better see this." Jimmy grabbed the remote to the kitchen flat screen and flipped it on to the local news channel. The scene that appeared on the screen was one of chaos and uncertainty.

The news that the press conference was being moved to the steps of the Temple provided a unique opportunity for a stampede of protest from a wide range of society. The area in front of the podium had just increased twentyfold over the space that was to be made available inside the Temple.

Janet and Thomas rejoined the others just in time to see a full crew preparing a podium with lights and a sound system. The two sphinxes guarding the Temple steps seemed amused by the flurry of activity that was spreading out before them. The line of police, which had hastily assembled across the base of the steps, did not appear to be amused.

What caught the group's attention was the waist-high steel barriers being erected about ten feet away from the podium itself. To everybody's amazement, various groups were already staking out their territory just beyond the barriers. "It's a veritable soup of protesters, ranging from the professionals to those who are just plain nuts." Jimmy could never understand the need to be subtle.

Judging by the placards, the alternative right—the white supremacists, the white nationalists, the neo-Nazis—had arrived the earliest, which was somewhat confusing, judging by past events. Obviously, they had totally confused Pike's message and were falling back on the age-old adage that America had lost its greatness due to the extension of human rights to blacks and the allowing of refugees into the country. Men dressed in the white mantles of the Ku Klux Klan had even dared to show up in full regalia.

It was certainly easy to spot the alternative right, with their fanatical dress, red Confederate flags, and chain weapons hanging from their studded belts. What really gave them away were the shaved heads and requisite bad tattoos. Some of the cleaner-shaven ones wore brown shirts and ties along with swastika armbands. Others were sporting long, scraggly beards like those of Confederate soldiers. Many of them, no matter what their affiliation, also wore yellow vests.

In sharp contrast, there was the alternative left, which contained a mixture of preppy types and older, back-to-the-earth hippies who appeared, from their placards, to be more concerned about environmental abuse by the big corporate machine. They no doubt associated Freemasonry with money and corruption.

Then there were the Christian evangelicals and creationists, waving Bibles in one hand and placards in the other, which condemned all secret societies and followers of the ancient mysteries. Interspersed among this group were several dozen Mormons. Everyone seemed to take exception to Albert Pike and Freemasonry monopolizing the limelight.

The group around the kitchen island continued to stare in disbelief as the street and square in front of the Temple steadily filled with every kind of activist, even though it was only midmorning. Several media trucks had arrived and were erecting their telescopic antennae in preparation for their live broadcasts. Food-vending trucks were selling everything from hot dogs and hamburgers to shawarma and falafel. One enterprising vendor had even taken a model of a knight on a horse and swapped the knight's pennant for a Confederate flag.

"What a zoo," Danny declared. "The crowd will be whipped into a frenzy by five o'clock. Who's this senator idiot who pulled rank on the Supreme Council and persuaded them that somehow this was going to be good for Freemasonry?"

While this was all going on, Janet had called up the senator's bio on the Internet. "Listen to this: The good senator is known for his tough stance against abortion, same-sex marriages, and gun control. He was raised in a very strict household and attended a private Jesuit school in his early years before college. Rising up through the political ranks, he's become the leader of a small religious caucus within the Senate. It's said that he is the official voice of a group of Catholic and Protestant creationists."

"And he sits on the Scottish Rite Supreme Council? How the hell did that happen?" Jimmy slammed his fist down on the kitchen counter.

Danny was much calmer. "Jimmy, you of all people should understand that Freemasonry is nonjudgmental from a religious perspective. All a candidate has to do is confess to a belief in a Supreme Being—a Deity. Freemasonry is all about taking good men and making them better. The senator, I'm sure, is seen as an upright ultraconservative, but he is a powerful and influential citizen. His opinion obviously carries a lot of weight within the High Council."

It was David's turn to draw everybody's attention back to the TV screen. "Now, who the heck are those guys?"

The group that appeared on the screen were dressed all in black; many of them were wearing black hoodies or full-length black cowls—if their spiked hair allowed them. Some wore red kilts and Doc Martens, and many of them wore black-and-white face masks sporting the Munch scream. As for what they were protesting, many of them probably didn't have a clue themselves.

"Well, the party really wouldn't be complete without the anarchists," Danny groaned. "Just where the hell did all of these people come from, and why are they protesting a press conference to announce the discovery of a bunch of letters?"

"Washington, unfortunately, has become a cesspool for humanity," David replied. "People of all stripes and sizes are drawn to the seat of world power like a magnet." He shrugged. "It's a sad state of affairs when a fraternity such as Freemasonry has become a lightning rod for all that is rotten in this world. I can see how so much of the population is longing for the day when the Catholic Church controlled the world and told people when, where, and to whom they should pray. I guess it's easier to follow and have blind faith in something than it is to reason the essence of God out for oneself."

"Well, if I haven't seen everything," said Sarah Cohen, directing everybody once again back to the TV screen. "Are those Native North Americans who are just arriving?"

It was Danny who answered Sarah's question. "Yes, you're right. And judging from the flags, many of those are militant warriors, all decked out in war paint. I would think that they're here in support of all of the work that Pike did on behalf of the indigenous peoples. He was quite successful in negotiating whatever rights that he could for the Native North Americans, even though it was futile in the end."

"I better get on to the police and see what they're doing to maintain order." Danny tried to sound confident, but the concern on his face said differently. "Someone or something has whipped these groups into a frenzy, and I believe that we know just who that person is. Darn it all, he appears to be one step ahead of us again!"

XXVIII

KNIGHT OF THE SUN, OR PRINCE ADEPT

4:00 p.m., Four days ago

ON THE STEPS OF THE SCOTTISH RITE TEMPLE

As Thomas stepped onto the front stone pedestal of the Temple, he thought: *This whole situation is madness! There must be over two thousand protestors just beyond the metal barricade and a single line of police. They're all waving placards or flags or Bibles, trying to outshout one another. Absolute insanity!*

Sensing Thomas's unease, Janet quickly moved to his side and intertwined the fingers of her hand with his. He turned to her and smiled. He could sense that she was just as terrified and confused, but she had a better way of concealing it.

Luckily, there was a throng of dignitaries from around the world eagerly waiting to be introduced to the two, and it was Thomas who first spied David Rose standing off to one side, resplendent in his own 33° regalia and tuxedo. Much to Janet's surprise, standing beside her grandfather were both Danny Sullivan and Janet's own father, sporting their own 33° regalia. As soon as Janet saw the three of them, she immediately relaxed a little and started to feel more comfortable.

But there was no time for conversation, as Thomas and Janet were expected to greet every esteemed guest who was present and to take their place at the center podium in preparation for a five o'clock start. Of course Janet made her way to her father first and greeted him with a big hug. She almost burst into tears when she addressed him. "Father, it is so good to see you here. I was afraid that you wouldn't make it. But it puts you in danger alongside all of us."

Janet's father held his daughter and let his energy melt into her as he stroked her hair. "I wouldn't miss this for the world. It really puts things into perspective. There are so many lost and angry people out there, searching for guidance. Maybe today you and Thomas can give them a little insight. People need to really stop and think for themselves, instead of being caught up in some misguided cause. Look at them. Most of them have no idea why they're even here."

Solomon Rose scanned the writhing mass. *My God, they're building themselves into a frenzy of hate. All that's required for this whole thing to go sideways is for one of the so-called leaders to give the command. Who in his right mind would have thought that having this press conference out in the open would in some way promote Freemasonry?*

The answer to Solomon Rose's unspoken question stood to the back of the group of dignitaries. He too wore the regalia of a 33° Scottish Rite Freemason and the additional regalia of its Supreme Council. He had done as he was told, of course, but at this moment was regretting his involvement in the whole affair. *Absolute fear has a way of opening a man's soul, exposing the primitive truth about himself.*

As the senator surveyed the scene, he focused on the crowd to the front and right of him. This was the slice of society that he feared most—the skinheads, the rednecks, the right-wing nationalists, the neo-Nazis, the Ku Klux Klan, and whoever else cared to join them. He had ignored their support in his rise to power and wanted to believe that their hatred had finally been buried. But here it was again, on full display, rising out of the ashes like a multiheaded snake.

Then he froze. Standing out in the midst of the foaming mass was a lone, stark figure, clothed in the red scarlet robe of the Imperial Grand Wizard. Most of his features were covered by the pointed hood that had been pulled up over his head and around his face, but the way he portrayed absolute power was unmistakable. The senator knew instinctively that here was the Jesuit priest who had visited him earlier, demanding that he persuade the High Council to move the press conference and ceremonies to the steps leading to the Temple.

It was as if the Wizard's eyes, although concealed, were boring right through him. The senator was sure of it. Philippe had insisted that the senator be present for the opening ceremonies in order not to raise suspicion. As the senator's bowels threatened to explode, he knew that something very sinister was about to happen. Although his followers thought him to be a very religious man, he hadn't really prayed for years. But afterward, the dignitaries who had surrounded him swore to the FBI that they could faintly hear him begging the Almighty for forgiveness.

Nobody on the podium had time to really assess the situation. Thomas and Janet were being ushered from one individual to another by the current Sovereign Grand Commander of the Southern Jurisdiction. A kindly, gray-haired gentleman, he was oblivious to the hatred that spewed in front of him. As far as he was concerned, this was a great day for Freemasonry, and he wasn't going to let a few protesters ruin this triumph of reason and logic over mass hysteria. In his mind, this event was comparable to George Washington's laying the cornerstone for the Capitol.

The Commander, cognizant of the time, managed to get in all of the introductions and have Thomas and Janet at their assigned position just before the appointed time. At the PR briefing held earlier in the afternoon, the TV producers had all insisted that the press conference be finished by 5:30 so that the stations in North America could carry it as a main news feature.

Stepping up to the podium, Janet looked at her prepared notes. She knew that what waited to be found within the Pike Letters would be shattering to the worldwide audience, but she also knew that she was the ultimate bait in a deadly game that was going to finish today.

Swallowing hard, she cleared her throat, and as she did, the crowd eerily fell silent. It was as though a cloud of thoughtfulness had settled on it. Every individual there was filled with hate and bias, but a glimmer of hope had come over them, as though they recognized the power and wisdom of the woman who stood before them.

It seemed as if Janet had once again become the High Priestess—the Prophetess—who was about to share the fate of the world with each and every one of them. The Masonic dignitaries who were present realized that something sacred was happening here. Even the photographers and reporters, who had been given a special area up front, stopped taking pictures and lowered their microphones, as if they too were honoring the Goddess.

Then she began, first talking quietly and then gaining strength from the words she pronounced. "Good afternoon. My name is Janet Rose, and I, along with my fiancé, Thomas Moore, have pieced together a mystery whose solution will cause the world's religions to question their very existence, and the existence of their God. I know that most of you will consider this blasphemous, but all we ask is that you consider the truth when it is presented to you."

Janet paused, allowing her words to sink into the crowd's collective psyche. She continued, "Throughout my doctoral studies in ancient philosophy and esoteric symbolism, one man has always appeared as an enigma: Albert Pike, who, after a tumultuous and misunderstood career before and during the Civil War, went on to become the life-long Sovereign Grand Commander of the Southern Jurisdiction of the United States of America in Freemasonry. In fact, his remains are entombed in a crypt right here behind me in this temple.

"For over a hundred years, Freemasons have tried to reconcile the public image of the man who was purportedly instrumental in forming not only the Knights of the Golden Circle but the Ku Klux Klan with the man who wrote tomes on the ancient mysteries and pre-Christian philosophies, all which have led to the evolution of what we see as the one and omnipotent Deity—the higher Being—the one true God."

Pausing a second time, Janet scanned the crowd for signs of De Smet's presence, but there was none. Sensing that her uneasiness was returning, Thomas slowly moved closer to her, as though to protect her from an invisible force. The crowd remained silent, but it was clear that everyone was waiting for someone else to make the first move.

Glancing to her left, Janet caught her father's eye, reflecting an assurance and pride she had never seen before. The energy between the two helped her to continue. "In 1871, Albert Pike published his magnum opus, which was titled *Morals and Dogma of the Ancient and Accepted Scottish Rite of Freemasonry*. This brilliant work reads as a reconciliation of the rituals contained within the thirty-three degrees of Scottish Rite Masonry and an understanding of God and Truth from the beginning. In Albert Pike's own words: 'Before the world grew old, the primitive Truth faded out from men's Souls. Then man asked himself—"What am I? And how and whence am I? And whither do I go?"'"

Janet paused for effect and then continued, "Pike was like every other man. He had sinned, and he had unwittingly committed evil. That is human nature. Yet at some point in his life he realized that he could repent. He could repent by providing the world with his profound understanding of the very essence of God. He realized that he could be reborn. Here is the question humankind of every race, color, and creed struggles with every day, including Freemasons.

"In chapter 28 of his *Morals and Dogma,* he wrote, 'While yet the first oaks still put forth their leaves, man lost the perfect knowledge of the One True God, the Ancient Absolute Existence, the Infinite Mind, and Supreme Intelligence; and floated helplessly out upon the shoreless ocean of conjecture. Then the soul vexed itself with seeking to learn whether the material Universe was a mere chance combination of atoms, or the work of Infinite, Uncreated Wisdom: . . . whether the Deity was a concentrated, and the Universe an extended immateriality; or whether He was a personal existence, an Omnipotent, Eternal, Supreme Essence, regulating matter at will; or subjecting it to unchangeable laws throughout eternity; and to Whom, Himself Infinite and Eternal, Space and Time are unknown. With their finite limited vision they sought to learn the source and explain the existence of Evil, and Pain, and Sorrow; and so they wandered ever deeper into the darkness, and were lost; and there was for them no longer any God; but only a great, dumb, soulless Universe, full of mere emblems and symbols.'

"This is where the Roman Catholic Church brilliantly realized, close to two thousand years ago, that it could monopolize the world's soul by presenting itself as the only entity that could interpret these emblems and symbols. The emperor Constantine, a lifelong pagan himself, realized that he needed to compartmentalize the new movement known as Christianity in order for the Roman Empire to survive. The first step was at the Council of Nicaea and then with the development of the New Testament did Jesus the prophet become the Son of God by the stroke of a pen."

With these words, the crowd started to stir. The writhing throng had waited for an attack on their personal beliefs, and Janet didn't disappoint. The various factions started to push and shove, jockeying for dominance. All it would take would be for a leader to emerge, challenging not only Janet's words but the words of the various protesting groups.

This was what had been planned. Danny and Jimmy and the rest of the Rose group had spent hours on Janet's speech, looking to orchestrate a performance that was guaranteed to drive Philippe De Smet into such a state where he would make his first mistake and, hopefully, his last. The group knew that De Smet considered himself to be the one and true Prince Adept—the heir apparent to the throne of Peter. How he would react to the double cross was the outstanding question.

The throng of dignitaries, who had been so eager to be present this day and to be associated with Janet's and Thomas's discovery, had by now developed a real sense of foreboding. They started to slowly back away from the crescent that they had first formed behind their rising stars, leaving Danny Sullivan, Solomon Rose, and David Rose as the only ones to remain anywhere close to Thomas and Janet. The five were now isolated and vulnerable.

Undeterred, Janet proceeded to deliver her pronouncement. "Through a tremendous spiritual synchronicity, I met my fiancé right here within the Scottish Rite Temple library and soon discovered that he was not only the great-great-grandson of William James Bury MacLeod Moore, the Canadian equivalent of Albert Pike, but had in his possession thirty-two letters written from Pike himself to MacLeod Moore. Amazingly, these thirty-two letters all correspond in some manner to the rituals of the thirty-two degrees of Scottish Rite Masonry of the Southern Jurisdiction that Pike has been widely credited with having reconstructed. But Pike himself never allowed his name to be attached as author of the rituals, as he indicated that he had used a variety of sources to extend them. We now know that one very important source of knowledge that Pike relied on was none other than MacLeod Moore."

The gathering of high-ranking Freemasons did not know how to react to this new piece of information. Even the current Supreme Grand Commander appeared perplexed.

Regardless, Janet stood as tall and upright as she could, standing up to the growing disdain of the entire crowd. "It has long been believed that within these letters there exists a secret—a coded secret—identifying the real location of a crypt, which contains the most important information discovered by the original Knights Templar just before their order was sanctioned by the pope himself in 1129. The key to the location is contained within a thirty-third letter, which I discovered within the Albert Pike Library, located in the Temple. The letters indicate that this crypt is located in western North America and is still protected by high-ranking members of an indigenous secret society known as the Mide'win—the Grand Medicine Society. Now I will reveal what is actually contained within the crypt so that mankind will now understand."

As if on cue, the alternative-right crowd parted to allow the Imperial Grand Wizard to be seen by the cameras. The figure, who stood ominously silent, took on the form of a Grim Reaper in scarlet, which cloaked his entire body, including his face.

As he raised his right arm, it was as though the Wizard's index finger had magically grown in order to more forcibly accuse Janet and Thomas of heresy. No one except Danny Sullivan realized that the form cloaked by the long scarlet sleeve was not a finger but a gun, equipped with a long silencer.

To anyone who was present, the next series of events would forever be a blur. There was a deadened thump, which sounded as though it came from somewhere near the Wizard, although nobody would be able to say for certain. In that same split second, Danny Sullivan launched himself sideways, trying to cover Janet's body as best as he could with his. The cameras would show Danny Sullivan taking the full impact of the invisible force right in the chest, being blown back into Janet and barreling both her and Thomas violently backward. The only thing really obvious to the millions watching was the small crimson stain that steadily spread across Danny's white formal shirt, resembling an eight-pointed Templar cross.

At this point the crowd realized something was terribly wrong. Some of the police jumped up on stage with guns drawn, while others tried to prevent half the crowd from rushing the barricades. At the same time, the other half of the crowd scattered in all directions toward personal safety. People were pointing everywhere, mostly at Danny Sullivan's prone, inert body, which was surrounded by the kneeling Thomas, Janet, Solomon, and David. The cameras even caught Janet's grandfather praying over Danny's body.

Members of the crowd later claimed that they saw everything, but nobody really grasped the truth. One young evangelical protestor who was later interviewed by the news outlet even said he saw the Wizard extend his wand like Harry Potter and that it had emitted a supersonic ray.

The commotion caused by the events on the podium prevented anyone from focusing on the Wizard. Even if they had turned their attention to him, they would only have seen the Wizard's second-in-command moving toward him, as if he was protecting the Wizard's back. As with the Wizard, all they would have seen was the white cloak with the emblem of the red, eight-pointed cross within a circle. Also like the Wizard, he had a magic finger, which silently pointed itself up against the base of the Wizard's head and blew it away.

Five minutes later, Jimmy O'Reilly, unseen and unchallenged, quietly made his way around to the back of the Temple, depositing the Klansman's white cloak where it belonged—in the dumpster.

XXIX

GRAND SCOTTISH KNIGHT OF SAINT ANDREW

7:00 a.m., Three days ago

GEORGETOWN

As had become their habit during the early morning hours, Thomas and Janet, David and Sarah, along with Solomon and his wife, Eliza, huddled around the kitchen island enjoying homemade coffee and a hearty makeshift breakfast. Occasionally one of them would glance at the morning newspaper or the news on television.

Surprisingly, given the events that had occurred over the past twelve hours, none of them had much to say. It was decompression time. It was also time to reassess the whole situation and to pay homage to the bravery of both Danny and Jimmy, acting like the warrior-monks that they were.

Thomas was leisurely enjoying a bowl of porridge topped with strawberries and blueberries and a sprinkling of white powdered gold when an in-depth feature on yesterday's events at the Temple appeared on CNN, starting with live-motion footage of Danny getting shot. At this point, everyone around the kitchen island stopped eating and watched the newscast.

"That was quite a performance, I must say so myself. I should get an Oscar!" The voice came from the hallway, but it was unmistakable. Stepping into the kitchen, wearing a plush white bathrobe and rubbing the remaining water from his hair with a towel—was none other than Danny Sullivan. Behind him was Jimmy O'Reilly, sporting one of the biggest grins ever.

Janet threw her arms around Danny before exclaiming, "Yes, my guardian angel, you do deserve an Academy Award for that performance. You were absolutely magnificent. You're so brave and yet so modest. How are you feeling?"

Danny blushed before answering. "To tell you the truth, not bad, all things considered. The doctor says that I have two cracked ribs from taking the shot so close to my heart, but the new Kevlar vest really did the trick. I was more afraid that the bastard wasn't that good of a shot and would miss my heart but, of course, he was deadly accurate, hitting the blood pack perfectly. Then I thought that the paramedics were going to drop me off the gurney before they got me to the ambulance, what with people running in all directions. It's a good thing that they were actually members of our own RCC security team. Wouldn't that have been something? Janet, crying over me all the way to the hospital was a nice touch. I really didn't think that you cared so much."

Janet punched Danny in the arm, but her broad smile gave her away. Jimmy chuckled. Considering that he had recently killed a man at close range, he was in a rather mischievous mood this morning.

Thomas spoke next. "Can either of you tell me how you knew that De Smet was disguised as the Imperial Grand Wizard? And how were you so certain that he would take a heart shot?"

"Elementary, my dear Watson!" Jimmy was definitely in a good mood. The victorious warrior was still running on adrenaline. "You just have to connect the dots. De Smet was a sadistic, egotistical narcissist.

He truly believed that it was his destiny to be anointed as the next pope. Given that he was an expert on the Spanish Inquisition, we figured that out of all the disguises that he could choose he wouldn't be able to help adding a little irony to the situation by dressing in a cloak and a hood that resembles a *capirote*. It's a pointed conical hat that is still used in Spain by the radically faithful. It is part of the uniform of some brotherhoods during Easter observances and Holy Week reenactments. Historically, the flagellants are the origin of the current traditions, as they flogged themselves to do penance. Pope Clement VI ordered that flagellants could perform penance only under control of the church. Rather coincidentally, the use of the capirote was proscribed in Spain by the Inquisition. It was the earlier pope, Clement V, who conspired with the king of France to annihilate the Knights Templar in 1307. You just have to connect the dots."

Everyone stared incredulously at Jimmy. David Rose was the first one to break out laughing; then everyone joined in. The laughter helped relieve the tension from the previous day.

Jimmy just shrugged. "Hey, what can I say? I'm more than a pretty face. I happen to study history!"

Danny patted Jimmy on the shoulder. "Don't worry about it, Jimmy. It's my turn to impress this crowd." Danny walked over and poured himself a mug of coffee and then leaned back on the counter. "Jimmy hit it spot on. What he didn't tell you is that we found it odd that the ultraright would be the first to show up for the party, staking out their turf like that. That really was unusual, and when we checked with our FBI friends, we were informed that they found it puzzling also, as the real Imperial Grand Wizard was known to be in Mississippi all day yesterday. That's when we put two and two together and figured out that somehow De Smet had infiltrated the alt-right in order to make them do his bidding. He positioned the ultraright mob perfectly to get a clear range of sight and to make his escape."

Danny took a sip of his coffee before continuing. "As for taking a heart shot, Philippe De Smet was a Jesuit, meaning that he believed that the soul was in the heart. That's why we knew he would look to shoot at Janet's heart. Besides, his hatred for everything feminine guaranteed that she would be his first target. We knew that he saw Janet as the biggest threat to a patriarchal society, especially as she was the only female on the podium. She was definitely the White Queen in this deadly game of chess."

Eliza was listening quietly but spoke up for the first time. "Danny, I don't quite understand. What are you saying? What is this notion that the heart is different from the soul?"

"Well, Eliza, the original Knights Templar believed that the heart was just an organ. They believed that the soul's reasoning came from the brain—the brain being capable of logic and reasoning. The Templars used the same reasoning and logic to determine their veneration of the feminine. It's widely believed that the so-called Templar Treasure contains evidence that Mary Magdalene was married to Jesus.

"That's why the skull, which encases the brain, is portrayed as a vessel in many earlier paintings and writings. The vessel came in many forms—the sacred feminine, the Grail cup, even the upended skull itself. To the Knights Templar, the skull and crossbones were a symbol that represented the soul of a man. The crossbones form the X symbol, which, when it's hooked, is widely seen to represent the purported Holy Grail Family. Christianized, it becomes the symbol of St. Andrew of Scotland, suggestive of the Scottish Rite, which leads us back to the ancient mysteries. Take it one step forward, and you get the skull and crossbones of the Jolly Roger and *Pirates of the Caribbean*. X marks the spot, don't you know?"

With that, Danny took his bow, to the continuing laughter of the entire group. But the laughter quickly died away as the newscast showed a close-up photo of Philippe De Smet from his seminary days. His frame was a little leaner and his hair a little longer, but the eyes were the same—almost jet-black and infinitely deep, full of hate and contempt for mankind.

The newscast then showed an amateur video of the murder scene, obviously shot with a cell phone. It showed the police slowly moving toward the body of De Smet with guns drawn, just in case he wasn't dead. He was still wearing the crimson cloak, and the dark red pool of blood surrounding his head was slowly expanding. Somehow the owner of the cell phone had had the wherewithal to zoom in on the white-and-black collar.

Below the scene, across the bottom of the flat screen, ran a ticker tape indicating that, although it couldn't be confirmed, De Smet was killed by a high-ranking Klansman who recognized him as an impostor. Another theory suggested that De Smet had been taken out by an FBI sniper positioned atop one of the nearby buildings when he saw him take aim and shoot Danny. Either way, the Klan wasn't going to openly complain about the killing of the impostor, as it would put the continuing existence of the Klan front and center on the world stage. The real Imperial Grand Wizard had quickly claimed that he was the real target of the attempted assassination.

At the same time, the broadcaster announced that the Vatican had just released an official statement regarding the incident. The pope himself denied any personal knowledge of Father De Smet and suggested that the priest had suffered from mental-health problems due to a traumatic childhood. The statement went on to say that Father De Smet appeared to have harbored delusions that the Freemasons were infinitely evil. It also said that the pope would pray for De Smet's eternal soul.

Somehow the whole charade seemed appropriate but was still unnerving. The Vatican had made De Smet out as the real victim.

Shaking his head at the absurdity of it all, Thomas reached out for Janet's hand and pulled her gently toward the living room, away from the never-ending information dump coming from the TV. They found refuge on the couch, basking in the morning sunlight.

Sitting down, Janet laid her head on Thomas's shoulder as he reached around her to draw her close. She closed her eyes and sighed, quickly falling once again into her trancelike state.

The High Priestess awoke to find herself still lying in the fields next to her lover. The Goddess had heard her prayers and decided to grant mercy to the couple. The captain of the guards slowly stirred from his deep sleep. Miraculously, the self-inflicted wound had cauterized itself, and the sunlight, which beat down upon them, had mended his damaged organs. They sat up and turned to face each other. Embracing, they gently kissed and looked to the sky, silently giving thanks for the mercy and glory of the Goddess. They both realized that they had been spared for a specific reason. From that point forward, they were to guard the Temple and its underground crypt forevermore against the usurpers.

Janet was asleep for only fifteen minutes: that was all it took for her to receive the vision. Somehow she had been able to share it with Thomas. From the smile and nod that he gave her, she could tell that Thomas understood everything. They were one again.

All that was left to do was to crack the coded Pike Letters once and for all, but the two had better things to do. They decided that they would go for a long walk in the morning sunlight through Georgetown's many streets and had gotten up to leave when Solomon called them back into the kitchen.

"Hey, you two, before you go sneaking off you have to come and see this. You won't believe it."

Thomas and Janet made their way back to the kitchen. The screen showed a lineup that snaked for at least two miles down the block away from the Temple. Yesterday's events at the Temple had resulted in a tenfold increase in interest in the exhibit. The broadcaster said it appeared as though people didn't mind waiting upward of five hours to view the Pike Letters. Nobody appeared to know that the originals weren't on display. Some note of optimism and free will must have sounded among the general public after witnessing the deadly fiasco that had taken place the day before.

It appeared to be a redemption for Freemasonry in general. After the chaos died down, the Scottish Rite Supreme Council had called an emergency meeting, with the senator leading the charge not to go ahead with the opening, but logic and reason finally won over. One immediate result was the senator's resignation from the High Council. He had quickly realized that if he didn't resign, he would be subject to a vote of confidence, which he would surely have lost. Eventually, someone would put together his involvement and relation with the Jesuits and De Smet. It would have meant permanent disgrace and eventually absolute devolvement from Freemasonry.

Danny's cell phone rang; so, almost simultaneously, did David Rose's. Danny picked his phone up and went into the hallway while David went to the living room. Everyone remaining in the kitchen raised their eyebrows. Seeing her opening, Janet grabbed Thomas's hand and dashed for the front door and outside before anyone could protest. They definitely needed some fresh air. The phone calls were an omen of some sort that nobody understood.

David was the first to come back into the kitchen with exciting news. "Never in the world would I have expected that call! It was from the chief of the Blackfoot—Chief Bull Bear—calling from Montana. It was as though we've known each other our entire lives, although I've never met him before. Anyway, he wants us to meet him in three days in Townsend, Montana. He says that he and his grandson—Little Bull Bear—will meet us at the airport. He guarantees that it will be life changing. He promises to provide us with the final answers to our search. God, I don't know what to make of it all."

Solomon had been quiet and pensive all morning but brightened up when he heard David talk about the phone call. "Dad, this is wonderful news. The Pike Letters at one point speak of Pike interacting with the North American Native elders on a very spiritual level. You remember; they're known as the Mide'win—the Grand Medicine Society. They're the equivalent of the Grand Council of the Knights Templar or the Supreme Council of the Scottish Rite—same concept of an inner circle within a secret society. The Templars, like all other secret orders, had two doctrines; one concealed and reserved for the master adepts, which was Johannism; the other, public, which was Roman Catholic. I'm willing to bet that you just received an invitation from the head elder of that society, which remains as the guardian of the crypt right to the present. What a tremendous honor for all of us! This really is a tribute to the Rose family. Don't you see? This confirms the blending of the bloodline between the Native North Americans and the Grail Family."

Finishing his call, Danny reappeared in the kitchen with a broad smile on his face. He was just as excited as David had been. "Now never in the world would I have expected that call. It was from a Monsignor Dominic de Valdes, the head of the business secretariat for the Jesuits, in Barcelona. I could hardly understand him because of his accent, but he provided me with some important information. He first apologized and indicated that Father De Smet had acted alone and was deranged and delusional. Then, in a rather suspect manner, he said that he would provide us with the probable location of the original Pike Letters if we agree to stop implicating the pope, the Vatican, and the Jesuits themselves in all of this."

Jimmy was the first to speak up. "OK, Danny, and how did you respond?"

"Well, of course, I said with the straightest of voices that we all understood how something so sensitive could be misconstrued as being a threat to the church and religion in general. Then I agreed that all of this sordid business should be put behind us, and we would very much appreciate the opportunity to retrieve the Pike Letters. In return, we would agree not to involve the Vatican, the pope, or the Jesuits any further; we were only interested in the historical value of the Pike Letters as they relate to Freemasonry. Finally, I politely declined the offer of assistance in our ongoing research, because we didn't want to prejudice the findings, if any, in any way." Danny spread his hands in what had become his trademark "I'm totally innocent" gesture.

"Hah, and what was the response to that?" Jimmy couldn't quite believe what he was hearing but was enjoying every moment.

"Oh, he indicated that the Inner Circle would be fine with that, as long as we kept our end of the bargain. The only qualification was that if we should discover something of a *religious* nature, they would expect the professional courtesy of informing them before we went public with the find." Danny sat down at one of the island chairs.

"Hah, and I'm willing to bet that if we informed them of anything of great significance, we wouldn't live long enough to inform anyone else. They play a very sly game, don't they?"

"Yes, Jimmy, they certainly do, which means that all of us are in danger as long as we pursue the issue to the end."

"I don't know about you two," said David Rose, "but I'm not going to give up. Now where did they tell you that we could recover the originals?"

"Apparently De Smet was using an old manse on the other side of the city that still belongs to the church. It's supposed to be developed for affordable housing in the near future. It's good that Thomas left for his walk when he did, because this information may trigger something in the back of his mind—something which may not be all too pleasant. I've already contacted the D.C. police and FBI and asked them to carefully check the place out. Knowing De Smet, he probably booby-trapped the place just in case he didn't make it back. Thanks to Jimmy here, he certainly won't be returning to his lair!"

XXX

KNIGHT KADOSH

7:00 p.m., Two days ago

GEORGETOWN

The rest of the day was spent as normally as possible. Janet and Thomas wandered about Washington for five hours, taking in the sights of the capital and trying to act like two normal tourists. Walking along the Mall toward the Lincoln Memorial, neither Thomas nor Janet could get out of their minds the essence of life and love, of truth and wisdom that had been revealed since their first meeting thirty days ago. The early Jewish mystics referred to it as *Kether,* the climax of the journey through the *sefiroth* of the Kabbalistic Tree of Life.

Meanwhile, Solomon, Danny, and Jimmy had made their way by limousine to RCC headquarters. A lot of work needed to be done to assure the many clients that everything was continuing to run smoothly and that the commodities market was stable.

The bulk of those tasks was left to Solomon Rose. Because he was CEO and chairman of the board, most of RCC's biggest clients would expect a call from him to provide the needed personal assurances. Even the Vatican Bank was a major commodities investor through an

RCC subsidiary located in Rome near St. Peter's Square.

Danny also had to coordinate the news of his future miraculous recovery with the help of the CIA, FBI, and local police. At this point, all that the media outlets knew for certain was that he had been rushed into surgery at an undisclosed private clinic and was in critical condition following a four-hour operation. However, the latest press release indicated that it was hopeful Danny would survive, as the bullet had missed his heart by a centimeter. Only time and medical care would tell.

The continuation of the ruse was necessary to allow the FBI to complete the murder investigation surrounding the concierge and De Smet's purported involvement without muddying the waters.

Throughout the day, Jimmy was doing his usual—using top-secret, live satellite imagery to coordinate the search efforts of the local police force and FBI. He was trying to detect any seemingly out-of-place things associated with the manse, which had easily been located using the directions of the Jesuit secretariat. So far the FBI had detected and defused three bombs meant to maim or kill anyone who showed too much interest in the activities of the manse. Even in death, De Smet had left a few deadly calling cards.

Back at the Georgetown brownstone, the mood was upbeat. As always Eliza had a way about her, taking over the general duties of the house and seeing to the preparation of a celebratory meal. She didn't even raise an eyebrow when Dr. Sarah Cohen arrived just after six o'clock. The two of them were immediate sisters, giving each other a hug before Sarah made her way down to David's lab, where he had spent the entire day. If Sarah and David had something more than a platonic relationship developing, Eliza wondered, who was she to judge how love works?

By seven o'clock, everyone had arrived back home and prepared for dinner. Present at the table were David and Sarah, Solomon and Eliza, Janet and Thomas, and Danny and Jimmy—the Rose family and its two guardians. As both modern-day Templars and Rosicrucians, Danny and Jimmy had devoted their lives to the preservation of the Grail Family, and here was living proof of that dedication.

Instead of a traditional Jewish prayer of thanks, David Rose stood and expounded upon a little bit of ancient mystical wisdom. "Some around this table will understand that the ancient adepts of the Rose-Croix, otherwise known as the Rosicrucians, became a mystical sect that united with many of the original Templars, with the doctrines of the two intermingled; and that this Inner Circle believed themselves to be the sole depositaries of the secrets of the Gospel of St. John. These Supreme Magi saw in it an allegorical account of rites for completing the degrees of initiation. There were nine degrees altogether. Once completed, the newly initiated magus will have learned the same ancient mysteries that were taught to Jesus by John the Baptist."

Danny and Jimmy looked at each other with raised eyebrows, somewhat surprised that Janet's grandfather would choose this moment to reveal the secret of the Rose-Croix.

Nonetheless, David continued, first raising a magnificent silver cross embedded with a ruby rose in its center, which he had hidden under his linen napkin. "The mystical meanings of the rose as a symbol are to be looked for in the Kabbalistic commentaries on the Song of Songs. The rose was, for the early initiates, the living and blooming symbol of the revelation of the harmonies of being. It was the emblem of beauty, life, love, and pleasure—all things attributed to the Goddess."

David paused for effect. "Now you may wonder why an old Jewish mystic is holding what at first may appear to be a very Christian symbol. Well, the early alchemist Nicolas Flamel, relying on the Book of Abraham the Jew, made it the hieroglyphic sign of the accomplishment of what was known as the Great Work. Such is the key of the *Roman de la Rose*—the Rose-Croix. The conquest of the rose—the sacred feminine—was the problem propounded to science by initiation, while religion was laboring to prepare and establish the universal triumph of the cross. The sacred rose, of course, is a symbol of the sacred feminine that just won't go away, in spite of two thousand years of suppression by the papists."

Everyone stared at David, trying to understand what he was getting at. Finally the mood was lightened by Sarah's laughter as she exclaimed, "My goodness, David, you truly amaze me. Are you suggesting that on one level the Rose-Croix is a secret sign signifying the eternal balance between the masculine and feminine? If this is true, why is there a secret *under the rose* that only a male Rosicrucian—a magus—understands? Wasn't Rosicrucianism first revealed by *The Chemical Wedding of Christian Rosenkreutz*—otherwise known as *CRC*—where the male and female are wedded into a perfect androgynous entity?" Sarah had been doing quite a bit of reading about alchemy and the Rosicrucians.

Before anyone else could remark on David's comments, the doorbell rang.

Jimmy and Danny popped up quickly and moved toward the front door, as if they didn't want David or Sarah to pursue the issue anymore. Everyone appeared almost relieved to focus on something else.

Danny and Jimmy appeared to know whoever it was at the door quite well, to judge by the hearty handshakes and backslapping that were going on. Laughter drifted down the hallway and back into the dining room. Those in the dining room could just make out something about Danny rising from the grave.

As quickly as they had arrived, the men left, and Danny and Jimmy reappeared at the table. Danny had a large brown envelope in his hand, which he put on the table next to his setting. Before anyone could ask what was going on, Danny dived into his plate of food. After the first bite, he looked up and said, "Let's finish eating before we get into the heavy stuff. Everything's just fine. By the envelope, you can see that our friends recovered the Pike Letters without serious incident. Of course, they were smart to be cautious around the manse. That bastard De Smet had worked it so that if he didn't return by midnight tonight, then the manse and the letters would literally go up in smoke. So let's just get back to normal and finish what is obviously a work of love, thanks to Eliza."

Responding to the compliment, Eliza supported Danny's wish. "You heard the wise man. Let's put aside these two-thousand-year-old questions until after dinner. I really did go to a lot of work making the meal and even made my father-in-law's favorite dessert—*crème caramel.*"

No one needed much encouragement to dive into the meal. At the same time, Solomon reached over to his wife, gently pulled her head to his, and gave her a sensuous kiss. Janet was shocked. She had never before witnessed true passion between her mother and father. As if to mimic her parents, Janet leaned over to Thomas, who willingly met her halfway with a sensuous kiss of his own.

Not to be outdone, Sarah leaned over to David and, to the surprise of everyone, planted the most sensuous kiss of all of them on the old man. Maybe it was the white powdered gold, or the adrenaline of the past few days finally working itself out, but David Rose responded as though he were once again a teenager.

Everyone broke out in laughter again. It was a perfect example of the undeniable attraction between male and female, between two spirits passing one another. The tarot card of the Lovers subliminally displays this connection for all to ponder.

Jimmy cleared his throat and spoke. "I know that the six of you are pining away for each other, and that's sweet. Thank goodness that all of this cloak-and-dagger stuff is over. But we still have a task at hand—to find the crypt. Then I imagine that the big question is going to be what will we discover, and whom does it belong to?"

Everybody perked up to the question. Albert Pike had obviously struggled with it, and this group of eight realized that the invitation from the Mide'win would require them to answer this question as well.

Those at the table were unusually quiet, as Jimmy's question had given pause for everyone to think. The original Knights Templar had realized that what they discovered under the Temple of Solomon was beyond priceless—earth shattering, in fact. They quickly realized that, if exposed to the world, the evidence for the marriage of Jesus and Mary Magdalene and the ever-growing Grail Family would shake the foundations of the Roman Catholic Church. They also realized that the Church would surely bury both them and the treasure before it could do any harm to the pope or the Church.

Sadly, the Dominicans were first to become the Vatican's secret bloodhounds and then the Jesuits assumed the role, pursuing the generational guardians of the treasure to North America.

Yet this secret was only a trickle of what was discovered. Because of their hidden Jewish mysticism the original Templars understood the teachings found among the many scrolls, which made up a key component of the treasure. The Templars, who not only understood the basic tenets of Christianity but the ancient mysteries upon which they were based, also understood the order of all things and the forces of nature. They knew how the ancients had learned to harness the very essence of the Supreme Being. The energy could be concentrated in a way that could move both heaven and earth—for evil or for good. And this ancient technology required a profound knowledge of alchemy— the basis of modern chemistry.

Consequently, the original knights agreed that it would be better to conceal and protect these discoveries for a time when the world was willing to accept a different basis of worship, even if it took over a thousand years. As a result, they set in motion a plan whereby the treasure would always be split to prevent its complete discovery by the Church or its agents. They knew that someday, somewhere, the whole secret would finally be put back together.

Danny put down his fork, playfully shaking his head at his own inability to block out the conversation and finish his meal. "OK, I might as well jump into the conversation." This caused everyone to put down their forks.

Danny continued, "Before we get into the question of who are the rightful owners of something that we haven't discovered yet, I want to remind everyone what the Knights Templar have become in the eyes of the public. It's certainly the opposite of what the original nine knights foresaw when they enacted their grand scheme. Outside of the Masonic Brotherhood, the Knights Templar are considered comic-book heroes. Even when Dan Brown wrote about them as the basis for *The Da Vinci Code,* it was fictionalized to the point where they're now part of a conspiracy theory that's generally dismissed. When *The Da Vinci Code* was first published, there were cries of blasphemy and heresy, and many predicted the downfall of the Catholic Church. That didn't happen. Then people began to focus on the so-called Templar Treasure. That became the subject of the movie *National Treasure,* which I found highly entertaining, but nothing more. Probably the most telling sign of how far the myth of the Templars has fallen is that they're portrayed as the bad guys in the video game "Assassin's Creed," where they're aligned with the Spanish royalty and the Jesuits against a secret sect of assassins, who strive to preserve the 'apple of knowledge.'"

"Danny's right!" Jimmy added. "If Danny or I stood up in a public forum and declared that we were modern-day Knights Templar and Rosicrucians who practiced the Christian mysteries, we would probably be burned at the stake."

"That's the point that I'm trying to make," Danny grimaced. "Say that we decipher the secret code within the Pike Letters, which leads us to the location of the crypt. And say that with the consent of the present-day guardians, we are chosen as the ones to open the crypt and expose the treasure once and for all. Are we worthy of claiming ownership of the contents? How are we able to prove beyond a doubt that our modern-day secret society is the direct descendant of the original nine knights? If not, who is the rightful owner?"

"I can tell you one thing. The Vatican will exert whatever pressure it can in order to be identified as the rightful owner of the crypt and its contents. The U.S. and Canadian governments will have tremendous legal and moral pressure exerted upon them. And most European countries that still acknowledge royalty will be forced to side with the Church. It's a moral dilemma that both Jimmy and I realized soon after being initiated into the Grand Encampment. Pike was a genius. He realized that it was well enough to leave the answers buried rather than expose them to the world."

David Rose solemnly stood up from the table. "And that is why, my friends, we must ponder the question some more. We haven't got too much time, though. We are expected in Montana in two days. Might I suggest that we all finish our dessert and then go to bed and sleep on it?" He winked at Sarah before continuing. "But before we do that, Danny, would you be so kind to pass me the letters? I think I'll go to my laboratory and ponder the question while I study them more closely, with a bit more perspective from the insight that we've gained over the last few days."

There wasn't much more to say. What first started out as a celebration in recognition of defeating De Smet only led to a bigger question. Danny nodded and passed over the envelope with reverence, as though the letters did contain the holiest of holies.

As everyone stood up from the table, Sarah leaned over to David and almost whispered, "David, can I join you in the lab? I believe that you will need a female's eye to help you find *that-which-was-lost*."

David brightened up considerably. "Of course, my dear, it would be a pleasure if you were to join me."

XXXI

GRAND INSPECTOR
INQUISITOR GENERAL

7:00 a.m., One day ago

GEORGETOWN

A semblance of normalcy had returned to David Rose's Georgetown home. So much had occurred in the last thirty-one days that everything from now on would be anticlimactic.

There was still much to accomplish, to comprehend, to share. That's why the everyday routine of gathering around the kitchen island in the early morning was so important. It brought the family together, refreshed and renewed, as the sun bathed everyone in its glory. The Deity's warmth assured everyone that life would go on and would bless them.

This was not the time for anyone to judge when Dr. Cohen appeared in a long, silk, purple gown while David bounded into the kitchen in his own silk pajamas like a teenage boy who has experienced sexual intimacy for the first time.

Thomas couldn't help but look up from his morning paper and smile. He was instantly reminded by the obvious love between Sarah and David of Pike's lamenting within *Morals and Dogma*. Pike himself had written that there are no exceptions to the great general law of attraction, "which binds atom to atom in the body of a rotifer visible only by aid of a microscope, orb to orb, system to system. The law of Attraction gives unity to the world of things, and rounds these worlds of systems to a Universe. At first there seem to be exceptions to this law, as in growth and decomposition, in the repulsions of electricity; but at length all these are found to be special cases of the one great law of attraction acting in various modes."

Thomas knew that he too had found his own balancing element in Janet. There was a sense of justice to his and Janet's bond, which had been strengthened by the evil they had faced together in the form of Philippe De Smet. The law of justice allowed Thomas to become Janet's yin to her yang, black to her white, cold to her hot.

Never one to challenge the universal laws of judgment and justice, Janet was next to come into the kitchen, looking every bit the High Priestess of the Major Arcana. Her white Chanel pantsuit accentuated her height. She glided across the kitchen floor to the stool next to Thomas and let out a cheery "Good morning!" to everyone present.

Not to be outdone, Solomon Rose appeared, resplendent in a custom-made black suit, a crisp white shirt, and deep blue silk tie. He looked ten years younger. Following closely behind was Eliza, looking resplendent in a flowered dress and matching camisole. Everyone admired one another all around. That which was good and loving had definitely triumphed over that which was evil.

Janet's grandfather was the first to break the mood, exclaiming, "Hey, what's going on with all of you? Did we miss something?"

Solomon was the first to laugh and then responded, "Well, Dad, you may not have heard the phone ring late last night after you and Sarah retreated to that wicked lair of yours. It was the White House calling. The president himself invited us to breakfast, of all things. It appears that he would like a firsthand account of everything that has happened. Danny and Jimmy will be picking us up at 7:30 in the corporate limo, so we don't have much time."

Sarah and David appeared put out by the pronouncement but quickly recovered. David was especially quick, considering that he hadn't gotten much sleep the night before. "Solomon, this is wonderful news. But why didn't you let the two of us know? Please don't tell me that you're embarrassed by your father and his newfound companion."

"Dad," said Solomon, "you know that's not the case at all. In fact, I was thinking of disturbing you just after the phone call, but my all-wise wife indicated that I should leave you and Sarah alone. Apparently, she believes that the two of you are two old souls who have finally found each other, wandering through the netherworld."

Sensing that David was still slightly uneasy, Solomon put his hand on his father's shoulder and continued, "Dad, you know that none of us can ever be judgmental over your relationship with Dr. Cohen. In fact, I think it's safe to say that we're all thrilled—and amazed. Mother, bless her soul, would encourage it; I'm sure of that. You've mourned her for too long. It's time that you start thinking about the happiness that you have left."

Eliza had moved toward Sarah, who stood off to the side apprehensively, and embraced her. Tears welled up in both of their eyes.

Tears were also appearing in Janet's eyes as she wrapped her arms around her grandfather and hugged him. "Oh, Grandfather, we're all so happy for you and Dr. Cohen! Though I hope that you didn't sprinkle her with some white powdered gold."

Sarah laughed and said, "Janet, how could you ever think such a thing? I am a woman of science but also a woman who deeply admires and loves all that is good in this world. I've fallen in love with your grandfather simply because of the quality of the man. I would never depend on stimulants of any nature to influence my judgment. As to his physical prowess, let's just say that some men take Viagra and chase twenty-year-olds, which is ridiculous. I actually prefer it that your grandfather takes his white powdered gold, which not only increases his physical stamina but stimulates his brain as well."

With that, there were tears all around, to be interrupted by the doorbell.

Janet flung the door open, squealing with glee as Danny and Jimmy stood there grinning. Danny entered first, followed by his fellow over-sized leprechaun. They seemed excited to receive the invitation to the White House. For old warriors to be honored in such a manner was never out of place.

The wisecracking Jimmy was the first to sense that something quite emotional and profound had just taken place in the Georgetown house. To lighten the mood, he declared, "God bless all here! Even if it is the wickedest den of impropriety this side of Murphy's bar. My God, Danny! Do you smell the animal musk floating around this place? They're going to have to fumigate the place."

Janet responded in her usual manner by punching Jimmy in the shoulder, except this time she put a little more strength in the jab, causing Jimmy to yelp. Grabbing his shoulder in mock discomfort, he couldn't help giving a comeback: "Hey! What was that for? I was just making an observation, which appears pretty accurate by everyone's wicked smiles this morning."

To get everybody back on track, Danny held up his hand and inter-jected, "OK, the two of you stop right now. I know that this is an excit-ing moment, but we need to get organized and to get going. I can tell you that the president of the United States does not like to be kept waiting."

By this time David Rose had wrapped a robe over his pajamas. He wasn't put out in the least that he and Sarah wouldn't be going to the White House. He knew what the president wanted to hear, and he wasn't prepared to tell him, at this or any other moment. He had played out a lot of things in his mind over the past few days and had some further thoughts about what lay within the Pike Letters. He issued a kind of patriarchal order: "I'm sorry, but as the head of this family, I want to ask each and every one of you to make me a solemn promise!"

Everyone stopped in their tracks.

David continued, "What I am about to say is not said lightly, but I must ask all of you to promise me that you will not reveal to the president the potential location of the crypt. I'm sure you realize that we've received a great personal honor by being invited by the Native North American guardians of the Templar Treasure, and I've given my word that we will keep its location secret. Even though we have not determined its exact location as yet, I don't think that will matter anymore. Tomorrow the eight of us will fly out to meet Chief Bull Bear and his grandson, and I believe that they have enough trust in us to reveal all."

"Yes, David!" everyone responded in unison. This again produced guffaws all round, although everyone felt the seriousness behind the request.

Surprisingly, it was Thomas who spoke up, asking the question that everyone was afraid to ask. "Mr. Rose, with the greatest of respect, I am somewhat confused. Should we not be looking to the president of the United States for some sort of guidance to how, if discovered, the Templar Treasure should be shared with the world?"

The Rose Family patriarch stepped forward a little bit more. "But that's exactly the point I'm trying to make, Thomas. We've seen how the power of the treasure swayed one of the world's three greatest religious institutions to the point of utter ruthlessness. History, of course, tells us that it was the Templars who first bore the weight of the Catholic Church.

"And now, I'm almost loath to say it, but even the head of the most powerful country in the world cannot be trusted to do the right thing. Albert Pike realized this, and that's why he never revealed where the true treasure lies. He saw what the U.S. government was capable of in almost wiping out the Native North Americans. I do not want this family to provide the catalyst to finish the job. Even though I haven't met him as yet, I believe that I will be meeting my blood brother tomorrow, no pun intended."

"OK, that's it." Solomon Rose assumed the family mantle. "The six of us are going to breakfast with the president of the United States of America. We're going to tell the story as completely as we can without revealing what we know about the probable location of the crypt and its potential contents. That shouldn't be too hard. Now let's get going. As Danny has already indicated, the president does not like to be kept waiting."

With that command, the six filed out the front door and headed toward the sleek black limo. None of the others noticed that Danny was out in front of the group and Jimmy was taking up the rear. The two modern-day warrior-monks were still wary and protective of the family.

As Jimmy hopped into the front passenger seat and signaled to his security-team driver to head out, he couldn't help but think of the potential events of the next day. His mind was already beyond the White House, trying to picture the Montana landscape from a bird's-eye view. *Would the location of the crypt be that obvious for those with the eyes to see?*

The excitement of those behind him contrasted starkly with the brooding melancholy that had just overcome Jimmy. Sensing that his partner was sharing the same premonition, Jimmy tried to push it out of both their minds. They had just cleared the chessboard of all of the pieces, but another game was already in play. This time, though, their opponent was none other than the commander-in-chief, who appeared almost too inquisitive about the activities of the Rose Family.

XXXII

MASTER OF THE ROYAL SECRET

5:00 p.m., One day ago

GEORGETOWN

At five o'clock that evening, the group arrived back at the Georgetown brownstone. Ready to greet them at the front door were David Rose and Sarah Cohen; to judge from their ruffled appearance and bright glow, the couple had made good use of their time alone. Arm in arm, they giggled at the thought that they had been caught in the act by the younger ones.

David and Sarah couldn't help noticing the excitement of those who piled out of the black limo. It was as though something extraordinary had occurred during their visit to the White House. Their mood was puzzling, given the apprehension that had been palpable earlier in the day.

Thomas was the first to tumble out the back door of the limo. Laughing, he gathered himself up from the grass and stood, extending his hand to his fiancée with a gallant gesture. Helping her extricate herself from the car, Thomas pulled her in close and kissed her.

Next to remove themselves from the limo were Solomon and Eliza. They too were beaming and appeared to have gained a sensual closeness. David went to the bottom of the steps and spread his arms wide, asking, "What is going on with you? Have you been drinking? And what have you done with your two guardian knights?"

Janet was the first to respond, dragging Thomas along as they made their way toward the front door. "Grandfather, of course we haven't been drinking, but the most outrageous and sublime thing has happened to us. As expected, our breakfast meeting with the president was rather strained and testy. To say that the president is everything less than we expected is to put it mildly. But let's save that bit until we get into the house and get settled. As to Danny and Jimmy, we dropped them off on our way home at RCC headquarters. They said they needed to make some last-minute arrangements for our flight to Montana tomorrow morning. We were delayed because they wanted to make sure that we wouldn't be tracked by all the president's men."

Janet's grandfather stopped in his tracks and exclaimed, "Why, Janet, what an odd thing to say. The mystery appears to have deepened. Well, then, let's get you into the house, where we can talk more freely. I thought that we would have all of the answers by now, but this mystery surrounding the Pike Letters appears to get even deeper, if that's possible."

With that, everyone scurried into the house, not noticing that the limo hadn't pulled away yet. Danny had instructed the driver to linger until the group was securely inside the house. Something foreboding must have happened during the meeting with the president.

As they gathered once more around the kitchen's granite island, Janet and Eliza wrapped their arms around Sarah. Thomas and Solomon lingered nearby, allowing the scene before them to unfold.

Janet's grandfather broke the atmosphere by asking once again, "OK, all of you, grab a stool, and I'll pour the tea. Sarah and I want to hear all about your adventures at the White House. Janet, I really can't fathom your mood, given your earlier comment that your time with the president was rather abrupt and short. What have you been doing since then?"

Janet smiled and nodded deferentially to her father. Gathering up his energy, Solomon took a stool and began to tell a very odd tale. "Father, Sarah, we had what can only be explained as a roller-coaster ride of a day. As you know, we were all apprehensive before our breakfast, especially after you asked us to not to discuss our trip tomorrow to Montana or to provide any more information about the location or contents of the Templar vault."

Solomon sighed before continuing, "Dad, you were bang on. I've never met such a narcissistic, self-centered, and self-absorbed man. God help us that he's in such a powerful position. Hopefully, his self-absorption will lead to the end of him. Anyway, I'm getting off topic already. We were greeted with all due respect and admiration, but it turned out to be false. We were first guided into the Oval Office, not to be congratulated in any way but, I think, to intimidate us. Then we were led to a private dining room that had been set to impress, with the presidential china and crystal laid out. It was almost too much to bear. Everything was excessive and over the top."

Eliza, sensing that Solomon was almost embarrassed by the thought that they had been included in the scene, quietly moved to his side and put her hand on his. This gesture appeared to renew Solomon's strength. Although the Roses were among the fifty wealthiest families in the world, the president's transparent display of wealth and power had unnerved him.

"Breakfast was nice enough, I suppose," he continued, "but I soon enough lost my appetite, because the president got to the point almost too fast. Clearly he was after one bit of information and one only. He almost blurted out the question."

Thomas interjected, "It was as though he hadn't even watched the scene for himself and had only been briefed on a few pertinent facts. I can only imagine the briefing that he receives on current world affairs.

How can a man with such limited comprehension run the most powerful country in the world?"

Nobody had an answer to this question, and Solomon picked up the speed of his tale. "When it became evident that we wouldn't give up the information he wanted, he quickly excused himself. It was clear that he had become bored with us. Frankly, I think all of us breathed a sigh of relief when that happened. It was about 9:30, and we were about to get up and see ourselves out when the door opened and in came a middle-aged gentleman who evidently had witnessed the whole debacle."

"He strode across the room with great power and elegance and extended his hand in greeting to each and every one of us. Much to our collective surprise, we immediately recognized him as a Freemason not only by the handshake but by his manner. I would guess that he was fifty or sixty years in age, although he looked to be in excellent physical shape. He was tall and lean, with a full head of dark, rich hair and had the most piercing blue eyes. He was quite tanned and carried a very spiritual air about him."

Solomon paused to get his breath. "He identified himself as Mr. Smith and immediately apologized that he could not provide any more information about his position within the White House or his relationship to the president. What was really odd was that he appeared to have free access to all parts of the White House. I looked to Danny and Jimmy for an explanation, but they stood there stone-faced, as though this was normal. I couldn't tell whether they recognized Mr. Smith, but there was an instant bond there, as well as with the rest of us. It was Thomas who noticed that Mr. Smith didn't wear any type of identification or security-access badge."

Solomon raised his hands and shrugged. Thomas picked up the story. "That's when Mr. Smith did the oddest thing. He held his finger up to his lips as if to silence us for a moment and then linked his arms with Janet's and Eliza's and started to escort them across the room toward another door. Only when we were out of the private dining room did Mr. Smith innocently ask us if we all wanted a personal tour of the White House. After this moment of intrigue, we couldn't refuse his offer. When we tell you of his commentary over the rest of the day, you'll understand why."

As if by tag team, Janet picked up where Thomas left off. "I'll try to condense what we learned over the next six hours, but please stop me if you want any elaboration on what we were told.

"Mom and I immediately felt comfortable with Mr. Smith. He was definitely an old soul. He knew about our entire ordeal at the hands of Philippe De Smet and also recounted details of our family back for generations. He even knew stories of some of our ancestors on both sides of the family that none of us knew. He told Mom and me that we were direct descendants of the union between Jesus and Mary Magdalene. It was as though he was exposing our very souls, but we completely believed him. It was as though he could read all of our blood memories. Then he asked me if I was still having dreams—visions—of being a High Priestess in ancient times."

Janet waved her arms, as if to mimic her father's and grandfather's earlier gestures. "We were enthralled and hung on his every word. He walked us down every corridor and through every room, rattling off so many interesting facts and sublime stories about the various presidents and their wives and families. He would always point out whether this or that president had been a Freemason and whether they were part of the Grail bloodline. Before we knew it, it was three o'clock and he had guided us into the South Wing of the White House. We found ourselves in a smaller room, and that's when he told us the most amazing story."

"Mr. Smith talked for an hour about Thomas Jefferson and his own quest for the Templar Treasure, to which he was first introduced as the United States ambassador to France following the American Revolution. Did you know that it is still rumored that Jefferson became a member of the Nine Sisters Lodge while staying in Paris, although it has never been proved? Rather surprisingly, Mr. Smith said that as soon as Jefferson became president, he immediately added the South Wing.

According to Mr. Smith, the construction included an elaborate vault based on early Masonic lore of what was found under the ruins of the First Temple by the three sojourners. Here's the kicker: the real reason behind the Lewis and Clark expedition was as a cover for Meriwether Lewis, who was a Mason, to check on the treasure, whose final resting place is in Montana. All of this was done through the direct instructions of the president himself."

Everyone fell silent. Here was confirmation of what they had suspected. It was now apparent that Albert Pike had been told of the final resting place—the hidden vault—by his Native blood brothers and that the burden of the secret was so great that Pike found solace in revealing it to the one man he could trust: MacLeod Moore.

Thomas couldn't stand the silence. "Following the expedition's triumphant return, Meriwether Lewis was appointed the western Indian agent for the United States, and he returned to the West, perhaps to recover the treasure, just as Albert Pike would do some sixty years later. Lewis became racked by guilt for his part in opening the West to white settlers. Then, mysteriously, he was murdered along the Natchez Trace in Tennessee while on his journey eastward to meet with Jefferson again. So the location of the vault died with Lewis, until Pike came along."

Janet jumped in once again. "That's not the end of the Jefferson story. The architect Benjamin Henry Latrobe, who worked with Jefferson on the design of the South Wing, was a Moravian. I've never heard of the term, but Mr. Smith obviously knew all about the movement. The Moravian Church originated in 1457 in Bohemia and its crown lands, Moravia and Silesia. It is one of the oldest Protestant denominations in the world and leans heavily on Hussite beliefs, with Lutheran Pietist influences. The name by which the Church is commonly known comes from the original exiles who fled to Saxony in 1722 from Moravia to escape religious persecution."

Janet inadvertently licked her lips before continuing. "Now this is where it gets really interesting. In 1722, a small group of Bohemian

Brethren known as the 'Hidden Seed,' who had been living in northern Moravia as an illegal underground remnant surviving in the Catholic Hapsburg Empire, arrived at the Berthelsdorf estate of Count Nikolaus Ludwig von Zinzendorf, a nobleman who had been brought up in the traditions of Pietism. Mr. Smith in fact believes that the Hidden Seed were descendants of the Grail Family, just like the Rose family.

"Fleeing persecution, Moravians under Zinzendorf, a reputed Rosicrucian, founded missions with Algonquian-speaking Mohicans in the British colony of New York. Now don't confuse the Mohicans with the Mohawks. The converted Mohican people formed the first native Christian congregation in the present-day United States of America. In fact, the Delaware Indians intermarried with the European Moravians and today still live on a reserve in Canada known as the Delaware of Moraviantown. Mr. Smith indicated that the Moravians clearly understood that the earlier Algonquin Nation had intermarried with the Knights Templar. The ultimate aim was to strengthen the Hidden Seed in order to continue to protect the treasure in perpetuity. On March 8, 1782, at the Moravian mission village in Gnadenhutten, Ohio, ninety-six Moravian Christian Lenape Indians were massacred by colonial American militia from Pennsylvania. Mr. Smith believes that the massacre took place to eradicate known members of the Grail Family. Isn't that the most extraordinary story?"

The implications of what the group learned that day was exhausting. It would take a long time before everyone could fully digest what they had been told by Mr. Smith. It was as if everyone had been left with the same thought: Could the Templar Treasure have been discovered by others who were in on the secret and brought to Washington to be deposited under the South Wing of the White House or another hidden vault in Washington? If so, what awaited them in Montana, and would the Rose family be constantly hunted until they were all dead?

XXXIII

(HONORARY) INSPECTOR GENERAL

2:00 a.m., Today

PRIVATE CORPORATE AIRPORT, JUST OUTSIDE OF WASHINGTON, D.C.

The previous day started with so much apprehension and ended with such a high that it left everyone emotionally drained. In fact, all three couples had gone to bed without having much of anything to eat. A cup of green tea and a few shortbread cookies were all that was needed. Mr. Smith's revelations were almost too much to fathom. Regardless, Danny Sullivan had insisted that the group be ready to go by two o'clock in the morning. He wanted to ensure that they would be able to meet their guests and greet the Montana sunrise with plenty of time to spare.

Almost in a trance, the group stumbled into the limo and then onto the RCC corporate jet in the dark hours of the morning. As instructed, everyone was casually dressed but bundled up for the expected cold morning air. The six of them also carried identical knapsacks provided by Jimmy. These displayed the RCC logo and contained the essentials for a wilderness hiking trip—dried fruit, water, coded satellite phones with GPS, flashlights, matches, and rain gear. What the six didn't realize was that sewn into the lining of each knapsack was a small homing transmitter, which Jimmy followed on one of his magical black boxes. The game would never be over.

Both Danny and Jimmy wore the quilted black jacket and pocketed cargo pants unique to RCC security members. These outfits were designed to conceal the bulge of sidearms and security paraphernalia, but also to provide easy access to them if required.

After the last thirty-two days, along with the ominous feeling left by the visit to the White House, nothing was left to chance. Something in the president's tone had suggested that if they wouldn't cooperate in sharing the location of the vault and its contents, they were on their own in terms of risk management.

The patriarch of the family was the one most concerned about the president's attitude. David's prior conversation with Chief Bull Bear of the Blackfoot, with whom they were all to meet within the next five hours, had done nothing to allay his fears. It was as if they were experiencing the same apprehension of the descendants of the original Grail Family who were the first to make their way across the Atlantic to the New World. Their guardians—the medieval Knights Templar—had to fight a rear-guard action across the expanse of North America against the same type of enemy that existed in the present.

David Rose reflected further on the past days' events as he sat quietly buckled into the jet's leather seat, staring out into the darkness, thinking about one of his current-day heroes—the late Stephen Hawking. He had such admiration for the strength of Hawking's mind over his lifelong failing body. Hawking had done it by sheer willpower, even without the magical powder.

David noted that there was still no sign of the faint glow of the soon-to-rise sun in the east. From the location of the stars, the family patriarch sleepily realized that they were heading southwest and that the sky would remain dark for a considerable time. At that point he awakened for good. "Hey, Danny, it appears that we're heading southwest instead of northwest. What's going on?"

Danny unbuckled himself from the last-row seat and made his way to the center of the cabin, where everybody had congregated, except for Jimmy, who had taken the reversed front seat facing the passengers.

Stopping midcabin, Danny leaned down and looked out the side window before speaking. "Mr. Rose, I'm surprised that it's taken you this long to comment on this. That sixth sense of yours, your inner compass, or whatever you want to call it, usually kicks in immediately. Could it be that the powder is finally clouding your mind for good?"

"I didn't want to alarm anyone, but we're taking a circuitous route to Montana. We're going by way of Oklahoma City, then San Antonio, then skirting the foothills and Rockies below a thousand feet, following the old Salt Lake City prime meridian from south to north. Our flight plan is actually filed only for Oklahoma City at this point. It seems overly precautious, but you can't take too many chances, even with your own government."

Janet had stirred beside Thomas by this time and poked her face out of the blanket. "Danny, are you serious? Do you really believe that the U.S. government might be following us?"

Danny glanced out into the darkness as though checking to make sure that a phantom jet wasn't following them. Seeing nothing that alarmed him, he responded, "Ms. Rose, as I've said before, the only way that Jimmy and I have survived this long is to trust no one. Philippe De Smet is gone, but someone will take his place. The current president will someday be gone, only to be replaced by another."

Danny glanced at Solomon and received the nod to continue. "That's why we've come to a very critical juncture in our lives' journey. For, you see, I believe that all of us are about to enter a harmonic convergence of sorts, where all of our souls become aligned with those of the indigenous peoples who have summoned us. We don't know exactly where this is to happen—maybe not for another two hundred years.

The chief and his grandson will show us the spot. At this morning's sunrise, I believe we will be standing on that very point, identifying a New Jerusalem, and that the sun will show us the ninth doorway. The question still remains of whether we'll choose to enter the spiritual gateway to what the Knights Templar considered to be heaven or we will remain on this Earth for a little while longer."

Evidently Solomon, Danny, and Jimmy had discussed the topic at length during some previous sojourn.

David Rose sat up straight, trying not to shift his new love too far away from him. Sarah had given him renewed strength and purpose. Almost sheepishly, he let out a slight cough to catch everyone's attention. "Ahem, excuse me, but I need to tell all of you something. I think that I know exactly where this gateway to heaven is located."

At first it was as if nobody heard him correctly.

Thomas had been quiet, enjoying his fiancée's warmth, but he was now animated. But Janet beat him to the question: "Grandfather, you sly old fox, are you telling us that you solved the puzzle within the Pike Letters and have waited this long to tell us?"

David Rose stood and removed a manila envelope from inside his quilted jacket. Grinning, he waved the envelope in the air. "I'm sorry, Janet. I only was able to finally piece everything together when all of you were at the White House and Sarah was having a nap. I can't believe that I didn't think of it sooner. Fortunately, it was my new-found love of Sarah that provided the key." He extended his free hand down toward Sarah, who readily accepted it.

Janet clapped her hands together like a schoolgirl. "Grandfather, this is wonderful. Please, can you show us what you've found?"

"Of course, my dear." David Rose was beaming as he activated the switch that swung the side table upward between the seats.

Janet and Thomas already occupied the seats directly opposite David and Sarah, while the rest all gathered around to see the family's patriarch unveil the ultimate mystery of the Pike Letters.

Slowly reaching into the manila envelope, David Rose extracted the one-page letter. From the odd composition of the paragraphs and the now-familiar handwriting, Janet immediately recognized it as the thirty-third letter of the Pike Letters. But she also recognized that it wasn't the original letter. Her grandfather had scanned the original and produced a copy.

In her mind, she immediately recognized why he had done such a thing. Imposed on top of the body of the letter was a proportional tau cross, which her grandfather had digitally drawn.

Nobody said anything for a moment before Thomas opened up. "Mr. Rose, I'm somewhat confused. You haven't explained why you imposed a symbol atop the main body of this letter. I think we all half-expected that an external key was required—maybe a keyword, a sequence of numbers, or a symbol relating to Scottish Rite Masonry. To tell you the truth, I'm not familiar with this type of cross. I would somehow have expected a Scottish Rite cross, a triangle or circle, an X, or even a star or compass hands."

Everyone else nodded in agreement. The application of the tau cross was completely unexpected.

David cleared his throat before he continued. It had taken him a lifetime of study of esoteric, mystical, and Rosicrucian teachings in order to decipher Pike's mind. He wanted to make sure that he had gotten everything right in his own mind before he explained it to those who were dear to his heart, for it was as much their journey of discovery as his.

"Please listen to me carefully. There are so many layers to my reasoning that it's very difficult to follow. First of all, if you read all of the thirty-three letters in their proper sequence, you would very soon realize that Pike's inner thinking toward God as a Deity, as a Supreme Being, in relation to religious tradition was forever evolving. Through the thirty-two degrees of what we now recognize as the Southern Jurisdiction Scottish Rite, he had his hand in remolding and directing the initiate through a deliberate process of self-reasoning—to the morals and dogma, if you like, of an enlightened one."

Everyone nodded to indicate that they were following so far.

David continued. "In this way, when a Scottish Rite Mason is awarded the honorary thirty-third degree of Inspector General, it declares that he has gained a lifetime of profound understanding and knowledge, which leads to the combined wisdom of the ancients. This in turn enables the fully initiated Freemason to apply his own reasoning and logic to the essential question of the existence of God. To put it more simply, Christianity's God—and through a mystical extension, the Son of God and the Holy Spirit, the Blessed Trinity—is the sum total of all religious beliefs that came before."

Jimmy scratched his head. He looked around and saw that everyone was deep in thought before exclaiming, "Now just what the hell is that supposed to mean?"

David wasn't the least put out by the question. "Jimmy, of all people, you must realize that the God whom Christians worship as the omnipotent one, is derived from the pagan gods of the Romans and the Hellenistic period, as well as from Jewish and Old Testament beliefs. The Holy Spirit was the Goddess, who became the Virgin Mother. The Son of God, dying on the cross for our sins, takes many attributes from the Norse god Odin, who hung from Yggdrasil, which means *gallows,* as a sacrifice for man's evil ways."

David paused before continuing, "In Norse mythology, from which stems most of the information about the god, Odin is associated with wisdom, healing, death, royalty, the gallows, knowledge, battle, sorcery, poetry, frenzy, and the runic alphabet. Now doesn't that sound a lot like Jesus's attributes, including his reputation as a prophet and a teacher? The Vatican has been fine-tuning the attributes of the Blessed Trinity and the Son of God's attributes for seventeen hundred years, ever since the Council of Nicaea."

Jimmy was as fascinated by David's reasoning as any of the others present. But he wasn't going to let him get away without a sarcastic comment. "Oh, please continue, old wise one!"

That lightened the mood all around and allowed David to pick up where he left off.

"I know, I know, cut to the chase," said David. "Isn't that what you and Danny say all the time?

"Of course, all of this led me back to the thought that Pike recognized that, prior to the Emperor Constantine, Jesus was considered to be a good man, a prophet at best. To Pike, the Mason, that would have been enough. As such, he studied the early Christian monastics—the mystics who took to the wilderness to resolve the connection between early Christianity and that which came before it. Said in another way, to find *that-which-was-lost,* to understand the word. For in the beginning there was the Word, and the Word was God.

"The earliest Christian monks believed that by taking to the wilderness, one could contemplate the very origin of God, who was defined as an ever-present spirit in everything surrounding them. Indigenous peoples have understood this from the beginning. The Supreme Being, the Creator, was the spirit of all things, from natural things to animals.

"One of the earliest monks, St. Anthony, had a revelation of sorts and wore the tau cross on his shoulder to remind himself of this evolution of God, because the tau is an emblem of immortality, of life in general. It is the mystic tau of the Chaldeans and the Egyptians. It represented the Roman god Mithras, the Greek Attis, and their forerunner, Tammuz, who was the Sumerian dying and rising god, consort of the goddess Ishtar. Conveniently, the original form of the letter T was the initial letter of the god of Tammuz. It is the last letter in the Hebrew and Phoenician alphabet and stands for eternity. This is why Pike chose to use the tau cross as his mystical key to the eternal question."

Danny held up his hand. Although he appreciated the traditional teachings, he was getting impatient. "OK, we accept the philosophical key and its application here. But Mr. Rose, you need to simply explain how the key is applied to the letter and why to the last letter only."

David smiled. "Ah, that's the beauty of it all. Just like Scottish Rite Masonry, the initiate's understanding builds as one moves through the degrees—*the sum of all its parts.* The simple beauty of it all is that just before dying, Pike disclosed the longitudinal and latitudinal coordinates of the secret vault to his friend using the simplest and most ancient of languages—numerology.

"It should have come to me sooner. What a fool I was! In 1803, Thomas Jefferson stressed to Meriwether Lewis that he needed to learn how to take accurate longitudinal and latitudinal readings. In fact, I can remember exactly his initial recorded instructions to Lewis: 'Beginning at the mouth of the Missouri, you will take observations of latitude and longitude, at all remarkable points on the river, and especially at the mouths of rivers, at rapids, at islands, and other places and objects distinguished by such natural marks and characters of a durable kind, as that they may with certainty be recognized hereafter.'"

Stretching his arms out to make his point, David Rose exclaimed, "Here's the hidden reason that Jefferson pushed the Louisiana Purchase through Congress, even though the U.S. government was virtually broke at the time. Jefferson had an inkling, if not direct knowledge, of where the last Templar sanctuary lay in North America. He understood that the medieval Knights Templar possessed even a better understanding of latitude and longitude than he did."

David then swung the letter around so that everyone could have a better look. "Here, everyone should have a closer look at the letter and you'll see what I mean. Once we land in Townsend, we're going to be looking for the hidden vault that is located at 46 degrees, 18 minutes north, and 111 degrees, 48 minutes west. That's what I took from the letter. I hope that you'll agree."

March 24, 1890

Most Illustrious Brother Macleod Moore, 33°, KT

Every day, I feel the very life essence flow out of both mine and your body. However, I ask that you do not mourn for either of us, my good and faithful friend, as we have both lived a full and rewarding life. As such, I believe that we must give thanks to I.H.W.H. for his wisdom and understanding, in allowing us to occupy our earthly vessel for so long.

I trust that you are of the same understanding as I, that our rituals link us to our antient origins. Indeed, we both follow in the footsteps of the Sumerian God-Kings, Egyptian Pharaohs, Biblical Prophets, Frankish Royalty and their guardians—the Knights Templar—and even those Great Adepts who came before the Great Flood.

I trust that you will also understand, my most illustrious brother, when I come to lie prone, stretched out from east to west, that I will lovingly remember the morals and dogma found within the sublime 11th degree, x 2, as well as the minute details, which can be found deep, deep within the 4th and 8th degree rituals.

Do not fear, for every minute that we still stand tall, able to gaze in all directions, in a complete circle circumventing earth, from south to north, again the Mystic Word, I.N.R.I., found within the sublime 18th degree – Knight Rose Croix.

Like Enoch, the hidden secrets within these holy degrees will enable us to ascend to the lodge on the highest hill, which overlooks the deepest valley. There, like RCR, we too will be entombed in a secret vault, awaiting a better time for our understanding and knowledge to be exposed to the universe.

Let us remember, however, that knowledge is power, and that the Source of all wisdom sustains our feeble steps on the journey that leads to eternal life.

Once again, I remind you of the 4th and 6th degrees and all of the degrees, with their remarkable latitude and zeal towards reaching the utmost pinnacles of wisdom. Most illustrious brother: Let those who have the understanding, use it with wisdom.

In God we trust, forever yours,
Albert Pike, 33°, KT
Sovereign Grand Commander

The group of eight fell silent, deep in thought. The spiritual enlightenment displayed in Pike's last letter to MacLeod Moore had taken everyone's breath away. Because of their own initiations, David,

Solomon, Danny, and Jimmy understood the deep speculative and oper-ative nature of Pike's words. Yet the words also had a deep meaning to Janet, Eliza, Sarah, and Thomas.

Not another word was spoken between any of them until they landed at their destination.

EPILOGUE
6:30 a.m., Today
TOWNSEND, MONTANA

The RCC jet landed seamlessly at the small airport in Townsend, Montana, at exactly 6:30. Seeking whatever sense of security they could find, Danny and Jimmy were certain that the plane hadn't been tracked using conventional airspace radar. The jet's pilots had performed a series of extensive, and exceptional, maneuvers after takeoff from Washington.

Of course the pilots were handpicked by Danny. The selected pilots had been with both Danny and Jimmy from the beginning of their military careers and welcomed the opportunity to keep the money and adrenaline flowing even after retiring from the air force. Besides, they all shared membership in both the military and the Masonic brotherhoods.

Although the jet's landing was smooth, the twinkling lights along both sides of the airstrip quickly brought the group's collective subconscious back to earth. Danny and Jimmy nodded to each other. Two silhouetted white vans slowly followed the jet as it made its way into a modern hangar sitting off by itself at the end of the runway.

As the jet slowly taxied into the hangar, the vans followed through the open doors, which then appeared to close by themselves. Once the jet was safely ensconced inside the hangar, a set of dim overhead lights slowly adjusted, presenting a diffused, somewhat surreal atmosphere. Thomas remarked out loud that the arranged meeting was straight out of a Bond movie.

The plane's stairs automatically dropped, allowing the group to disembark, but not before Solomon silently signaled to Danny and Jimmy to allow his father to be the first to deplane. As patriarch of the family, it was proper and just that David Rose be afforded the opportunity to be the first to meet his counterpart, his mirror image: for the Native elder who stood waiting to greet the Rose family was indeed the mirror image—an absolute doppelganger—of David Rose. The similarity between the two elders wasn't lost on anyone who was present. In fact, the only ones who appeared not to be shocked were David Rose and his counterpart—Chief Bull Bear.

Immediately recognizing a longtime spiritual bond, David approached the chief and embraced him as an equal, as a Brother, as a kindred spirit. The two even exchanged whispered secret greetings, long lost in the mist of time. David went first, "Golgotha." The chief replied without hesitation, "Place of the skull."

Satisfied that he hadn't made a mistake in inviting the Rose family, the chief, standing remarkably straight and tall for his ninety years, extended his arms forward and exclaimed, "*Kwey, nanabashoo!* Greetings, my brothers and sisters, In the name of the Creator, I welcome you to the traditional territory of the Blackfoot—of the larger Algonquin Nation. *Ayeway!* A short time ago, I was visited by our mutual ancestral spirits and instructed to show you the final path in your journey, for my family is the last guardian of the sacred vault. We are the offspring of the unions between our warriors and our princesses, of the Knights Templar and the Goddesses, who came and intermarried a long, long time ago in order to keep our blood strong. That is why I carry the name Baldwin. *Kwey, kwey!* Many thanks and prayers must be given to the Creator for arranging this meeting between two such families and giving me such a funny name. *Meegwich*!"

Everyone in the group, suitably honored, gathered around, introducing themselves individually. Once they had done this, the chief stepped back and quietly summoned the two figures who stood in the shadows of the vans.

The chief turned slightly and waited to be joined by the two, saying, "And now I would like to introduce you to my son and grandson, for they continue the guardian bloodline."

Here was another unexpected surprise. Mr. Smith walked forward with the slightest of a grin on his face, accompanied by his son—the chief's grandson—who was a spitting image of both his father and his grandfather.

Before anyone could comment, Mr. Smith held up his hand, palm forward, which stopped everyone in their tracks, including Danny and Jimmy, who had actually been in on the game from the start. Mr. Smith then quietly spoke. "Greetings, Rose family. I see from the shock on all of your faces that our little ruse worked." Janet walked over to Jimmy and gave him the requisite punch to the shoulder before Mr. Smith continued, "I'm sorry that I had to fool you back at the White House, but it was necessary to determine your ultimate desire with respect to the Templar Treasure. I never was in doubt because of my Masonic relationship with your guardians, but my father instructed me to determine your true nature for myself, and I must say that you passed with flying colors. The day that I spent with you was truly memorable. The capital has become a cesspool of contradiction lately. By the way, my real name is Hugh St. Clair, and my son's name is Godfrey St. Clair, although he much prefers Little Bull Bear."

Curiously, no mention was made of how Hugh had free rein of the White House or how he had appeared almost invisible to the security personnel. The group had already moved on, surging forward as one to greet not only Hugh but his dark and handsome son, who sheepishly grinned at the mention of his name. Obviously the three indigenous leaders had been assigned European names to remind them of their Templar heritage.

Danny suddenly spoke up, again breaking the euphoria that had appeared to accompany the group ever since Philippe De Smet was dispatched. "Enough of this camaraderie and jubilation. We need to be at the site of the sacred vault before sunrise, and from my timing, I would say that we have less than half an hour."

Having received their orders, the group quickly fell into line and split themselves between the two vans. The first had Hugh driving and Chief Bull Bear riding in the front passenger seat, while the middle seats were occupied by David Rose and Sarah Cohen, who stole the opportunity to squeeze each other's hand. Following up in the rear seat was Jimmy, who appeared to be busily studying one of his little black boxes.

The second van was driven by Little Bull Bear. Seated in the front passenger seat was Danny, who produced a military-grade automatic rifle. This quieted Janet and Thomas, who now occupied the second row of seats, with Solomon and Eliza occupying the third row. Even though they were bundled up against the cold morning air, the sudden appearance of Danny's deadly weapon seemed to have sent a chill down the backs of everyone, including Little Bull Bear.

As the small convoy silently moved forward, one of the hangar doors opened just enough to allow the vans to exit. Nobody noticed except Danny and Jimmy that the van's headlights hadn't been switched on until they gained access to the main road adjacent to the airport. After that, they proceeded very quickly westward to where the main road ended and a rough dirt road began. Slowly gaining elevation, the two vans made their way into the foothills, skirting a large limestone outcrop, which was taking on a faint glow from the dusky rise of the sun over the horizon to the east.

Time was now of the essence, and the occupants of both vans remained silent. It was apparent to everyone that there would be ample time for a full explanation by both parties once they arrived. Upward the vans climbed, using what appeared to be a little-used logging road, which zigzagged back and forth, following the hilly terrain. In some instances, the vans slowed to a crawl, bouncing from side to side, trying to avoid craterlike potholes obviously developed by the repeated passage of all-terrain vehicles.

Once on top of the plateau, which overlooked the high plains, the vans sped forward toward a small circular copse of woods. From his GPS, David Rose immediately realized that the site was located exactly where the Pike Letters had indicated the secret vault lay. As the vans circled the copse to the west, it readily became apparent that the outer ring of trees concealed a circular clearing in the middle that was large enough to accommodate the vans and much more. Surprisingly, within the immediate center of the circle remained a stone foundation of sorts, round in nature with a diameter of about thirty-three feet.

The occupants of the two vans quickly disembarked and made their way to the center of the ancient stone foundation. As everyone silently followed Chief Bull Bear, Thomas noted what appeared to be a smooth flagstone flooring underfoot, covered by moss and rough field grass. This ancient stone circle, concealed by the outer ring of mature trees, hadn't been visited for some time.

As the visitors marveled at the site they had penetrated, they failed to notice that the chief's grandson had gathered enough dry kindling to start a small fire in the exact center of the structure.

That's when it began to happen. Everyone quickly positioned themselves in a way to face direct east, anxiously anticipating the first sign of the sun's rising.

As the faint upper crescent of the sun began to appear along the horizon, the extensive plains before them began to glisten in the early morning dew. The dew provided a prism of sorts, diffusing the ever-increasing light into a rainbow of colors. As the plains' field grasses began to sway in the morning breeze, everyone pictured a giant snake making its way toward them. But instead of being afraid, the group realized that here was the snake of knowledge—of the knowledge and virtue of those who came before them.

Suddenly, Chief Bull Bear dipped his hand into a small pouch hanging by his side. The pouch, made from the skin of a small animal, was covered with beadwork denoting the carrier as a shamanic Mide'win— an elder of the Grand Medicine Society. When he pulled his hand out, it contained a mixture of tobacco and cedar and another ingredient, which nobody recognized. The chief immediately threw the mixture into the small fire, and it burst into flames, sending sparks and smoke in all directions, causing both Janet and Thomas to jump back a little.

The chief smiled faintly and then began his pronouncement. "*Kwey, kwey.* The path to enlightenment reveals herself to us this morning. Mother Nature has embraced our souls. It is a good sign. Here we stand within the remains of the last sanctuary of those Knights Templar who fled Jerusalem a thousand years ago. Having arrived on the eastern shores of Turtle Island, they were befriended by our brothers, the Mi'kmaq, who passed them along to the various Algonquin Nations who reside between the eastern shores and these foothills. In doing so, many fine and strong little people were conceived over several generations. It was here that the guardians finally decided to remain with their blood brothers, building a stone tower not only to defend their treasure but to conceal their activities deep within the earth below our feet. The source of Bear Creek is below our feet—the source of all life-giving waters to the east. They also used the tower to chart the stars and to establish their astronomical position."

The chief threw another handful of the mixture into the fire. This time a spiral of smoke resembling DNA made its way into the sky.

The chief continued: "The guardians indicated when they reached this site with their Blackfoot conductors that signs were left by those ancients who had come before them, ancient mariners who sought the riches of the earth—gold and silver, ruby and sapphire—destined to adorn Solomon's Temple. Below our feet and all around us are the remnants of those ancient mines, many of which the Templars continued to mine. But it was not the ferrous metals that they sought. They had rediscovered the key to an ancient technology below the ruins of the Jerusalem Temple that, using other minerals that were also present—

cobalt, manganese, titanium, and other rare earths—possessed a power to destroy the world."

Sensing that his father was being a little too dramatic, Hugh took over and continued with the story. "Thank goodness that the guardians realized that mere possession of such a weapon would strike fear in the hearts of the church. Instead of activating such a weapon of destruction, they deposited the sacred things that the original nine knights had discovered in Jerusalem into a sacred vault, which was constructed in accordance with instructions secretly passed down by Solomon himself. Then they booby-trapped the vault's entrance with some sort of bomb, if you like, which only could be penetrated by those who have achieved the highest of the highest levels of Masonry or the Mide'win, for the highest levels are mirror images of each other. Your Sovereign Grand Commander, Albert Pike, and Supreme Grand Master, William James Bury MacLeod Moore, were two such men, as were our Sitting Bull and Tecumseh. Meriwether Lewis only discovered a few remnants, which were intentionally made obvious. This is what lies below the White House today. In reality, my father and Mr. Rose are the only two remaining supreme guardians who we know have the true knowledge of the ancient alchemical technology."

Janet gasped at the pronouncement, as did both Eliza and Sarah. Everyone realized the enormity of what Baldwin and Hugh had just said. Solomon Rose remained quiet but immediately moved to his father's side and lovingly put his arm around his shoulders, which sagged a little with the tremendous responsibility that had just been placed on them. Even Danny and Jimmy appeared to have momentarily dropped their guard, stunned by what they had just learned.

David Rose held up his hand. The sun's rays slowly embraced the entire group, as though it too knew what David was about to say.

"Yes, it is true. I believe that Chief Bull Bear and I, as Supreme Magi, are the only two who, combining our knowledge and understanding, would be able to penetrate the vault. However, I feel in my heart that Baldwin already knows the answer to the question. For over four hundred years, the real secret has remained below our feet, safely guarded by the Mide'win, who understand the truth of the matter. To an alchemical master such as myself, I realize that the mystical white stone has already been found. It is all around us."

David raised his arms and twirled 360 degrees. "Here is the New Jerusalem that so many seek. It is the navel of the world and should not be penetrated, for it provides life and light to Mother Earth. We have witnessed this morning the living and breathing umbilical cord that joins all men. Albert Pike must have carried a tremendous burden, knowing the information that he possessed could have led the South to rise again and defeat the North—to defeat the world, for that matter. Instead, he chose to honor the faith entrusted to him by his Native Brothers. I've decided to do the same. It is an easy decision to make. We shall keep the sacred vault's location a secret and instead rejoice in our newfound brotherhood. As we previously discussed, Sarah's and my charitable foundation will put all of its resources toward developing life-saving medicines that will look to eradicate cancer and other diseases that afflict all of mankind."

Janet quickly moved to her grandfather's side and gave him a big hug. Tears fell from her eyes as she whispered to him, "Oh, Grandfather, what a wonderful thought. I am so proud of you. You've such a beautiful soul."

Then, as if on cue, the rising sun burst from the horizon in its full splendor. The oldest Deity to be worshipped once again cast his blessing upon the face of the earth. Its warmth spread across the land as if announcing another day.

Absorbing the sun's warmth as he waited, Thomas respectfully stood off to one side until he felt that the intimate moment between grandfather and granddaughter had passed. He then walked over and spread his lanky arms around both Janet and David. Leaning in, his face met Janet's, and they locked eyes. There were tears of joy in their eyes. For today, at least, love will triumph over evil.

ACKNOWLEDGMENTS

As one grows older, one comes to realize that no single individual has ever lived long enough to have figured out the true meaning of life. That's not to say that some great and illuminated men haven't come close to discovering the Holy Grail. Certainly, I pale against such figures such as Francis Bacon, Nicolas Flamel, Albert Einstein, and Albert Pike.

However, after sixty-four years of constant learning, I believe that I've gained just enough knowledge and understanding of all the sixty-four squares of the chessboard to allow me to think along a different plane than most people. Even if you understand all of the squares, you must still gain the wisdom to master the game. To God, the Supreme Being, the Creator, the Force, I will be forever grateful to have been offered a glimpse into the cosmos that lies between man and the spirit world.

This is not to say that I would not have found my life and career rewarding enough without having been immersed into a world of mystical Christianity, Freemasonry, and Native tradition and ceremony. Actually, it is a unique pathway that I was destined to follow all along, now knowing and understanding the ancestral connections that are embedded deep within my psyche. Once I discerned what lay in my blood memory, the movement to a higher level came easily, using the degrees of Masonic, Rosicrucianism, and Mide'win ritual as stepping-stones to the clouds.

With that said, I could not have accomplished any of this without the perpetual assistance and support of the family members, friends, and colleagues who have surrounded and supported me over my many years. First and foremost, I give thanks to my wife, Marie, to whom forever I will owe a boundless amount of gratitude. She is my constant, my rock, forever challenging me to maintain my two feet on the ground and to remain within this world. Simply stated, she is the love of my life.

As are my two sons, William and Thomas. To watch them grow into the fine young men they are is reward enough, but to see them take an acute interest in their father and their heritage is bewildering and amazing at the same time. Whoever coined the phrase, "The apple doesn't fall far from the tree" certainly knew what they were talking about!

I wish to also give thanks to my two late parents, Bill and Doreen Mann. Even though I grew up in a household where more often than not the cupboards were bare, there was such an abundance of love that it sustained and cultivated my lifelong desire to live and to love. Their spirit will forever linger with me, for which I am eternally grateful.

A large thank-you must also go to my two sisters, Vicki and Cheryl. Their enthusiasm for all things is infectious, and their constant search for proof of our ancestral roots must be embedded within all of us. Their habit of searching out long-lost relatives is something to behold, especially if there's a Native casino or two along the way.

My soul has also been enriched by my many close friends, including Scott and Janet Wolter, Mark and Wendy Phillips, along with my 4 Skies partners: Michael Thrasher, Steve Brant, and Bob Watts, all of whom share my quest for truth and reconciliation. Then there are my many Masonic Brothers and Cousins, including Gary Humes, George Fairburn, David Warren, Bill Koon II, and Jeff Nelson, along with the remaining, living past Supreme Grand Masters of the Sovereign Great

Priory—Knights Templar of Canada: Gerry Tetzloft, Doug Draker, David Hardie, Joe Marshall, Job Parsons, Gordon Stuart; and all of those who came before them, including Reginald Vanderbilt Harris and my great-uncle, Frederic George Mann.

Many thanks must also go to the current Grand Chancellor of the Sovereign Great Priory, David Walker, who rather unknowingly rescued the Pike Letters from the flooded basement of the old chancellery office in Toronto. Hopefully, this book will pique the hidden esoteric interest of a younger generation, resulting in a renewed interest in the Masonic Brotherhood, including the Knights Templar.

Finally, I could never have written this book without the support of Jon Graham, acquisitions editor, and Ehud Sperling, owner and publisher, of Inner Traditions and Bear & Company. They are the largest publisher in the world of "alternative, hidden history and the mysteries of consciousness" nonfiction books, so I was pleasantly surprised when they took a chance on a work of fiction that was centered on a set of historical letters written by such a mysterious and controversial figure as Albert Pike. They truly share an enthusiasm and bravery for seeking the alternative truth in history.

Among the many staff members of Inner Traditions, I would be amiss if I did not thank Jeanie Levitan, editor-in-chief; Mindy Branstetter, editor; Patricia Rydle, editorial assistant; Kelly Bowen, contracts and royalties; and Manzanita Carpenter Sanz, publicist extraordinaire. Without their insight and conviction, this novel would not possess the level of energy and spirit that it does.

Somewhere, Albert Pike must be winking.